WEB OF PASSION

"Please, Cord, help me," Floryn cried.

His hand curved around her nape and he tugged her to him. The space separating them melted away until the distance between his lips and hers was immeasurable.

"Ah, yes, I love to hear you begging me to help *you*. The sound is music to my ears, although it's ten years too late."

As she closed her eyes, she shut out his words. She let darkness with its velvet softness enfold her as his lips whispered against hers. In the darkness it was easy to float in time and place so that she recaptured the magic of their love.

"Cord." Her palms moved up the chest she remembered so well, exploring what she had dreamed about time and again. But this was no dream.

She swayed closer to him as he kissed her. She was stunned by the web of passion enclosing her, the same hot passion she had felt the first time they had made love . . .

LET ARCHER AND CLEARY
AWAKEN AND CAPTURE YOUR HEART!

CAPTIVE DESIRE (2612, $3.75)
by Jane Archer

Victoria Malone fancied herself a great adventuress and student of life, but being kidnapped by handsome Cord Cordova was too much excitement for even her! Convincing her kidnapper that she had been an innocent bystander when the stagecoach was robbed was futile when he was kissing her until she was senseless!

REBEL SEDUCTION (3249, $4.25)
by Jane Archer

"Stop that train!" came Lacey Whitmore's terrified warning as she rushed toward the locomotive that carried wounded Confederates and her own beloved father. But no one paid heed, least of all the Union spy Clint McCullough, who pinned her to the ground as the train suddenly exploded into flames.

DREAM'S DESIRE (3093, $4.50)
by Gwen Cleary

Desperate to escape an arranged marriage, Antonia Winston y Ortega fled her father's hacienda to the arms of the arrogant Captain Domino. She would spend the night with him and would be free for no gentleman wants a ruined bride. And ruined she would be, for Tonia would never forget his searing kisses!

VICTORIA'S ECSTASY (2906, $4.25)
by Gwen Cleary

Proud Victoria Torrington was short of cash to run her shipping empire, so she traveled to America to meet her partner for the first time. Expecting a withered, ancient cowhand, Victoria didn't know what to do when she met virile, muscular Judge Colston and her body budded with desire.

Available wherever paperbacks are sold, or order direct from the Publisher. Send cover price plus 50¢ per copy for mailing and handling to Zebra Books, Dept. 3845, 475 Park Avenue South, New York, N.Y. 10016. Residents of New York and Tennessee must include sales tax. DO NOT SEND CASH. For a free Zebra/ Pinnacle catalog please write to the above address.

Emma Merritt

ZEBRA BOOKS
KENSINGTON PUBLISHING CORP.

ZEBRA BOOKS

are published by

Kensington Publishing Corp.
475 Park Avenue South
New York, NY 10016

First printing: August, 1992

Printed in the United States of America

One

"LOVE FOREVER," Floryn whispered. "JUNE, 1855."

With her fingertip she outlined time and again the words on the tree trunk, words Cord had carved there only minutes before. Eventually she pressed her palm over the pledge and turned her head to look tenderly at him. Her lips trembled. Her honey-gold eyes shimmered.

"I love you, Cord."

"I love you."

"Forever," she vowed.

"Forever," he vowed.

The sweet fragrance of first love, of passion first discovered, her whispered confession caressed Cord like the kiss of the summer wind. From her cheek, he kissed away a tear. From her forehead, he brushed a lock of hair, the same shade of brown as her eyes.

"I'll never forget this summer," she murmured.

"Me either."

Intoxicated on love, bubbling over with happiness, they gazed deeply into each other's eyes. Laughing, they ran hand-in-hand across the meadow, beyond the buckboard and Cord's tethered roan, until she stumbled and both fell onto a bed of red Indian paintbrushes. Cord held her in his arms.

Even when the breeze turned into a nipping wind that alerted them to the coming shower, he was loath to move, loath to let her go. Pearl gray clouds swirled through the sky to cover the sun. He held her closer. Picking up momentum, the wind rustled through the grass. Droplets of rain splattered on them.

"We'll get wet." Her laughter danced with the wind.

"Do you mind?" He turned her so that she lay on her back; he leaned over her. Her hair blew across his face, around his neck, binding him to her in honey-gold silk.

"No." The word merged into their kiss.

Again they celebrated their love, this time in the rain.

Cord Donaldson wiped the moisture from his face. Tears? Of course not! He had no tears. He was perspiring. Heavy, humid air pressed in on him. He brushed his arm across his forehead, wiping the perspiration with his shirtsleeve. It was always like this before a summer storm. He pushed back on his bunk, against the mildewed rock wall, and looked through the window at the turbulent sky. Lightning periodically illuminated the darkened room; thunder boomed.

His gaze fell to the calendar fastened to the wall. June, 1865. This was one hell of a summer, and Huntsville, Texas, was a hellhole. He wiped the perspiration from his face again. God, but it was hot!

Ten years had passed since he had seen Floryn. Ten years since they had made their confession of forever love.

Forever love! The thought was repugnant. Not the forever part. He believed in that. Only God knew how much. He had been here forever. He rose and crossed the room. His hands curled around the bars that imprisoned him, and he pressed his forehead against the cold metal. Texas State Penitentiary metal.

Yes, he believed in forever. He no longer believed in love.

Down the corridor he caught his reflection in the

wall mirror, but did not have to gaze at it to know what he looked like, to know he was not the same man who had made love to Floryn. Not only had his outlook and beliefs changed, so had his appearance. He placed a hand against the black leather patch that covered his left eye. Slowly he brushed his fingers back to touch hair that had once been black, jet black, that was now streaked with gray.

Boots clipped an even cadence down the corridor until a portly guard stood in front of Cord's cell. Fat hands tugged on the waistline of trousers that, since Cord had been here, had never topped the protruding belly. Cord doubted they ever would. Yet, as if a believer in miracles, Alvin Ainsworth tugged again.

Snarling the words, he said, "Warden wants to know if you changed your mind about seeing your visitor."

Cord shook his head.

With unchanged expression, Alvin shook his head and snorted. As if to put himself into gear, he yanked on his trousers a third time, spun on his heels, and retraced his steps.

"She can go to hell for all I care," Cord muttered.

"Hell will freeze over quicker than I'll leave." Floryn pushed back in the straight-back wooden chair, clamped her hands around the armrests, and stared at the warden.

Jack Willowby shoved his hand through his hair and paced the floor of the small waiting room, finally coming to a halt in front of Floryn. "Look, ma'am, I understand your desire to speak to the prisoner—"

Desire to speak with the prisoner! What an understatement, Floryn thought. She had to make a deal with him and immediately. Time was her worst enemy.

"No, Mr. Willowby, you do not, or you wouldn't be trying to talk me out of seeing him."

7

With practiced ease he pulled a timepiece out of his vest pocket, clicked the lid open, and stared at it. He clicked it shut, returned it to the pocket, then looked at her.

"You've been here thirty-six hours and have accomplished nothing. It's evident Donaldson doesn't want to see you."

With gloved fingers Floryn lifted the watch that hung suspended about her neck on a black velvet ribbon, the gold disk and ribbon a decided contrast to her white high-necked blouse. With what she hoped was the same deliberation that Jack Willowby had exhibited, she studied the little gold hands and numbers. She listened to the ticking . . . to the passing of time, but needed nothing to remind her how long she had been here, how long she had been waiting for Cord. She had marked each day of each passing year—all ten of them. She blinked back tears of frustration and longing.

"You're wrong, Mr. Willowby. I've been here thirty-seven hours, and I'll remain here as long as it takes for me to see Cord Donaldson. I *will* talk to him."

She snapped shut the lid and dropped the timepiece so that it once again rested against the bodice of her blouse. Jack Willowby resumed his pacing. The atmosphere in the room was tense, so tense that when a knock sounded, Floryn jumped. Before the warden could speak, the door opened, and an elderly man entered, a tray of food balanced on one hand.

"Brought lunch for the young lady," he announced.

"Why not, Rule!" Jack Willowby threw his hands up in defeat and walked toward the door. "I certainly don't want her death on my hands! It's not enough that I put up with criminals. I must run a hotel. Did you bring her a cot with blankets and pillows?"

"Well"—Rule carefully placed the tray on the long table that sat in the center of the sparsely furnished

8

room—"to be honest, Warden, I did. They're in the hall. Couldn't get more than the tray through the door on this trip."

"Damn!"

Jack walked out and slammed the door.

"Don't pay no mind to him." The old man chortled through a thick, unkempt beard. "He's not a bad 'un, just a little edgy. Being a warden at a state penitentiary ain't no easy job. Specially for Jack. He's a good and honest man. There ain't much place for them in our world today. And he's got to work with the likes of—" He cut himself short and gave Floryn a wary gaze; then he shrugged his shoulders. "Well, ma'am, it just ain't easy for a man like Jack Willowby to be herding outlaws."

The aroma of food beckoning, Floryn dragged the chair closer to the table.

"I cooked this special for you, ma'am." He removed the lid from a cracked ceramic serving dish. "Hope you like stew with new potatoes and onions and carrots."

"Oh, yes—" Floryn's words died, and her stomach churned. Swimming in a greasy, thick broth were more lumps of fat than meat or vegetables.

"Fresh milk." Rule picked up the pewter pitcher and filled her glass. "And butter for your bread."

She leaned back in the chair. "Mr.—"

"Compton." He returned the pitcher to the tray, the clang of metal against metal echoing dully through the room. "But I don't rightly take to being called Mr. Compton. Call me Rule."

"Rule, do you know Cord Donaldson?"

"Yeah, I reckon I know him about as well as anybody here knows him." He never looked up from slicing the bread. "Which ain't saying much. Donaldson's a law unto himself, but I reckon you know that, ma'am."

"Yes," Floryn murmured, "I knew that. I guess . . . I

9

suppose . . . I want to know how much he's . . . if he's
. . . changed."

Rule laid the knife down and wiped his hands on the
dishcloth he had brought in with him. Thunder
boomed, the reverberation rattling the windowpanes in
their casement. Wind whistled through a crack fluttering the newspaper that lay in one of the chairs.

"Time changes all people. Prison petrifies 'em,
ma'am. A man's never the same once he's been in a
place like this. He may look the same but inside where
it counts, he ain't nothing but rock. He don't know
what emotions are anymore. Guess that's 'cause he
don't rightly have any."

Rule walked to the window and looked out. "Most of
the time the men in here don't have nobody waiting for
'em either. Donaldson ought to thank God he's got a
good woman like you. Don't know what his game is,
not wanting to see you."

But Floryn knew.

She, too, stared out the window but saw beyond the
bleak, storm-ridden sky to another time, to another
morning, a long-ago morning. A summer morning of
forever love.

She was returning to the ranch after a visit to the
neighboring village to care for a sick child when she
noticed the dark clouds gathering. Trying to outrun the
storm, she was in the lower meadow when a bolt of
lightning, followed by a resounding boom of thunder,
frightened the team and she lost control. Cord, out riding the prize roan he had recently purchased, had
come to her rescue, subduing the runaways. His face
white with anxiety, he had climbed into the buckboard
and gathered her trembling body close to his, holding
her, assuring her she was safe.

Slowly, certainly not premeditatively, resolve to fight
her growing feelings for this man fled as genuine comforting turned into passion. She forgot marriage vows

10

and commitments. She surrendered to the moment, to the man. Not even the summer storm had been enough to dampen their newfound ardor. Closing her eyes, she could still see Cord as he sat beside her beneath the oak tree after the shower.

"This is the happiest, yet the saddest time of my life," she had said. "I'm happy because I found you, because we love each other, but I'm also sad."

"Because of Hal," Cord said rather than asked.

"Yes," she murmured, "because we've hurt him."

Hal. Hal Donaldson. Floryn's husband. Cord's uncle. It amazed Floryn how the thought of him, of what she had done to him, could shatter the beautiful world she and Cord had created from their love. Yet it did and proved how fragile their world was.

"I've broken my marriage vows," she confessed in the same soft voice.

"I didn't plan this, Floryn," Cord said. "I wouldn't have come had I known this would happen. I would have stayed in San Francisco. Anywhere, but here."

Floryn brushed the unruly shock of black hair from his forehead. "I know," she whispered, also feeling guilty because in loving one man, she had betrayed another.

By law she was Hal's wife, but both she and Hal knew theirs was a marriage of convenience, not love. Aged and confined to a wheelchair, he wanted a nurse, housekeeper, companion, and someone to manage the ranch. He had found it in her—a sixteen-year-old orphan and the daughter of a whore, a young girl who desperately wanted security, who wanted to escape her mother's kind of life—before it was too late.

When Hal had asked her to marry him, he explained that it would be a union in name only. He would love her like a father. He would protect and provide for her. Too young to weigh fully the consequences, too lonely to care, and too happy to be rescued from her present life she had quickly accepted. For the first time in her sixteen years she had a real home; she had respectability.

She and Hal had enjoyed their honeymoon in Paris, where he had delighted in taking her shopping and in buying her new clothes. Money was no consideration where she was concerned. He delighted in making her wishes come true. Lavishing her in luxury and attention, he had teasingly called her his little fancy lady.

As much as she had enjoyed the excitement of Paris, New York, and New Orleans, however, she was glad when they returned to Texas. Immediately she had loved the ranch. Previously called the Donaldson Ranch, Hal now christened it after her . . . the Fancy Lady. For two years she had been his little lady, his honorable little lady. Then three months ago his nephew had arrived at the ranch for a visit. From the first moment she saw Cord, Floryn had been attracted to him. Until the ride in the meadow, she had kept the attraction to herself.

Cord seemed to have read her thoughts. "Hal's my only family, Floryn. God, what have I done to him?"

"Not you. Not me. But us," Floryn said.

She regretted she had been weak where Cord was concerned, but would not allow him to shoulder the blame alone. For three months she had fought her attraction for him, and until today had maintained her distance. However, the unsettling events of this morning had pushed her over the edge of sanity, had carried her from denial to passion and to love. On all counts, she was as guilty as Cord.

In a way she despised herself for what she had done to Hal, but did not regret for one instant the happiness and fulfillment loving Cord had given to her. Nor would she judge herself too harshly. She truly wanted to be Cord's wife, but that could not be unless . . . She left the thought unfinished because the dilemma presented no honorable solution.

Because she respected Hal as a father, a part of her wanted to confess her love for Cord. Because she knew the workings of his mind, the greater part of her did not. Hal was an old man, and while he might understand her indiscretion and would probably release her from her promise, he would be lonely. He would feel betrayed by the one person on whom he completely depended. Now she must face the consequences of her loving Cord.

"What am I going to do?" she murmured.

"We'll tell Hal," Cord said and captured her hands in his. Intense, startling blue eyes, full of love, stared into hers.

"I can't."

"We have to." Now the eyes pleaded with her. "When he knows we love each other, he'll give you a divorce."

"Oh, Cord, what you're saying sounds so wonderful." Tears turned her voice husky. "I wish doing it were as easy as talking about it. If we had to think about ourselves only, it would be easy. But we must think about Hal."

"I didn't say it would be easy," Cord corrected. "I'm just saying it's what we have to do, Floryn. It's the only way."

"No, there's another way." The words were a painful whisper. "The way we must go. Hal doesn't love me the way you do, but he's come to depend on me. He can't live without me. If it weren't for him, I'd be in a whorehouse today. I owe him too much to hurt him."

"What about me, Floryn? What about us?"

She said only, "I swore before God I wouldn't forsake him, Cord, that I'd take care of him until he died."

"He'll understand. I know he will." She began to cry, and Cord held her even tighter. "Honey, it's unfair to Hal if we don't tell him."

"He's been in that wheelchair for nearly twenty years, Cord. Unable to live a full life like you and me. I can't subject him to more suffering, not when he's been so kind to me."

"In not telling him, Floryn, we're being unkind to him," Cord argued.

After a thoughtful pause, she murmured, "It's—it's not like Hal and I are really husband and wife." She gazed into his face. "I'm really more like a daughter to him, or a housekeeper, or a friend."

Agreeing with her, Cord looked expectantly into her face.

"Not a wife. Not a lover," she added, pressing her cheek against Cord's chest. Her argument, however, paled into nothing as she thought how helpless Hal was, remembered all he had done for her, wished there was an honorable way out of her marriage. "What about the ranch? Who'll take care of it for him?"

"He'll manage," Cord said. "He did before he married you."

She raised her head and gazed into Cord's face. "He wasn't doing a good job of it."

"That was before he hired George Greeve to be his foreman," Cord said. "Not only is George young and strong, he's interested in ranching. He's a good manager, and he'll take care of the Fancy Lady for Hal."

"George might take care of the Fancy Lady," Floryn reluctantly admitted, thinking about the dark-featured man Hal had hired several months prior to Cord's arrival, "but he's not going to take care of Hal. Besides, Cord, George is a drifter. He told us so when we hired him, and one of these days he'll be moving on."

Floryn really liked George Greeve but suspected he more than liked her. When he thought she was not looking, he would stare at her with an interested gleam in his eyes. Still he kept his distance and was always respectful. Never once did he step out of line.

"There are others Hal can hire," Cord said.

She shook her head. "No, Cord, I can't leave him. I won't. He can't run the Fancy Lady by himself, and others might take advantage of him. We'll lose everything."

"The ranch. That's it." Cord slowly removed his arms from about her. "You're saying you can't leave him, but it's the ranch you can't bear to leave, isn't it?"

She shook her head. "No."

"Yes, it is. It's this damned ranch." He spoke in an ominous undertone. "And the agreement the two of you made before you married. You can't deny it."

"I'm not going to," she said. "I'm not ashamed of what I did. Hal offered me respectability and a home if I would take care of him."

"In return he's willed you the Fancy Lady." Cord rose and stared at the words he had carved into the trunk hours earlier. "You can't stand the thought of losing the ranch."

"Be reasonable, Cord." She stood also, reached for him, but he moved away.

"You don't want me because you think I'm poor. Certainly by Hal's and your standards I am, but I own my own company, Floryn. Donaldson's Dragoons. We're the best guard service in the west and we're growing larger every day. More and more companies — on the east coast as well as the west — are hiring my men to escort and to protect their shipments. I'm saving my money, and I'm going to expand. One of these days, I'll own a big spread, a big hunk of California. I'll be rich like Hal."

"I can't, Cord." Her whisper was teary.

He glared at her, finally saying, "You and your damned promise of forever love."

He walked toward the tethered roan. Floryn followed.

"What are you doing?" she asked.

15

"Leaving." He unsnapped the reins.

His words were final, cold.

"We . . . we haven't finished talking, Cord."

"Believe me, we're finished, Floryn."

"You can't go back to the ranch now," she cried.

"Ranch, hell. I'm leaving for good." He swung into the saddle and guided the roan around the buckboard, past Floryn.

She followed him. "Back to San Francisco?"

"Away, Floryn. Far away. The way I feel about you, I can't stay here. The way you feel about Hal, you can't leave."

No! He could not go, could not leave her.

She could not imagine life without him. She ran to the side of the roan and grabbed Cord's leg. She clung to him. "What about Hal? Aren't you going to tell him goodbye?"

The brim of the black hat shadowed his eyes. "The only way I can look Hal in the face is to tell him the truth. He and I haven't been close since my parents died, but we've been honest with each other."

Devastated, she sobbed, "We can't tell him, Cord. It would break his heart."

"Giving up the ranch wouldn't break yours?" he asked but did not wait for an answer before he said, "You can lie to me and to Hal all you want, Floryn, but be honest with yourself. Admit you want the ranch."

"I want you, Cord."

"Yeah," he drawled. "You want me here so you can have more of what we did. Well, think again, Floryn, I'm not playing the role of stud."

Tears trickled down her cheeks. "I'm not asking you to."

"But you are." Strangely his voice was gentle, almost reconciled. He lowered his hand and brushed his fingers against her cheek. "If I thought I had a chance in hell, I'd return to the Fancy Lady and fight for you, for

16

your love. I'd tell Hal about us, but I can't fight both of you, Floryn. If I don't go, neither of us will have any honor, and we'll grow to hate ourselves and each other."

He removed her fingers from his leg and rode away. Looking ahead, his back straight, his shoulders squared, he lengthened the distance between them. Finally she slid to the ground where she sobbed his name and pressed her face into the rain-wet grass. Then in despair she pounded the earth with her fists.

In anger he had left her, left her with memories of one beautiful morning. She had never seen him again. Never heard from him. They had both been young . . . so very young, but knowing that, admitting it did not diminish the pain she felt. She died a little when he left, a little more each day thereafter, but forever locked within her heart was Cord's love.

The lock clicked into place, and Jack Willowby stepped back from the safe.

"Damn it, Pruitt!"

He shot the attorney a cutting glance as he raked his hands through his hair, not for the first time since he had walked into his office that morning. He accorded most attorneys little respect, Pruitt none. The only cause the man fought for was his own. He gave selfish a new meaning.

"If you do this, you're luring an innocent into a deadly game. Mrs. Donaldson is a nice person. She could be hurt, and I'm not talking about her heart either."

Webb Pruitt picked a piece of lint from his black suit coat. "You're too soft for your own good, Jack. We have to use her. It's the only way. In nine years nothing we've done has persuaded Donaldson to utter one word about the robbery."

17

"You should know. You've done everything short of killing him," Jack muttered.

"Your way sure as hell hasn't worked," Pruitt snapped. "You're worse than an old mother hen when it comes to these prisoners. Paying whores to come up here every so often to sleep with them." He shook his head in disgust. "Christ, Jack!"

"The prison is my concern. My strategy has served me well. Even you have to admit, things are peaceful."

"Yeah. Yeah," Pruitt mumbled, ambling around the office. Finally he pulled up short. "Donaldson is one obstinate man. I always questioned Nellie after she visited with him, but she claims he never talked about the robbery. Claims he never talked period. Not one word about the robbery to me or to her."

"He never discussed the money, you mean," Jack said.

Pruitt nodded. "And he's the only one who knows where it's hidden. I would have thought Nellie could get the truth out of him, but she didn't."

"Maybe she's keeping the information to herself," Jack suggested.

"No, Nellie's too smart for that. She understands that a little is better than nothing."

"Like you say, Nellie's a smart woman," Jack said. "One of these days she's going to get tired of you using her, Webb, and she's going to leave you."

"That's wishful thinking on your part. I've seen the way you look at Nellie. I've seen the wanting in your eyes."

"If she ever leaves you," Jack promised, "I'll sure be in line for her. I'd treat Nellie real good."

"Nellie likes the way I treat her." Webb laughed. "Even if Nellie left me, Jack. She wouldn't get involved with someone like you. Nellie wants an exciting man." His laughter mocked the warden. "I'm not worried about Nellie," the attorney bragged. "I have her in the palm of my hand."

"Just make sure you don't ever spread your fingers, Webb, or she's gone."

"Well, I don't have time to argue the point with you. I need to be thinking about Cord Donaldson," Webb said. Sliding his hands into his pockets, he began pacing again. "I know it's risky, but we're going to have to take a chance on letting him out. Once he's free, he'll eventually lead us to it. The money is what keeps him going."

Jack shifted in his chair. Thinking about the young woman who sat in the receiving room, he picked up a sheaf of papers and thumped them against the desktop. "Maybe. Maybe not. From what I've learned about Donaldson during the four years I've been warden, I'd say he's predictably unpredictable."

Pruitt laughed. "You might say that, Jack, but I wouldn't. I know people. I know Cord Donaldson. And he'll eventually lead us to the San Domingo treasure."

The San Domingo treasure. Not a day had passed during the past four years that Jack had not heard about this treasure, and each year its value grew, its denominations changed. At the moment, the latest assessment was a million dollars in gold bars.

"Jack," Pruitt drawled, "I'll wager you a thousand to one we'll have the San Domingo treasure within the year."

"A thousand dollars," the warden murmured. "You're willing to wager that much?"

Pruitt blinked, hesitated, then bobbed his head. "Why, yes, Jack, I am. I'm that sure of my prediction."

"But first you're going to have to get Mrs. Donaldson and Cord together. How are you going to do that?"

"I'm not going to have to do anything," Pruitt answered. "Mrs. Donaldson is playing right into our hands and will soon have Donaldson playing into hers.

She retained me to petition the court for Donaldson's pardon. While I've assured her a pardon is out of the question, I advised her to seek a parole. A pardon delivers him out of our hands, but a parole . . ."

Letting the unfinished sentence trail into silence, Pruitt walked to the wall mirror and studied his reflection. He ran the tip of a finger down the middle part of thickly greased, straight hair.

"In fact, Jack, I've already begun the paperwork. The judge took it under advisement and has sent me here to let her know he's in agreement. Of course, considering the enormity of the crime Donaldson committed, it'll take a large sum of money to guarantee his release."

Money that a corrupt judge and attorney would divide between themselves! Disgusted, Jack dropped the papers to the desk and gazed at Pruitt. With unscrupulous men like Webb Pruitt running the government, what was the world coming to? he wondered. Swiveling in his chair, he straightened out his legs.

"Well, Jack, I guess I'll be going." Pruitt walked across the room and lifted his hat from the pegged rack. Lightly brushing the impeccably clean crown, he said, "If you'll tell me where the young woman is, I'll give her the good news."

Jack stood, took several steps around his desk, and stopped at the front side of it. "Donaldson's a smart man. He's not going to ride straight out of prison to the money."

"You underestimate me, Jack." Pruitt clicked his tongue. "Shame on you. I have my ways."

"Which are?"

Pruitt opened the door, paused, and said over his shoulder, "I'm not at liberty to say, but we have the smallest of details worked out."

From the hallway Jack heard footfalls he quickly identified as belonging to Rule. During his time as warden, he had come to know the old man's gait well. His crisp, hurried steps were as distinctive as his coarse voice.

"Afternoon, Mr. Pruitt." The prisoner's greeting echoed into the warden's office.

"Afternoon, Rule. Jack, here, tells me that you'll soon be getting out. Finished your term, huh?"

"Yep. Reckon so."

"How long have you been with us?"

"Nigh on twenty years."

"Jack says he's really going to miss you. Seeing as you're a model prisoner and the best cook the penitentiary ever had."

Rule grinned. "Well, sir, don't wish to cause the warden no hardship, but I certainly ain't desirous of staying just so's he'll have a cook. Reckon he'll have to find another prisoner willing to take over my duties."

Pruitt laughed with him. "Understand you've been taking care of Mrs. Donaldson?"

"Yes, sir."

"Aren't you afraid Donaldson will take his spite out on you?"

"Not really," the old man drawled. "Right now he probably hates me and believes I'm not the friend he thought I was. But give him time to get over his anger, and he'll see I did what was best. Well, sir, I gotta go. Got lots of work to do to get dinner ready." Footfalls, in accompaniment to whistling, faded down the corridor.

Pruitt turned, looked at Willowby and smiled slyly. "I guarantee you, Jack, we'll know everything Cord Donaldson is doing, with him none the wiser."

Two

Pondering the wisdom of her announcement to stay until hell froze over, Floryn still sat in the hot, humidly oppressive penitentiary. Four days and nights and one storm had passed. Cord still refused to see her. *Adamantly* refused, the warden reported more than once. The temperatures soared. Hell would not be cooling off any too soon, much less freezing.

She moved out of the shaft of afternoon sunlight that gleamed hotly through the small, barred window. Long since having shed both gloves and vest, she flexed her shoulders to work out the stiffness. She wiped perspiration from her face. The doorknob rattled, and she spun around. Rule poked his head around the door through an ever widening crack.

She took a step and eagerly asked, "Did you see Cord?"

"Yes 'um. Sure did."

"Will he see me?"

"No, ma'am, he weren't having none of it. He shouted a string of cuss words, the likes of which a lady like you shouldn't be hearing. Mixed up in 'em was a no."

"You gave him the message?"

"Sure did. Told him you had a plan to get him out

22

of here, but he weren't interested. Said he didn't need no woman to take care of 'im. He'd do it hisself."

Floryn's spirits sagged. She moved back to the table, bracing both hands against the worn top and bowing her head.

"Now, don't you go getting depressed." Rule crossed the room to pat her shoulder reassuringly. "I got a plan myself. I figured out how to get you to him."

"Oh, Rule," she breathed, "I don't know what to say."

He held weathered, vein-strutted hands up. "Don't reckon you ought to say anything. I ain't promising nothing. I'm just gonna take you to him out on the work line."

"Where's that?"

"At the quarry quite a ways from here. Where the chain gang works. You'll hafta walk. And, ma'am—"

She waited.

"I don't guarantee he'll talk to you."

"I know." She felt the prick of tears in her eyes.

Opening her reticule, she fumbled for a handkerchief. Before she found it, Rule pressed a clean white one against her cheeks. She clasped it, her hand closing over his. For a second she took comfort.

"Thank you. I don't know how I would have handled this if it hadn't been for you."

"I was married once," he said. "She died. She might'a had a chance if the doctor had seen fit to come treat her. But he was too busy drinking and dancing at a social." Rule moved away from her, picking up the empty pitcher from the washstand. "She was all I had. When she died, I was so angry I lost my mind. I shot the doctor and wounded him. He died later."

"Is that what you're serving time for?" Floryn asked.

He nodded. "If I had been thinking straight, I wouldn't have done it, 'cause she never loved me like I loved her. I knew she was seeing other men, but I pretended I didn't know 'cause I was afraid I'd drive her away from me, and I couldn't of stood that. She was the prettiest thing you ever did see. She was the light of my life." He smiled sadly. "I figure I must'a loved her like you love Donaldson. A deep, hurting kind of love."

Without her saying a word, the old man had aptly described her feelings for Cord. She wondered if her emotions were as transparent to others as they had been to Rule.

He smiled kindly. "Now, I'm gonna bring you some water, so's you can freshen yourself up. I know you'll want to look your finest when you see him."

As soon as Rule left the room, Floryn quickly unpinned her hat and laid it on the table. Moving to the aged mirror that hung on the wall, she fluffed the curls that framed her face. She ran her fingers over her cheeks, letting them linger on the mauve semicircles beneath her eyes — one sign of her exhaustion. She brushed the tip of her finger over her bottom lip. She was pale, her features almost gaunt. Would Cord recognize her? Would she recognize him?

Abruptly she was assailed with doubts and wondered if she should go to the quarry to see him. Mr. Pruitt had emphasized the importance of her letting him handle the situation, of her working through proper legal channels. Perhaps in setting up this visit without the warden's approval, she and Rule were jeopardizing Cord's chances of being paroled.

The door opened, and Rule reentered the room. After setting the pitcher and a small bar of soap on the washstand next to the basin, he removed a towel and washcloth from his arm.

"Rule, perhaps we should discuss what we're doing with the warden."

"I don't think that's the right thing to do, ma'am. The warden, good man he is, hasn't been able to convince Donaldson to see you, and he ain't gonna see you. Donaldson's mind is made up, and it ain't gonna be changed. Only a surprise attack will work."

"Mr. Pruitt promised me he would take care of everything. I don't want to antagonize him. He's assured me he can get Cord a parole." And too much rode on his freedom, on his returning to the ranch for Floryn to mess it up with impulsive behavior.

"Told you what I thought," the old man said as he moved toward the exit. "You better make up your mind quick. We don't have no time to dilly-dally. I'll be back to get you in about thirty minutes. You can let me know what you've decided."

The door had not closed behind him before Floryn made her decision. She knew exactly what she was going to do, what she had to do. Her resolve diminished not a whit. She wanted to be careful where the authorities were concerned, but she had to talk with Cord to see if he would accept her conditions. If not . . . She refused to entertain the thought.

She had to talk with him immediately. Already she had wasted precious time. She doused the cloth in the warm water and began to wash her face. She had not traveled this far to turn back without telling him her reason for coming.

Her long journey from Donaldsonville to Huntsville, Cord's constant refusal to see her, the warden's impatience with her, exhaustion — none of this had lessened Floryn's resolve, but this trek to the quarry threatened to do so. The terrain was rough, the path-

25

way up the hill steep and jagged. Stopping to catch her breath, she brushed dust from her skirt, then pushed a strand of hair from her face, knocking her hat askew. She straightened it. A lot of good her toilet had done! As she lowered her hand, she noticed she had snagged her kid gloves — the new ones imported from France. That matched her new dress. That were meant to impress Cord.

In fact, her entire wardrobe had been bought with Cord in mind. She had spent hours pouring over the patterns, standing for the fittings, and ordering accessories. Cost had been a major consideration, but Floryn had felt the clothes were worth the extravagance. She wanted to look her best for him when she asked for his help. A world of good it had done her since he had refused to see her.

"Can't stop now, Mrs. Donaldson," Rule called over his shoulder.

"I'm not."

Disregarding the pointed rocks that cut into the delicate leather gloves, she climbed higher, closer to Cord, closer to the completion of her goal. When she and the old man reached the top of the incline, she narrowed her eyes against the glare of the afternoon sun and scanned the column of men off in the distance.

Chained together at the ankles, weighted down with iron balls, they pounded rocks with large picks and sledgehammers. Each thwack of the tools jarred the earth and echoed harshly against the hewn walls of the quarry. Dust filled the air, forming a hazy cloud around the men.

Eagerly Floryn's gaze moved from one to the other, but it was difficult for her to tell them apart. All wore faded, nondescript uniforms that made them look the same; the hair that escaped the bibbed caps they wore was chalky with dust. Yet she strained to find Cord. He was here. He had to be.

Leaving her, Rule walked up and down the line. Finally he returned, shaking his head. "Cord's gone," he announced. "They must have him working somewhere else."

Floryn went numb with disappointment.

Rule caught her hand. "Now, now, everything is going to be all right. We'll find him. You just come with me. I'll take you to a place where it's a little cooler. You can wait there while I search for him."

She followed, vaguely aware of the wooden cistern and nearby water trough. She slid down to sit on a rock and to wait . . . longer. The sun climbed higher in a sky that was conspicuously devoid of clouds. A lone bird fluttered overhead, finally lighting on the edge of the cistern. In the background she heard the pounding of the hammers and the picks, the hacking coughs, the loud raucous conversation among the inmates.

Thinking she could cope better with the dry heat of Donaldsonville than this East Texas humidity, she blotted her face with her handkerchief. She closed her eyes and leaned against the boulder. What was she going to do if she did not see Cord? Strange, she had not allowed herself to think of this possibility . . . until now. Even so she refused to dwell on the thought. Her entire future depended on Cord. He was the only one who could help her. She had to see him. She would see him. He would help her. Surely he would.

Boots crunching on loose gravel caught her attention. Her eyes opened, and she stared at the back of a man, a tall man, as he bent above the trough, sloshing water over his head. Broad, muscular shoulders stretched the faded material of the uniform shirt. Long sleeves were rolled up to reveal firm, muscular sun-browned arms. His head of hair, soon washed clean of the white dust, gleamed raven black.

He grabbed the towel hanging on the rod attached to the cistern. After he dried his hair, he returned the towel to the rod and picked up a black leather band which he tied around his head. A sweatband, no doubt. The man turned to gaze into the distance, and Floryn saw his profile — a profile that was indelibly imprinted in her memory.

Cord. She straightened and laid her hand at the base of her throat. Her breath caught in her chest. She struggled to breathe. This had to be him. This had to be Cord.

She was not aware she had spoken his name until the man, his tall, lean body captured in the sun, completely turned in her direction to stare in surprise at her. Silver winged his temples, and Floryn thought how apt that she had compared him to the raven. Black hair with silver wings.

Her gaze fastened to the piece of black leather tied about his head. Not a sweatband as she had supposed but a shield over his left eye. She knew she should not stare, but could not help herself. Pain, acute pain, washed through her at the thought of his having lost an eye. While she hurt for him, she was also fascinated by the black patch. On others the loss of an eye might have been maiming, might have detracted from their looks. Not for Cord. It added to his ruggedness, to his toughness.

"Hello," she murmured, only now allowing her gaze to move over the rest of his face.

He stared intently, saying nothing, giving no indication that he recognized her. She almost felt the progression of his gaze, from her eyes to her lips. She watched it lower to the lace jabot that adorned the front of her blouse, to the pull of material across her breasts. She forgot her anxiety over her new clothes, over wanting to impress him. She was aware only of his penetrating gaze upon her. Her breathing quickened so that she could not disguise the rapid rise and fall of her breasts. They held his attention.

Finally his gaze—full of mockery—settled on her face. Confused, embarrassed, she again concentrated on the black leather patch that covered his left eye, that touched the line of beard stubble on his cheek. Strangely, it was an extension of him, an intimate part of him. As much as she longed to feel his flesh beneath her fingers, she wanted to touch the leather shield.

Cord smiled, drawing Floryn's attention to his mouth. Although the shape of his lips was as she remembered, as she had dreamed about, they were different. Instead of gently lifting at the corners as if on the verge of a smile, they were straight and hard, almost clenched together in the beginning of a frown. Now his lips—these lips that had kissed her so tenderly, that had declared his love for her—these lips were twisted in mockery.

"I—I—it's been a long time," she finally managed. Their first meeting was not as she had imagined. Nothing close to what she had imagined.

Ignoring her completely, he glanced down, pulled the bibbed cap from his shirt pocket, and settled it on his head. Wrapping a hand around the handle of the sledgehammer, he easily slung it over his shoulder, causing muscles to ripple across his chest. He turned and, impeded by the ball and chain, walked slowly away.

"Cord! You can't leave me. You must talk with me." Floryn ran, caught him by the arm, and tugged. Her first contact with him in all these many years. If

29

she had grabbed the end of a red hot branding iron, she could not have been more aware of sensation. The mere touching of their flesh caused dormant emotions to leap to life and to tug her heart strings. Memories of that long-ago summer resurged with such force Floryn's hand began to shake.

He stopped walking. The ball rolled back, stopping short of her foot. She felt his tenseness, the hardness of his muscles. She looked down at his arm. He did, too. Was he experiencing the same emotions as she? She could not tell because he kept his back to her.

"Please, Cord," she begged softly, "hear me out. Don't turn me away without giving me a chance."

He prized her fingers loose and turned. Closer to him than she had been previously, she saw the ravaging marks of time on his lean face. It was empty, bleak, stripped of emotion. The features were glacial. The years had grooved heavy lines around his mouth and the corners of his eyes . . . of his eye, of his ice-blue eye. Overcome by what she saw, giving in to her earlier desire, Floryn reached up, but Cord moved his head aside. She quickly withdrew her hand, yet continued to stare at him.

"Say something," she begged. "Please."

"You said it's been a long time since we saw each other. I say it hasn't been long enough."

Floryn felt a rush of hostility toward her so strong it formed a barrier, invisible yet impenetrable.

"Surely you can't mean that," she cried. Mentally she saw the carving on the trunk of the oak tree; she remembered their pledge. Had she not touched the words nearly every day for the past ten years? "Remember our summer, Cord?"

She searched the dark countenance and saw a tightening of his jaws, but not a flicker of remembrance crossed his face to soften his features. This

30

man, this silent, bitter stranger was defeating her, was stripping all her control away, exposing and leaving her vulnerable.

"Goodbye, Floryn."

In the face of such open hatred and rejection, she felt helpless. Tears swelled inside, but she would not give them release. Pride demanded she leave; therefore, she sacrificed pride. Cord was the only one who could help her; she needed him desperately. No matter what happened, she would not let him make her lose her composure. She would not give up in her efforts to persuade him. She chose her words carefully, keeping her voice low, not wanting him to hear her vulnerability.

"Love forever. June, 1855."

"June, 1865." He spoke harshly. "Ten years have passed, Floryn. That summer is long gone."

"Not the memories," she cried. "Not what we shared."

"But you and I have changed. I'm not the same man you knew then. Certainly not the romantic fool."

"I didn't think you were a fool."

With each word they spoke the distance between them widened, the barrier hardened. More than years separated them. Bitterness tarnished and distorted what they had once shared. Again silence hung oppressively between them.

Eventually she said, "Hal is dead."

Cord lowered the hammer and drawled, "No wonder you wanted me to hear you out and to say something. This definitely calls for a response, but I'm unsure which word to use, not because I haven't had a stimulating conversation with a woman for the past nine years but because I'm unsure of your feelings." The sarcasm in his voice equaled that in his smile.

"Which shall it be, *Aunt Floryn,* congratulations or condolences?"

"How can you be so cruel?"

"You don't know the meaning of cruel."

Cord turned the hammer loose, letting it topple to the ground. In a swift unwinding of powerful muscles, he stood in front of Floryn, his austere face filling her view. She saw the beard stubble shadowing his cheeks, the texture of sun-bronzed skin and a dust-glazed leather patch. She felt the full force of his anger, his hostility. Like flames, it flared between them. If she moved a fraction of an inch she feared she would be incinerated.

He grasped her by the upper arms, the material of her blouse offering no protection to the biting grip or to the heated touch. Either he had no such fear or wanted her to burn. She decided it was the latter. The ball rolled closer, nipping the tip of her toes, but her awareness of Cord was too acute for her to be concerned with her feet.

"Don't play the innocent with me, Floryn. I know who and what you are."

He was close, too close, and his anger blazed against her skin, hot and powerful. She shook, but not from fear. She was so hot, she thought she was ablaze, burning, yet not consumed. Her body recognized Cord's touch. It yearned for this and more.

His fingers tightened to send waves of excitement undulating through her body. As if guided by a force outside herself, she leaned forward, face lifted, lips parted in expectation. He released her. Still she remained where she was.

"I know what you want, Floryn."

Fear curled around her heart and squeezed.

"I know why you're here."

"You—you do?"

32

"You taught me well. I know how women like you operate. I know what you want from life. You wanted all that your impotent husband promised — power, respectability, and wealth. But you're also a young and passionate woman and wanted more. You needed a stud in your life, or shall I say studs?"

Hateful words from the past spilled over into the present to hurt her anew. Still in love with him, she wanted to penetrate this facade of hatred and bitterness. Surely love was stronger than either of those emotions. Surely *their* love was stronger.

"There have been no others," she said. "Only you."

Disregarding her denial, he forged ahead. "The lovers you have, those you can have no longer thrill you, so you want a new challenge. What better way than keep it in the family. The uncle's gone, so it's back to the nephew, back to your first plaything. How thrilling to see if you can arouse the first man who stirred your passions."

Puzzled, Floryn stared at him. Like every other word he had spoken to her since they met, his declaration was hard and cynical. He was using a fabrication to make her feel cheap and conniving. For the most part he was successful. It revealed a facet of Cord's personality Floryn had not even begun to imagine existed.

Softly she said, "Maybe that's your fantasy."

"Lady, that doesn't begin to compare to my fantasies."

She heard his breathing, felt the warmth of his body, smelled the chalky dust that clung to his clothing. He no longer touched her with anything but his gaze, yet he compelled her to come nearer. She swayed closer. He stepped back. She stumbled, but he made no offer to steady her.

A hateful grin twisted his lips and coldly grooved

his mouth. The gesture should have made him ugly, repulsive, but it did nothing to diminish his virility, his animal magnetism.

"Perhaps I'm wrong," he said. "Maybe there haven't been other men. You act as if you're starved for loving."

No, she thought, *starved only for your love.*

"Again it could be that you're playacting. You want me to believe I'm the only one. It heightens the pleasure of the game. You were good at playacting, Floryn, but you're not going to fool me a second time. You made your bed—without me—now lie in it—without me." Dry laughter ended the sardonic pronouncement. "Women like you have no trouble finding someone to lie in their beds, do they?"

She slapped him hard. Her palm stung, but she felt no regret, not even when she saw the reddened imprint of her hand on his right cheek.

"Don't begin to judge me." She spat the words. "You have no idea what kind of woman I am."

He tugged the brim of the cap so that it rode low on his forehead and shadowed his face. "You've satisfied your curiosity. Now leave."

"Not without telling you why I came."

"I'm not interested in hearing. Go on back to the ranch and play the part of the grand lady."

"Even if I wanted to, I can't." She lifted her chin and bravely made her admission. "The Fancy Lady doesn't belong to me."

Again Cord laughed, the sound loud and mocking and abrasive. "So your great sacrifice didn't pay off? You lived with an old man twelve years for nothing."

"Hal betrayed me."

"Don't tell me he left the ranch to George Greeve."

"I'm—surprised you would remember George."

"I liked him," Cord answered. "He was a good man."

"Yes," she said. "Perhaps too good."

Cord's mouth thinned, his jaws clinched; otherwise, his expression remained unchanged. His gaze, his scrutiny of her intensified. "What happened to him?"

"Last I heard he was working in New Mexico."

"He was interested in you."

"He was interested in people period."

"In you period. I saw him looking at and wanting you. It was written all over him. For all I know he gave you a shoulder to cry on after I left. Maybe he gave you more."

Floryn caught her breath, held it a long time before she slowly released it. "Maybe I didn't cry after you left."

Cord did not laugh again, but a smile continued to curl his lips. She stared at this man, at this stranger who stood in front of her, almost hating him. She had come to him in love, but had been reduced to admitting only need. In everything Cord did or said he attempted to hurt or humiliate her.

This man standing in front of her was as hard as the rocks around him, sculpted by hatred, chiseled out of anger and bitterness. Gone was that innate gentleness of the soul that tempered the dark side of his nature, that subdued the primitive man within. As Rule had warned, Cord's emotions were petrified.

The wind riffled his hair, black strands — burnished in the sunlight — blew across his forehead to remind her of the Cord she had known long ago. The Cord who was strong and indomitable like the Forever Tree in the meadow, the one on which he had carved their pledge of love. The Cord who had loved her, and it was love that had put gentleness in his strength, that had subdued the beast within.

"What did Hal do with the ranch?" Cord asked.

His question startled Floryn, and she jumped. "He left half to you and half to Hope."

"Who's Hope? The woman who replaced you in Hal's affections?"

Anger surged within, but during her marriage Floryn had learned patience. She was an expert in aplomb. "She's our daughter."

For the first time during their conversation his composure changed. Floryn had gotten the best of him and was glad. She waited through the shocked silence. He lowered his gaze to her stomach, stared, then raised his head to look into her eyes.

"*Your* daughter?" he asked. Without waiting for an answer, he spoke again, his voice harsh and accusing. "Yours and who else's?"

Softly she said, "Our daughter, Cord. Yours and mine."

Three

"Our daughter."

The words brushed past numbed lips. Cord took several steps toward Floryn, tugging the heavy ball with him as if it were a toy. Was it possible that he and Floryn had a daughter? That *he* had a daughter? He reached for Floryn, then realizing what he had done, dropped his arm.

Strange as it was, during all these years, in all his wondering, he had not thought of the possibility of a child. Maybe he had subconsciously pushed the idea aside.

He could not have tolerated his imprisonment, the injustice done to him, had he known he had a child. He would have hurt all the more to know his child had a mother who was accused of infidelity.

"I wrote you. Several letters," Floryn said. "They were returned with no forwarding address."

"How old is she?"

"Nine. I—I still have the letters, Cord. With me. I also have her christening papers. She was . . . she was born March 14, 1856. Almost nine months after you left."

He digested the words, calculated the time. He had a daughter. His own child. A part of him. A part of him that spoke of a future, that guaranteed him one. Floryn was the past. A child—their child—was the future.

"Describe her. Describe Hope to me."

A gust of wind tore the hat from Floryn's head and it dangled from its ribbons down her back. Strands of honey-brown hair blew across her face. A hand, covered in a soiled and tattered glove, brushed them back into the chignon of curls. Her arm dropped. His gaze returned to eyes the same shade of brown as her hair.

She smiled, her expression soft when she spoke, "In actions and looks she's very much like you."

No, she must be more like you. He envisioned his daughter as a miniature version of the woman he had loved so many summers ago.

"She has black hair and brown eyes."

"Eyes like her mother," Cord murmured. His daughter. His flesh and blood.

"Hair like her father," Floryn said. "She's beautiful."

"Yes," he said, "she would be. Where is she?"

"At home with Leanor—Leanor Santico, her nanny whom she adores and who adores her. Leanor delivered Hope and has been with us ever since. I thought about bringing both of them with me, but I wasn't sure about . . . about anything." Floryn held her hand out. "Here are the letters. I wrote you all about Hope."

He brushed the bound packet aside. "I don't need proof, Floryn. I know you were a virgin and Hal an impotent cripple when we made love."

"When we confessed our forever love."

"Forever love," he repeated softly.

He remembered the beauty of that morning. Then pain and disappointment rushed in. Reality replaced nostalgia. Rumors had filtered in to him about how long she had remained true to Hal . . . and to him . . . to this sacred memory of forever love she had thrown up to him since she arrived. He had heard

38

about the endless string of men in her life, and he had hated all of them. Had hated her.

But he had heard nothing of the child! Of his daughter!

After ten years Floryn walks back into my life and blithely announces that I'm a father, that I have a daughter. In an instant, before I can snap my fingers, I've accepted Hope as mine. Am I this easy to fool?

No, he was not. He had known the answer to that before he asked himself. But Floryn was intelligent, always had been. She had known what he craved, what he needed—forever love epitomized by a child, their child. Floryn had taken the reality and the concept of forever love away from him when she refused to go with him years ago. Now she offered it back to him in the form of their daughter. He gladly accepted because Hope filled a void in his life and he would make sure Floryn did not take it away from him this time.

"Forever love," he murmured the second time, extending his thoughts into words. He looked at her, noticing the expectant expression on her face, the hope, the eagerness, both underscored by her anxiety. "Yes, we confessed that, didn't we?"

On one level his words sounded like a declaration of love. Certainly they had been a statement of intent on his part, a forever commitment. On another level they were an accusation. The shadows in her eyes assured him he sliced her to the quick.

"Strange how short forever is, Floryn. A mere four or five hours." He hoped he hurt her even more, that he hurt her as deeply as she had hurt him. "What did you tell Hal?"

"The truth." She drew a breath. "You were right. We should have told him we were in love. He would have let me go."

39

Cord felt an ache in his chest, an ache for what could have been, for what could never be recovered. Lost love. Lost years.

"Hal loved Hope as if she were his own child. I named her Hope because I hoped you would come back and know your daughter."

He ached for lost opportunities.

"I would have come to you sooner," she said, "but it's taken all this time for us to find you. Hal and I were concerned about you, but you . . . you never wrote."

"No, I didn't want *you* to find me."

Only her eyes gave way to momentary discomfort.

"So how did you find me?"

"I hired a New York detective. His fee was quite high, but he promised favorable results."

At twenty-eight she still retained an innocence that was reminiscent of the eighteen-year-old he had known, but she was even more poised and confident. Although wind-blown and dusty, she held herself with dignity, her back straight, shoulders squared, her chin uplifted slightly.

"Even had I known you didn't want me to find you," she said, "I would have searched for Hope's sake."

They lapsed into silence.

Finally she said, "Rule delivered my message?"

He nodded.

"I can get you released, Cord."

Cord said nothing because he could not. The idea of being released from prison, following so quickly on his having learned about having a daughter was overwhelming.

"Freedom, Cord. You can have your freedom. Think about it."

As if he had not for the past nine years. To hear

her utter the word—the most wonderful word in the entire American vocabulary—gave him new heart. Freedom! The greatest gift one could bestow upon him. What he had dreamed about day and night. He glanced at her, almost unbelieving. The reflection of the sun cast her in a halo. An angel. He had thought she looked like an angel when he first saw her. He thought so now.

Damn it to hell! What was wrong with him? She had never been an angel and never would be! He could not afford to let her beauty and softness, her promises get to him.

"I've retained an attorney," she continued, her voice seemingly undetached to any emotion, "who for a fee is willing to petition the court for a parole for you. He said the judge is sympathetic to your case."

"Webb Pruitt?" At her nod, Cord said, "You may not have the best of the profession, but you have the best for the job. If Pruitt's working with you, God help those working against you."

"He's been kind to me," Floryn defended.

"I'm sure he has. He has a strong motivation for his *kindness*," Cord drawled.

"My money?"

Cord nodded.

"I figure he's not quite as upright in his profession as he may claim and probably the parole guarantee is going into his pocket. That's not what matters now, Cord. He's willing to and can help us."

"So he thinks he can get me a parole?" Cord said.

Not a pardon, but freedom, nonetheless. If Cord accepted Floryn's offer, it would serve his purpose. He could prove his innocence, discover the secret of the pendant and the San Domingo fortune, and find the person who had framed him. And reclaim what he had hidden so long ago . . . if it were still there.

41

Floryn took a step, moving into the shade cast by the cistern. The burst of radiance around her head—her halo—disappeared. Just as well. Cord no longer believed in God, miracles, or justice. He was unsure what he believed about Floryn Donaldson. He had learned that if anything good came along in life, it had conditions.

"What's in this for you?" he asked.

"I want you to marry me," she answered forthrightly with no hesitation, her gaze locked to his, "so I can have guardianship of Hope, and I want one fourth of the Fancy Lady."

He studied her.

"One fourth when you were bargaining for the whole thing," he mocked. "Wasn't that a letdown?"

"Yes," she admitted, "it was . . . and is."

"Why didn't Hal leave Fancy Lady to you?" he asked. "That was your marriage agreement, wasn't it? The ranch in exchange for your taking care of him until he died."

"He believed me guilty of infidelity."

"Which was true," Cord said, "considering what happened between you and me. Was your fidelity part of your marriage agreement?"

She winced—that was what he wanted—but her voice was steady when she said, "He forgave me that, so he said, but as time passed, he taunted me. He believed that once a woman—especially the daughter of a whore—has been awakened to passion she could not remain celibate. My indiscretion with you gave him basis for believing that I continued to be promiscuous."

"Of course you weren't?" he said sarcastically.

"You're fully aware of my only indiscretion." Her steadfast gaze demanded that he believe her.

"I'm fully aware of one indiscretion," he corrected.

During the past nine years nothing—none of the rumors Shelby had repeated to him—had been unable to erase Floryn's face from his memory. Despite knowing she had had many lovers, he had been unable to make love to the prostitutes that were brought to the prison without thinking about her, without wishing the one with him were she. All these years he had had sexual release but never gratification. Forever she had left her mark on him, he thought bitterly. She had reduced him to a life of loneliness, a life without fulfillment.

And it made him furious. It had eaten away at him all these years.

All Floryn had ever wanted or needed was the ranch. Always it was the damned ranch.

His thoughts turned to the Fancy Lady—endless acres sprawling along the Rio Grande River east of El Paso and close to the small border town of Donaldsonville. "How big is the ranch?"

"Five hundred thousand acres," Floryn replied. "After I became manager, I doubled our holdings and expanded our operation. We utilize part of the acreage for farming—"

"In West Texas?" Cord asked.

"We had to. I've been studying and going through the early Spanish records. Just like they did in the early missions, we've built aqueducts to irrigate small garden plots. The rest of the property is used for our stock—cattle, horses, and mules."

"Sounds like you have things under control."

"I did until Hal became obsessed with the idea that I was a whore, until he took guardianship of Hope away from me," she said, a bitter tinge to her voice. "He had me declared an unfit mother which wasn't difficult considering my mother was a known whore, considering Hal owned everyone in Donaldsonville

43

and for hundreds of miles in all directions of the ranch. I have absolutely no say in our daughter's welfare."

"Who's her guardian?"

"She's a ward of the court, but she's allowed to remain at the ranch under Leanor's supervision until the two-year stipulation on Hal's will expires or you return to become her guardian."

"Two years?" he said.

Floryn nodded her head, then raised a hand to brush perspiration from her forehead. "You inherit and become Hope's legal guardian only if you return to the ranch within two years of his death, and eight months of that is already gone. If you don't return, Hal's attorney, Kern Wallis, will become her guardian and the executor of the estate until she reaches the age of twenty-one."

Cord removed his gaze from Floryn and stared into the distance. He saw the haze of chalky white smoke that hovered above the quarry. He heard the blur of noise, a mixture of the prisoners' conversation and the pounding of the hammers and picks.

"Whether you or I like it," Floryn said, "we are mutually dependent on each other."

Returning his attention to her, he raised a brow.

"Is it correct that you no longer own your company?" she asked.

"Donaldson's Dragoons," Cord murmured. Memories he had long since pushed aside were returning, and they still hurt him. His company of armed guards. He remembered his successful business venture, his plans, his dreams. Fate, coupled with injustice, had stripped him of this.

"You sold the company and used everything you got and had to finance your defense." The crisp cadence of her voice reminded Cord of Alvin

44

Ainsworth—the fat guard who always delivered bad news with such flourish and pleasure.

"Where did you learn that? Pruitt?" When she nodded, he said, "He's a thorough bastard."

"We're not discussing him," Floryn said. "We're discussing us and how we're going to handle this situation."

"How *we're* going to handle the situation," he said sarcastically. "The way you're talking, you're handling everything. I'm a pawn, necessary but easily dispensed with."

"I didn't mean for it to sound that way," she said, giving him a stricken look. "We need to discuss how we're going to handle the financial aspects, and—"

"The bottom line is always money, isn't it?" he said.

Her gaze intensified; then she sighed. "No, the bottom line is Hope. I want to save the ranch for her, but I'm not going to waste my breath and energy trying to make you believe it. It's evident that you're closed-minded and are going to believe whatever you want to."

Cord reached out to lightly rub Floryn's temples. When she gazed at him in surprise, he said, "I was right?"

She raised her thick arched brows.

"A moment ago, the way the light was hitting you, you looked like an angel. Now that I feel the horns, I believe you're the devil I've always thought you were. A beautiful one, but a devil, nonetheless."

"This is no time for jesting."

"No jest. According to the stories I was told when I attended Sunday school, the devil wanted it all—just like you."

"I have never compared myself to the devil," Floryn answered. "I have my dreams and one of them is security for me and our daughter. It's not a sin."

He leveled a studious gaze on her. "Security, yes, but I'd say more for yourself than anyone else." Before she could respond, he asked, "Do you know why I'm in prison? Why I'm out here in the quarry with the work gang?"

Even as he spoke, in the distance he heard a guard yell a command. His gaze scanned the horizon. Although hidden from view, armed guards were posted. They watched. They waited for someone, anyone to make a charge for freedom. They delighted in bringing them back, mangled and alive. Ready sport for another day, Cord had always sworn.

"Yes, I know why you're here," Floryn said, again speaking forthrightly. "The warden told me. You were sentenced to serve twenty years for the murder of Sanchia Guilbert and for stealing the San Domingo fortune she was smuggling out of Mexico."

"Believing that, you still want to marry me?"

"You ask me what I knew, not what I believed," she replied.

When she remained silent, he asked, "What do you believe?"

"You're innocent."

"All evidence points to my guilt."

"I don't care. I know you. I once loved you."

Once loved you. The words assaulted Cord's senses. He did not want to care about her. He was determined not to care. But it hurt, hurt like hell, for her to admit openly, flatly that she really did not care about him. Like ten years ago, she wanted to use him again. Both times her purpose had been the same: the Fancy Lady.

"I know you couldn't have killed that woman—for that matter—anyone," she said.

"Mrs. Donaldson!" Rule ran up. "Time to go. The

46

guards will be changing soon. Cord, you better get back to work."

Floryn stepped away. "I'll be leaving on tomorrow's stage. I'll need your answer before then."

She followed Rule Compton past the cistern to a large boulder that marked the path down the hill.

"Floryn!"

She turned. Rule remained where he was, slightly hidden behind the outcropping of rocks.

"I want my letters."

Returning, she opened her reticule. "I — I thought you believed me."

"I do where Hope is concerned."

Again he qualified his answer and made Floryn wonder anew why he doubted her so, made her wonder if Kern Wallis had already found him. The thought filled her with trepidation.

When she pulled the bound packet from her purse, her hands shook so she dropped it to the ground. By the time Cord knelt, Floryn was already kneeling. Their hands met and intertwined over the letters. At the instant of contact, despite Floryn's kid gloves, lightning flashed between them. It was elemental. Sensual and intense.

Her eyes flew to his face. Their fingers still intertwined, she felt the brush of his thumb over the top of her hand. Her heart fluttered — this time from excitement — as she looked at him. As quickly the hard, calloused expression wiped away her joy. She strongly responded to him; he hardly responded to her. He brushed a strand of hair from her forehead, to send a fresh tremor of excitement through her body.

"It's a shame things turned out as they did, Floryn. You and I were good together." A slow smile twisted his lips. "We still could be."

"Could we?" she murmured.

47

"Yes," he drawled, raising a hand to touch the crook on his nose, "if you were willing to be one of my prison women."

The statement rudely shattered the hypnotic spell he had woven about her. Her heart as shattered, Floryn's hand flew up. Cord caught her wrist, his fingers biting into the tender flesh.

"You slapped me once, Floryn, not again." The smile turned to sarcastic laughter. "You always were spirited. I liked it when you were younger. I like it now. I like and still want you."

"I don't like or want you," Floryn gave voice to a lie — a defensive one spoken to protect her broken heart, to keep her spirit from being broken as well. She twisted her hand, but his grip did not loosen. "As much as I wish it were different, all that's important to me is marriage to you."

"At one time, Floryn, marriage to you was all that was important to me. Today I don't return the sentiment . . . at all."

Cord had mocked her, attempted to humiliate her, yet Floryn would do it all over again. Hope was her life — her entire life. Floryn would willingly give her life for her daughter. Closing her eyes, she saw Hope. The large brown eyes, sparkling with life and surrounded by long curling black lashes. The lips that always curved into a teasing smile — like the one Cord had had when Floryn first met him. Hope would never be without a home, would never be forced into a marriage of convenience. Would never be forced to be dependent on a man or suffer abuse at his hands. Floryn would see to that. She would persuade Cord to help her. She would!

"Marriage is the only way I can save my daughter," Floryn said bitterly, "and she's worth whatever price I have to pay."

48

"There are those who say I'm worth the cost," he taunted.

"I'm not counted among them," Floryn retorted. "I've told you my deal. What's your answer?"

"It appears to me that I'm on the short end of the stick," he said. "Without marriage to you I inherit half the ranch and have guardianship of Hope. With marriage I stand to lose my bachelorhood, one half my inheritance, and guardianship of Hope. The price of a few nights in bed with you is high, Floryn. I wonder if you're worth the cost."

She had been looking for the gentle man who made love to her in the glade, who had introduced her to the magic of love, the man who had fathered her daughter. A man who loved her. Instead she had found an embittered man she could barely recognize.

"You're not getting one night in bed with me, much less a few," Floryn said, her voice as hard as steel. "I'm promising you nothing more than your freedom and one fourth of the ranch. That's one hell of a lot more than you have right now."

Cord laughed cynically. "Considering your hot nature, do you think you can keep your distance if we were to be married?"

Honestly Floryn had given no thought to keeping her distance, but she was determined that this bitter man would not dictate the terms of their agreement. Certainly he would not blackmail her into his bed, into an intimacy that lacked love.

"It's my way or nothing. I'm your only hope for freedom. Without me and my money, you'll stay here for the next ten years and you'll lose your half of the Fancy Lady."

"Without me," he taunted, "you'll lose everything. The ranch. Your daughter. Your empire."

Before Hal died, he had tried to control and manipulate Floryn. Now Cord was attempting to do the same, and she felt helpless to do anything about it.

No, that was not true. For Hope's sake, she willingly made this choice. She willingly placed herself in this position.

"It sounds to me like you have more to lose than I do."

Her world crumbling beneath her, she stared at him. He had ridden away and left her, but surely he would not allow her to lose Hope, to lose their child.

"If I remember correctly, you were quite a lusty woman." He paused, letting his blatant gaze roam her body. "Of course, ten years can dim the memory."

He attempted to reduce their love — the one beautiful memory she had — into lust. The very memory that had given her strength to endure her marriage of convenience, to remain true to her wedding vows. Cord would take it away and leave her nothing.

"If you're not willing to do this for me," she said, "please think about Hope."

"Don't use the child to try to manipulate me into doing what you want. It seems to me that Hal was thinking about Hope more than you."

His accusation hurt, but Floryn strove not to give way to her emotions. During her marriage she had suffered greater indignities and accusations than this as Hal had grown more and more jealous and had accused her of having numerous affairs.

"No" — wearily she shook her head — "that's not true."

Dear Lord, but it was not true.

From the moment she learned she was with child, with Cord's child, Floryn's life had taken on new meaning. The sun shone brighter; the world was more beautiful. When she held the newborn in her arms, she fully understood the encompassing love of

50

a mother. Hope was her life. Hope was a product of Cord's and her love, their flesh and blood. In Hope, Floryn would always have a part of Cord with her. Everything Floryn did was for the well-being of her child.

She cared that Cord thought she had been unfaithful to Hal, that he thought she was obsessed with keeping the ranch, but not enough that she would abandon her fight to get guardianship of Hope. Not enough that she would abandon her fight to keep her daughter's inheritance intact. This man be damned!

Cord moved closer to her. She heard the clinking of the chain, the scraping of the ball across the rocky surface. "You haven't changed. You always were materialistic and selfish, ready to use anybody who can help you get what you want. You'll never change."

Floryn felt as if she were losing the battle. She despised it when hot tears slid down her cheeks. "Please, Cord, help me."

His hand curved around the nape of her neck, and he tugged her to him. The space separating them melted away until the distance between his lips and hers was immeasurable, until his warm breath fanned her face. He was so near to her now that his face was a blur. Only his touch, his smell was real.

"Ah, yes, I love to hear you begging me to help *you*. The sound is music in my ears, although it's ten years too late."

As she closed her eyes, she shut out his words. She let darkness with its velvet softness enfold her as his lips whispered against hers. Delicate visitations. Misty dreams. Summer ten years ago. With her eyes shut it was easy to float in time and place so that fantasy and reality merged, so that she recaptured the magic of their love.

Again she felt the touch of the summer wind.

51

"Cord." Her palms moved up the chest she remembered so well, exploring what she had dreamed about time and again, for which she had yearned as long. But this was no dream. Cord was real. The lips teasing hers were warm and very much alive.

His arms held her close to his body as his mouth tempted but did not settle. His caresses were slow and inevitable. They were a planned and welcomed seduction. Floryn had not expected this kind of gentleness from such an embittered man, the same kind of gentleness he had shown ten years ago. The intoxicating warmth of his mouth drove her to distraction as he continued his tempting explorations. And then he was finally kissing her. Really kissing her. Still he made no demands. But by coaxing and teasing, he won her response.

Her lips parted and she swayed closer to him. She was stunned by the web of passion enclosing her, the same hot passion she had felt the first time they had made love. The shell that had enclosed her for so long cracked, splintered, shattered about her feet. She leaned against his body, sighing her passion into his mouth as for the second time in her life he whirled her away in a hurricane of sensations.

"My God, Cord," Rule called. "Make love to her some other time. I gotta get her out of here before she's discovered, and you better get back to the gang."

Jarred to reality, to the present, Floryn attempted to pull back. Cord would not let her. He capped her shoulders with his hands and tugged her closer to him. Her eyes locked to his, she willingly complied with the silent command.

"You'll not convince me you want a marriage of convenience."

I won't try because I really don't, she thought. *I want a real marriage, Cord. One based on love, on our love.*

52

"If I were to marry you, I'd sure as hell not accept one."

Again he kissed her, and the old magic was there as powerful as it had been ten years ago. When she realized this was reality, not fantasy, she turned traitor to herself. She parted her lips, granting him access. He explored her with a raw passion that made her weak at the knees. The first kiss had been gentle. This one was hungry, the thrust of his tongue sensual and demanding. The kiss was darkly inviting and Floryn willingly allowed herself to be caught in the passionate blackness. Refusal was not an option she considered.

His lips lifted from hers, and she stared first into the warm blue eye, then at the black patch. Ever since she had first seen it, she had been intrigued by and had wanted to touch it. Now she did, her finger moving first over the patch, then sliding to touch his cheek.

She forgot the point of contention between them. She remembered only the sweet flow of passion. She floated high on memories of what had been rather than what was, what would be.

"Your eye?" she murmured.

"A battle wound."

"I'm sorry."

"Don't be. You should have seen what happened to the other fellow." His voice was cold, brittle. "The women sort of like it. They say it makes me look more virile. What do you think?"

More like the devil! Her hand trembled against his cheek. "I—I wouldn't know."

He laughed and sounded like the devil.

"Floryn Donaldson," Cord said, "it looks like I'm going to have to marry you. You really do need me."

"A marriage in name only," she murmured, determined to hold her ground.

"A marriage in every sense of the word." He tugged her closer as if to demonstrate his hold over her.

Fighting for her last vestige of independence, fighting the attraction that drew her to him, she pulled away. "No."

"No?" He was surprised.

"I have one more option."

She really did not, but the fabrication was her last measure of defense against Cord. He was her only hope, but he was not going to call the shots in this agreement. She loved him, would always love him, and knew if they consummated their marriage on his terms, she would become his pawn. She would be beholden to him in a way she had not been to Hal. Cord would own her body and soul. This she would not allow.

"Hal's attorney," she heard herself saying calmly, "will be executor of the estate only, never the owner, and when Hope reaches the age of twenty-one he won't even be that. He's a reasonable and greedy man, always willing to strike a deal. He and I can negotiate. He'll agree to a marriage in name only."

"One man or another will do." Cord sneered. "It doesn't matter to you, does it?"

Dear God, but it does matter, Floryn wanted to cry. Instead she stared at him, holding her emotions in check.

"I'm determined to save my daughter, but it'll be on my terms, Cord."

She walked away, her heart heavy in her breast. He was a stubborn man, and she figured he would rather rot here in prison than help her . . . or their daughter.

She had almost reached the outcropping of rocks when Cord called.

"You were willing to negotiate with Wallis. Why not me?"

She turned. Neither moved. Finally he walked to her.

"A marriage of convenience until you say differently."

Floryn celebrated her success. "Which will be never."

Cord laughed softly. "If your definition of never is as long as your definition of forever, I'll have a short wait."

"You're despicable," Floryn hissed.

"That's my final offer," he said.

He walked back to the trough, picked up his hammer, and slung it over his shoulder. One step. Two. The ball scraped along the ground. Three. She recognized the set to his back and shoulders. She knew he would leave without a backward glance. He had once. He would do so again.

"I'll accept," she called out.

Cord nodded, but never turned, never stopped walking.

"Cord—"

He stopped.

"Why did you change your mind?"

He faced her, and in the distance that separated them she could see the hatred etched on his face. She heard it in the hard tone of his voice.

"I want out of here, Floryn, and you've offered me the quickest and easiest way." Again his laughter mocked her. "If I learned anything from you that summer, it was to use people."

Floryn's moment of elation was eclipsed by her disappointment. Why in getting her way did she feel like the loser? She quickly pushed her apprehensions aside. She had handled tougher situations than this. Whatever she had to do, she would do. Marriage was a necessity, her only way to save Hope, and no matter what the consequences, she would save her daughter.

Four

"I now pronounce you man and wife." In a large receiving room at the prison and from the elevated makeshift podium — really a platform that was sometimes used as a gallows foundation — the minister smiled at Floryn and Cord who stood below. "You may kiss the bride."

Cord leaned down. Floryn tensed. Out of the corner of her eye she could see the people who had assembled for their wedding, who stood behind them. Jack Willowby. Rule Compton. Webb Pruitt. Several of the inmates. All of them were smiling broadly.

Then she saw only Cord as he pulled her fully into the tight circle of his arms and pressed his lips to hers. He gave her a kiss that quickly progressed from gentle to fiercely hungry. She insinuated her hands between them and tried to separate herself from him, but he held her even more tightly.

He lifted his lips from her enough to murmur, "Don't make a scene in here."

He laughed softly, then before she quite knew what was happening, he kissed her again. Longer this time, and she did know what was happening, but did nothing to end the pleasure that swirled through her body, that warmed her heart.

Again he barely lifted his lips. "I wouldn't have done this, but the minister ordered it." His husky words whispered against her lips allowed her to feel as well as to hear them. "Far be it for me to disobey a man of God."

Floryn pushed doubts and misgivings aside to take the moment. His embrace was tight but not painful. His kiss was devastating. It conveyed his desire and needs. It aroused her to a fevered pitch. She allowed him to rekindle her desire as she remembered his hands moving all over her body. She wanted to feel that again; she ached for that again.

He buried his head in the curve of her shoulder and neck. In an undertone for her ears alone, he said, "I asked this once. I ask it again. When you react to my kisses like this, how do you intend to keep your distance from me? I believe this marriage of convenience is already falling apart."

How easily he shattered the beauty of the moment. His hold slackened, and she pushed out of his arms. Her desire, flowing so heatedly, so freely through her body only moments ago, now turned to lead. It choked out all sensations but disappointment and hurt. It gave rise to pride and arrogance.

"As you said the last time we saw each other, I am a woman, a young and passionate woman. Just because I responded to your kiss does not mean I'm ready to jump into bed with you."

He laughed. "No? Lady, since the minute you laid eyes on me in the quarry you've been begging me to make love to you."

"Your male pride wishes I were," she answered.

"No, my male pride knows as well as you know that you will. It's a matter of when, not if." The bleakness in his eyes belied the harshness of his words. "I don't know what happened in your past, I don't know if Hal's charges of infidelity are true or not, but from now on, Floryn, I promise I shall be the only man in your life."

His promise had been her dream for ten years; yet now it sounded more like a punishment than a joy.

Before she could reply, the minister had walked to the end of the platform and descended the four steps that brought him to the main level of the room. He moved to where Cord and Floryn stood. The Warden and Rule were across the room supervising the refreshments, and the inmates, enjoying a day of liberty, were milling around.

"Mr. Donaldson," the minister said, "may I congratulate you on your marriage? This is my first time to see a man walk out of prison with a new bride beside him. You are indeed fortunate."

"Indeed." Cord's cold gaze settled on Floryn.

The minister began to lecture Cord on the virtues of a reformed man, of a man who has been given a second chance to redeem himself with society. Letting Cord fend for himself in this conversation, Floryn was soon lost in her own thoughts.

She gazed at the white cake — their wedding cake — that Rule had baked for them. The large bowl of punch. In a prison she had married a convict!

While she would not change the course of events she had set in motion with her marriage to Cord, she was apprehensive. This was her second marriage of convenience. That did not bother her. The idea that Cord could play her emotions as if she were a finely tuned musical instrument did.

She had had no fear that her first marriage would be more than one in name only. Hal's impotence guaranteed that. She knew this one would be different. Cord's virility guaranteed consummation. Hal had been predictable, not so Cord. She had not loved Hal in the wifely way. She loved Cord. No matter that he vilified her, that he mocked her, her body responded to his demands.

She had lived to regret her first marriage, but was able to defend her choice by blaming it on youthful ignorance. This time she did not have that excuse. She had walked into this marriage moon-eyed. She had known from the beginning that Cord intended to push her over the edge, that he intended to make love to her. Yes, she had been fully cognizant of the possible consequences. Until now she had thought she was strong enough to keep him at a distance. But her greatest weakness, her tragic flaw that would guarantee her giving in to his passionate demands was her love for him. Her forever love.

Some people might be destined to have more than one love in their life, but Floryn knew beyond any shadow of a doubt that she was destined to have only one . . . Cord Donaldson.

In many ways Cord reminded her of Hal. His accusations about her infidelity smacked of his uncle. Had her eyes been closed when Cord had spoken, she would have sworn she was hearing her husband again. Had she married a second man who was obsessed with the misconception of her infidelity? Would he eventually resort to punishing her with abusive verbal outbursts as Hal had done? She shivered, contemplating life with her husband, with Cord Donaldson . . . with this hard and embittered stranger.

She looked at her hand lying against the dark material of his coat, then her gaze moved from the pristine white shirt to the narrow black necktie. Her throat grew dry as her eyes traveled up the column of tanned neck, to the granite features of his face. Finally she rested her attention on the patch that fit over his left eye. It gave him a roguish quality, an added mystique.

It did emphasize his virility.

Cord was not handsome, had never been. He had been more. He was rugged and enduring. He had a forever quality about him that most people, men in particular, lacked. His face was angular, with sharp cheekbones and a hawk's nose, its austerity broken by his rakish smile and a head of thick black hair now winged with silver. Even the character lines that furrowed his forehead added to his ruggedness.

His dark coloring was striking, and his skin which she would have expected to be pasty, had the healthy burnish of sun and wind, making his eyes . . . his eye . . . appear even bluer—an intense and startling blue.

"Mrs. Donaldson?"

Floryn looked at the minister.

"I was saying I pray you and Mr. Donaldson have a long, happy, and prosperous marriage with many healthy children. May God bless you both."

"Thank you, Reverend," she murmured.

When he was out of hearing distance, having joined Rule and Jack Willowby at the serving table, Cord said, "What the man of God doesn't know is that for you to consider the marriage a happy one, it must be a prosperous one, not a long one."

"You have no idea what I believe comprises a happy marriage," Floryn said. "And since you're not interested, we won't waste time by discussing it."

"The one ingredient I don't guarantee is happiness. The one I expect is fidelity."

This was it. Floryn would accept no more insinuations about her character. "Except for one indiscretion which you know about, in which you were a willing participant, I was faithful to Hal, yet you continually harp on my infidelity. Why?"

"I first heard about your string of lovers from a friend who drops in to see me occasionally."

"This *friend* of yours, the one who told you about my *string of lovers,*" Floryn said scathingly, glancing around to see if anyone were close enough to over-hear them, "did he ever mention our child to you? Did he tell you about Hope?"

"No."

"Of course not. He wanted only to talk about the sordid and untrue."

"Sordid, I agree, but untrue? I hardly think so." Harsh tones corresponded with his harsh gaze. "Hal's attorney wrote to confirm the rumors."

The friend repeating rumors aggravated Floryn. Kern Wallis frightened her. "Kern Wallis?" she whis-pered.

"Right. Your other option for a marriage of con-venience." Again his lips curled into that damned sar-donic smile Floryn was beginning to despise. "Seems to me that the two of you were running a race to see who could reach me first. Both of you were full of good deeds as long as I signed the ranch over to you."

Ignoring his innuendo, she asked, "Had you re-ceived his letter when you agreed to marry me?"

"No, I received it several days later. I had time to change my mind if his terms had appealed to me."

"What were his terms?"

"He was willing to petition the state to get my re-lease from prison and to give me custody of *your* daughter if I would sign over one half of my share of the ranch to him. He felt that was just compensation. It was almost the same deal that you offered." Cord tucked his fingers beneath her chin. "Only you in-cluded a challenge I couldn't afford to pass up."

For a moment they gazed at each other before she twisted away from his touch.

"What did he say about me?"

"Nothing more than you said. Hal accused you of

62

infidelity and had declared you an unfit mother."

Apprehension gnawed at Floryn. Kern Wallis had promised to ruin her, and past actions proved to her that he would go to any length to do so. Right now he was playing with her, holding back his ultimate accusation, intensifying the tension by making her wonder when he would land the killing blow.

Although she had taunted Cord with the idea that she was willing to negotiate marriage with Hal's attorney, she had been bluffing. She hated the man. She despised all he stood for. Yet she may have been wiser to have struck a deal with him than with Cord. As reprehensible as Kern Wallis was, she understood him and his motives. Because of this knowledge and her hatred for him, she could have handled him.

But romantic fool that she was — to borrow the phrase from Cord — she had not. In her own way she was as deluded as Cord. Foolishly she had thought she could turn the hands of time back. She had believed in the enduring strength of her and Cord's love.

Floryn was not one to wallow in self-pity. When she returned home, she would have to face the attorney and his accusations. She would, but she was not going to allow thoughts of him to clutter up what she must do now. At the present her task was dealing with her new marriage, her new husband.

"The only reason you heard from Kern at all was because he found out I had located you and set out to talk to you, to bring you back to claim what Hal left you," she said. "If it weren't for me, he wouldn't have let you know about your inheritance."

Cord laughed softly. "My, my, Mrs. Donaldson, you do have long and sharp claws, and you know how to use them. Only time will prove which one of you is telling the truth. Until then, I give you warning. You will not find me as lenient a husband as Hal. Nor as loving. I repeat what I said earlier. From this moment on, there is no man in your life but me. Unless I'm the one to make love to you, you've begun to lead a celibate existence. Until death do us part, we swore before God and man. Do you understand?"

"You think you're smart," Floryn said, "but you're not going to force me into your bed. No amount of begging or badgering on your part will persuade me."

"I'm not going to beg or badger," he said softly. "You are, and that I promise. If you've really been faithful to Hal these past ten years as you claim, I shouldn't have to wait long. I didn't the first time."

"You're a bastard," Floryn exclaimed, clenching and unclenching her hands.

"But lovable," Cord said, his tight mouth suddenly curling into a smile.

"Cord. Mrs. Donaldson" — Jack Willowby moved to where the couple stood — "I wanted to let you know how happy I am for you."

As Cord had done, when he had evidently seen the warden's approach, Floryn forced herself to smile, but she was shaking within from anger and disappointment. She had known all along that Cord was not professing to love her, yet deep down she harbored hope that they might have a friendly relationship.

Now she had the darkest feeling that Cord had married her to punish her . . . forever.

"Where are you going from here?" the warden asked.

"Eventually to our ranch some miles from El Paso," Cord answered.

Jack frowned. "Does this mean you're going to make more than stage stops along the way?"

Cord nodded.

"Stanton Norwell," the warden said.

"He has something that belongs to me."

"Go easy," the warden admonished. "You don't have a pardon, Cord, only a parole. It'll be easy for someone who dislikes you and who has clout with the government to have you returned to prison. Stanton Norwell is such a man."

"Thanks for the advice, Jack," Cord answered. "I'll be careful. I won't be coming back. That I promise."

A big grin spanning his bearded face, Rule Compton joined them. He caught the lapels of his suit in both hands and rocked back on his heels. "Beautiful wedding," he said. "You and Mrs. Donaldson make one handsome couple. Don't you think so, Warden?"

Jack nodded.

"You were quite a best man, Rule," Floryn said.

Cord fondly clapped the old man on the shoulder. "Rule's always been my best man. If it hadn't been for him, I wouldn't be alive today."

"I know you'll always believe that," Rule said, "but it ain't quite the truth. You survived because you wanted to, because you're tough." The old man's voice took on a teary gruffness. "Remember that, boy. Don't trust nobody but yourself. That's the—"

"First and most important law of survival," Cord finished, almost as if it were script he and Rule often acted out. Cord cast his friend an affectionate grin.

Webb Pruitt broke into their circle. Smiles faded from the men's faces and their eyes grew wary. Floryn felt her husband tense. About the same height, the two men measured each other as only opponents do. Deadly opponents, openly hostile to each other.

"Donaldson," Pruitt said, a stiff smile on his lips, "I want to congratulate you on your freedom. I'm glad I was able to play a role in it."

65

"Yeah," Cord drawled sarcastically, "I'm sure you were."

"I hear you're leaving on tomorrow's stage."

"That's right."

Pruitt extended his hand. "I wish you well."

Cord's hand remained at his side. "Keep your wishes for me to yourself, Pruitt. You've given me more than I ever wanted. I'll never forget you and your *kindness,* and I promise to repay you in kind one of these days." He looked down at Floryn. "It's time we were going."

Repay it in kind! The words whirled through Floryn's mind. She had the feeling this is exactly what Cord was doing to her.

"Yep," Rule said. "Time you two was going. Time you was headin' home, boy."

Floryn agreed it was time for them to leave, but she disagreed on the destination. Home was more than a house. It was family. Love and laughter and warmth. Home was friendship.

"Straight home," Rule admonished.

Floryn feared Cord was headed straight to hell, her in tow.

Five

Hellsville! This was the name that many Texans were giving to Huntsville since the ending of the War Between the States, and Floryn thought the name described the town perfectly.

Standing at the window of her second-story room in the boardinghouse, she gazed at the collection of people who gathered in the street below. She spotted a familiar sight—soiled and tattered gray uniforms. Many of the drifters were ex-Confederate soldiers with no place to go, no place to call home. A lawless breed they were proving to be. Reports of violence done by them swept through the state.

She lifted the hair from her neck, letting the afternoon air touch her moistened skin. Although the temperature was probably lower than that of West Texas, the humidity was greater and she perspired more. She was hot and tired and wanted to go home. She was homesick.

Although beautiful, the huge evergreen forests of East Texas pressed in on her. At times they choked her. She longed for the wide open spaces, for the small mountain ranges that surrounded the *hacienda,* for the brilliant sunlight.

Yes, she was ready to go home.

Turning from the window, she looked at Cord who

sat at the desk writing letters. "I'm glad we're leaving this place. I can hardly wait to get back to the ranch."

She moved to the dresser where she picked up her brush. While she stroked her hair, she closed her eyes and thought about the Fancy Lady, about home. About Hope and Leanor. About Antonio and the *vaqueros*. She could imagine them as they went about doing their chores.

"Oh, Cord," she murmured, "you're going to love the Fancy Lady. It's changed so much since you last saw it, but we have much yet to do."

"How have you managed to keep your head above water during this war, when other ranchers are going under?"

"I employed Mexican cowboys," she answered. "*Vaqueros* who had experience working the Mexican spreads. They're tough and good and loyal."

"And they had no allegiance to either the North or the South," Cord said dryly, "so you didn't have to worry about them leaving to fight in the war."

She nodded. "I have so many plans, so many things I want to do. I want to branch out. Along with the stock, I want to raise sheep and goats."

"Are these *vaqueros* of yours also experienced sheep-herders?" Cord asked.

She paused before she said, "Yes."

He was gently mocking. "Always the business-woman."

His smile made her feel like butterflies were fluttering in her stomach. "Is that so wrong?"

He shook his head and reached up to rub his thumb and index finger down the sides of his nose. His fingers rested at the corners of his mouth, drawing Floryn's attention to his lips, causing her to forget the conversation, to concentrate on him.

Lips that sometimes seemed hewn out of stone. Today they were gentled by his smile, his teasing. Masculine lips neither too full or too thin. Lips that possessed the power to fill her with fire and vibrancy, that worked magic with her sensations. Lips she wanted to kiss. Lips she wanted to feel on her body . . . all over her body.

"Sheep farm and ranch," Cord drawled.

The words should have dragged her thoughts from his body back to the conversation, but they did not. He dropped his hand, the movement pulling his shirt tight around his chest and guiding her attention to shoulders that looked impossibly wide. As if aware of her fascination with his body, Cord crossed his arms. His sleeves were rolled up over his biceps, and the springy hairs on his forearms were burnished blue-black in the sunlight.

"Sheep and cattle," he drawled a second time, shaking his head. "I've been out of circulation for quite a while, but not that long. I'll bet the ranchers in the area love your idea."

His words merged into a blur, the only distinguishable one being love. Floryn's face went hot as desire burst into life within her.

"Is something wrong?" he asked, looking at her strangely.

Floryn realized he was staring at her, and the heat suffusing her face turned to embarrassment. He had caught her daydreaming. "No," she quickly denied. "I was—"

His lips, those lips that had been the instigator of this embarrassing moment, quirked into a smile. A knowing smile. Her face felt ever hotter.

She spoke. "I was thinking about what you said."

Floryn had to push thoughts of his lips and arms and chest, of his virility out of her mind. He was driving her to distraction, and they had been married for only hours. How could she maintain her distance when she was her own worst enemy?

"And?" His lips still softened by his smile, he hiked a brow.

"The Spanish mixed sheep and cattle," she answered, unable to douse the fire in her body but quite capable of controlling the timbre of her voice. "Granted the colonials were still living under the feudal system on their manors, but they proved it could be done and done successfully."

Cord leaned back in the chair. "You won't get one rancher in the state of Texas to agree with you."

"I only need the agreement of one," she replied.

He reached up and rubbed the corner of his mouth with his index finger. "You'll find that on some subjects I'll be in agreement with you."

The expression in his face spurred her heart into a gallop. His gaze was sultry as it moved from her hair to her face. It lingered so long on her lips, they began to feel swollen with the memory of his kisses. Flares of response prickled the skin of her neck.

She caught her breath when his gaze moved slowly downward to caress her breasts. Her nipples tightened against the bodice of her dress. The sensation was as explosive as the firecrackers they exploded during fiesta at the *hacienda* and rushed straight to the low, soft core of her body. She shivered over an ache of raw desire.

Cord's smiling lips parted. "But I'm not in agreement with this one."

"This one?" Again Floryn almost lost herself in the wondrous sensations racking her body and dropped the thread of conversation. She reluctantly dragged her gaze from his and moved across the room.

"I'm not in agreement with raising sheep and cattle

70

on the same ranch." His soft chuckle touched her raw, exposed nerves.

She regained her composure, her thoughts. "I do have an interest in the ranch. I'll own one fourth of it."

"But I'll control three fourths, mine and Hope's."

"Cord, it can be done. Just listen to me."

"Not now, Floryn." He bent back over the desk, pen in hand. "I want to finish this."

Irritated, Floryn pulled the brush through her hair so roughly tears smarted in her eyes. She had worked hard to build the Fancy Lady. She was the one who had taken risks, who had insisted they try new ideas. She was the one who had had the courage to fight Hal every step of the way. Eventually she had triumphed, until in death Hal had scored the ultimate victory.

Now she was being rebuffed by Cord. Like Hal, he was not even willing to listen to her ideas. The fighting would start all over again, and she was not sure she could win any of the battles against Cord. It seemed that ultimate victory belonged to him from the beginning.

"You're writing a lot of letters."

"Are you surprised that I can write or that I have this many acquaintances or both?"

"Just curious," she answered.

"I'm writing to some men I need to help me."

"We don't need extra ranch hands," she said. "If we do, Antonio will hire them. I made him *gran vaquero* and gave him that responsibility."

"Antonio may be the foreman," Cord said, "but from now on I'll do the hiring. To set your mind at ease, I'm hiring these men to help me in San Antonio."

Her irritation over the first part of his statement

went without comment as she gave in to curiosity. "Why San Antonio?" she asked. "What are you going to do there?"

"Spend a few days and visit with an old acquaintance."

"Cord, I'm running short on money. Outside that which I've set aside to buy Hope some new clothes which she badly needs, I only have about three hundred dollars left. Not knowing how much I would need, I brought all the cash I have to buy your freedom."

She did not tell him that she had gone deeply in debt to the local stable owner, Lyle Hackett, in order to get the money or that part of it was spent on a wardrobe she had bought to impress him.

"You're not going to be out that money," Cord said. "I plan to repay every cent you've spent on me."

"Until you do," Floryn said, "we have to live on what I have. So far, we still need to purchase our fares to El Paso, and I need to buy supplies once we reach the ranch. We simply can't afford a long delay in San Antonio!"

"You can go on to the ranch if you choose, but I'm staying. Keep a count of all the money you're spending on me. Consider it a loan that will be repaid with interest."

"Even if you could, that's not the point."

"You seem to be making it one."

"Can't you take care of your personal business later?"

"We're going through San Antonio. I see no reason why I shouldn't take a few extra days and do what needs to be done."

"What about Hope?" she asked.

"You're the one who told me she was safe at the ranch with her nanny. But if you're that worried, go directly to the ranch. I'll follow later." Rising from the desk, he returned the pen to the holder, then folded and sealed several envelopes.

Floryn loosened her grip on the brush handle and flexed her fingers. He spoke to her as if she were a child, as if she needed his permission to travel on without him. She was the one who had begged and borrowed so that she could get the cash to get him out of prison. His first loyalty should belong to her. She itched to tell him, but bit back the words. This thirty-year-old, prison-hardened man was not an easy one to deal with, certainly not a man to be manipulated. She doubted the word "loyalty" fit into his vocabulary.

"Your business is saving the Fancy Lady for Hope," she snapped, letting her frustration get the best of her. "But anytime I mention the ranch, you brush the subject aside. You always say we'll talk about it later. When is later going to get here, Cord?"

"Now we get to the heart of the matter. It's always the ranch. It gets monotonous talking to you because the Fancy Lady is all you know, all you want to know. Put your worries to rest. I've written Wallis informing him of our marriage and our arrival. We'll be there well within the two-year time limit."

His nonchalance only heightened her level of aggravation.

"There's work to be done, and the longer we're away the farther behind we're getting. We have to round up the cattle and get them ready for market. We have to move fast, Cord, because time is running out. Not for the time limit of Hal's will, but for our valley, Cord. It's not going to take ranchers long to find out our beef is worth a fortune in the East. I want to be one of the first to send my herds to them."

73

He sighed. "Floryn, I'm only talking about a few days, not a lifetime."

Realizing the futility of arguing with him, Floryn moved to the window. "I suppose this business you must take care of in San Antonio is that Stanton Norwell Mr. Willowby was talking about this morning?"

"No other."

In answer to the knocking that sounded in the room, Cord walked to the door and opened it to see a young boy.

"Hi. I'm Jason Renshaw." His arms were filled with packages and from one dangled a man's hatbox. Round-eyed, he stared at Cord. "I have the clothes you bought at the dry goods store this morning."

Cord took the purchases and handed him a coin.

"Thank you, sir." Staring at him, the boy slid the money into his pocket. Finally he turned and slowly walked down the corridor. When he reached the landing, he stopped. "Sir."

"Yes?" Cord swung open the door again.

Jason returned to where Cord stood. Brushing a shock of red hair off his forehead, he said, "I ain't never seen anybody wearing a patch over their eye until you soldiers started coming home from the war."

"I wasn't a soldier."

"What was you?"

"A prisoner," Cord answered.

"Here?"

"Yes."

Floryn moved to the door to take the packages from Cord, her gaze moving to Jason. He was staring so intently, so worshipfully into Cord's face he caught her full attention. She remained where she was.

Jason's gaze lingered on the patch. "It makes you look tough."

Cord studied the boy a long while before he said, "Well, Jason, this little piece of leather doesn't mean I am. It means I lost an eye in a fight."

"Did you win?"

"I gave as good as I got," Cord answered, "but I'm not sure I won, Jason. For the rest of my life, I'll be without one eye."

"I'm gonna be tough when I grow up," Jason said. "Just like my pa was. Everybody's gonna be scared of me."

"Where is your pa?" Cord asked.

"He's dead." Jason blinked several times, but his voice was steady. "He was killed protecting me and Ma from outlaws that robbed us when we was moving from Illinois to California. Pa told me before he died that I'd have to take care of my ma from now on, and I am. After Pa died, me and Ma had to stay here 'cause we didn't have no money."

The boy's confession touched Floryn deeply. She set the cumbersome load on the bed but continued to look at Jason.

"Sounds to me as if your pa was a brave man," Cord said.

The child nodded. "I'm gonna be brave, too. I'm gonna wear two pistols and be a dead shot. Nobody's gonna push me around. Why, you ought to see how I can throw a knife. And I'm gonna buy me a black hat and a black leather vest like the ones you bought this morning. They make you look real tough."

Cord smiled. "You like the hat and vest?"

"Sure do," Jason answered. "When I get enough money, I'm gonna buy 'em for myself." His face fell. "But that's gonna take a long time 'cause I have to help my ma. Since Pa died, I'm the man of the house."

"How old are you?"

"Eleven." The boy puffed out his chest. "Well, almost eleven."

"As the man of the house, you have a big responsibility," Cord said. "Anybody can have people scared of them, Jason, but it's a wise and tough man who can have their respect."

The child blinked at him, clearly not comprehending what he was saying.

"It's better for people to trust you, Jason, and to like you. That's what makes a tough man."

"People like my ma," the boy answered slowly, "but they don't think she's tough."

Floryn and Cord laughed. He leaned down to tousle Jason's hair. "I'll bet your ma is a tough lady. She doesn't let anybody get the best of her, does she?"

Jason grinned. "I don't reckon."

"Just think about what I've said, all right?"

Jason nodded. "Well, I better go before Ma gets mad at me." Turning, he skipped down the hall.

Cord closed the door and followed Floryn to the bed where she deposited his clothes.

"You handled the boy quite well," she said.

"I hate to see him grow up thinking weapons and toughness are the answer to every problem when most of the time they're really what instigate the problem." He opened the box and pulled out his hat. "I guess, too, I began to think about Hope. As I looked at him, I wondered what she thought about, how she thought."

"You were curious about her?" Floryn said, quelling the excitement she felt.

"A little," he answered absently, his attention centered on his purchases.

76

Floryn wanted to pursue the subject of Hope, but felt to do so would not be wise. She could not force Cord to be interested in their child or to love her. He had to take the initiative, and she had to be patient, answering his questions when he raised them. He had raised the subject once; he would do so again.

She watched as he tore through the string and several layers of brown wrapping paper to lift out black trousers and leather vest, shirts, handkerchiefs, and several pairs of socks. The clothes, the best Huntsville offered, were not exceptional. Yet Cord gazed at them as if they were custom-made by one of the world's most renowned tailors. A knot formed in her throat as she watched him touch each.

"Do you realize how long it's been since I've been able to have clothes that were not provided and chosen by someone else?" he said. "Clothes that were not identical to every other man I saw or worked with?"

He picked up the vest, kneading the soft leather in his hand. Mesmerized, Floryn studied the sensuous movement of fingers and leather.

"Clothes chosen by me. Clothes that belong to me." He glanced up, his face stark. "Such a little thing for a man to be raving about, isn't it?"

"No," Floryn whispered, a lump in her throat, tears forming in her eyes.

She felt like an interloper. The moment was Cord's and his alone. Forcing her thoughts away from him, from the intimacy of the scene, she walked to her portmanteau that rested on a straight chair opposite the bed. Opening it, she gave him some privacy, herself time for composure. She extracted several ribbons and matched them to the various colors in her dress.

"What does Stanton Norwell have that belongs to you?" she asked.

"A pendant," he answered.

"It must be important."

"It is."

He watched as Floryn held the ribbons, one by one, against her hair, letting the length drop to the bodice of her dress. Looking at her filled him with pleasure. If prison had given him anything good, it was an appreciation for the simple, for the here and now. He took nothing for granted . . . not even the way she looked when she dug through her luggage for her ribbons and collars and those silly little lace things she sometimes wore on her hair. She moved to the mirror and continued to play with the ribbons.

"Are you going to wear all of them?" Cord asked curiously.

"No. Only one. Which matches best?" Studying her reflection in the mirror, she held up two.

"The brown one." He looked at a discarded one that lay on the dresser.

She furrowed her brow. "I'm not so sure. There's so little brown in the dress."

"But so much in your eyes. It's the exact shade," he said.

Their gazes caught in the mirror.

"It's supposed to match the dress." She smiled at him.

"I'd rather it matched your eyes." He smiled at her.

She lowered her head and continued to study her ribbons.

He sat on the edge of the bed. Crossing his legs one over the other, he unlaced the high-top shoes he wore — prison issue. One by one he dropped them to the floor. Next he peeled off his socks — the same vintage as the shoes. He would never wear prison issue again. Never.

He inhaled deeply. He inhaled life itself. Freedom.

He dragged it into his lungs, feeling its cleansing coolness all the way to his toes. He would never get enough of life, of freedom. No longer anyone to watch or goad or crowd. No one to eavesdrop on him. No one trying to ferret information on the San Domingo treasure. He was free, and by God he was going to stay that way.

He rubbed his ankles. They ached, and the skin was tender and brightly pink. When he removed his hand, he glanced up to see Floryn staring at him, at the scars, the telltale sign that he had worn leg-irons, that he had been an inmate at the penitentiary.

"I have something that will help," she said.

Laying the ribbons aside, she lifted a small jar from the dresser and moved to kneel beside him. After she unfastened the lid, she dipped her fingers into a thick salve, but Cord caught her hand before she touched him. She looked up.

"I don't need a nursemaid," he said.

"I don't intend to be one."

"I don't want your pity."

"I have none to give. I was doing for you what I do for horses or cattle. This ointment is made from herbs," she explained. "It heals wounds and soothes scarred tissue. The *curandera* gave it to me for the *vaqueros* to use at the ranch. If you don't want me to use it on you, I won't."

His grip tightened on her hand. His every nerve ending was attuned to her, attuned to the faint trembling beneath his hands, to the warmth of her touch. Somehow freedom, sunlight, and life became synonymous and were all around him. She was all around him. Her wide questioning eyes staring up at him. The fragrance of her rising up to fill his nostrils. A sweet, sweet woman smell in the sultry morning heat.

"If you're afraid you'll become further indebted to

me or that my rendering you aid will insinuate you further into my life, rub the ointment on yourself," she said. "And if you want to be bullheaded, then don't do anything for your legs. You're a strong man. Endure the pain if it makes you feel like a martyr."

"You have little esteem for me," he said.

"No, you have little for yourself."

He was unsettled by her ability to read his thoughts, angered by his yearning to bury his face in the silk curtain of hair that fell about her face, that caressed his fingers. A yearning so strong he turned her hand loose.

"Go ahead," he said.

"Lie down," she suggested.

His gaze turned quizzical.

Exasperated, she said, "I can get to your ankles better."

He grinned. "This promises to be interesting."

He shoved his purchases aside and did as she bade. He felt the mattress sag when she sat down at the foot of the bed and began to rub the cool ointment onto his ankles. How quickly her gentle touch chased the pain away. Combined with the softness of the mattress, her ministration lulled him into a peacefulness he had not known since he left the Fancy Lady ten years ago, a peacefulness he had not thought possible again.

"Would you tell me about Sanchia Guilbert?" Floryn asked, her faraway voice as hypnotic as her touch.

He fluffed the pillows beneath his head and burrowed his shoulders deeper into the mattress. "I don't know much about Sanchia," he answered. "She and I spoke two or three times at the most. Generally we spoke through her servant."

He allowed his body to relax completely, a luxury

he had been denied since he had been in prison. "After I left the Fancy Lady in '55, I headed back to San Francisco. In El Paso I met Mathieu Guilbert — a young Frenchman, recently married to a Spanish grandee's daughter. Her parents — the San Domingos — died from an epidemic of cholera, and she inherited a large *hacienda*. One of Sanchia's distant relatives, wanting the estate, contrived charges of treason against Mathieu and Sanchia."

"Her own family?"

"Umhum. They seemed to be a greedy lot. But I don't have to explain that to you, do I? Look at what lengths and expense you're going to to get your ranch back."

"It's hardly the same," Floryn said.

"Close enough." She rubbed harder, and Cord chuckled. "Mathieu found out about the plot and offered to pay me a large amount of money to escort Sanchia and their servants from Mexico City to New Orleans. Mathieu's family was to meet Sanchia in New Orleans, but he couldn't get away at the time. He intended to meet her later."

Cord had refused to accept Mexican currency. He had insisted on U.S. or either gold or silver. Having no available cash, Mathieu had given him priceless Guilbert family heirlooms. In New Orleans, the Guilbert family member who was meeting Sanchia was supposed to give Cord U.S. currency for the jewels.

That had not happened. They had never traveled beyond Laredo, Texas. The night Sanchia had been killed Cord buried his jewels for safekeeping. Now he was glad that he had. Everyone would think his retainer was the San Domingo treasure.

He mentioned the Guilbert jewels to no one — not to his two closest acquaintances — for fear they would be stripped from him as everything else had. They were his secret and would remain his secret.

Thoughts of the Guilbert jewels drifting away, Cord listened to the simple sounds of the town drift in through the opened window. People talking and laughing; wagons rumbling by; the whinny and snorting of horses. Sounds he had missed. Floryn dipped more ointment on his ankle. It was cool, then warm as her fingers gently massaged the abused flesh. A gust of wind swept the sultry odors of summer through the room. He luxuriated in the sounds, the feel, the scent of freedom.

"And?" Floryn gently coaxed.

"Not far out of Laredo on the Texas side of the border," he continued, "the wagon train was ambushed. I was wounded pretty badly, but knew if I didn't get Sanchia out of there, she would be killed. She, her personal maid, and I rode away together, headed for the Fancy Lady. I figured she'd be safe there. We were followed, and I was getting weaker from loss of blood."

Again he lapsed into silence. In his mind's eye the ruins of the church were as vivid as they had been that evening when they camped at the Church of the Angels.

He spoke again, his voice low. "We had traveled a long way but were an even longer way from the ranch when I passed out. I don't know how long I was unconscious before I came to. I found Sanchia dead. A knife through her heart. Her maid was gone, and someone had swept all the foot and hoofprints away."

"I'm sorry," Floryn whispered, her eyes misty with tears. "She was so young to have died in such a barbaric way."

"Death is death," Cord said, "but I agree it's a tragedy she had to die so young. As much for me as for her, I intend to find the person responsible for this."

"Whatever happened to Mathieu?"

"I don't know," Cord said. "I never heard of him again."

Relaxing and for the time being pushing aside past concerns and vowed revenge, he enjoyed the feel of her soothing hands on his ankles and feet.

Then from afar came a quiet question that jarred him. "What about the San Domingo treasure?"

"The San Domingo treasure," he repeated. "Has it got you hooked too, Floryn?"

"You might say so. Everyone who talked to me about you mentioned it. In fact, they were more interested in talking about it than you."

Cord laughed. "And like them, you're more interested in it than in me."

"Now that I have you, perhaps it's time I turn my attention to the treasure."

"Did it entice you to pay the parole guarantee?"

She smiled. "Let's say your value went up considerably when I heard about it."

Six

"Exactly how much did my value go up?" Cord asked.

Golden brown eyes focused on him. "Over one million dollars in gold."

"That's what it was the last time I heard. I thought maybe I was worth more." He feigned disappointment. "I'm afraid you're in for a big disappointment. As far as I know, the treasure is nonexistent. Certainly none was found in the wagon train, and we didn't have it with us when we ran for safety."

"Rumor has it you killed the two women, took the treasure, and buried it."

"Rumor being Pruitt?"

Floryn nodded and pressed ointment on to his other foot.

"Did the good attorney enlist your help in his search for the stolen goods?"

"He tried."

"But you were a step ahead of him. Why divide the treasure when you stood a chance of having it all?" he taunted.

"Why indeed?"

Mercenary little cuss! Just what he thought. He had hoped he was wrong, that she had changed. God, but he wanted to believe her. He wanted to believe in her innocence, wanted to believe she had been faithful to Hal.

He was a fool! Why was he so preoccupied with her innocence, with her morals? Before today, he had not been married to her. She owed him no loyalty, no fidelity. Yet he remembered their pledge of forever love. To him that had been as sacred as wedding vows. That day when they made love, he had felt as if they were married. When Shelby had told him the rumors about other men in her life, he had felt her betrayal.

First she had betrayed him in love, then in greed. Strange as it was, it hurt him even more now they were married.

"Isn't that what you expected me to say, Cord?"

The question pulled him from his thoughts. He raised his head to stare into her face. Floryn's features were delicate and natural. He had forgotten how delicate, how natural. She reminded him of the wide open spaces, sunshine, and fresh air.

And her eyes. Her golden brown eyes. They were irresistible. Framed by silky eyelashes, they gazed innocently at him. Her smile was warm . . . and . . .

"You believe I'm conniving enough to have married you for the ranch. Why not for the San Domingo treasure also?"

Mocking! Laughter danced in the depth of those golden-brown eyes. He had always admired her astuteness. Reluctantly he smiled. She had gotten the best of him this time.

"You aren't going to tell me that you're really not interested in the treasure, are you?"

"I wouldn't go that far," she replied.

Her attention centered on his foot, she trailed her fingers up his instep to his ankle and back down to the sole of his foot. Desire like fire lapped through his body. Intentional or not, the message she was sending his body at the moment was anything but soothing. Certainly not relaxing.

He had told her he would not beg her to go to bed

with him, and he would not. No matter how intensely he wanted her. And every stroke of her hand, every sniff of her perfume reinforced his desire, made him want her more than intensely. He knew he would have to exert all his willpower to keep his hands off her. Perhaps, he would not be so strong. He might not keep his promise. She really did not expect — did not want — him to. Neither did he.

"But I will admit that right at this moment," she said, "I have more a personal than monetary interest in you. All—"

"And the moment is *all* that counts," Cord said. "That's all we have. And I've learned to take it."

He caught her wrist in his hand and gently tugged so that she was lying beside him. The rustle of material filled the room — the sweet and beautiful rustle of the only woman he had truly wanted, the sound of the woman so long denied him. The clean smell of her skin was heady, the warmth and softness of skin pure pleasure. Being with her was heaven. Taking the jar from her, he set it on the table next to the bed.

Picking up one of the handkerchiefs, he wiped the ointment from her hands, his fingers covered in the white material dipping sensuously between hers, then sliding up the length of each. He felt her slight trembling and turned her hand over, slowly stroking her palm . . . slowly stroking her palm even after all traces of the medicine were gone. The handkerchief slid from his hand; he continued to stroke her, flesh against flesh.

"Turn me loose," she said in a breathy voice. "I don't appreciate what you're — doing to me."

"No? Perhaps I can do something else that you would appreciate more." He ran his fingers lightly up her arm.

She shook her head. "I don't want you touching me at all."

"That's an outright lie." His expression reflected his

86

laughter. "Your rubbing sent a different message to my body."

"You misinterpreted it."

Thick brows hiked. "Really."

He released her hand, scooted to the foot of the bed, and lifted her skirt.

"Don't!" she exclaimed, yet did not move.

Cord chuckled at her expression of outrage. "Mrs. Donaldson, must I remind you that you're my wife."

"But not in the sense—not like—"

"I'm not going to do a thing more to you than you've been doing to me." He unlaced her shoes, pulled them from her feet, and dropped them to the floor. He slipped his hand beneath her skirts again to catch her garters and roll down her stockings, slipping them off also. The tantalizing brush of his fingers on her skin sent shards of pleasure through her body. "In fact, I won't be doing as much, because I'm not going to fight my way through all these layers of clothing that you're wearing."

He had no need to remove her clothing. He was setting her afire without it.

"You took your own clothes off," she snapped, her gaze inadvertently settling on his chest, on the mat of crisp black hair, the muscular pectorals. "You wanted to flaunt your half-naked body in front of me."

"So that's it. You're jealous." His suggestive gaze deliberately settled on her bosom. "Why not . . . tit for tat?"

The cad! He was laughing at her!

"Take yours off," he softly enticed. "Flaunt your half-naked body in front of me. I didn't say you couldn't. Fact of the matter, I would thoroughly enjoy it. I said I wouldn't do it for you."

Her face turned crimson. He began to trail his fingers around her ankles, the side of her foot, the bottom.

87

"Cord"—her voice trembled slightly—"this is unfair."

"I never said I'd be fighting fair," he said. "Certainly it wasn't one of our points of negotiation."

She tugged on her foot. "I would rather you stopped."

Liar, his smile said. "Why?"

"It's—well—it's uncomfortable." Well, it was uncomfortable!

He continued to grin, continued to torment her feet with his strokes.

"When I"—she gulped—"when I said my interest was you, I really meant—"

His hand swept above her ankle. She gasped. Up the front of her leg, behind her knee, down the calf.

"Yes, Floryn?"

She closed her eyes and rolled her head back against the pillows. "I really meant"—her voice sounded wispy even to herself —"all the gold in the world wouldn't get my daughter back for me. It won't save Fancy Lady for Hope. That's my interest in you. Hope means more to me than my own life."

He wrapped his hand around her ankle and flattened his palm against the bottom of her foot. She felt the calluses against her tender skin, the heat. But his roving exploration had stopped, not so the fierce rush of blood through her body, the accelerated beating of her heart.

"Could it be, Mrs. Donaldson, that your body was turning traitor on you just like mine did? Maybe you're *misinterpreting* the messages I'm sending you?"

She opened her eyes, her gaze locking to his. "I don't think so," she whispered. Well . . . perhaps.

"No, you didn't misinterpret them. Neither did I." The humor fled from his countenance. "Floryn, both of us are mature adults who understand passion, who have experienced it. Both of us feel it between us again.

88

Why can't we be honest about it and enjoy ourselves? We are married and have legal license."

Legal license but not moral license, she wanted to scream. She would not agree to make sex without love. She would not consummate a marriage with a man who considered her little better than a whore. She jerked her foot away from him, away from the tantalizing strokes.

"A marriage in name only."

"If that's what you truly want," he said, "I strongly suggest you keep your hands off me. The rubbing you were doing sends messages that are answered." He raised up, caught her chin in his hand, and gazed into her eyes. "I promise you that sooner or later I'll answer them and feel no remorse."

Deciding she had had enough advice and too much intimacy, she pulled away from him. At this precise moment, she did not trust herself or her reactions, and she was suffering under no delusions as what to expect from him. Sliding off the bed, she picked up her shoes and moved to the rocker on the other side of the room. Cord slipped into his new clothes, black trousers, then socks and boots.

Floryn asked, "Why were you accused of murdering Sanchia?"

"One of my dragoons who survived the attack testified that I smuggled the San Domingo fortune out of Mexico and that I was responsible for the ambush that resulted in the deaths of all the people on the wagon train. The jury bought the story, and I was sentenced to twenty years hard labor."

"No one believed you?"

"One man. Shelby Martin. After I came to and discovered that Sanchia was dead, I tried to make it back to Laredo but was too weak. I passed out again. When I regained consciousness the second time, I was in a doctor's office. Shelby had found and brought me in.

89

By this time, the dragoon had already testified against me, and I was under arrest."

"Why would he lie about you?" Floryn asked.

"Maybe he thought he was telling the truth."

"You can question him now that you're out."

Cord's face shadowed. "He was killed several months later in El Paso over a gambling dispute."

"You have no one, nothing else?"

"Only Shelby," Cord answered. He was quiet for a moment before he said, "But even he believes in the San Domingo treasure."

Floryn looked at him in surprise.

Cord nodded. "There are many things I couldn't remember after I regained consciousness and still can't. Shelby thinks the treasure is one of them. He's done everything he can during the past ten years to jar my memory."

"But you don't sound as if you believe in it?"

"I don't," Cord answered with conviction. "I believe something would have jarred the information loose. Something would have triggered the memory. But nothing — not even the pendant — has."

"It could be part of the treasure."

Cord shrugged. "Whatever it is, it's the only clue I have to that part of my past." Picking up his shirt, he slipped into it, fastening the buttons. "That's why we're going to lay over in San Antonio to visit with Norwell."

"Why does Norwell have it?" she asked.

"I kept it with me when I was sent to prison," he answered. "When Stanton Norwell — he was the warden then — saw it, he wanted it. It and the treasure he thought it represented. So, he took it away from me."

Fascinated by this piece of jewelry that was so important to Cord, she said, "What does it look like?"

"It's a pie-shaped silver medallion inset with a large ruby. About twenty carats."

"Sounds as if it's valuable."

90

"More to me than to anyone else. It's all I have left. Sanchia was killed, and her servant disappeared."

He walked to the mirror and brushed his hair, raven locks defying the brush to spill across his forehead.

"I looked for the woman but couldn't find her. Later, after I buried Sanchia, I saw signals that looked like sunlight reflecting off a mirror and thought the servant might be trying to send me a message. Again I searched, this time to find the pendant caught in the bushes. It was dangling from a chain and gently blowing in the breeze."

"Sunlight had been reflecting off it," Floryn murmured.

Cord nodded and laid the brush on the dresser. "When I held it, I saw the ruby, the size of it. I knew it was valuable, but what struck me most wasn't its size or beauty, but its placement and the marks around it."

"What about it?" Floryn had never heard of the pendant until a few days ago, but the more she learned about it, the more it captivated her attention.

"You would think the ruby would be symmetrically placed on the triangle, but it's not. It's to one side, and the marks look more like a code than a design. It must mean something, but I was never able to figure it out. It's the only clue I have. The only one."

"It's doubtful Norwell still has it." She thought for a moment. "Well, he may have the pendant, but might have sold the ruby."

"I don't think so," Cord answered. "First, he's a wealthy man in his own right. Second and most important, he would be afraid to get rid of any part of it. He believes it's a clue to the San Domingo treasure. Neither of us ever let Pruitt know he had it. Norwell kept it secret because he wanted all the treasure for himself. I kept it secret because I felt the pendant was safer with him than with Pruitt."

Cord slipped into his vest and adjusted the collar of

his shirt. "I haven't seen Norwell for four years. It's time he and I visited."

"During which time he's going to return your pendant. Then the two of you will shake hands and part friends."

"I'm not sure about the parting friends," Cord said. "Otherwise, your little outline is about the way I see it happening."

"He's not going to give it to you, Cord, not without a fight."

"I can be pretty persuasive, but in case my powers are not enough, added persuasion is meeting me in San Antonio."

"Guns?" When he nodded, she said, "Don't do anything that will put you back in prison."

"I'm not."

"Don't let him do anything."

"I won't."

Cord moved to the dresser and, picking up his gun belt, fastened it about his waist. After he secured a holster to each thigh with a leather thong, he opened a long, narrow mahogany case that lay on the dresser. He gazed at two pistols — Navy '51 Colts that Floryn had purchased for him only that morning from the local gunsmith. Her wedding gift to him lay in a bed of lustrous wine velvet. He lifted the pistols by their high-relief horse-head ivory grips and twisted them so that the sunlight accentuated the scroll engraving on the highly polished metal. After he loaded each, he slipped them into the holsters.

Opening the hatbox, Cord pulled out a black John B. He ran his hand around the flattened crown before he settled it on his head and tugged the brim low on his forehead so that it rode just above the eye patch.

Floryn's gaze moved from the black hat, over his face, down the front of the white shirt to the trousers.

Low-waisted, snug in the hips, with slim legs, they fit his muscled body like a second skin.

Reminiscently, she said, "You look like the Cord I used to know."

"I may look like him"—in the reflection of the mirror Cord captured Floryn's gaze—"but I'm not the same man and will never be. You made love to the other Cord, but you're married to me—to the man I am today. I want you to remember that."

Yes, she must remember that for her own salvation! No matter how much she may wish he were the Cord she remembered, the one hewn out of the majestic oak tree. He was not. This man, her husband, was solid stone.

"You make it sound ominous." Fear—or was it excitement?—caused her heart to beat erratically.

"No"—his voice was low—"when you decide to make love to me, I want to make sure you're making love to me, not to a memory."

"*If* I were to make love to you," she replied, "it would be you I was loving, not the memory."

He walked toward her. For a big man he moved quietly and quickly. He stood directly in front of her—close enough that she could smell his newly purchased after-shave cologne, close enough she could see the texture of his cheeks, the texture of the leather patch he wore over his eye.

Her body still thrumming from his recent caresses, Floryn wanted to move away from him, but sensations, newly awakened, kept her feet planted to the spot. "You keep insinuating that I'll eventually initiate our lovemaking. You seem to labor under some delusion that I can hardly wait to get into bed with you, that I have spent the last ten years pining away for you. Be assured I have not."

He was altogether too close, making coherent thought impossible. She backed up a step. "I can understand your tendency to misinterpret everything I say or do."

He advanced a step.

She was inundated with his presence, the warmth of him. Sheer willpower kept her voice steady. "Your . . . er . . . your socializing with women has been limited during the past nine years. I imagine that because you're in . . . in dire need of one—of a woman—you imagine that if I have truly been without a man for the past nine years, I have the same . . . the same dire needs."

Again she moved.

Again he closed the distance between them.

She drew a ragged breath. "Let me make something clear here and now, Cord Donaldson, I am not in such need that I will go to bed with any man without love. Our marriage is a business arrangement, and despite what you want, what you think I want, that is exactly what it will remain. I think my terms are overly generous . . . without our sleeping together."

"I find your sense of generosity grossly overstated," Cord said. "I want you to know I'm not laboring under some delusion. I'm just honest enough to admit that both of us are still attracted to one another. Part of that attraction comes from our having made love ten years ago. We wonder if we made love again would it be as exciting. Another part of our attraction is simple. You're a woman. I'm a man."

"God forbid if every man and woman who find themselves thrown together should think like you," Floryn scoffed.

"I find you damned attractive and tempting. It's all I can do to keep from throwing you on that bed, ripping off your clothes, and making love to you until time ceases to exist . . . perhaps longer. While my desires have all to do with my *dire* needs, they have nothing to

94

do with my having or not having led a celibate life for the past nine years."

Floryn felt the heat radiating from her face. Never had she participated in such blatant sexual conversations as she and Cord had shared recently. Her mother may have been a prostitute, but she had shielded Floryn from the wicked, sinful side of life. After Floryn married Hal, he had continued to shelter her from the world.

"For your information, I had a woman fulfill my *dire* needs only a few days ago. Jack Willowby, astute warden he is, believes in keeping trouble down to a minimal. He makes women available quite often."

He moved slightly, enough that his chest was rubbing against Floryn's bosom. She sucked in a painful breath and hastily took a step backward, her last, for she was jammed against the wall. He edged closer. His warm breath blew against her skin.

"I want to make love to you, Floryn Donaldson, because you're you, because I desire *you* . . . not just a woman. Sooner or later I will, whether you or I initiate it." A smug smile played on his lips. "The way you react to me, I'd say we'll be doing the coupling sooner rather than later."

Seven

I want to make love to you, Floryn Donaldson, because you're you, because I desire you . . . not just a woman!

Although Cord's words sounded like a confession of love, they were not. Lustful, they undermined her purpose, corroded her dreams and hopes. They reinforced his bitter and distrustful outlook on life, his hostility and anger. They insinuated these same negative emotions into her life now that they were married.

His compelling gaze searched, drilled straight through to all the secret parts within her. She forced herself to return his stare. She did not wish to give him the satisfaction of forcing her to look away. She did not want him to know she felt so naked under his gaze. So her eyes met his in open competition.

The room crackled with silent tension. The walls seemed to press in on Floryn. Her entire body tightened inside, and her intense need to see him smile tenderly at her, to listen to his deep voice whispering words of love, to feel the gentleness of those capable hands, all grew.

No matter what he had done to her, no matter that he did not believe her, she wanted him.

Damn!

A cutting shout outside pierced the moment. The words did not register, only the noise. She walked to the window on the pretense of investigating the commotion, but saw nothing unusual. The distance between her and Cord made her feel more in control, made her feel safer. Cord returned to the bed and began to sort through his clothes.

Street noises drifted into the room, people talking to one another and children laughing; horses whickering, dogs barking; wagons lumbering by. A warm breeze, stirring the gauzy curtain, blew tendrils of hair against her cheek.

She saw a little girl about Hope's age accompany her mother into the general store.

"I told you I saved enough money to buy Hope some clothes. I have some extra. I thought I'd buy her a gift," she said.

"A doll," Cord said absently. "I think I saw one at the general store this morning."

"She doesn't play with dolls."

Floryn watched as he folded one of the handkerchiefs and tucked it into his trousers pocket.

"She's rather a tomboy."

Agile fingers slipped the pocketknife into another pocket. He picked up his timepiece, an ornate one—the only possession he had brought with him from prison—and wound it before sliding it into the small slit on his vest. He hooked the gold chain.

"I'll probably get her a new shirt or material for a pair of trousers," she said, wondering if Cord was listening to her, wondering if he would ever show any interest in his daughter.

Floryn looked out the window to see a prison supply wagon moving up the street toward the general store. She smiled when she recognized the driver to be Rule. She was about to mention this to Cord when he spoke.

"Does Hope know about me?"

The tone of his voice was casual, but Floryn heard the underscoring of interest. She turned. "Yes."

He raised his head quickly, his expression one of surprise.

97

"Hal didn't want me to tell her because he wanted to be her papa, but she's an intelligent, perceptive child. About a year ago she questioned me, and I told her the truth."

"She knows her father—me, Cord Donaldson," he clarified, "is coming home with you as your husband?"

"Yes."

"You were pretty damn sure of yourself." His voice was cutting.

"No, I was pretty damn sure of you."

"Exactly how is she responding to this truth?"

"With my confession followed closely by Hal's death, she's not sure what she thinks, Cord. She's curious to see you, but she's also frightened and lonely. She loved Hal deeply."

His expression was unexpectedly desolate. "She's probably going to view me as an interloper. She's too old to accept me as her father, Floryn. I think you're spinning yourself a fairy tale if you believe otherwise."

"You're underestimating your daughter."

"You're underestimating the situation. When you told me about her, I—I wanted it to work out between us. I wanted to know Hope."

There was a sadness to his voice, a hesitancy as if he wanted to say more. Floryn was consumed by the need to reach out and touch him, to chase away the shadows that had appeared so quickly in his face.

"I have a dark past, one that wishful thinking and wanting isn't going to erase. I'm not the proper father for her."

Floryn was shaken by the strength of the emotion his confession stirred within her, by the power that made her care so deeply. That made her care so deeply when he obviously did not care about her. It made no sense.

"Proper or not, you are her father." Floryn stepped closer to peer into his face shadowed by the John B. "The only father she'll ever have. The one she needs."

"Floryn, I've been in prison for nine years. I've been exposed to a reality you've never imagined, much less seen. A reality I pray you never see." His voice reflected the same bleakness that she had witnessed in his face.

"Don't talk to me about reality. What do you think I've been doing for the past ten years?" Floryn exclaimed. "Playing with dolls? Well, I haven't. I've experienced this reality you're so fond of talking about. I've run the Fancy Lady, managed the household and *vaqueros,* rounded up stock. I've reared our daughter. I'm the one who tried to make our household seem like a normal one, even when Hal became mentally ill."

She paused, then said, "Even when he began to hate me. For the past few years I've lived with a crazy man who has reviled me, shouting and screaming at me the majority of the time. You can't imagine the horrid things he has accused me of."

"I apologize, Floryn. I'm not making excuses for myself or saying you had an easy time of it, but you could make choices. At any time you could have left Hal. I could not walk out of prison. You could have created a new life for yourself. Injustice created a new life for me. My road was chosen for me, not so yours."

"Oh, no," she said bitterly, "that's not true. Making love and the possibility of our making a baby was your choice as well as mine. I couldn't and didn't do it alone, and refuse to accept the blame for it. Had you really cared about me, Cord, you would have kept in contact with me. You would have been interested in knowing whether or not I became pregnant. You knew the possibility existed."

Cord rubbed his cheek below the patch. "You're right," he said. "I should have found out. Again I apologize."

"I should have found out. Again I apologize," she mimicked. "Let me tell you, apologies don't stretch far

99

enough to cover such a flagrant oversight."

"I wasn't implying that you chose to become pregnant," he said. "I was talking about your choosing to stay with Hal."

Floryn crossed her arms over her breasts. She fought to control her temper, her voice. She cursed the tears that had been so close to the surface since she had met Cord again. Always there, waiting to be unchecked, and he seemed to be doing his best to release them.

"Yes," she admitted, weary of always having to defend her choices, of being accused of ulterior motives, "I chose to stay with Hal, but I was young, inexperienced, foolish. Most of all, I was an idealist. I chose a road that could have left me bitter and disillusioned like you, but I didn't allow it to. You can overcome your past, Cord. You'll see that once we get far away from the prison."

"I'm not willing to forget it, Floryn. I want the person who did this to me to suffer as I've suffered. It's been eating away at me for nine long years."

"Revenge is double-edged," she cautioned.

"I've had my edge and it sliced me to the bone," Cord said. "Now it's time for them to have theirs."

"Cord, please think about Hope."

He made no reply.

"I understand clearly your feeling—rather your lack of feeling—for me. I'm not suggesting we take up where we left off ten years ago, but we have Hope to think about. We have an obligation to create a future for her."

"You'll get your ranch, Floryn, and your daughter."

Your daughter! The phrase slit Floryn's sensibilities like a sharp knife. Not their daughter, but her daughter!

"Just stop using the child as a pawn."

"I'm not," Floryn said. Instilling her voice was a calmness she was far from feeling. "I'm fighting for her.

She's the innocent victim in this series of tragic events. And whether you want to admit it or not, you are a part of Hope's future. She's a part of yours."

"The word future is no longer in my vocabulary, Floryn. All I'll promise is one day at a time. That's all I've come to expect from life. That's damn well all I give." He strode to the desk. Picking up his letters, he said, "I'm going to post these. Then I'm heading to the saloon for a drink. I'll be back in a couple of hours to take your luggage down."

"I can manage myself, thank you," she snapped.

"Whatever." Cord walked out of the room.

Floryn moved back to the window to gaze into the street below. It was more congested than it had been earlier. She looked farther up at the prison wagon parked in front of the general store. Rule, moving around the vehicle, supervised the loading of supplies. She liked the old man and was going to miss him when they left Huntsville.

She heard the entry door of the boardinghouse slam. Boots clipped on the boardwalk, then Cord stepped into the street. His black leather vest shimmered in the sunlight. The handles of his Navy '51 Colts glinted dangerously. He walked with a confident stride, his head held high, his back straight.

He had changed all right, she thought, but not in appearance. He was still darkly handsome, a commanding figure. Of all the men along the street, Cord stood apart. Not because he was necessarily taller or his shoulders broader. It was his carriage, his bearing. Confidence made him a veritable giant among men.

She returned to the bed to begin packing her valise. She was eager to be away from Huntsville, away from Cord's past.

Still reveling in his freedom, Cord stepped onto the

boardwalk in front of the saloon.

"Howdy, Donaldson!" shouted a man.

The voice was familiar, but Cord had not heard it in years, had wanted never to hear it again. It made his flesh crawl. He stopped walking, turned, and stared.

"It's been a while." The man hitched his thumbs over his gun belt and grinned, exposing tobacco-stained teeth. "I'm Orwen. Orwen Baxter."

As if he could ever forget, Cord thought. "What are you doing in Huntsville?"

"Heard you were out of prison, and I wanted to see you."

"Well, you've done that."

"We got a score to settle."

"Not me," Cord said. "I settled mine."

Orwen's grin turned into a malicious sneer. "Last time we fought I took that eye. I should of took 'em both."

"You should have."

Orwen took a faltering step, dragging his right leg. His ankle turned; he stumbled and grimaced.

"The leg bothering you, Orwen?"

"It's worse on some days than on others," he answered.

"Be glad you can walk at all," Cord said.

"Reckon you're right about that." He spat, but his raisinlike eyes remained on Cord's face.

Cord turned his back on the man and took several steps toward the saloon. He was standing in front of the swinging doors when Orwen shouted.

"Donaldson! You said you already settled your score. I ain't. Reckon I'll do that right now."

Cord faced him.

Orwen pushed away from the porch column, his right hand lowered to hover over his revolver. He brushed his left palm down his dirty shirt and limped toward Cord. Head and shoulders taller than Cord, he was built like a locomotive. A man who reasoned like a locomotive, who depended on brawn to get him through life.

As they stared at each other, Cord remembered the first time he had seen Orwen Baxter in prison. Orwen had ordered him to empty his slop jar. Cord had refused. Orwen sicced his thugs on Cord, and he had barely whipped them. The older man determined to break Cord. Cord had been equally determined not to be broken.

As a young man and new prisoner, Cord had feared Orwen more than any of the other hardened prisoners. Although he had won the first battle against Orwen, he was wise enough to keep his distance. But Orwen, self-proclaimed king of the prison, goaded and pushed Cord. He was determined that Cord would be obeisant to him, getting more determined the longer Cord opposed him.

Even now, remembering those first days at the penitentiary, Cord felt the perspiration run down his back. He felt it gathering beneath his eye patch. This time it was not caused by fear of Orwen, but by the anxiety of recalling those hellish days when he had been locked up. He had felt no fear since the night he and Orwen Baxter fought.

He had lost an eye and suffered several lacerations, but he had been victorious. He had slashed Orwen's right leg from the hip to his knee—a deep slash that had rendered the leg almost useless. From that day forward, Orwen Baxter never tried to lord it over him again. All the prisoners gained a new respect—or perhaps a fear—of Cord and left him alone.

Cord probably would have died from complications to the eye wound had Rule not taken care of him. Later when he had recuperated, he and the old man had become fast friends.

When Orwen finished serving his time, Cord hoped

he had seen the last of him. He, of all people, had made the mistake of forgetting how deep hatred and revenge run.

The two men stared at each other.

Cord never moved, never gave indication of his discomfort. He flexed his right hand. It was stiff. Nine years since he had used a handgun, had really held one.

"Let it be, Orwen. Neither of us has anything to gain by this and everything to lose." Cord realized with the saying of the words that he really meant it. Orwen Baxter was a part of his past, not the present, not the future. "You're not going to goad me into a fight. I'm out of prison and intend to stay out."

"Cord!" Footfalls echoed loudly on the boardwalk as Rule ran to where the two men stood.

"It's all right, Rule," Cord said.

Orwen shifted his gaze so that it rested on Rule. As Cord watched, Orwen played with his straggly mustache. His jaw bulged when he moved his cud of tobacco from one side of his mouth to the other and back again.

"Still taking care of Donaldson," Orwen jeered. "Well, this ain't yore fight, so why don't you get outta here?"

Out of the periphery of his vision Cord saw a crowd gathering. At the prospect of a fight, they circled tightly about him and Orwen. By this time Rule was out of Cord's line of vision. The door to the dry goods store opened, and Jason ran out. Adults crowded in front of him, and he quickly shimmied up a portico pillar and perched on the hitching post.

"Why you damn liver-bellied coward!" Rule shouted from behind, breaking the tense silence.

A shot immediately followed the shout. Another. Cord whirled around to see Rule catch his shoulder and collapse against the porch column. Another man, a stranger, a frozen expression of disbelief on his face, staggered into the street. His revolver slipped from his hand as he fell, face down.

"He was gonna shoot you in the back," Rule gasped. He jerked his head. "Look out behind."

Cord spun around, his gaze catching Floryn who stood in the opened door to the boardinghouse.

"Over there, Cord," she shouted and pointed at Orwen.

A bullet grazed Cord's arm. Before Orwen could shoot a second time, Cord whipped out his Navy '51 Colts and fired. He found his target. Orwen dropped his revolver, clutched his chest, blood oozing through his fingers, and crumpled into the street.

Frightened by the shooting, the team of horses hitched to the prison supply wagon snorted, their nostrils flared. No one to control them, they lurched forward, soon in full gallop. Cord jumped out of the way, but heard a commotion behind him. Jason tumbled from his perch into the street. Unmoving, evidently dazed, he lay in the path of the runaways.

"Jason!" A woman pushed out of the mercantile store toward the fallen boy.

Cord bolted to his feet. Grabbing her by the waist, he swung her onto the boardwalk out of harm's way.

"My baby. My only child. Dear God, don't take him away from me." The anguished cry of the mother touched Cord's heart.

In the split second as Cord raced into the street, he again saw the child standing in the hall with his purchases. Large, inquisitive eyes set in a freckled face framed with red hair. Almost eleven years old. About the same age as Hope, as his daughter.

Cord scooped Jason into his arms. He seemed so small and defenseless. He felt like a limp doll. Cord, protecting Jason's body with his, rolled them to safety on the other side of the thoroughfare and lay there as the team galloped by. When he was sure they were safe, he rose, bringing Jason with him.

"That was a foolish thing to do," he grated, his voice gruff with fear. "Are you all right?"

Freckles stood out in relief against the boy's white face. His lips quivering, he nodded.

"Jason!" The woman rushed to where they stood, throwing her arms around the boy. She hugged him tightly. "Oh, Jason. I was so worried."

"I'm all right, Ma."

Looking embarrassed, Jason struggled out of his mother's embrace. He dusted the front of his shirt and brushed the errant strand of hair from his forehead.

"Next time," Cord advised, "be a little more careful where you stand."

Having regained some of his color, the child breathed in deeply a time or two. "Yes, sir," he said quietly, "I sure will. You really are tough, Mr. Donaldson. Nobody could have done what you done."

"Thank you, Mr. Donaldson," Mrs. Renshaw said. She wiped tears from her face. "I don't know what I would do if something happened to Jason. He's all I've got in the world."

Quite the adult, Jason held out his hand. "Thank you, sir, for saving my life."

Cord clasped the hand and shook it, one man to another.

Cord grinned as he watched Jason and his mother walk away. This was his first experience with children. They were different, but he liked the difference. He was eager to meet Hope. From what Floryn had told him about her, he expected she would be spunky enough to climb on a hitching post to watch a duel.

As Cord walked to where Rule lay in the street, slumped against the portico column, Cord wondered about Hope. Who was she? What was she? He knew what Floryn had told him. Hope had black hair and brown eyes, but that was what she looked like. It was not the substance of Hope. He wanted to hear her laughter and see the sparkle in her eyes. He wanted to know this daughter of his.

He looked at Floryn bending over Rule. He had first become aware of her presence when she had shouted, when she had saved his life. "How is he?" Cord asked.

"His shoulder. I think he'll be all right."

Rule coughed, and his face twisted in pain. "I ain't dead or unconscious," he said. "You don't have to talk like I'm not around."

"The bullet went straight through," Floryn answered, her gaze anxious, searching. "How about you?"

"I'm fine." He knelt beside his friend. "You old fool, your first week out of prison, and you've gotten yourself wounded. You could have been killed."

"What about yourself?"

"Orwen involved me. You involved yourself," Cord said.

"You don't have to be so gentle with an ailing old man. I'll probably live to see another day. None of my vitals is damaged." Rule's lips twisted into a smile.

Cord laughed. "We'll take you to the doctor's office and have this tended to. I guess I'm going to have to take you home with me, old man, and watch out for you."

"You mean, you want me to go home with you, so's I can watch out for you."

"Yeah, that's what I meant. Somehow I can't imagine life without your meddling."

Floryn caught Cord's arm and looked at the bullet-torn shirt. "You're not all right," she accused.

"There's more damage to it than to me," he said.

Looking closely as if assuring herself, she said, "I was scared. When I heard the shooting, I ran out, and I saw. I thought—"

He could handle Floryn better when she was brisk

and all business. When she became the doting wife, she bothered him. She touched a tender, sensitive area of his heart, an area he was protecting at all costs, an area he wished were as hardened as his emotions.

"I'm fine." His words sounded brusque even to him.

She gave him a trembling smile. "You look a sight."

Both glanced down at his torn and dirty clothes.

"Nothing mending and a good washing won't take care of."

"I'll do it after we've taken care of Rule," she said.

"Thank God, you finally thought about me," Rule muttered. "I don't know if I'm going to that ranch with you or not, Cord. I'll spend the rest of my life standing around while the two of you make goo-goo eyes at each other."

Cord swept the old man into his arms. "Why don't you admit you're enjoying all this?"

Rule grunted. "To be honest, I am getting some pleasure out of it, and I think I'm gonna get more when I see you toeing the line for the little lady."

"That'll be the day," Floryn murmured dryly.

"There was a day," Cord said, his gaze catching and locking to Floryn's. "Never again."

"Hey, Mr. Donaldson." Jason came running back. "I'll show you the way to Doctor Pritchard's office."

The boy in the lead, Cord moved down the boardwalk, turned into an alley, and climbed a side staircase. Floryn, his hat in hand, ran behind him. In answer to their knock, an older man opened the door.

"Doctor Pritchard?" Cord asked.

The man nodded his head and threw the door wide, his gaze fastened on Rule's shoulder as they passed by. "Put him in the back room. The door to the right."

Walking through the house, Cord laid Rule on a small day bed, then moved away. Floryn remained in the entry room. After shutting the door, the doctor pulled a chair up to the bed and examined the wound.

When he leaned back, he said, "Nasty but clean. Looks like you're going to heal up just fine."

"Sure will. Take more than this to kill me."

The doctor straightened and walked to the cabinet where he extracted bottles and bandages. Rule beckoned to the boy.

"Run to the warden's house," he said, "and fetch him for me. Tell him what happened and let him know the prison supplies have been held up."

The child bobbed his head, then raced out of the room.

The doctor stopped in front of Cord and pulled at the sleeve fabric. "You're wounded, too."

"It's nothing," Cord said.

"I'll determine that. Now let me have a look-see." After Cord rolled up his sleeve and the doctor looked at it, he said, "You're right. It's nothing. But just in case, I'm gonna clean it and put some salve on it."

When his arm was bandaged, Cord rolled down his sleeve and buttoned the cuff.

"Now," the doctor ordered, "get out of here while I take care of this man."

Floryn waited impatiently in the small room. When the door opened, she ran to it and looked anxiously into Cord's face.

"How is he?"

"Fine."

"You—" she said. "You're not hurt?"

He shook his head, and they stared at each other for a long time, saying nothing.

Finally the tears trickled down her cheeks. Tears because he was all right, because she loved him, because he made such a pointed effort to misunderstand her. They were for the times that had been and would never be again.

"Are these for me or Rule?" he asked softly, so softly she cried even more.

He sounded like the love of her life, the man she had met in the meadow so many years ago. A man who cared for her.

Not trusting herself to answer his question, she posed her own. "You love Rule, don't you?"

He lifted a hand, brushing the moisture with the knuckle of his index finger. "I owe him. He took care of me when I first arrived at the penitentiary. He taught me the rules of survival." A partial smile touched his lips. "He told me that was his duty. That's why his name was Rule."

"You owe me, too." She gave him a teary smile and pressed her hand over his.

"I'll make sure you get the ranch." Without moving his hand from her cheek, he twined his fingers through hers. "I promise."

"I wasn't thinking about the ranch."

He searched her face with such hard intensity her stomach contracted with the most primitive kind of awareness.

"I wasn't thinking about it altogether," she said.

"I'm glad you added that. For a minute there, I thought you had forgotten our promise to be truthful with each other."

His hair was disheveled, his body radiating heat, his shirt open at the throat. She saw the hint of black chest hair in the opening. His gaze shimmered on her as if she were a priceless possession, something of great value to him.

For this moment in time she felt as if she belonged to him, as if he loved her. But she knew he did not. He had made plain his feelings on that subject.

He was close enough for her to see the pulse at his throat. He slowly lowered her hand without releasing it. The silence was suddenly intimate, the morning sunlight reflecting on his face, on the leather eye patch. His smile disappeared and his gaze rested on her.

He unsettled her the way he stared at her. He brushed a strand of hair from her cheek. He ran the tip of his finger along her lip, from one corner of her mouth to the other. She curled her fingers around his, holding it against her mouth. She kissed his fingertip.

His palm cupped the back of her head, and he pulled her closer to him as he leaned closer to her. "I always repay my debts."

Her nostrils quivered with the tantalizing mixture of his scents: sweat, street dust, masculinity, and his after-shave cologne. She felt the warmth of his breath, saw his eyelid shutter down. The first touch of his lips was more a stroke than a kiss. Then they settled down, soft and warm and moist. He kissed her again, this time deeper and more intimately.

It did not end, that kiss, until Floryn was a mael-strom of emotion. At the same time she felt as if she had been run over by the runaway team, as if she had climbed the highest mountain and were surveying the kingdoms of the world, as if she were swirling in an endless eddy of passion. The excitement shooting through her was borne from something magical and terrifyingly powerful that promised they would inevita-bly make love.

When Cord raised his head, his features were stark. Unsmiling, his gaze burned into her. His mouth was wet from their last kiss. Embarrassed by her wanton behavior, she dug her handkerchief out of her skirt pocket and raised it to his face.

"You—you probably want me to—"

"I want you, Floryn." His voice was low and thick with desire. "Plain and simple."

She never touched the handkerchief to his face. He planted a hand against the doorjamb, the sleeve of his shirt evocatively brushing against her cheek, and shoved away from her.

"Go back to the boardinghouse and finish your packing." His voice was yet low. "After I post my letters and have a drink, I'll come get you."

She nodded and said, "I'll get your hat."

Returning the handkerchief to her pocket, she crossed to the clothes rack and unpegged the black John B. She handed it to him and watched as he resettled it on his head.

She inhaled his herbal cologne and fought the desire to run her finger around the outline of the leather shield to feel at the same time beneath her finger the texture of leather and his skin. Again he gazed at her. Again he caught her chin and tipped her head up.

"Sooner or later," he said.

Floryn did not pretend to misunderstand his words. She accepted their truth. They would make love, and she would be willing. For her it would be total commitment, total love. For him, it would be sex. No emotional involvement. No love.

He was gone. The slamming of the door echoed through the silent room. Floryn heard his receding steps as he descended the stairs. Alone. Alone and frightened. Cold, despite the summer heat. She had not felt this alone since he had left her once before in a field dampened by the rain. She wrapped her arms about herself . . . but that was not enough to console her or to warm her body or soul.

Eight

Cord stood alone at the bar. Even if the saloon had been filled to overflowing, he would have been alone. He braced his foot on the brass rail and held a half-filled glass of whiskey in his hand.

He had married Floryn because they had a mutual need. In effect they were using each other. As Floryn had said, they were mutually dependent on each other. In actuality, he felt used more than he felt that he was using. But he could and did not blame Floryn. His own emotions were playing him for a fool.

He quaffed the remainder of the drink. Setting the glass on the bar, he lifted the bottle and refilled it.

He had promised himself that he would not become emotionally involved with Floryn again. But he had known from the beginning that he was lying to himself. He had never been uninvolved with her. He had been allowed to have sex with prostitutes periodically during his time in prison, but he had not made love to a woman since Floryn.

He had searched for but never found her. Not until that day he turned and saw her sitting beside the cistern.

He was not sure he loved her. He was not sure what love was anymore. But he wanted her.

His hand tightened around the glass!

"Cord Donaldson," a masculine voice called from the door.

Cord set the glass down and turned.

A tall, lanky man walked into the saloon. A smile edged through a brown beard and mustache. His hat, once white, was sweat-stained and soiled. A cloth vest, worn over a faded, checkered shirt, brushed against gray trousers tucked into knee-high boots. Around his waist were fastened two Colt pistols.

"Hello, Shelby," Cord said. "What are you doing here?"

"Delivered a prisoner."

"What'll ya be a'having?" the bartender asked.

Shelby Martin picked up the bottle on the counter and said to Cord, "Is this what you're drinking?"

Cord nodded.

"I'll join him," Shelby said. When the bartender sat a second glass down, Shelby lifted it and beckoned to Cord. "Let's move to a table where we can drink and talk in comfort."

Cord followed him to a secluded corner of the saloon where they seated themselves. Shelby sprawled back in the chair and gave his friend a hooded stare and a lazy smile.

"Heard you were married." He filled both glasses.

"I am."

Shelby lifted his glass. "To a long and happy marriage."

"Don't know about the length of it, but it's going to be fun while it lasts."

"I have to admit it took me by surprise."

"Me, too."

"Then why?"

"Marriage to her was a way out of prison." They

drank in silence. Then: "You spend much time out in West Texas?"

"How far west?"

"Around the ranch."

Shelby shook his head. "Nine years ago was the last time I visited. I haven't been back since you asked me not to. Why?"

"I was just wondering."

"What I told you about Floryn was rumor. Just that. Nothing more or less. Nothing that can be proved or disproved."

"Did you know about the child?"

Shelby took a swallow of his drink. "Not for a long time. When I did find out, I had heard so many rumors about her infidelity that I figured—" He ended the sentence with a shrug. After a lengthy pause, he said, "Is Floryn claiming she's yours?"

Cord nodded.

"I never made the connection," Shelby said.

Not wanting to discuss Floryn or Hope any longer, Cord asked, "How long you staying in town?"

"I'm on my way out now. Where are you headed?"

"San Antonio."

Shelby cocked a brow. "So you're going to pay old Norwell a visit. And once you have the pendant, you're gonna start investigating the massacre."

"Plan to."

Interest sparked in his eyes and he leaned forward, settling his folded arms on the table. "Have you remembered something?"

"No."

"Got a new clue?"

"No."

The animation dying from his face, he pushed back in the chair. "Hell, Cord, the trail was cold by the time I found you nine years ago. By now there isn't one. Sanchia's dead. The dragoon was killed in a drunken brawl. The maid and Mathieu Guilbert disappeared without a trace."

"Pruitt let Floryn buy my parole," Cord said.

"I heard. He's hoping you'll lead him to the treasure."

Cord leaned back in the chair. "Why is he so convinced there is a treasure, Shelby? What does he know that I don't?"

"The pendant, Cord," he said. "It's got to be part of the treasure. If only you could remember."

"How many times must I tell you —"

Shelby held up his hand. "You don't. If you hadn't insisted on keeping that damn pendant with you when they transferred you to the penitentiary, I could have had it, instead of Norwell. Maybe those odd scratches on it have meaning."

"Since I haven't looked at it in a long time," Cord said, "maybe I'll see something new, something different."

"Yeah," Shelby drawled, "maybe it'll jog your memory. That is, if you see it at all. You don't have a clue what Norwell has done with it. God, by now he's probably sold the ruby."

"I hope not, but I'll be glad just to have the pendant."

"If I didn't have to go to Austin, I'd ride with you," Shelby said. "You're probably going to need some extra guns."

"I'll have them. Rule's going to meet me there."

"A lot of good an old, wounded man is going to do you."

"He's not hurt that bad," Cord answered. "And he's not the only one who's going to join me. I've sent out several letters."

Shelby's eyes narrowed. "Anybody I know?"

116

Cord grinned. "You should. You brought them in. Kid Ferguson and Tony Esteman."

"Heavy guns! You trust them?"

"As much as I trust anyone."

"I trust I'm not disturbing you, Mrs. Donaldson?" The woman's voice was low and husky. "I'm Nellie Stratford."

Standing in the opened door of the boardinghouse room, Floryn stared at the beautiful, young visitor. Her expensive pale green dress, trimmed in a darker shade of the same color, enhanced jade eyes and contrasted with auburn hair.

Oh, yes, Floryn thought, *you disturb me very much.* She had no idea why the woman was here, she had no idea who the woman was, but Floryn knew — yes, she knew — her visit did not bode well for her.

"I don't want to sound inhospitable, Mrs. Stratford, but I don't have much time. My husband and I are leaving shortly."

"Miss Stratford," the woman said.

"I beg your pardon," Floryn murmured.

"Not Mrs.," she clarified with a smile. "I'll only take a moment of your time. Please let me come in. I don't think you want this conversation to take place in a public place like the corridor of a boardinghouse."

Her suspicion concerning the woman's visit confirmed, Floryn waved to the love seat at the foot of the bed. "All right, then. Please be seated."

Nellie did so, and Floryn sat in the chair across from her. Nellie removed her gloves, straightened and laid them on her lap. On top of them she placed a smooth, dainty hand with shapely fingernails that had been buffed to a high sheen. The creamy hands

117

looked as if they had been pampered with care and lotions.

Nellie looked up, a cherubic face peering at Floryn from a hat that was mounds of delicate lace and dark green feathers. A face that also had been caressed with creams and cosmetics. The woman's perfume—a fragrance similar to the ones Floryn had sampled when she had honeymooned in Paris—touched her nostrils. It was a scent that hung heavily in the room, one Floryn would not soon forget.

Floryn looked at herself. Her clothes were new and expensive, but they did not disguise what Floryn was, a working woman. She looked at her hands. Unlike Nellie's manicured nails, Floryn's nails were clipped short and clean. Nellie's skin was milky white; Floryn's was tanned. Kissed by the sun and wind, Leanor often said. More like burned by the sun and wind, Floryn thought.

"I suppose you're wondering why I'm here," Nellie said.

"Yes, I am."

"Cord came to see me, to tell me he was married and I wanted to meet his bride. I wanted to meet the woman who was taking Cord away from me."

All kinds of retorts rose to Floryn's lips, as anger and jealousy swelled within her heart, but she curbed them. She had handled worse situations than this during her life. She curled her lips into a semblance of a smile, a practiced gesture she had used often when dealing with undesirables.

"Well, you've met me, Miss Stratford. You can leave now."

Nellie rose and took a step, moving in front of the window where sunshine gleamed brightly on her. Although she was still a beautiful woman, Floryn saw

118

an artificialness about her that she had not seen before.

Everything about the woman was exaggerated. Too many feathers on her hat. Too many frills and furbelows on her dress. Her cosmetics too thick. Her perfume too heavy. Her smile too wide.

"If you think Cord loves you," Nellie said, "you're stupid as well as . . . as well as . . . old and ugly. I'm the woman who has made love to Cord during the past four years. He and I understand one another. No questions asked. No commitments." She gave Floryn a patronizing smile. "He married you, but he's not married to you. I'm Cord Donaldson's woman."

Looking directly into those green eyes, hoping fire was burning in her own, Floryn said, "You may have been his woman, Miss Stratford, but that was the past. Today is the present, and I am his wife, his woman. Now leave before I forget my manners and the meaning of civility."

"Not before I give you your wedding gift." After slipping on her gloves, Nellie unpinned a gold watch from her dress. A malicious smile curved the full lips; it glittered in the depth of her eyes. "I had this and another crafted three years ago in New Orleans. One was for a woman, the other for a man. Do you recognize it?"

Puzzled, Floryn accepted the watch from her. Holding it in her palm, she looked down at it. She turned it over several times. It was a smaller replica of the one Cord wore.

"I gave Cord his," Nellie said, "on November 12, 1862, for his twenty-seventh birthday. It was a special gift to celebrate not only his birthday but our feelings for each other."

Floryn held her hand out to return the watch.

119

"You keep it," Nellie said. "It matches the one he uses now. Keep it as a special gift to celebrate your marriage. When I take him away from you, you can return it to me."

"I don't want your watch," Floryn said. "I have one of my own. If I were to take it, Miss Stratford, you could rest assured you would never get it back."

"Because you're a sore loser?"

"Because I'm not a loser. Cord Donaldson will never leave me for you."

Floryn was amazed at the many times she had *mishandled the truth*, as Leanor would say, during the past few weeks.

"We'll see." Refusing to take the watch, Nellie brushed past Floryn to stop when she reached the door. She turned around and leaned back. "I don't like you, but since you're married to Cord—for whatever reason—I'm going to give you some advice. He had better be careful. His life could be in danger."

"How do you know?"

"I overheard bits and pieces of a conversation between Webb Pruitt and some of his associates. In case you're wondering, Webb and I are friends." She smiled sarcastically as she lowered her veil, opened the door, and departed. "Good day, Mrs. Donaldson."

Long after Nellie Stratford had departed, her perfume remained to taunt Floryn. Knowing it was an odor she would hate for the rest of her life, she paced the room, her mind awhirl with thoughts of Cord and his *woman*—his woman for the past four years.

Floryn knew she had no right to expect Cord to have led a celibate life during the past ten years, but to be confronted by his . . . by his . . . by the woman he had been sleeping with for the past four years was more than she could tolerate.

Nellie's carriage and demeanor was not that of a

woman who was generally referred to as a lady of the street. Nellie Stratford definitely was not the kind of woman Floryn had envisioned Cord spending his time with during his stay at the penitentiary. She had never imagined him having any woman, much less the same woman during this time.

Jealous of whatever had gone on between Cord and Nellie, Floryn could not block out images of them together, of their talking, of their holding one another and making love. In her imagination she could hear Cord whispering endearments in her ear as he loved her. Floryn no longer questioned the reasonableness of her feelings, she only experienced them.

By the time Cord appeared, Floryn had worked through disappointment and anger to white hot fury.

He glanced at her hat still sitting on the dresser. "I thought you'd be ready for lunch."

"I was delayed. I had a visitor." She spoke in staccato tones. "Nellie Stratford. Perhaps you'll recognize the perfume she wore. The room is full of it."

That he evinced no curiosity fueled her anger. "She wanted to let me know you had been to see her."

"She lied." His voice was cool, his expression closed. He unfastened a valise and pulled out a clean shirt and trousers.

"You've been sleeping with her for the past four years."

"What I did before you and I married is my business."

How true! Floryn thought. She fell to the earth hard and knew she would carry the bruises for the rest of her life. When she had come to Cord, she had expected, had hoped they would rediscover their love. Now she knew that probably would never be. Cord was so hard and cold, almost angry at her for mentioning Nellie. Yet Floryn persisted.

"Nellie Stratford made what you did before you married me my business." Floryn glared at him, unable . . . or unwilling . . . to take her eyes off him as he changed clothes. "For God's sake, Cord, we're married."

"In name only," he reminded her, sharpness again evident in his tone.

Nellie's words taunted Floryn. *No questions asked. No commitment. He married you, but he's not married to you. I'm Cord Donaldson's woman.*

But, I'm his wife, Floryn silently screamed to still the taunting litany.

She had him in marriage only, but she was losing that tenuous bonding to him. Damn it! She was losing him altogether . . . to this woman, to his past.

"It matters not whether we are married in name only or not." Floryn tried to keep her voice as cold and hard as Cord's. "We are married, and that in itself is a commitment. I will not be subjected to . . . to this kind of treatment from the women in your life."

"Woman," Cord corrected. "Not women. She was enjoyable in bed, and we spent many pleasurable nights together."

Despising his confession, although she had demanded it, she said, "What about the watch?"

"What about the watch?"

She held her hand out, Nellie's watch on her palm. "She gave the matching one to you."

"I never noticed." He cradled in his palm the watch he was about to slip into his vest. After a long pause in which Floryn continued to stare at him, he said, "Yes, they are quite similar."

"That's not what I meant," Floryn said.

122

Again he looked at her darkly. Finally he said, "I wanted a watch so that I could tell time without having to ask. She gave it to me."

"Such an expensive one?" she goaded sarcastically.

"She has good taste."

"She doesn't think you do."

Floryn marched to the dresser, slammed the watch down, and plopped on her hat.

Cord was behind her, his hands on her shoulders. He looked at her reflection in the mirror.

"She was a part of my life before you showed up," he said. Their gazes locked. "You don't have to be jealous of her."

"Jealous!" Floryn spun around and sputtered. "Jealous."

"I can't imagine a woman of your strength being afraid of someone like Nellie," Cord said.

"I'm not afraid of her or jealous." Floryn fudged on the truth on both counts, but she felt justified. "I'm angry. The woman—the slut—she told me I was old . . . and *ugly.*"

"She spoke out of jealousy."

"She's a beautiful woman," Floryn said, unable to erase the woman's image from her mind.

"Yes, she is," Cord admitted, and Floryn's spirits sank lower.

He brushed back the veil to reveal her face. "But you're also beautiful."

He kissed her lightly on the lips, and pleasure curled through her body.

"I'll never forget your sitting forty-eight hours in that prison receiving room just so you could speak to me. I can still see you as you stood in front of me at the rock quarry, your gown dirty, your gloves torn to shreds, your hat about to fall off your head. You were proud and dignified, determined to fight for

123

what you wanted. You were honest, admitting that you wanted to save the ranch for yourself and Hope." He smiled gently. "Let's forget Nellie. She's a part of my past."

No, Floryn thought, it is not that simple. Nellie, in coming to see her, had insinuated herself into Cord's present. Floryn must struggle to push her out of their lives, must struggle to forget the woman. She wondered if Cord could, if he would. Yet she would be making a fool of herself if she pressed the issue. She had to appear as unconcerned about the incident as Cord was.

"She claims that you may be in danger from Webb Pruitt."

Cord shrugged the warning aside. "Since there is no treasure, I don't fear him. You shouldn't either."

"I do," she confessed. "Until you arrive at the ranch to claim your inheritance and until the guardianship of Hope is returned to me, I'll be afraid."

Her fear was jagged, rasping anguish.

"You're shivering." He moved to the sideboard and poured her a drink. Returning, he pressed a glass with a small amount of whiskey into her hands. "Take a sip or two of this."

She stared at the glass, knowing whiskey could not cure her fears, could not diminish them one iota.

Nine

"Whiskey Saloon," Cord said. "Sounds as if a lot of thought went into the naming of that place."

The only other passenger in the swaying, westbound stage, Floryn sat across from him. She pulled back the leather flap and through the haze of dust, stirred up by clopping hooves and rolling wheels, looked at the crowd gathered in front of the ramshackled building on the outskirts of San Antonio.

"It seems to be popular," she said. Dust swirling through the window, she quickly dropped the flap and fanned her handkerchief through the air.

"At least the name sounds inviting," Cord said.

Leather creaked, metal groaned, and wood snapped as the driver let loose a few choice phrases he had been using with regularity since he left Huntsville several days earlier. The coach jolted to the side of the road, throwing Floryn forward.

Cord caught and held her, their gazes locking, before she slid her hands between them and pushed back in her seat. She grabbed the leather strap hanging from the ceiling. A crack of the whip and another lurch of the stage to the right told her they had dodged yet another pothole.

Cord, raising his arms and locking his hands behind his head, stretched out his legs. Coat and vest long since shed, his posture pulled the material of his shirt tautly across his chest. His slow, lazy smile teased her; it taunted her. "My throat's bone dry. Shall we ask the driver to turn around and stop so we can rest awhile and get a drink?"

She returned his smile. "No, thank you."

"Ladies don't drink whiskey?"

Cord's gentle teasing, his overall gentleness since the gunfight, was steadily destroying her wall of defense, exposing her vulnerability. She had to be wary of sweet-talk.

"Oh, they drink," she answered softly, "they just aren't permitted to drink in public."

Cord laughed.

Taking off her hat, she placed it on the seat beside her, then reached up to fluff the curls around her face. Then she said, "Hal tried to make a lady out of me, but didn't succeed. Somehow I missed that step in my development. I went directly from girlhood into womanhood."

"I'm glad." He leaned over and picked up her hat. He twirled it on his hand, then gently ran his fingers up the feather. "I would soon be bored with a lady."

"My being a woman has nothing to do with your likes or dislikes," she said, no edge to her voice, just flat honesty. "It was something I did because I had to."

"Or perhaps because you wanted to." He set the hat beside him.

Honesty was easier accepted when one was dishing it than when one was receiving, Floryn thought.

With a twinge of bitterness, perhaps jealousy, his words propelled her thoughts back to Nellie Stratford, to her softness, to her femininity. Although in the strictest sense of the word, Nellie was no lady, she had ladylike qualities. Qualities, which to a certain extent, Floryn had been denied. Or, as Cord suggested, had denied herself.

Floryn admitted that she had discarded ladyhood

and all its implied restrictions to ride with the men and to work beside them. She had shed expensive dresses for work clothing, trousers, shirts, boots, and broad-brimmed hat. Branding irons, ropes, and revolvers replaced jewelry. Heavy, durable leather gloves shoved fashionable kid ones aside.

She would do it all over again. The Fancy Lady was hers. She had loved it the first time she saw it, although it was in a deplorable condition. Hal had owned property and a house, not a ranch and home. He had neglected the land. She, not Hal, was the one who loved it, who had turned it into what it was today.

It was her home. It was Hope's home. Both loved it.

Floryn renewed her vow that Hope would have a mother and a home, the Fancy Lady. She would not be abandoned, her care entrusted to strangers. Hope would never know what it was like to wonder where her next meal would come from.

"With all the work I had to do around the ranch," she said, verbalizing her thoughts, picking up on the thread of previous discussion, "I had little time to pamper myself with lotions, creams, milk baths, and cosmetics."

"No, I wouldn't imagine," Cord said.

Moving across the coach to sit beside her, he encircled her hand with his. She dropped her gaze and watched him slowly rub his thumb over the top of hers. Through the material of her gloves she felt the roughness of his hands, the strength, the determination. Warmth, sweet and protective, emanated from his touch to spread through her body. Oddly his touch was more comforting than arousing.

"My mother was a prostitute," Floryn said softly, "and I loved her, but I don't remember her ever looking as beautiful as Nellie Stratford. My mother — she worked the cribs in El Paso."

"Nellie isn't a common prostitute," Cord said. "She's

127

really Pruitt's mistress, and as such is well provided for. Also she's young, Floryn. Age hasn't taken its toll as it had your mother. It will. Sooner or later it catches up with all of us."

Floryn said nothing, for she did not trust herself. Emotions were riding the surface, ready to erupt at the least provocation. Not tears, but confessions. Cord had been too gentle during the past few days, since they had left Huntsville, and she had dropped her guard. She was fearful of exposing too much of herself to have him reject her, to have him revert to the hardened and embittered man she had witnessed so shortly ago.

He began to pull one of her gloves off, but Floryn curled her hand into a fist to stop him. She remembered how soft and smooth Nellie's hand had looked. A hand that had intimately caressed Cord. A hand that he had caressed.

Firmly, but gently, Cord pried open her fingers, slid the glove off, and held her hand in his. He turned it over, running a thumb over the small calluses. Calluses he would not find on Nellie's hands, Floryn thought.

"Nellie would give anything to change places with you," he said quietly.

"To be married to you?" Floryn asked.

"To be married period," he answered, again reverting to teasing. "Of course, I'd like to believe married to me. She's a lonely woman, wanting the same things in life as most people—I imagine. I tried to persuade her to leave Pruitt and to look for a man who loved her, but she seems to think no man will want to marry her because she's sullied." He added, "I told her that I believed Jack Willowby was interested in her, but she wouldn't believe me."

"I'm surprised that the two of you talked," Floryn said, her vulnerability giving a sharp edge to her words. "I thought the two of you had other, more important, things to do."

Humor softened Cord's features. "We did that, my wife, but we spent a lot of time talking, too."

Floryn, inundated by what she considered the injustices of the past, leaned her head against the leather cushion of the coach seat and closed her eyes. Even so, she could not close out the memories; they crushed in on her today—heavy and oppressive.

"Twelve years," she murmured, unable to hide her bitterness, not really wanting to. "Twelve years I've given to the Fancy Lady, and Hal took it away from me. He knew the ranch and Hope were my life, what I cared about most."

"Yes." Cord sighed. "It always has been. I'm sure he figured it always would be."

"Yes," she murmured. Tired of fighting, tired of trying to vindicate herself, Floryn said nothing. She would allow him to think what he would. During this time she had not changed his mind; she doubted she could. "The Fancy Lady provided me with a much better life than my mother led in the cribs of a slummy saloon in El Paso, of a saloon like the one we just passed."

"But you could have had a different life without becoming a whore had you chosen to leave the Fancy Lady. You chose to remain there, Floryn. One of these days you're going to have to admit that."

"I stayed after Hope was born because it guaranteed her a different future than I had. She won't ever have to marry a man in order to escape a life she hates. She'll be free to make her choice, to marry for love, to be courted. She'll be a lady, Cord. I promise."

Twining their fingers together, he pressed the top of her hand against his thigh. "Tell me something about this little girl you're determined to make into a lady."

Her eyes opening in surprise, Floryn rolled her head over, her gaze pinning on him. She was glad she had been patient and had not pushed him. Now he was asking about Hope, wanting to know her.

Visions of her daughter, of the most precious thing in her life, flashed through Floryn's mind. She smiled. "She's shy, but highly intelligent. She loves her books and studies and the ranch. She enjoys riding and spends a lot of time with Antonio as he goes about his duties. You ought to see her ride, Cord."

Floryn continued to talk about Hope, her accomplishments, her aspirations. Cord listened.

A long time later, when their laughter over the child's latest escapade died down, Cord asked, "Sounds like our daughter is stubborn."

"Just like her father."

"I was thinking how much like her mother she was."

They looked at each other, smiling, savoring the moment, savoring the joy of parenthood.

"How is she with her sewing and embroidering?" he asked.

"She's not as highly motivated with it as she is with riding and shooting."

"Nor with cooking and housekeeping?"

Floryn shook her head.

Cord reached up and tweaked the ribbon on which her timepiece hung. "Does she wear all these ribbons and lace and ruffles?"

Floryn laughed. "I buy them for her, but she much prefers her trousers, shirts, and boots. She loves her freedom."

"This child, the one who doesn't want to sew or cook or keep house, the one who wears trousers, rides horses, and brands cattle, is the one you're insisting on making into a lady?" Cord hiked a questioning brow.

"At least, I want her to have the choice."

"She will either way. When we arrive in El Paso, I'll help you select a gift for this little daughter of ours."

The phrase *little daughter of ours* had a wonderful ring, but Floryn had no time to revel in its beauty. He ran his fingers up her arms, and she shivered with pleasure. A tiny part of her, the reasonable part wished he had never moved to sit beside her. The woman in her was glad he had.

During the next few minutes, the comforting strokes of his hand on hers turned into provocative touches that she felt throughout her body, that set her afire in certain places. She tugged her hand to withdraw it, but his clasp tightened.

His head lowered, his attention seemingly focused on the movement of his thumb on her hand. "Even if you had the opportunity, Floryn, I don't believe you'd make any substantial changes in your life."

"Yes," she said, "I would."

He raised his head. They stared at each other, the world around them forgotten, time locked into place.

"One important change," she whispered.

One hand holding hers, Cord used the other to tilt her chin and to gaze somberly into her eyes. Her lips parted as she saw the darkness in him, the passion in his eyes. So much for the flimsy barrier she had thought to erect. She knew that soon he would make his demands. That soon she would comply, willingly, probably wantonly. She felt the hardness of his body as his mouth descended upon hers. His lips firmed and claimed hers in an intense, shattering kiss.

The touch of his mouth was fiery, potent to her. Evidently to him. He exhaled. She inhaled, taking his breath into her body, freely taking the passion that flowed from him to her. She was lost to her long-denied need.

His arms circled her, brought her closer to him. She raised her hand to the thick hair at the back of his neck and kept his lips pressed against hers. His lips softened. The kiss gentled; it was softness and warmth spiraling through her body.

His lips lifted. They stared at each other. She lowered her lids and rested her cheek against his chest.

131

Ironclad, it rose and fell against her face as he breathed. She snuggled closer. She burrowed into his warmth, his strength. She felt the smooth coolness of metal against her cheek. Wrapped in the hazy layers of sensation, she moved her face to one side. Still the metal touched her. Then she remembered. The watch chain. She heard the ticking. The watch Nellie gave him.

Nellie. Young Nellie Stratford. Floryn thought of Nellie in Cord's arms. Nestling her face against his chest. Beautiful Nellie naked in his arms, making love to him. Floryn tried to push the thought aside, but could not.

Instead she pushed away from him.

"What's wrong?"

She shook her head, loath to admit her jealousy, to admit her weakness. Her gaze fell to the watch chain. She stared at it. He touched it.

"Nellie!" he exclaimed softly. "Damn it, Floryn!"

He caught her hands in his.

"I never took a personal interest in her, Floryn, and not really a sexual one either. Mostly I wanted female company. A woman to look at, to hear, to be with. Someone besides fellow convicts. I wasn't lying when I said Nellie and I talked. We did. We spent most of our time together talking."

"Nellie cares for you," she said.

"Her only interest in me is the San Domingo treasure. She let me know she would team up with me for its recovery, but she would not have been happy sharing such wealth with me or anyone. She would have wanted it for herself and would have found a way to get rid of me at her earliest convenience."

"Why have you kept the timepiece?"

"I had no reason to get rid of it. It's expensive. The craftsmanship is excellent, and it keeps accurate time." After a lengthy pause he added, "Probably the most important reason why I've kept it is that it's a personal belonging the prison authorities allowed me to keep. Something that was mine. A trophy of sorts. Strange as it seems—"

His confession was so intimate, so touching, Floryn's heart filled with compassion. She laid her hand over his mouth to hush him. "Don't," she murmured. "I didn't think, and I had no right to question you about it or your life."

"I've attached no sentimental value to it." His lips brushed against her fingers as he spoke. "It's simply a timepiece."

She removed her hand from his mouth and leaned forward to kiss him softly. But Cord would have no tender kiss. His mouth crushed hers, and his desperation flowed into her with a desolate, dark passion that took away her breath, that painted her as darkly, as desperately. The force of his tongue bore into her with a fierce, but welcome urgency.

Rather than the violence frightening her, it drew her into a depth of feeling as primitive as his and just as defiant. She reacted with the swept-away need of emotions too long controlled. She responded with a vehemence as devastating as his. His harsh invasion of her mouth spoke not of wine and roses, of moonlight and softness. It was fury, majesty, the elemental danger of a raging summer storm. Rather than slowly exploring and building intimacy, his tongue raided her mouth, searched for and found the woman in her.

At the same time she was being plundered, she was also being wooed by a desperation that seduced her. Her body cried out for this harshly sensual man whose ragged breath threatened more pillage. Responding to that promise, she opened her mouth to receive more of him.

Cord's chest heaved at her invitation. His embrace tightened. His tongue probed more deeply in an amorous race that had no winner. Relinquishing the sparring, his tongue made a short trip across her lips before he lowered his head to her neck and its fragrant valley. Nipping gently, he tasted her flesh, knew the lobe of her ear.

She turned her head, accommodating his titillating exploration. She silently pleaded for more, her supplication answered when he claimed her mouth once more, kissing her, kissing her until she thought surely she would pass out from sheer pleasure.

He tangled his fingers in the coil at the nape of her neck. The hair came loose and tumbled down her back. He forced her mouth from his.

"I'm not mistaking you for Nellie, nor am I using you as a substitute for her. I'm kissing you, Floryn. You. You're the woman I want to make love to, have wanted to make love to for ten years." He held her at arm's length, and his gaze softened, quickly turning to molten-silver. "Don't you be mistaken about who or what I want."

Or why you want me, Floryn silently added. Yet she did not dwell on the thought. She chose fantasy to reality. She used little imagination to transform the interior of the coach into a suddenly wonderful world. It was one draped with the trappings of love, a world that was theirs alone.

Slipping an arm around her shoulder, he sheltered her for a moment, his expression soft. She nestled against him, enjoying the subtle way the swaying of the coach caused their bodies to brush together. Today, this very minute, the sounds of travel—the creak of the leather traces, the ping of the coach springs—were music to her ears. Her body radiated the pleasure his lovemaking had given her.

Yet she was unsettled. He had talked about their making love, and she knew, as well as he, that this marriage of convenience was short-lived. He had convinced her that his passion was for her alone. But he had not once mentioned being in love, and probably would not since love was not an integral part of what he wanted to share with her.

The coach slowed down and the driver yelled, "San Antonio."

"I want you, Floryn. Only you."

She said nothing.

"Do you believe me?"

Her soul aching, her heart empty, she murmured, "Yes."

The stage lurched to a stop. Cord slid across the seat, flung open the door, and leaped out. He caught Floryn about the waist and swung her out, then around. She threw back her head, letting the afternoon sun warmly touch her, letting the breeze blow the moistened tendrils of hair from forehead and temples.

Cord still held her. She felt the hard muscular chest pressed against her. Laying her hands against his shoulders, she lowered her head, and gazed into his face. Not granite. Not bronze. Flesh and blood. Hard, hot, flesh and blood. Beneath her palm she felt the steady thumping of his heart.

These past few days of travel had been wonderful. Almost idyllic. In the light of what had so recently transpired between them, she could almost believe hostilities and bitterness were ended.

"You don't know how I've longed for this," she murmured.

"So eager for me to keep my promise?"

A twinge of pleasure swept through her. "Eager to be in San Antonio. Eager to be out of the stage and closer to home."

He lowered her. She heard the swish of material as his hands slowly slid up from her waist. She felt the heat generated by the brushing together of two bodies. When her feet touched the ground, his hands rested immediately below her breasts. He did not touch them, he did not release her, nor did he allow her to move away from him.

"We need to get a room," she said.

"Yes."

"The Menger?"

He nodded.

Reluctantly she pulled away from him. She heard a click, and both looked down to see her watch case opened, the lid caught on his waistcoat button. Reaching for it at the same time, their fingers touched. In one hand he clasped hers, with the other he moved the offending button and held the opened watch in his palm momentarily before he clicked it shut and let it fall back to lie against her bodice.

Clearing her throat, Floryn withdrew her hand from his and stepped away. In a prim voice that was totally lacking in conviction, she said, "It's time we were—"

"Yes," he murmured, and she looked up into a darkly handsome face filled with sensual promise, "it's time."

Ten

"What time shall I expect you back?" Floryn strove to keep the disappointment out of her voice as she laid her hat on the dresser next to her gloves and reticule, as she meticulously lined them up one against the other. Her gaze returned to the folded sheet of paper Cord held in his hand. The note the clerk had given to him when they registered. The message that was taking him from her.

"What?" He looked at her absently. He had been preoccupied since he had received it.

"Must you"—she cleared her throat—"must you go now?"

He nodded and walked to where she stood. "It's business I must take care of."

The tender tone did nothing to appease her hurt. "Is it the gunfighters?"

Again he nodded.

"Cord, remember what your friend said about them."

Floryn could not forget the lawman's warning as he had bid them goodbye in Huntsville only minutes before the stage departed.

"I know them better than Shelby does," he answered. "I served time with them. He only brought them in."

"Cord, I feel it. These men are dangerous."

137

"Thank you for your concern, Floryn, but when it comes to my business and my friends, I know what I'm doing. I'll be back shortly."

"All right," she said and turned her back to him.

She heard the soft thud of his boots on the hardwood floor. He stopped, touching her shoulder as if to urge her around. She flinched from him. He moved to stand in front of her. He tipped her head, looked at her, his warm breath on her face.

"It's something I can't put off. Surely you understand."

But she did not. She could hardly stand the disappointment. Their trip from Huntsville had been so idyllic, so promising. She felt the brush of fingers through the curls that framed her face, the graze of his flesh against hers.

"I'll be back as soon as I can. Promise."

"Take your time." She wished she really meant the words. "It doesn't really matter. If you're not concerned about your safety, why should I be?"

His fingers slid down her cheek, her neck, to hook her collar. Fingertips glided over her skin as he traced the high, round neckline of her dress.

"It matters, I am concerned and am taking care of myself, and I'll be back as soon as I can to take care of our needs." He kissed his finger and pressed it to the tip of her nose. He removed his hand, stood for a moment in which they gazed at each other, then walked out of the bedroom, through the parlor.

Long after the front door had closed behind him and the lock clicked into place, Floryn stood in front of the mirror. Eventually she walked to the head of the bed to the bellpull. When the maid answered, she ordered a bath. Until it arrived, she kept herself busy by unpacking their luggage and placing their clothes in the matching wardrobes.

138

But no matter how busy she kept her hands, she could not still the gnawing hurt. She had dropped her guard and had allowed herself to believe Cord cared for her. She had been so hopeful. And as he had done repeatedly since she had come to him, he had hurt her, had reduced her expectations to ashes.

When he received the note, he had left her.

Cord had told her he had learned to live a day at a time, to expect no more. Although she had argued with him, taking the opposing view, she knew full well what he meant. Only by taking life a day at a time had she been able to endure her years with Hal, especially the final ones.

This was exactly the same way she would have to handle her second marriage.

For dinner that evening she selected her favorite dress, a deep yellow poplin gown trimmed in brown grosgrain. Only when she was searching through her valise for a ribbon did she remember Cord's telling her he would rather her ribbon matched the color of her eyes than her dress.

She wadded the ribbon in her fist, and for a moment contemplated changing her dress. But she would not allow Cord advertently or inadvertently to manipulate her. She was a strong woman. She would wear a ribbon that matched both her dress and her eyes. Cord be damned!

By the time she had spread her clean clothes across the bed, her bath paraphernalia arrived. Soon she luxuriated in warm sudsy water in an oblong copper tub. Resting her head against the rim, she closed her eyes.

"This is what I call a provocative scene!"

Her lids flying open, Floryn turned her head. Asleep, she had heard no key turn in the lock, had heard no door open. Yet Cord, dressed only in his shirt and trousers, stood in the doorway, leaning against one side of the jamb. One arm hung to his side. In that hand he held a bouquet of flowers, their fragrance now filling the room. He rested the other palm on the opposite jamb. He stood far from her, letting that blue gaze wander over her, but like the scent of the flowers he was all around her.

From his lounging pose, he stared at her with an intensity that caused her to tingle with awareness, that filled her with confusion. Her thoughts conflicted. She wished she was fully dressed at the same time that she wished he was holding her in his arms, making wild, passionate love to her. His very presence touched her. It seduced her senses, making her forget her resolve to be strong, to resist him.

She straightened up.

"I like this view even better." He grinned at her. That mischievous grin that erased all signs of hardness from his face and overwhelmed her with its pure masculine enjoyment.

She followed the invisible line of his gaze to the exposed upper portion of her breasts. Soapsuds slid down the rounded mounds. She slipped lower in the water.

"I wasn't expecting you back so soon." Embarrassment tinged her voice with a defensive edge.

"I told you I wouldn't be gone long."

The rakish grin still twitching his lips, he walked across the room and dropped the flowers into the pitcher of water on the washstand. Then he was kneeling beside the tub. Cornered, she had no place to run to. He brushed bubbles from her neck. His fingers trailed to her breasts. She caught his hand to stop the movement, to stop the quivering in her stomach. The heat rushing through her body no longer had anything to do with embarrassment.

"How much longer before you're through with your bath?"

Before we're through playing this game? he really said.

He was so near, his touch so devastating, she could hardly think. The clean odor of his body, mixed with the cologne he wore, filled her nostrils. He pulled his hand from hers, his fingers once again exploring, this time brushing across her collarbone, close to her breasts, not quite touching them.

"A long time." She answered both of his questions, the one he uttered, the one she assumed.

"I don't think so."

He picked up a washcloth and, holding it in front of her, wrung it out. The water trickled over her skin to wash away the suds and to leave exposed the fullness of her breasts. He dropped the cloth to the floor and stared at her. She felt as if this were the first time he had seen her nudity. She experienced an innocence and vulnerability she had never known before, had not experienced when they had made love all those years ago.

His head angled toward hers. Reason fled in the wake of desire. She moved toward him. Their lips touched, tentatively, then fully. His hand slipped into the water to cup her breast, his thumb to brush over the sensitive flesh.

When he removed his mouth from hers, Floryn traced his lips with her finger. Her hand moved over his freshly shaven cheek to the edge of the black patch that she outlined with her fingernail.

"I've never seen you without it," she said.

"It's not a pretty sight."

"But it's you." Now she lightly brushed her fingertip over the soft leather. "Someday you'll have to let me see it."

"Maybe."

141

She looked down to see both his wrists resting on the edge of the tub, water dripping from the tips of his fingers, from his shirt cuffs. She looked back into his face. She heard the mantel clock chime in the parlor.

"It's time, Floryn," he said.

She moistened dry lips. Pride demanded she resist, that she say no. The needs of her body far outweighed pride. She wanted him. He had said she would beg. She would if it were necessary.

"Yes." The word was as soft as his expression.

He caught her hands in his. They rose, their gazes locked together. He tugged. She stepped out of the water. She heard the water dripping on the floor, pooling around her feet, yet she never looked away from his face. His hands whispered up her neck to the top of her head to free the coil of hair that toppled down her back to brush against her buttocks.

"You're beautiful." He lifted her hands, palms upward, to his mouth. He kissed the calluses. "All of you is beautiful."

Again his gaze caught hers and something flared in his eyes, dark and dangerous, but today Floryn no longer feared the darkness or the danger. She reveled in them. She wanted to be one with them.

His mouth trailed quick kisses over her face, teasing, never satisfying her. She breathed heavy and fast. He ran a finger up and down her bare spine, smiling when she shuddered.

She unbuttoned his shirt, parted it to press her mouth to the heated skin beneath. Heated because of her. The thought was heady. The tip of her tongue left a moist trail across his chest before she lifted her head.

"Kiss me," she whispered.

His lid closed. Thick lashes fell in a raven black

crescent on his sun-baked cheek. He kissed her. So gentle was his touch, yet he branded her lips with his. Her hands slid slowly up his chest through the mat of crisp hair to his shoulders to push the material aside. Her fingers tightened, then went lax as he softened the kiss, deepened, then gentled it. Willingly she rode the wave of passion, going where it took her.

He lifted her into his arms and held her there a moment. Heavy lids opened and she saw that he watched her with an intensity that set her stomach muscles to quivering.

His body tensed; he groaned. With feather-light kisses, his mouth teased and tormented hers as he carried her to the bed. She felt the flexing of his muscles as he moved with her. She experienced his strength and power.

He sat, cradling her in his lap. His mouth continued its quiet devastation of her reason. She felt each tender touch, the stroke of a fingertip, the brush of his palm, the gentle and patient quest of his lips. Her body seemed as light as the flower-scented air, yet she felt as if she could not move. Certainly she had no wish to.

Soft music from the plaza below wafted through the opened window. It, his murmurs, the violent roar of her own racing pulses all merged into a song of seduction. Floryn knew she had never been more vulnerable or more willing to go wherever he chose to take her.

Here in Cord's arm she was in heaven. Vaguely she remembered thinking at one time that he would take her to hell. Instead this angel of darkness had carried her to the very portals of heaven. She should have known that Cord Donaldson dared do anything. No realm was safe from his possession.

She gasped when his lips whispered over the tops

143

of her breasts. Slowly, erotically he teased her hardened nipples, the abrasive texture of his tongue driving her wild. His fingers played over the skin of her legs, beginning with her knees, moving to her thighs. Lightly, so lightly, gliding up on the outside, and around and up . . . to the inside.

His lips covered hers. His mouth captured her moan of ecstasy when his hands reached their destination. His fingers magically touched her, time and again, until he sent her over the first towering peak. She arched, then melted against him. Breathless, almost delirious, she reached for him.

"Cord—"

His fingers moved against her again. Again his mouth captured her stunned cry, letting it become the essence of their kiss. While she was still shuddering, he laid her on the bed.

His knuckles brushed her skin, making her jolt as his mouth moved along her leg in openmouthed kisses toward the secret place where only moments ago his hand had been. His tongue glided over the back of her knee, down her calf, over and around her ankle until she was mindless with pleasure.

Trapped in soft, hazy layers of sensation, she reached for him again, only to have him evade and repeat each devastating delight on her other leg. His mouth journeyed up, lingering, pausing until it found her.

Floryn felt as if she had fallen off a high precipice and was falling, falling. Her stomach quivered. Sensations, delicious, wonderful sensations rolled through her entire body.

At the first touch, his strength poured into her. His sweet, gentle mouth . . . his fiery, violent mouth loved her and pushed her toward a height of passion she had only dreamed about.

"Cord!" She reared up. Nearly weeping she grasped him, pulling him up against her.

Summer hot, covered in a sheen of perspiration she could see in the waning afternoon light, her flesh met his. But it was not enough, not nearly enough of him. She pulled at his open shirt, uncaring that it was one of the new ones, tearing seams in her desperation to find more of him. As she ripped the material away, she nipped into his shoulder. His stomach muscles quivered. As she tugged the waistband of his trousers, she heard his quick intake of breath.

"I've been so long denied you," she whispered when at last the offending material was gone, when they were no longer separated by any kind of barrier. "I must have you, Cord."

Reminiscent of their first coming together, he laid her on her back and leaned down to kiss her. As his lips touched her, she felt the glaze of the leather patch on her cheek. Rampant desire seized her.

Tears blurring her vision, she caught one of his straying hands and held it tightly. "Now, Cord. I want you right now. All of you."

Quick movements placed them in the middle of the ravaged and damp bed. One moment he was kneeling over her, the next he was sliding down the length of her body. She gasped with pleasure when she felt him ease into her, stretching, filling, and satisfying. Cord stroked slow and deep, but needing him desperately, Floryn arched, wrapped her legs around him and spurred him. Every nerve in her body screamed for release. In answer to her whimpers and thrusting, Cord thrust, plunged deeply, rapidly, and fiercely.

Her breathing sporadic, her fingers digging into his back, she moved beneath him. She heard her own cry, her gasp of relief as something wonderful shattered inside her. Sharp slivers of passion turned into soft, fragrant petals of satisfaction.

Claiming her lips in a kiss, Cord thrust himself even deeper into her. On a sob she tightened her arms and legs about him, holding him close when that same splintering occurred within him, when he cried out. He lay on top of her for a moment, dragging in deep breaths of air. Then he rolled off.

Satisfied — wonderfully, completely satisfied — she lay on the bed, one arm tossed across her forehead, the other lying limply on the mattress. She thought perhaps she would never move again. Yet when he kissed her shoulder, passion again surged through her. She shuddered.

"I meant to be gentle the first time," he said.

There was to have been no first time.

"I will be the next time."

There would be a second time, a third . . . and only God knew how many more.

Floryn brushed the dampened hair from his forehead and traced in the fullness of the shield. How soft his face was. No longer were his features harsh and forbidding. No arrogance in it now, only the deep enjoyment of a man who has touched something precious and fragile. And she was that something precious and fragile.

With him still leaning over her, she moved her hands to the back of his head and untied the leather cord. He tensed slightly, but made no attempt to stop her. He relaxed. The shield slid down his face to land on her breast, at once hot and abrasive against her tender skin.

She looked at the sunken hollow, at the scar that dented the corner of the socket. She touched it tenderly, then raised herself. Before her lips could touch it, Cord caught her chin in a painful grip.

146

"You don't have to do this." His voice was raspy. "I know it's an ugly sight."

"No, I don't have to," she answered, "but I want to." She prized his fingers from her face and kissed the area. She picked up the patch and retied it around his head, not quite tight enough because it slipped down.

The tension of the moment dissipated in their laughter. He sat up, redoing the task himself.

"You told me the women thought the patch added to your look of virility." She smoothed her finger over it. "Well, it does. It makes you look quite roguish."

Satisfaction licking through her body, she lay down and closed her eyes. She heard the chiming of the clock in the other room and knew another hour had passed. She snuggled into the covers that smelled of her soap, of his after-shave cologne. She inhaled the drugging fragrance.

"Don't get too comfortable," Cord said.

"Why?" she murmured, her lids growing heavy.

"We're going to be having some guests in about an hour."

"What?" she bolted up, wondering how he could sound so casual about the announcement.

"The two men I wrote when I was in Huntsville."

"The gunfighters are going to come here to visit us?"

He nodded and slipped off the bed, walking out of the bedroom into the parlor. When he returned, he had his vest and coat draped over one arm. Taking his watch out of its pocket, he laid it on the dresser alongside his vest and coat.

Still lying on the bed, covered with a sheet, Floryn said, "You're really going to go through with this, aren't you?"

"Did you ever doubt it?"

147

"No, but I hoped."

She slipped off the bed and cleansed herself. She was standing at the dresser, clad in her dressing gown and combing her hair when she noticed Cord's watch. She leaned down and looked at it more closely. She whirled around.

"You have a new watch!"

"I traded." He spoke offhandedly.

She was so excited she pressed her hands against the dresser to keep them from shaking. She felt the muscles in her face move as her smile widened. She was sure it stretched from ear to ear, maybe farther. Her heartbeat quickened.

She dared hope again.

"It's not—it doesn't look as expensive as your other one."

"I liked this one better." His tone was nonchalant, not so his gaze. "Don't you?"

"Yes," she murmured, "much better."

Eleven

"Much better," he murmured. "Golden brown ribbon to match golden brown eyes."

Beginning at her shoulder, he ran his fingertip along the brown grosgrain trim of the yellow poplin gown she now wore, across the collarbone.

"Just what you wanted," she whispered.

"Almost." His hands slowly moved until they cupped her breasts. A naughty grin tugged at his lips. "Now, this is more like what I want."

Floryn made no attempt to hide her trembling. She enjoyed her breasts swelling against his hands.

"While you've shown remarkable strides in your wifely duties"—his face moved closer, his gaze an irresistible magnet—"you still need instruction."

The words had become a whisper, a promise. Breathless, she closed her eyes and waited for his touch. His lips tenderly kissed each eye. The leather patch brushed against her brows.

"If we were not expecting guests, I would continue with the instructing. I would show you all over again what I want."

His lips moved down her nose to her mouth. He kissed her, and she felt his hardness against her, as demanding, as possessive as his mouth. Her arms circled his waist and brought his body home to hers.

He lifted his head and whispered, "Floryn."

She raised her hand to the thick hair at the back of his neck and urged his head down. She watched his lips descending, until their lips met. Then she was irretrievably lost.

His arms held her close, yet she strained to be closer. The fierce urgency flowed from him into her as his body melded to hers, covering and protecting her. His lips softened, and he kissed her slowly, gently. His tongue tickled her lips, teased her tongue, searched her mouth. One of his hands circled her waist. The other stroked her back, caressed her bottom, and rotated her hips against him.

She moved her mouth, her lips brushing his. "Am I doing as good with wifely duties as you are with husbandly duties?"

"Sweetheart," he murmured hotly, kissing her again. "If only we weren't having company."

She slid her hands around his waist and brushed her hands up his shoulders. "But we are."

They kissed again. They parted.

"After they leave," he promised.

After another long, thorough kiss, she turned her cheek into his shoulder and held him . . . just held him. Holding him, being held by him was the most wonderful, most comforting feeling she had ever experienced. She wanted it to last forever.

But nothing lasted forever, did it?

Fear washed over her. She had lost Cord once before, and she had no guarantee that she would keep him now. The threads that bound them were tenuous at best. She hugged him tighter and shivered slightly.

"What's wrong?" he asked.

Her fear that she would lose him . . . again, this time forever.

"I was thinking about Nellie's warnings and wondering how long—how long—"

"How long we're going to be chased by my past," he

said. When she nodded, he sighed. "I don't know. That's why I must find the pendant. It holds the answer. Once I have it, my past will cease to be shadows. It will be people whom I can fight."

She felt his desperation when his arms tightened and he nuzzled his face in the hollow of her neck and shoulder. Neither saying more, they held each other.

After the two men greeted Cord, they walked into the parlor and looked around. Although they were cleaner and more neatly dressed, they reminded Floryn of Orwen Baxter. These, too, were gunfighters.

Cord was different. He moved through the room with a grace that gave pleasure to Floryn. The blue suit enhanced the broadness of his shoulders, while the trousers emphasized the lean tautness of his buttocks and thighs.

"Gentlemen, my wife, Floryn," Cord said. "Kid Ferguson and Tony Esteman."

"Glad to meet you, Mrs. Donaldson." Tony Esteman, the older of the two gave her a friendly smile.

"Mr. Esteman."

Kid Ferguson also smiled warmly. "I heard about the wedding. Cord's a mighty lucky man to have married you, ma'am."

"Thank you," she murmured.

Keeping his hat on, his mouth curled into a half smile, Kid sat on the settee. After he removed his leather gloves and tucked them into his belt, he leaned back and crossed his legs. Tony sat beside him. Dropping his hat to the floor to one side of the settee, he leaned forward, his legs straddled, an elbow resting on each leg. He twined his hands together and let them dangle between his legs.

"So," Tony said, looking directly at Cord, "you want us to go with you to Norwell's?"

151

Cord nodded.

"Expecting trouble?" Kid asked.

"No, but I want to be prepared for any eventuality."

Tony sniffed and twitched his nose. He scratched a forehead that was furrowed with wrinkles and ran his fingers through tousled, prematurely gray hair. "Heard Norwell has his ranch fortified. If he knows the three of us are riding out, he could be dangerous. He never liked any of us."

"He was always scared of us," Kid said.

Cord said, "The fee takes into consideration the high risk."

Kid flipped his hat back on his head, a shock of blond hair falling across his forehead. "Thought Compton was going to be with you."

"He was," Cord answered. "He's been temporarily detained."

Kid laughed. "Had trouble with Orwen Baxter, I heard."

Cord said, "You heard right."

"Considering how much Orwen hated you," Kid said, "I don't suppose his showing up was a surprise."

"Not really," Cord drawled, "just an unnecessary encumbrance."

Tony bridged his hands together and pressed them under his chin. "I'd like to help you, Cord, but . . . Well, me, I ain't got no quarrel with Norwell, and I'm free, going straight."

"I'm not asking you to do anything that would result in your going back to prison, nothing illegal," Cord said.

Tony shook his head. "Fooling around with Norwell. That's enough, Cord. The man is dangerous." The gunfighter's gaze shifted to Floryn, and he smiled tentatively. "I don't want to do anything that will mess me up. I'm about to get hitched myself. We're going out west and buy us some land. Going to start a new life."

"How much you paying?" Kid shifted positions, the pearl handle of his gun gleaming in the fading sunlight.

"One hundred each," Cord answered.

"That's a lot of money," Tony said.

It certainly was! Floryn tensed in her chair. Granted Cord had said everything she gave to him was a loan that he would repay, but she had no idea when he would have the money with which to repay her. And she knew she was going to have to repay Lyle Hackett as soon as she could. The stable owner was a good friend, but he, like the rest of the people in the valley, needed his money. Although the papers Floryn had signed stipulated the loan in dollars, Lyle had agreed that she could repay him in horses. She had promised that he could take his pick from her herd.

"Sure is a lot of money," Kid added sarcastically. "Especially in times like this. It's not Confederate, is it?"

Cord and the Kid stared at each other before Cord rose and walked into the bedroom. Although Floryn heard him moving about, although she knew what he was doing, she remained seated. When he returned, he laid two hundred dollars in United States currency on the table.

"Count it," Cord ordered.

Tony shoved it back to him. "I didn't question you."

Cord looked at Kid who shook his head.

"Half when we ride out, half when we return," Cord said.

Queasy with worry about Cord's safety, about their future, Floryn stared at the money. Excusing herself, she walked into the bedroom, her gaze sliding to the dresser where her reticule lay opened. Cord had used nearly all the money she had left to finance his gunfighters. She could believe he would do it, but not without discussing it with her.

She looked around the room, at the bed, still ravaged

153

from their frenzied lovemaking only hours before. She had thought they had begun making headway on their relationship, that they were communicating with each other. How wrong could she be! The only communication they shared was sexual.

The conversation from the other room drifted in to her.

"What's this all about, Cord?" Kid asked.

"A pendant Norwell took from me. I want it back."

"The pendant I've heard so much about," Kid said. "The one that's a clue to the San Domingo treasure."

"There is no San Domingo treasure," Cord said.

"Yeah," Kid slurred. "You're out of prison on a parole because there is no treasure. Look, Cord, I'm your friend, and I'll throw in with you, but I want the truth."

"You have the truth, and it's my deal or nothing."

Floryn walked to the door to see the Kid and Cord staring at each other.

"I can't accept that, Cord." He shrugged, gave a jaunty wave, and pulled his gloves from his belt. Slipping them on, he swaggered to the door. "See you around."

When Kid closed the door, Tony said, "I'll ride with you."

"Thanks, Tony," Cord said. "Here's your fifty."

"You're using my money." Floryn never looked up from the bed she was straightening when Cord walked into the room.

"I'll pay you back."

Keeping her back to him, Floryn picked up his shirt, wadded it up, and tossed it across the room. "It's not a matter of your paying me back. It's a matter of your doing it without discussing it with me."

"We had already discussed it. You knew since I didn't have the available cash, I would be using your money. How many times must I tell you that every cent you spend on me, Floryn, I'll repay?"

A knock sounded. Surprised, they looked at each other.

"Kid," Cord said, snapping his fingers. "I'll bet he's changed his mind. He's a hothead who always acts impulsively."

More raps on the door.

"I knew once he'd thought about it, he'd be back."

By the time Cord opened the front door, Floryn was in the parlor also. She expected to see Kid. When she heard an unfamiliar and deeply masculine voice, she knew it was not.

"Hello, Donaldson."

Cord stood as if transfixed.

"May I come in?" the visitor asked.

Cord threw open the door, and an older, distinguished man entered the room. On seeing Floryn, his lips lifted in a tight smile — one that did not emanate from his eyes — hooked his cane over his left arm, and removed his hat.

Stepping forward, he said, "Good afternoon. I'm Stanton Norwell."

Reality coldly dashed all her preconceived notions of Stanton Norwell. Tailored clothes, dignified carriage, and white hair gave him an air of refinement.

"I'm Floryn Donaldson, Cord's wife."

"I'm happy to meet you, Mrs. Donaldson."

Taking his hat and cane and putting them on the hall tree, she waved to the vacant chair across from the settee. "Please be seated, Mr. Norwell."

The gray eyes assessed her. "Donaldson is a fortunate man to have found and married a lovely woman such as you."

"Thank you," she murmured and was surprised at how much the man seemed to differ from the descriptions she had heard of him. She had the distinct feeling, however, that the words he spoke were memorized from a script rather than spoken sincerely from the heart. "Would you like some coffee or something stronger perhaps?"

"Coffee, please."

"Some cake?" Floryn suggested. "I understand the Menger chef is renowned for his chocolate cake."

Norwell's gaze fell to his protruding stomach that was not so subtly hidden by finely tailored clothes. "A weakness of mine," he admitted. "I would enjoy having a slice."

"Then chocolate cake it shall be."

"By all means," Cord said dryly.

Floryn glanced up to see him leaning indolently against the mantel, his gaze — as dark as the patch he wore over his eye — pinned to Norwell. Hostility — closely akin to hatred — was written in his expression, in his stance. Although not directed at her, the full impact of his expression hit her full face. She turned to walk to the bellpull.

He moved to the settee where he sat across from their guest. Appearing to be quite at ease, he leaned back and placed one arm along the back, the other on the padded armrest. His coat parted to reveal the new waistcoat he wore.

"I suppose you're surprised to see me," the ex-warden said.

"Not really."

"Your letter left me a little unsettled."

Stanton Norwell looked uneasy, Floryn thought as she sat beside Cord. A feeling, she decided, that was unfamiliar to him.

"Being a man who likes to look ahead rather than over his shoulders all the time," Norwell said, "I decided to take matters in my hands, to make my own time, if you know what I mean."

Floryn studied Norwell. His eyes were narrowed, his

gaze wary. His hand tightly gripped the end of the armrest; his gaze shifted around the room. For all his refinement, his aloofness, he was not in charge of this meeting. Clearly Cord was, and was enjoying every moment of it.

"I was surprised to hear about the parole," Norwell said. "I shouldn't have been. That's the way Webb Pruitt works."

Cord said nothing.

Norwell shifted in the chair and raised a hand to his necktie. "You know he's after the treasure and has been since the beginning."

"As are so many others," Cord said dryly.

Norwell seemed unable to find a comfortable position. He moved again. Stretching out his legs, he crossed them at the ankles, then pushed back in the chair to prop his elbows on the armrests. He bridged his hands in front of him. "I suppose so."

Unobtrusively, Floryn answered the soft knock and quietly ordered coffee and dessert.

"I'm too old to play games, Donaldson," Floryn heard him say as she returned.

Norwell reached into his coat pocket and withdrew a small box. Snapping open the lid, he set it on the table in front of the settee. Sunlight reflected off the gold, pie-shaped medallion, off the deep red ruby, the largest Floryn had ever seen, the most beautiful. Mesmerized, she stared at the piece of jewelry.

The San Domingo pendant she had heard so much about, the only clue Cord had to the events that landed him in prison. The hundred facets of the ruby caught and reflected the sunlight, but as Cord had said, the stone did not comprise the beauty of the pendant. Its unique shape and design, the geometrical markings, set it apart.

With a touch akin to reverence, Cord lifted it from the velvet bed, letting it hang from the long chain.

157

With rapt attention his gaze followed its gentle sway.

"It's beautiful, isn't it?" Norwell murmured, his eyes also fixed on the swinging medallion. "I often sit in the sunlight and look at it. For the past four years I've studied it almost daily and have never figured it out."

Floryn held her hand out, and Cord slid the chain over her fingers. Smooth and silver, polished to a brilliant sheen, the pendant spun around. She captured it in her other hand and looked at the marks, at the placement of the ruby.

"Why did you return it?" Cord looked directly at the ex-warden. "Because you're no closer to finding the San Domingo treasure today than you were the day you took it from me?"

Norwell said, "I figured you would appreciate my having cared for your property all these years and for my cooperating with you. As you can see, I returned it intact — ruby and all."

Cord grinned, a gesture that touched his lips only and accentuated his cynicism, that reminded Floryn of the prisoner she had met only weeks ago at the rock quarry.

"I wasn't worried about your getting rid of the ruby. I knew you were a wealthy man, and the war made you even more so, since you sided with the North. You had no need for the money."

Cord leaned forward, so that he was closer to Norwell. With a stone-chiseled expression on his face, Cord stared at the visitor.

"I also knew that you were convinced there was a San Domingo treasure and that you would do nothing to damage the only clue to it. I have no doubt you had the ruby removed to see if it contained a clue itself."

Floryn observed the twin spots of color on Norwell's cheeks.

"No," Cord drawled with satisfaction, shaking his head, "you weren't going to destroy the clue, especially when you have been unable to unravel its secrets yourself. You have no choice but to rely on me to find the treasure for you."

Cord's sardonic laughter filled the room. "Now that you're convinced you can't find the San Domingo treasure by yourself, you're willing to become my business associate?"

Norwell squirmed in his chair. "Just a small reward for my efforts in preserving the clue for you intact, no matter what my reason was for doing so."

Floryn returned the necklace to Cord who cradled it in the palm of his hand. In answer to a knock, she rose and opened the door to allow the maid to enter with a serving cart. After she departed, Floryn poured the coffee and served the cake.

"Cream? Sugar?" she asked Norwell.

"Cream."

She looked at Cord. He looked directly at Norwell.

"Black. I don't want anything in it to mess up the flavor of the coffee."

"I disagree," Norwell said. "Sometimes a blending can enhance the flavor of something."

Floryn handed each their cup. Norwell stirred in the cream; Cord set his cup on his knee. She offered cake to Norwell. He accepted, spreading a white linen napkin over his lap. Floryn turned to Cord.

"Dessert?"

He shook his head.

No, she thought, he wanted only the pendant.

Norwell ate several bites of cake and took a swallow of coffee. "You should have a slice of this, Donaldson. It really hits the spot." He took another bite, chewed and swallowed. Spearing a piece of cake, he held out his fork. "Chocolate cake. Nothing I appreciate more."

Tracing the rim of his coffee cup with his fingers, Cord said, "What if I don't show my appreciation?"

Norwell picked up the napkin and dabbed the corners of his mouth. He lowered the fork to the plate and returned the napkin to his lap, but his gaze rested on the black leather patch Cord wore. "I would say you better watch your back at all times." He added in a quiet tone, "As best you can . . . with one eye."

The ominous declaration sent a chill of fear over Floryn. It reminded her of Nellie's warning, the warning Cord had laughed away when she repeated it to him.

"I've learned to overcome my handicap, Norwell. I protect my backside pretty good."

The cup of coffee, untouched, yet rested on Cord's knee.

"Since I have a lot of political influence," Norwell said, "I could be of help in getting your parole changed to a pardon."

"Why didn't you make this offer before?"

Norwell leaned forward to set the empty cake dish on the table. He laid the napkin on top of it. "I couldn't have initiated the parole or pardon. That took someone else. Now that the forces have come together, I can help you. I can certainly assure that you keep your parole, and I'm almost as sure I can get it changed to a pardon."

With her fork Floryn pushed the cake around on her plate and listened to the conversation.

"I'm sure you know that Pruitt manipulated the parole, so he could control you," Norwell said, "so he could have legal recourse if you don't play by his rules. With a pardon you would be free, no chance of returning to prison unless you are found guilty of committing another crime."

Cord returned his cup of coffee — still untouched — to the tray. "Thanks for saving me the trip to get my pendant, but no thanks to your offer. Now that I'm out of prison I'll take care of myself. I don't want a pardon, I want acquittal."

160

Norwell stood also. "As I said, keep your eyes . . . your eye open. All the time. You never know who is friend, who is foe."

Twelve

The pendant was Floryn's greatest foe, so far her greatest competitor. She truly despised the power it had over Cord. Since Norwell's visit hours ago, Cord had been quiet and withdrawn, sitting on the sofa, looking at the pendant, lost in memories. She had attempted to talk to him, but his answers, if any, were either absentminded as if he had not really heard her or sharp and abrupt as if she were intruding.

She walked into the bedroom where they had made love earlier. The odor of the flowers permeated the room, and the warm sultry air blew in the opened window, but the atmosphere had changed. It was no longer warm with love and sharing; it was lonely and cool. Off-putting. Gone was the tenderness she and Cord had shared. Gone was the tingling awareness, the sweetness of their having made love.

At this moment she felt as if they had not made love, and the man who had teased her was gone. Maybe never really existed except in her imagination. She was no closer to knowing this man to whom she was married than she had been ten years ago. Always there had been a barrier between them. First it was Hal; now it was Cord's shadowy past.

The anticipation that had blazed between them for the past few days quieted in the face of his discovery.

She lifted her watch. She snapped open the lid, looked at the time, then closed it. Putting on her hat, pinning it in place, she slipped the drawstring of her reticule over her arm and marched into the parlor.

"I'm going to dinner," she announced.

Cord looked at her. "I apologize. I completely forgot about dinner. I made reservations at the restaurant up the street." He jerked the chain lightly and caught the pendant in his fist. "Would you like to wear it?"

Her first inclination was to say no. She wanted nothing to do with the pendant, but reason quickly washed away her anger. It was only natural that he, not having seen the pendant for nine years, should be engrossed with it. She could not, would not, deny Cord the right to discover his past. Paradoxically the pendant was symbolic of both his past and his present. It represented the injustice that had been done to him; it was the key to finding justice. No, Floryn could not deny him the right to bring to light his shadowy past.

Also Floryn recognized that she had been consumed with jealousy, not anger. She wanted to share Cord with nothing, with no one. Selfishly she wanted his attention, all of it. Nothing that was happening between her and him was as she had imagined. One by one her daydreams were being burst.

"Well," Cord said impatiently, "do you want to wear it?"

"It doesn't really match my dress."

"This" — Cord held the ruby so that it captured the light — "matches anything."

"I'll wear it."

She quickly pinned her watch to her bodice and allowed Cord to fasten the chain about her neck. Afterward she walked to the mirror and looked at it. She ran her fingers over it, caressing first the gold, then the ruby.

"It's beautiful," she murmured.

"Sometimes I think it casts a spell."

"It does. Norwell admitted he studied it every day, and you've been doing the same since he returned it to you."

"I did the same before he took it from me," Cord admitted. "It's as if it has a message to tell, as if it's begging us to understand."

She turned to face him. "I know you feel you must find out who framed you, and deep down I want you to. But I fear your past, Cord. You've been out of prison for only days and already you've had warnings from so many people, beginning with the warden and ending . . . ending with . . ." She studied his face as if she could find the answers. "Is it going to end, Cord?"

"I'm not sure. When I was in prison, my goals were simple. I knew exactly what I was going to do when I got out. But the longer I'm out, the more questions I have, the fewer answers. Those answers which I have are fuzzy."

In silence they walked out of the room and down the stairs.

When they reached the lobby, Cord said, "I've always known the past was shadowy, but the longer I'm out of prison, the more I realize that it's black, Floryn. Jet black. I can't see anyone, anything. I'm walking, but I don't know where and I don't know who I'm liable to meet or when. Norwell was correct when he said I didn't know friend from foe."

He stopped walking, turned, and lifted the pendant. Holding it in his palm, rubbing it with his thumb, he said, "I never understood how the rumor of the treasure got started."

164

"If it is a rumor," she said.

He nodded. "Now everybody wants a share of something that I'm not even sure exists, and all of them, including my friends, are capable of killing me for it, of killing anyone who stands in their way of getting it."

"I've been thinking about that also," Floryn said quietly. She, too, looked at the pendant. "Now that you have it, will we be leaving for the ranch?"

He dropped the pendant and stepped back. "On the morning stage. I'll get the tickets when we return to the hotel. Then I'll let Tony know my plans have changed."

When they exited from the hotel, the sun had settled. Brilliant oranges and purples spread across the dusty sky. Enjoying the cool of the evening, they strolled to the restaurant.

Floryn glanced across the street to see a man standing in the shadows. He stared at them. After several more steps, her hand tightened on Cord's arm.

"What is it?" he asked.

"That man over there," she said and nodded with her head. "He's been walking with us and staring for a good while."

Cord looked in the same direction as she and stepped off the boardwalk to cross the street. The man moved further back into the shadows until he was lost. Then he stepped forward, lifted his hand and waved. Both Cord and Floryn turned to see a woman down the street wave back. The man and woman walked toward each other.

Embarrassed, at the same time relieved, Floryn laughed. "I'm sorry. I guess Norwell's warning has me a little jumpy."

At the restaurant they did little talking, and despite her announcement that she was hungry, Floryn did little eating. She felt as if she and Cord were under a dark cloud that was pressing lower, that was heavy and dangerous. By the time they began their return journey, darkness had settled over the city.

Light filtered through opened windows and doors to cast its pale glow on the boardwalk and streets. Several buggies rolled by. Horses and riders trotted up and down the thoroughfare, while pedestrians, laughing and talking, strolled the boardwalk on both sides of the street.

Although she had eaten little, Floryn's spirits lifted by the time they neared the hotel. She decided she had overreacted to Norwell's visit.

"I'll get our fares to El Paso," she suggested. "You let Tony know about tomorrow."

Cord agreed, and once he had seen her safely into the lobby, he left. After she purchased the tickets, she walked toward the stairs. She stopped when she passed an ornate mirror and gazed at her reflection, at the reflection of the pendant.

Again she was captivated by its beauty. As she stared into its blood-red depths, she saw the fires of hell. It frightened her; at the same time it excited and drew her into its flames, into its mystery, making her a part of its secret. All Cord had said about it and more were true. It was a spell caster.

She forcibly pulled her gaze away from the stone and shivered. She could not afford to become a victim of its spell. Although she had advised Cord to forget his past, she knew this was possible only if he learned the secrets of the pendant. These secrets were the key to his past which in turn was the key to the future, to his, to theirs . . . if they were to have one together.

And she prayed they would have one together.

166

She unlocked and opened the door, returning the hotel key to her reticule when she entered the parlor. She held the chimney of the entrance wall lamp and was about to strike the match when she felt a presence in the room. An eerie presence. She stood stock-still. Fear gripped her.

She took a deep breath, then with shaking fingers struck the match and whirled around, holding it up so the light would illuminate the room. She saw a movement in the bedroom before the flame burned out. She heard a noise to her left.

Were two people in the suite?

She dropped the chimney and ran toward the door. Heavy steps sounded behind her. She groped for the knob. Hands dug into her shoulders.

"Mrs. Donaldson, please give me the pendant," a muffled but familiar voice said.

Floryn began to turn her head, but a hand stopped the movement. She felt the brush of rough material against her neck and cheek and knew her assailant was masked and wore gloves.

"I don't want to hurt you," the person said, "but I want the pendant."

"No."

"Please."

Floryn squirmed and struggled, but her adversary was much stronger than she.

Sadly the voice said, "Then you leave me no choice."

She felt excruciating pain as something hard hit the back of her head. Gray shadows spinning around her, she slid to the floor.

"All I want is the pendant."

No. She tried to scream the denial, but the sound, lodging somewhere between her chest and mouth, never came. She wrapped her hand around the pendant. She had to protect it.

"Turn it loose," the voice said.

Her strength fading, she felt the pendant slipping out of her hand.

"Ah, yes, that's it," the voice said gently.

She felt the tug, and the back of her neck burned. Peace, sweet peace closed in on her.

Rather pleased with the turn of events, Cord threw open the door, lamplight spilling into the darkened and strangely quiet parlor. This was odd, he thought. He would have expected the entry lamp to be burning and noises in the other room as Floryn prepared for bed.

"Floryn, it's me."

Closing the door, he took several steps into the quiet room. He halted.

"Floryn?"

He took another step. Something crunched under his boot. Another step. The same crunching noise. He moved back to the door, reached into the lamp base for the matches. They were gone. He groped for the chimney. It was gone also. Cord rushed into the hall and in the pale light that filtered into the room he saw slivers of glass.

He grabbed a match from the wall container and returned to the parlor, lighting the wick. Soft, sputtering light soon dispelled the shadows and he saw the form on the floor, the hat and reticule lying nearby.

He ran to her. "Floryn! Dear God. No!"

His hands moved over her body gently, thoroughly, until he assured himself she was alive. She moaned, and he touched the back of her head. Her hair was wet and sticky. Blood. Further examination revealed the swelling and the cut.

"Floryn," he spoke softly, hiding his desperation, his fear, "can you hear me?"

She mumbled. He lowered his head, placing it close to her mouth.

"Cord?" Her lips brushed the word against his ear.

"It's me, Floryn. I'm here."

"My head." She reached up, but he clasped her hand before she felt the blood. "It's—hurting."

He could see her trying to open her eyes, her lashes fluttering before the lids revealed slivers of brown eyes. There was pain and confusion in them, and also relief.

Her lips barely moved. "Someone . . . hit . . . me."

"Did you see who?"

"No." She tried to shift and gasped. She closed her eyes and swallowed hard. Cord had enough experience with pain to recognize it.

He took her hand and held it tightly, feeling her fingers close around his as a drowning person's might. Despite her injury, the clasp was strong and warm, and a sudden surge of electricity ran through him . . . had always run through him when Floryn touched him. He fought burgeoning feelings of protectiveness, of tenderness, feelings he did not want again, feelings he could not afford again. He steeled himself against such emotions, but she looked so vulnerable. . . .

She was saying something again, and he leaned closer to hear the words. "I saw someone in the bedroom. The next thing I knew he was in here. Or—"

She wrinkled her forehead as if in thought.

"Or what?"

"Or maybe there were two." She tensed and struggled to sit up. Pain shadowed her face. Her lips tightened with concentration, and her eyes glazed over

169

with pain. She lay back down and closed her eyes again.

"It's all right," Cord murmured.

"No," she mumbled, "it's not all right. It's not."

Assured her only injury was the blow to her head, he reached down, picking her up carefully. In his arms, nestled against his chest, she was slender and light. She nestled closer to him; she brushed her cheek against his chest, and he caught his breath. He smelled the light, flowery scent of her—the scent of the bath oil she had used earlier—the bouquet he had bought her in the plaza.

As his arms tightened about her, she opened her eyes and their gazes met. Despite her wound, despite her pain, the spark of attraction that had always been between them ignited. Cord tried ineffectively to brush the sensation away. Now was not the time for them.

There was no time in his life for them period. Having sex with Floryn was one matter. That was a physical involvement. He swore he would not become emotionally involved with her again.

Yet he was . . . he wanted to take care of her.

Floryn's dark eyes wrenched away from his face, as if she, too, were feeling that same connection, as if she were also fighting it. As if she could read his thoughts and were hurt by them.

Cord laid her on the sofa, and feeling a terrible loss, stepped back. He almost trembled as her eyes searched his face with an intensity that scorched him. Then as if she found no answer or perhaps the wrong one, the light seemed to dim. Again he felt a terrible sense of loss that sent shivers through him. He felt that perhaps he had only imagined all these sensations on her part . . . just as he had imagined the depth of her love ten years ago.

170

Pushing the conflicting thoughts away, he busied himself taking care of her. As soon as he had a towel and the bed pillows propped around her so that she could rest her head comfortably without putting any added pressure on it, he gave the bellpull a tug.

"Cord," she mumbled, "he sounded like someone I knew. I mean, his voice was familiar." She rubbed her forehead and furrowed her brow. "I think I've heard it before."

He returned to the sofa and sat on the edge beside her.

"You rang, sir," a man called from the opened door.

Cord glanced up to see the night manager. "We've had a burglary, and my wife has been hurt. Please send for a physician and the sheriff."

"Yes, sir. Right away sir."

"I'm fine." Floryn sniffed.

"I want to be sure." Cord carefully brushed his hand through her hair, mindful not to tug the tangles too hard.

The man peered into the room at Floryn. "Is there anything else I can do for you, sir?"

"Close the door, please."

"I should know the man, Cord," Floryn said, her voice stronger now, escalating with frustration. "I should recognize the voice."

"Don't push it," he said, knowing what it was like to search his mind for a tidbit of information that surely must be there. He remembered the frustration, the irritation. "You'll remember in time."

"What if I don't?"

"Then you don't."

He walked to the sideboard and poured a glass of brandy.

"But you will." He brushed hair from her face,

171

then placed the glass to her lips. "Drink this."

Tears ran down her cheeks as she cupped the glass with both hands and sipped the brandy. "I shouldn't have worn the pendant, Cord. I should have let you keep it in your pocket. It's lost now, and you'll never find out what happened. We'll never know."

"Don't worry about it. A human life is more important than a damned pendant." He pulled his handkerchief from his pocket and dabbed the tears from her cheeks. "Don't cry about it. It's not worth it."

"It is, Cord." She sobbed. "It was your only clue."

It was, and losing it hurt but not nearly so much as the thought of losing her. He did not want to be responsible for the death of any human being, but especially not the death of his child's mother. He pulled Floryn close to his chest and held her, resting his chin on the top of her head. Eventually her tears stopped and the racking sobs turned into soft sniffs.

Floryn pushed out of Cord's arms and smiled tremulously at him. Out of the stark face, large golden-brown eyes peered at him. Light from the lamp behind glowed around her head like an aura. Again he was reminded that she looked like an angel. This time he did not argue with himself. Tonight she would be his angel. He tucked a stray curl behind her ear. She touched her hair, long since freed from the coil, hanging down her back.

"I must look a mess," she said. Light flickered over the honey-gold strands, transforming them into silken treasure.

"Never."

"I'm fine. Really I am. We don't need the doctor."

"I'd rather be sure." He noted that her mouth was pinched with pain. "Lie back down and rest."

"Cord—"

172

"For me, please."

She nodded, inhaled deeply, and closed her eyes. While they waited for the physician, Cord walked through the suite to make sure nothing else had been stolen. When he returned to the parlor, he picked up her reticule. Nearby lay her coin purse.

"Damn," he muttered.

"What's wrong?" Floryn asked. "Is our money gone?"

"No, everything is here."

"What's wrong then?" she murmured. She lifted her hand to her forehead and Cord noticed her wedding band. He saw the watch pinned to her dress.

"Something worries me. The thief didn't take your watch or ring or the money," Cord said, "just the pendant. This is no ordinary theft, Floryn."

She lay quietly for a long while. "Right before he hit me, Cord, he said something about not wanting to hurt me. He just wanted the pendant."

"Well, he got it." He smiled at her. "I'm just thankful you're not hurt any worse."

Sighing, she closed her eyes and mumbled, "Me, too."

While she rested, the maid came up. She swept up the broken glass and replaced the lamp chimney. Floryn was still resting on the sofa, Cord standing in front of the window, when the doctor arrived.

After he examined Floryn, he said, "A nasty blow. Looks like he used the butt of his revolver." Long fingers probed. "The back of your neck is bruised, and you'll probably have a headache for awhile." He rose and moved to the sofa table. "I'm going to give you this headache powder now, and I'll leave some for you to take tonight and tomorrow."

While the doctor stirred the powder in a glass of water, the sheriff made his appearance and took a full report from Floryn. After he departed, Cord carried her into the bedroom and laid her on the bed. The doctor followed.

"Mrs. Donaldson, in order for you to sleep the night through, I'm going to give you a small dose of laudanum."

Floryn protested, but both Cord and the doctor insisted.

After she drank her medicine, Cord turned down the lamp.

The doctor said, "Mr. Donaldson, I'd like to talk with you. I'll wait in the other room while you take care of your wife."

By the time Cord had undressed and tucked her into bed, she was asleep. He stripped out of his vest and jacket before he returned to the parlor where the doctor awaited him. Cord poured them a glass of whiskey.

Sitting down, the doctor took a pipe and tobacco pouch from his jacket pocket. After filling the pipe bowl and lighting it, he leaned back, leisurely smoking.

"I wanted to let you know that your wife's behavior may be a little erratic for the next few days. She'll probably be prone to depression and bouts of crying."

"The wound is worse than you led her to believe?"

Shaking his head, the doctor rested his elbow on the arm of the settee, a thin line of smoke curling up from the pipe. "No, it's the aftermath of being unconscious from a blow to the head and the fear of being attacked in the dark by an unknown assailant. She'll be fit as a fiddle after a few days of rest."

"We're leaving on tomorrow's stage for El Paso."

"I recommend that she take it easy for the next few days," the doctor answered. "Being jolted in that stage won't do her any good. Bed rest tomorrow, at least.

174

Then for the next couple of days, I would suggest you walk along the river. It's quite peaceful and is conducive to regaining one's health."

After the doctor left, Cord walked onto the balcony and sipped another drink. The pendant was the reason for the robbery, and the only ones in town besides him and Floryn who knew about the pendant were Ferguson, Esteman, and Norwell. Cord immediately scratched Tony's name from the list of suspects. Cord had been with him during the time Floryn was attacked. The second name scratched off was Norwell's. He had no reason to give Cord the pendant, then steal it back. That left Ferguson. But Cord did not believe the kid would steal the pendant—not when he was interested in bigger game.

Still contemplating the situation, he returned to the bedroom to sit in the chair close to the bed so he could watch over Floryn, so he could look at her. A lamp on the night table, the wick turned down low, cast a soft light on her.

Although she was pale from her ordeal, she was beautiful. Her skin was ivory, and long black lashes framed her closed eyes. Her cheekbones were high, her chin strong and determined. He leaned forward and slid his fingers through her hair. It felt like silk and smelled like fresh flowers.

His gaze returned to her lips that were nicely sculpted and begging to be kissed. He imagined them curving into a smile. He imagined them warm and soft and pliant beneath his.

He sighed. She moaned. He moved closer to her.

"You're going to be all right," he murmured. "Sleep now. I'm here with you, I'll take care of you."

Thirteen

Floryn wore the San Domingo Pendant around her neck as she rode the black stallion across the Fancy Lady. A wild Texas wind blew. It lashed her face; it whipped her hair.

But the pendant was hers. She held it in her fist. If she could keep it, freedom belonged to her and Cord.

She heard a rider behind her. Cord? She turned to see. No! A shadowy figure chased her, one who wanted to steal her necklace.

She urged the stallion to run faster, but the man chasing her gained. Closing a hand around the pendant, she again spurred the stallion. But no matter how fast the horse galloped, the pursuer's galloped faster.

She could not outrun him.

Then she was on the ground running herself. Stanton Norwell was chasing her. Then Nellie. They were one, and both of them were laughing. Floryn ran faster, ran until her chest felt as if it would burst and her legs as if they were cast from iron, the rusted joints unable to bend.

A warning voice drifted in. "You never know who is friend, who is foe."

Floryn was on the stallion again. He was galloping wildly. The wind blew harder, again lashing at her, again whipping her. Her pursuer drew closer, along side of her. He reached for Floryn. She screamed.

She blinked her eyes several times, felt her bodice to see if she were still wearing the pendant. She was not. Then she remembered. The pendant had been stolen.

She had awakened from a dream. She was not being pursued. Knowing she was safe in her hotel room, she settled back into her cocoon, let out her breath, and closed her eyes. But once consciousness began to awaken, it would not be denied. Memories stole back to replace nightmarish dreams.

The pendant was gone. Although in the deep recesses of her mind, Floryn knew she was not to blame for the theft, she yet carried the guilt. If only she had insisted that Cord keep it himself. If only. . . .

Trying to push the troubling thoughts from her mind, Floryn sighed, stretched out, then curled up again. She ran her tongue around a mouth that felt full of cotton. Barely opening her eyes, focusing on nothing but the night table, she reached for the glass of water. She sloshed and gargled before she swallowed.

Lying back down, she tucked her hand beneath her chin. A breeze touched her face, as if kissing her good morning. Again she opened her eyes, wider this time, to see the sheer curtain billowing away from the window. She heard the door open, soft footsteps, and she was peering into the concerned face of her husband.

"Good morning," she murmured.

"Good morning."

It was amazing how wonderful Cord could make those words sound. Almost seductive.

"How are you feeling?" he asked.

"My head and neck are sore, but I feel better than I did last night," she answered.

"Breakfast is here. Do you want to eat in here or in the parlor?"

"In the parlor." She yawned and stretched, then reached for her dressing gown.

Before Cord could reach her, she sat up and swung her legs over the side of the bed. At the abrupt and total movement of her body, her head began to swim. She went still, bracing the palms of her hands on each side of her.

"Are you all right?" Cord asked, sitting beside her.

Her eyes closed, her world righting itself, she smiled weakly. "I was a little dizzy. I'm going to have to move a little slower."

"No pain?"

"No, just dizzy."

Taking her wrapper from her, he said gently. "You're going to have to let me take care of you for a while."

The words had a devastating effect on Floryn. She knew Cord was being kind and considerate because of her wound, but she took him at face value. She wanted him to take care of her. For a little while she wanted her bruised and battered spirit to be cosseted. In ways the world had been cruel to her, and she was tired of fighting it. She wanted a shoulder to lean on, a hand to hold. She wanted someone giving her encouragement . . . and love.

She rose and slipped into the robe. Gazing into her eyes, he pulled it together, his hands innocently grazing her breasts. He fastened it, his large callused fingers again brushing against her highly sensitized skin—her collarbone, her breasts, her abdomen, her stomach—as he awkwardly tied the little bows.

She watched him patiently fighting the material and winning the battle, and her vulnerability increased. The door to her heart, always ajar where Cord was concerned, opened wider.

Their gazes caught and held. His hands stilled

178

their movement, the warmth of his fingers penetrating the fabric to touch her skin, to make her tingle with awareness. A shadow crossed his face, and she wondered what he was thinking.

She lifted her hand, touching his cheek with the tips of her fingers, outlining the patch. She leaned forward and kissed his forehead, then brushed her lips down his cheeks and felt him tremble against hers.

"Thank you," she murmured.

He smiled, then bent his head and resumed fastening her wrapper. As he bent his head, she gazed at the thick black hair, the temples highlighted with silver. As his fingers whispered against the material, against her stomach, lower, she softly brushed her fingers through the white hair at his temples.

"I've never told you," she said, "but your hair is beautiful. You're beautiful."

Again he lifted his head, his expression enigmatic.

"Can a man be beautiful?" he parried.

"You are."

As it had happened to her that day in the meadow when comforting had turned into passion, Floryn's vulnerability turned into desire. She wanted Cord to take care of her . . . of all her needs. Her body clamored with need, a desperate urgent need she had never felt before, one that surprised her with its intensity. Her blood pulsed so hard, she felt dizzy. But not from the wound. She moaned.

Cord's face creased with concern. "What's wrong?"

"Nothing," she whispered.

"Are you all right, Floryn? Do I need to get the doctor?"

"No, I'm not all right," she murmured, wondering if the thick, husky voice she heard was hers, "and no, I don't need a doctor. I need . . . you. Just you."

179

And that was the truth of the matter. She had always just needed him.

She locked her hands about his neck and strained against him. She lifted her face, pulling his head down, as she sought his mouth.

"Floryn"—his voice was gentle as he spoke, his hands gentle as they tried to unlock hers—"you don't know what you're doing."

"Yes, I do."

He pulled her hands between them, binding them in one of his. "Don't do this to me. You're hurt, sweetheart. And I'm only human. I can only stand so much."

Tears misted her eyes. "I want you, Cord."

Something in her face must have alerted him to the intensity of her desires. His gaze darkened, and she saw an answering passion.

He loosened her hands, caught her in an embrace, and rubbed her back with his hands. "I want you," he answered, "but not now. Not like this."

She leaned against him, her cheek resting against his chest, her hands settling on his hips. With both hands he cupped her cheeks, gently tilting her face up until her eyes met his.

"Your head—" he began.

"My entire body," she whispered. "It's on fire, Cord."

"It's—it's the medicine."

Cord was on fire also, slowly burning. The one part of him wanted only to comfort and take care of a patient. The other part—the greater part—wanted to make love to her—gentle, tender love. The hidden man, the one Cord seldom allowed to surface, wanted what had been denied him all these years.

"No," she murmured, "it's passion, Cord. Plain and simple, I need and want you."

The doctor had said she would need reassuring. Cord could do that without hurting her. But reassurance was not what she was asking for. Reassurance and comfort were not what he wanted to give; they were what he must give. Hardly conscious of what he was doing, wanting only to ease her hurt, Cord's embrace tightened. Light was the touch of his mouth as it touched hers. He meant only to comfort.

"Yes," she softly cried.

Whatever his intentions, no matter how good, they were quickly scattered into oblivion by her response. Her arms moved from his hips to lock about his neck, her fingers splaying in the thick hair at the collar of his shirt. She firmly pressed her body to his, the fire of her need flowing into him.

Despite their having made love the day before, Cord was thrown off balance by the way passion exploded between them. In the space of a heartbeat, everything was forgotten — the pendant, his need to take care of her, her wound. All he knew, all he wanted to know was the feel of Floryn in his arms, the taste of her on his lips.

Still Cord was not a man ruled by emotions. Too long he had disciplined himself. Too long he had exerted the utmost control. He surfaced the drowning eddy of passion. His hands slid to her waist. He lifted his head and drew a deep breath of air, sanity rushing back.

"I can't do this to you," he said.

"Then let me do it to you," Floryn murmured. Her hands twined about his neck and brought his mouth back to hers.

"Your head," he mumbled, his lips grazing hers as he spoke.

"My body," she countered, in the most beautiful

181

desire-laden voice Cord had ever heard. "I want you, Cord. I need you now. Right now."

Her cry that day in the meadow.

"I don't want to hurt you."

"You will if you don't take me."

She was so honest in her wants, Cord so heated with desire, he could not have refused her. He dared not.

Easily he lifted and laid her on the bed, her hair pooling golden brown on the white pillowcase. "I want you," he said, "but I don't think—"

"Don't think." Her ivory skin glistened with a sheen of perspiration; her eyes had darkened to a deep and passionate brown. "Just make love to me."

He lowered his head and covered her mouth with his. Their lips touched, tentatively at first, then hard and demanding. Her fingers curled into the thickness of his hair, dragging him closer still.

She had told him not to think. She gave him no time to think. He wanted no time to think. No time to wonder if this was the right thing for him—for them—to do. No time to draw back.

He must seize the moment. Imprisonment had taught him that. That particular moment never came again. Tenderly, gently so as not to hurt her, he would feel her with every fiber of his being. She would feel him. The blood pounded in his temples to drown out conscience and argument. He had to have her. He was no longer concerned about keeping his distance. It was too late for that.

Involvement! From some part of his brain the word leaped out. It ricocheted about, but the fires of desire soon burned away his fear of it. He no longer cared that his involvement might be emotional as well as physical. All that mattered at this minute was easing the burning ache in his body, an ache created

182

by his desire for Floryn and for her alone, an ache that only she could assuage.

He had gently, meticulously tied the bows that fastened Floryn's dressing gown. Now urgency and passion made his hands rough and uncaring. He unfastened some of the ties; others he tore loose, the rip of the fabric a sensual sound in the room that was quiet except for heavy breathing.

Cord's hands came up, cupping her sweet breasts, feeling the nipples hard and taut against his palms. He wanted to taste them, but Floryn's hands were already divesting him of his garments.

"Hurry," she whispered. When the buttons defeated her shaking fingers, she cupped her hand over his arousal, drawing a guttural groan from him.

"Hurry, Cord," she said again.

Cord moved away from her, slipping out of his unbuttoned shirt. Under her hooded gaze, he quickly if somewhat awkwardly shed his boots and socks. He stood, his fingers undoing the buttons of his trousers. He shoved them and his undergarments down to release the heavy, thick length of his manhood. When he returned to stand at the side of the bed, she curled her hand around him and gently stroked. He did not think he could contain his passion.

He eased back onto the bed. His hands stroked the smooth planes and curves of her sides, savoring the silken feel of her skin. But Floryn wanted no foreplay. She twisted beneath him, opening her legs, her ankles coming up to press against his hips.

Cord groaned and fought the urge to take her invitation. This was not how he wanted to take her, not while she was hurt, not when he could hurt her. He wanted to slow the pace, to be tender.

"Floryn," he muttered, his voice hoarse, "I'm afraid I'm going to—"

183

She stared up at him, her eyes dark with need. And he saw another emotion there—a bleakness of some sort—that he could not identify.

"Now, Cord. Please, now."

She reached between them again to close her hand over his swollen need. She drew him forward until he rested against her dampness.

"Now," she whispered fiercely, her hips rising up as if to force him to take her.

When the warm dampness touched him, his tenuous hold on control snapped. With a soft curse that was almost a prayer, he slid into her, her body rising to accommodate him, her softness surrounding him, her flesh enfolding him in the sweetest of embraces. Intense, wonderful pleasure coursed through him, and he pressed his forehead to the pillow beside her head. He struggled to regain a shred of control.

But Floryn was not interested in his taking his time, in a gentle coupling, in a controlled coming together. She forcefully arched her hips into his, drawing her legs up to circle his waist so that she took him even deeper.

"Don't." Cord lifted himself on his arms, his fingers knotted over the blankets as he struggled to regain control. He breathed deeply, the very effort hurt. He tried to clear his mind, tried to take charge of his body. "Slow down, Floryn."

"No." Her hips rose again as her fingers trailed the indentation of his spine from his shoulders to his buttocks.

He was on fire as he had never been in his entire life. His entire body was moistened with perspiration.

"I want you now, Cord."

"You have me."

"No, I want all of you."

184

She planted soft kisses across his chest, until her mouth found his nipple. Her tongue tasted it, laved it. Cord shuddered, feeling the last fragile vestige of control slipping from him like water running down his body after a swim. And he knew as he allowed himself to become one with desire that he would struggle to regain it no more this day. Her teeth scored him lightly and he made the ultimate surrender to passion.

"You want all of me, sweetheart," he murmured thickly. "Then you shall have all of me."

He stroked in and out, again and again, his pleasure building until he knew he could not contain himself. The intensity of his release made more wondrous by the knowledge they had reached it together.

He tensed, gasped, then collapsed on the top of her. He laid his head on the pillow beside hers, feeling the silken strands of her hair against his cheek, smelling the flowery scent of her hair once more—a scent he would always identify with Floryn—a scent that reminded him of the Indian paintbrushes in the meadow, their meadow. Breath shuddered in and out of him.

She dropped her legs to the bed to release him from his sweet prison. He rolled away from her, the full impact of what he had done hitting him. He was also startled by his comparing her body being wrapped around him to a sweet prison.

Some of his wonder, his pleasure was diminished. He had not left one prison to be enslaved by another, to be enslaved by a woman who wanted to use him.

They lay there without speaking, the room completely silent but for the whisper of the summer wind against the curtain.

"Thank you." Floryn's whisper joined that of the wind. "I don't know why—what made me—"

Without moving, Cord asked, "Did I hurt you?"

"No." She turned her head on the pillow. "I just felt sad and alone."

Cord laughed dryly. "I think maybe we could do without this confession. It's not doing a great deal for my ego."

Tears misted her eyes. "Cord, I'm so sorry about the pendant."

So that was it! he thought, his pleasure completely gone. She had begged him for this, yet to her it was atonement, nothing more. In one sentence she had stripped their act of love of all meaning and substance.

"I told you last night, a human life is much more important than a piece of jewelry."

"Not just a piece of jewelry," Floryn argued.

"It's gone," he said. "I regret it, but my life isn't going to end because of it, and thank God your life didn't end either."

A tear slipped out of the corner of her eye to run down her temple and dampen the pillowcase. "How are you going to find out about your past?"

"I don't know." He turned his head to look at her. "But I'll let you in on a secret; I didn't know how when I had the pendant, so I'm no worse off."

She laughed shakily and lifted her hand to touch his eye patch. "I'll help you," she promised.

Cord knew that he was going to have to be more careful in the future. For his heart's sake, he could not allow his involvement with Floryn to develop beyond mutual desire, mutual need, and fulfillment.

"How about breakfast?" he said.

"All right," she mumbled, adding a little later, "Who could have stolen the pendant?"

He shrugged.

"Surely not Norwell or Pruitt," she mused. "That

186

would be a stupid move on their part. Both of them want the treasure, and they know you're the only person who can take them to it. How about Kid Ferguson or Tony Esteman?"

She turned, propping up on an elbow, her honey-brown hair spilling over his shoulder and arm, oozing pleasure through his body. "You know, Shelby warned you about them. Remember, Cord, he told you, you couldn't trust either Ferguson or Esteman. Both of them are admitted thieves. That's why they were serving time."

Cord rolled off the bed and walked to the washstand. Water splashed as he filled the basin. "It couldn't have been Tony," he said, as he washed himself. "I was with him at the time you were robbed. Maybe Kid. I can see him doing it quicker than Tony, but I wouldn't have thought it even of him. He's out for more than the pendant."

"He's rather cocky. I can still see his arrogant exit out of the parlor yesterday."

"But he's young. Besides why steal the pendant and the money if he could have had the money simply by riding to Norwell's with me, by remaining with me to see if there were more than a pendant. Kid's too intelligent to have done this."

After Cord redressed, he set the washbowl and a clean cloth on the night table so Floryn could cleanse herself.

"There's more to this—much more—than we know at the moment," he said.

"I know you won't agree with me," Floryn said, "but I'm almost glad to be rid of the pendant. It's responsible for so many deaths."

"No," he said, "I don't agree with you. I wish we had the pendant, and we can't blame man's greedy nature on it."

After she bathed, Cord noticed she sat on the bed and held her hands to her forehead.

"Head ache?" he asked.

"A little," she confessed.

"I'll get you some medicine." He walked to the table and quickly dissolved the powder in a glass of water.

She drank it and lay down. "Let me rest a few minutes," she said, "then I'll get dressed."

Cord sat on the edge of the bed beside her. "The doctor advised that we not travel today," he said. "I'm going to reschedule us on the stage leaving next week."

"No—" she shook her head, wincing.

"You're hurting aren't you?" Cord asked, guilt settling heavily on his shoulders. He should have been firmer in his resolve not to make love to her.

"Just a little pain in my neck and shoulders."

"All the more reason for our staying a few more days," he said.

"Please, Cord," she begged, "let's go home. I'm all right really."

"Floryn, I know how concerned you are about our using the rest of the money, but—"

"It has nothing to do with money," she answered. "I want to leave here, Cord. I want to get back to the Fancy Lady and to Hope."

"You're frightened?"

"Not exactly. I'd just feel better if we were home." *I just hope we can make it back to the Fancy Lady with you alive.*

"Are you sure?"

She nodded.

His hands brushed over her back in soothing motion. "All right," he murmured, "we'll leave today."

* * *

Although only a couple of hours had passed since they made love, Floryn felt as if it were a lifetime. Once again Cord had retreated behind a facade of cool, almost brusque, indifference. He seemed solicitous of her health, but he also distanced himself from her, mentally and physically.

Floryn was not too happy with herself either. In a manner of speaking she had forced Cord to make love to her. In her urgency and desperation she had seduced him.

Once they reached the Fancy Lady, once they had miles and miles between them and Huntsville, she wondered, would Cord change? Would time and distance gentle the sharp edges? Soften his bitterness?

Hearing voices in the other room, she figured Cord was having their luggage taken down. She picked up her hat and walked across the room. When she opened the door and entered the parlor, she saw Rule sitting on the settee, Cord standing by the darkened fireplace.

"Rule!" she exclaimed. "I'm so glad to see you."

His face lit up and he rose, walking to meet her. "I'm kind of glad to be a'seeing you, too, ma'am."

"When did you get in?" she asked. She laid her hat on a nearby table.

"Last night," he answered. Like an uncle, he held both of her hands in his and studied her face. "It was late, so's I figured I'd visit with y'all today. Cord, here's, been telling me what happened. I'm real sorry. Real sorry I didn't come over last night."

Floryn smiled, and they stepped apart. "I'm already feeling better now that you're here and we're getting ready to leave for the ranch." She glanced at the cart of breakfast dishes. "We've eaten, but—"

189

"No, thank you, ma'am. I ate a bite on my way in."

"Are you riding in the stage with us?" Floryn asked Rule.

"No, ma'am. Ain't one for closed in places if'en I kin help it, ma'am. Figure I'll ride on over by myself." Returning to the sofa, he grabbed his hat and held it in both hands. "Well, reckon I'll find Tony and see if he's ready to go."

Question in her eyes, Floryn looked at Cord.

"I hired him," he said. "I figured Donaldsonville was pretty far west and a good place for a young couple who wanted to make a new start."

Floryn smiled. Her faith in human nature was well-founded, and perhaps some of her questions were already being answered. She had always maintained that Cord's personality would change when he gained his freedom, that he would revert to old traits and characteristics. Already it seemed that his cynicism was diminishing. This gave her hope that home would work wonders with him.

"I'll see you at the ranch," Rule said.

He crossed the room and opened the door. Kid Ferguson stood on the other side, holding his fist up as if to knock. Both of the men glared at each other.

Frowning, Kid looked up and glanced anxiously at Floryn. Hastily taking off his hat, he smiled at her. Then he spared Cord a cursory glance before he again looked at Rule, his frown returning.

"I see that you managed to get here after the damage has been done. Just like it was when we were in prison, huh, Compton?" He did not bother to disguise his dislike of the man.

"You don't know what you're talking about." Rule was also openly hostile. "And never did."

"I sure do," Kid drawled. "You were in town last

night. At the time Mrs. Donaldson was robbed."

"How do you know what time she was robbed?" Rule asked.

Kid hesitated. "Word's around town."

"Yeah, I bet. Who put it out? The thief what done it? Get outta my way, Ferguson, before I tear you into pieces."

Floryn was astonished at the enmity between the two men, at the accusations. She felt the kid's suspicions were misplaced. Rule was kind. He had been her friend when she was visiting Cord in prison, the one to arrange her meeting with Cord.

Rule said, "I'll be a'seeing you and Mrs. Donaldson at the ranch, Cord." His face drawn in harsh lines, he walked out of the room without a backward glance.

"Come on in, Kid," Cord invited.

"I just heard about the robbery." When he looked at Floryn, his face was filled with concern. Gone was the cocky arrogance. "I was worried about you, ma'am."

"Thank you." This abrupt and solicitous change discomfited Floryn. "I'm quite all right."

"I'm glad, ma'am, I sure wouldn't want you hurt because of that pendant." The soft words were reminiscent of the ones the thief had spoken last night.

Or were they?

Floryn wondered if her imagination were running rampant.

Kid twirled his hat nervously in his hand. "Cord, I figure not many knew about the pendant outside of Tony and me, but I—"

"I didn't think you did it," Cord said.

"I have a witness," Kid rushed on. "I was with her all afternoon and all night. You can talk with her if you want."

"I believe you," Cord said.

After a long searching gaze, Kid said, "Well, I guess I'll be going. See ya' around."

With a wave of his hand, he moved toward the door.

"Kid," Cord called, "I know you turned down my offer yesterday, but I want to make you another."

Kid's eyes widened, so did Floryn's.

"Since nothing but the pendant was taken, I'm worried. This robbery was unusual. I'd like to hire you on to work at the ranch."

Kid scrutinized him for a long time before he laughed softly. "To think I complained about the pay yesterday. I have a feeling that the offer will be even less today."

"Room and board and a monthly salary," Cord said.

"And probably plenty of trouble," Kid added.

"Probably."

"Rule gonna be there?"

Cord nodded.

Kid frowned. "You know that old man and me never did get along. He was always too cozy with the prison bigwigs for me."

"You know how I feel about him," Cord said.

Kid nodded. "I sure thank you for the offer," he said, "but I need some time to mull it over."

After the Kid left, Cord walked onto the balcony. Floryn followed.

"You don't trust either Tony or Kid, do you? That's why you want them to work for you, so you can keep an eye on them."

"Something like that," Cord said.

After a reflective moment, she said, "You don't trust anyone, do you?"

"Only myself," he answered.

Floryn gazed at the plaza below, an assortment of cantinas, general stores, livery stables, dance halls, and saloons, that was quickly filling with vendors, plying their goods.

"You're playing a dangerous game, Cord, one I don't like. I don't mind being a part of it because in a way I asked for it."

"In a way hell," Cord said. "You begged for it, as you've begged me for a lot of things, Floryn. Begged me to marry you, to help you save the ranch and our daughter."

She chose to ignore him. "Hope didn't ask for it."

Cord folded his arms and settled them on the balcony railing. "You knew I came with a heavy past, Floryn. I told you, and so did everyone else you talked with. You knew I was not a fit father for Hope. Yet you insisted."

"I had no idea—"

"Yes, you did." The voice was soft but not his accusation. "But you were determined to save that ranch for yourself as much as for Hope."

He turned, moved closer to her. He caressed her face.

"It's too late to renege now, Floryn. We've made our deal and we'll stick with it. You're going to have to take the bad with the good. I'm not going to let anyone hurt Hope," he said. "I promise."

Looking into his face, she nodded.

"I don't want my past to hurt you," he said.

The words whispered across her frayed nerves to remind her again of the thief's words. Her eyes opened wide. How soft and caringly the words were spoken. Dear God, Cord was not the burglar? He could not be. He was with Tony.

Agitated, unsure what she believed anymore, she

193

stepped away from him. The morning breeze touched her face.

"What's wrong?"

"My—my head it's—"

"Do you need some more medicine?" he asked.

"No, I'll be all right." She could not look at him.

"You're frightened," he said. "Of me."

"No. Yes. Oh, I don't know. It's just that when you said you didn't want your past to hurt me, you sounded just like the person who attacked me."

He caught her shoulder and pulled her so he could look directly into her eyes. "Floryn, I didn't attack you. I would have no reason to steal my own pendant. It was already mine, and I wouldn't have taken the chance of hurting you. No matter what our feelings are for each other, I don't beat women."

"I know," she whispered. "I'm so confused. It's true I knew about your past, about the San Domingo treasure, but I didn't know it was going to be like this. I believe that pendant is a curse."

Cord put his arm around her shoulder and guided her to the sofa in the parlor.

"I'm sorry, Cord," she said. "I don't know what's happening to me. I've never been like this before. I can't control my emotions. One minute I'm afraid, the next I'm not. I'm sad in one breath, happy in the next."

"It's all right," he said. "The doctor said you'd be confused, maybe depressed for a little while. He warned that your emotions may vacillate from one extreme to the other."

She supposed that was why she had insisted, had forced their lovemaking. One of the extremities of her emotions as a result of her accident. "I suppose . . . I am."

He poured a glass of water which he handed to

194

her. After sips, she pressed the cool glass to her forehead, wishing the dull pain would go away, wishing
she could turn back the clock. She was suspicious of
everyone she heard speak words similar to those the
thief had used. She imagined everyone to be guilty.

Floryn knew she would feel better only when
Cord's past was revealed, and perhaps not even then.

She set the glass on the table.

Fourteen

Looking at the empty glass on the table, Hope Donaldson made a face, but even that did not distract from the child's beauty. Thick, naturally arched black brows were drawn together, and golden-brown eyes flashed her challenge. She planted her hands on slender hips and bobbed her head as she declared, "I don't like sassafras tea, Leanor. It tastes horrid."

"True, but *La Curandera* says it is good for you," Leanor said. "Your body gets all clogged up during the winter, and these herbs help to cleanse you."

Hope sighed her exasperation and tossed her head, thick black braids swinging from her shoulders to her back. "How does Angelita know my insides are dirty or clogged up? When I grow up, I'm not going to drink any more of these teas, and I'm not going to make my little girl drink them. I'll have more faith in her insides than you do mine."

Laughing, Leanor captured the child's face in her hands and gave her a smacking kiss on the tip of her nose. "I love you."

Hope threw her arms around Leanor, giggling and hugging her tightly. "I love you, too. And when I have little girls, they're going to love you, too, just like me."

"*Sí, mi hija,*" Leanor said quietly, running the two words together so that the middle vowel was dropped and she spoke only one word, me-ha, a loving and tender diminutive for daughter.

Large brown eyes, eyes like her mother's, peered at Leanor. "I like it when you call me *mi hija*. It makes me sound so special."

"You are special," Leanor said. "And so is your mother. I think of both of you as my daughters, so I call you *mi hija.*"

"I'll probably call my little girl that, too," Hope said.

Leanor smiled and straightened. "Now I must see to dinner."

Hope gazed into Leanor's face. "Are you crying?"

Leanor shook her head. "No, it's the fumes from the onions. They always make my eyes water."

"Oh," Hope said.

"Antonio will be home soon," Leanor said, lifting her apron and wiping her eyes. "And he will be tired and hungry."

"Leanor!" a male voice shouted from the backyard.

Her boots snapping on the hardwood floor, Hope ran to the back screen door to see one of the *vaqueros* dismount. Flapping a letter through the air, holding the crown of his *sombrero* with the other hand, he jumped on the back porch and rushed into the kitchen.

A broad smile creased his face. "A letter from the *Señora.*"

"*Gracias,* Pedro." Leanor wiped her hands on her apron and sat at the table. She was eager for Floryn to be home. She missed her dearly, and she was needed at the *hacienda*. Quickly Leanor opened

197

the envelope and unfolded the letter.

The minute she saw the writing, she said, "No, Pedro." Her gaze swept over the first few lines. Her heart beat a little faster. She had been praying that Floryn's faith in Cord Donaldson was well placed. Evidently it had been. "It is from *El Patrón* not the *Señora*."

Hope pressed against Leanor. "The letter is from my—from my—"

"*Sí*," Leanor said, holding the sheet of paper in one hand, placing the other around Hope's shoulder, "it is from your papa. He is writing to let us know that he and your mama are on their way home. Your papa *is* coming home, *mi hija*. He and your mama will be here by the end of the week." She looked up at Hope. "That is wonderful, yes?"

A grave, almost doubtful expression on her face, Hope gave Leanor a halfhearted shake of the head. "Mama said he would come home when he learned he had a little girl."

"*Sí*." Leanor nodded her head. "And your mama was right. He'll soon be here."

"I will tell the others." Pedro hastened to the door, stopping to throw over his shoulder before he exited from the kitchen, "A fiesta, Leanor. We are planning a fiesta?"

"*Sí*, Pedro." Leanor chuckled softly and pulled another folded sheet of paper from the envelope. "Your papa included a letter for you, Hope."

Reluctant hands took the letter from Leanor. The child stared at the sheet a long time before she said, "He writes different from Papa Hal. Papa Hal's was wobbly."

Leanor looked at the bold and dark handwriting, that was so different from Hal Donaldson's. "*Sí*, your Papa Hal was a much older man. Because he was so sick, he could not hold his pen steady."

"I know he yelled at Mama a lot, but I miss him."

"I'm sure you miss him. He was a good papa to you." Leanor sighed. She tried so hard to be careful in what she said to the child about Hal. Although he had treated Floryn abominably, heaping all his hatred and bitterness on her, he had truly doted on the child, lavishing all his affection on her.

"I don't love this man. I don't even know him."

"Read your letter," Leanor gently prompted.

Hope lowered her head to look at the paper.

After a moment the housekeeper asked, "What does it say?"

"When they stop in El Paso, he's going to help Mama select a gift for me," Hope answered, then added, "He's looking forward to meeting me."

"Soon we will be a family again," Leanor said. Leaning back in the chair, she mopped her forehead with her apron and drew in deep breaths.

"Is something wrong?" Hope asked, little eyes peering anxiously from their frame of thick curling lashes.

"I get winded easily," Leanor replied, smiling away the child's worries. "I am not a young *niña* like you." She pressed her index finger lightly against Hope's nose.

"You mustn't work so hard," Hope said. "I'll help you more."

"It's not the work, *mi hija,*" she said, "it is the age."

"You're not going to leave me," Hope cried.

"I will one of these days," Leanor replied softly, keeping the serious subject light by adding, "The

Lord wants me to come supervise the cleaning of his mansions, but I told him I had to see after you first. When you're taken care of, I shall go."

Reassured, Hope grinned. "I'm never going to be taken care of, so you can't go."

Leanor smiled with her.

Hope returned the letter to the envelope, then slid into a chair. Folding her arms on the table, she laid her chin on her hands. "A while ago, you said we would be a family again. How can we be a family again if we've never been a family before?"

Leanor ran her hand around the braid that circled her head. "I did not say that well," she answered. "It is time for you and your mama and papa to become a family."

"Do you think he'll like me?"

"Ah, *mi hija*," Leanor murmured, "he will more than like you. You will be the apple of his eyes." Leanor brushed the bangs from Hope's forehead. "Your papa will love you."

"He never answered Mama's letters," she said.

"No, but he will explain this to you when he arrives."

"Maybe he didn't love me."

"He didn't know about you."

"But he could have found out if he'd loved Mama and had come back to see her."

"Ah, but that was impossible."

"Was it?" Hope asked with a childish simplicity that was full of adult wisdom. "Mama said he could not come back as long as Papa Hal was alive, but I wonder."

"This is something you must discuss with your mama and papa."

Stuffing the letter into her apron pocket, Leanor

rose and moved to the counter, where she picked up her bowl of potatoes. She rested a moment, holding her hand over her chest, breathing quietly until the tightness in her chest dissipated. Sitting down, she began to peel them.

"I heard Mr. Wallis telling Antonio that my papa was guilty of murdering lots of people so he could have the treasure they were carrying from Mexico to New Orleans."

"You cannot believe all Mr. Wallis says. He's a lawyer, and they mishandle the truth."

"Mishandle the truth!" Hope leaned back and grinned at her nanny. "I like it when you say things like that, Leanor."

"And I like it when you are happy. Now, we must move quickly if we're going to have the fiesta planned in time for your mama and papa's home-coming."

"I'm not going to wear that dress Mr. Wallis bought for my birthday," Hope declared.

"It's a pretty one," Leanor said.

"I don't like it. It has so many ruffles that if I wore it, I'd look like one of those silly dolls in the dry goods store in El Paso."

"Dolls are not silly," Leanor said. "And the dress looks beautiful on you, and you look beautiful in it."

"Can you see me riding Grandee in that dress?" Hope scoffed. "Or roping calves."

"There is more to life, *mi hija*, than riding your horse and roping cows. One of these days you will discover that for yourself."

"Not if it means being like Agnes Jennings."

"Agnes is not such a bad little girl."

"Yes, she is, too," Hope exclaimed. "Yesterday at school she said Mama was a whore and that her

201

mama and papa wouldn't ever come to see us again. Her mama doesn't want her to play with me."

"*Dios mía!*" A sharp pain sliced through Leanor's chest. She gasped, then dropped the paring knife into the bowl and placed it on the table. Her darling girl. *Niña de los ojos.* She pulled Hope to her. "We know what kind of woman your mama is, don't we?"

Hope's eyes misted. "But other people don't think she's good."

"What other people think does not matter, *niña de los ojos.* We know what the child says about your mother is not true. That's all that matters."

"Agnes always wears ruffled dresses like the one Mr. Wallis gave me." Hope lowered her head and stared at the toe of her boot. She lightly kicked at the table leg. "I'm not going to wear ruffles."

"No," Leanor said, her gaze slowly moving from the checkered shirt, down the brown trousers, to the boots, "you will not, *la niña de la corazón mía.*"

No, child of my heart, you will not wear ruffles.

"Hope doesn't like ruffles."

Floryn eyed the green and white gingham dress doubtfully. She really did not want Cord to buy the dress. While Floryn had set aside some of the money she borrowed from Lyle Hackett to buy Hope clothes, she had to be frugal and buy those Hope would get the most wear out of, and the child certainly would not wear this dress. But Floryn could not tell Cord this without confessing that she had an extremely large outstanding debt. Not that she was worried about it. By the time the note came due she would have the horses to Lyle, and come next spring she would have the foals. He would get his pick of them.

"Shall we buy her something else?" Floryn said.

"No, I want to buy this," he answered. "She may surprise us one of these days by deciding she wants to wear something besides trousers and shirts." Cord handed the garment to the store owner—a plainly dressed woman who patiently followed them around—and looked at Floryn, a teasing glint in his gaze. "It may come as a surprise to you, but little girls have a habit of growing up."

"Do you want the shirts?" the woman asked.

"Yes," Floryn answered, looking at the items she must have, "and the socks and sewing notions I selected and set on the counter."

"Floryn," Cord said. "Look at this."

She turned to see him walking toward her, holding up a small leather vest, quite similar to the one he purchased for himself in Huntsville. A strange smile touched his lips.

"Who does this remind you of?"

"Jason." She reached out to feel the soft, worked leather.

"If you'll take that thing, I'll give you a real good price on it," the woman said. "That was a special order, and the man was shot dead before he could pay for it. Ain't been another through to buy it who's as small as he was."

"Let's buy Hope two shirts instead of three, so we can get this," he said.

"Nobody's been willing to buy it for their kids."

"I am," Floryn said crisply, pushing aside worries about money, thinking about the little boy who wanted a black vest like Cord's but who did not

203

have the money to buy one. "We'll take it."

"Wrap it separately for mailing," Cord said. Moving to the counter, he picked up a pencil and pad and wrote a note to Jason for enclosure in the package.

When he returned to where Floryn stood, the store owner remained behind the counter.

Floryn said, "I'd like to see Jason. I think of him often and sort of worry about him. He's so determined to be tough."

"I think about him, too," Cord said as he and Floryn wandered through the store. "I understand how he feels. My dad died when I was quite young, leaving my mother and me alone. A loss like that forces you to change. By years you're reckoned a little boy, but in responsibility you're not. You're a man."

"You never talked much about yourself," Floryn said, surprised at his mentioning something so personal to her. "I always wondered why your mother didn't come to Hal. He often spoke of you and her. He would have taken care of you."

"For some reason my mother never liked Hal and she didn't want to be dependent on him. She chose to return to Philadelphia to be near her stepsister. She took in sewing and washing and I did odd jobs while I finished my schooling." He grinned at her. "Can you imagine? My mother actually wanted me to become a physician."

"Why didn't you?"

"It takes special people to be doctors," he said. "People who have tough souls but gentle natures. Me, I'm just a warrior, primitive in soul and nature, but I didn't even have a chance to prove my mettle in the army."

204

"That's why you organized the Donaldson Dragoons."

"I guess." Again he lost himself to memories. "My mother had grown weaker through the years, having lost the will to live after my father died. When I was seventeen, she caught pneumonia and didn't pull through. After she died, I felt like it was time to move on. Aunt Linney wanted me to stay but understood I needed to be on my own. So I headed west, ending up in San Francisco where I eventually started an armed guard service."

"And from there to Donaldsonville and the Fancy Lady."

"From there to prison," he added.

By now they had returned to the material a second time, and Floryn again looked at a piece of teal blue taffeta. It was the most beautiful piece of material she had seen in a long while. She ran her hand back and forth over it. Cord reached out and pulled closer another bolt of material that was a darker shade of the same color.

"They look good together, don't they?" he asked.

"Yes. I'd buy it if we weren't running low on money." She pushed the material aside and reached for the pattern book, flipping through the pages.

"If we weren't buying as much for Hope, we could afford this for you. Let's get her the dress and one shirt."

"How about two shirts and no dress?" Floryn suggested.

"I'm buying the dress."

Feeling a little guilty about the clothing she had splurged on prior to her trip to see him, Floryn said, "Hope needs the clothes more than I do."

"I don't have to get Jason the vest," he said. "That would pay for the material."

"No, I want him to have it." She remembered the round, freckled face peering so worshipfully into Cord's. "Probably by the time I need a special dress, more material will have arrived. Probably prettier material, too."

Floryn did not mind being a little unwise in her spending when it came to the children, but she would not spend on herself.

"What about want?" Cord asked.

Floryn looked at him blankly.

"You'll buy a dress if you need it, you said. Why not buy one simply because you want it?"

"My wants"—she paused, knowing he would misconstrue her admission—"have been the Fancy Lady and my daughter."

Again she thought of her clothing extravagance, but did not mention it. Cord would see the gesture as a self-serving one, as a move on her part to get the ranch by hook or crook, which in a way it was. She had been foolish enough to think she could have it all—the ranch, her daughter, and the man she loved. Now she was beginning to wonder if she would have any of it. Leaving him standing at the counter, she slowly meandered to the front of the store where she gazed out the window onto the street.

The closer they came to home, the more her fears grew. She felt as if all she wanted, all she had worked for—Hope and the ranch—were slipping out of her hands. No matter how careful she was, how diligently she fought, she was losing. Concerns she had left behind returned to haunt her. She would have to face them soon, and so would Cord. She had no doubt about herself, but she worried about his reaction.

She felt his presence before she heard him say, "I seem to remember Hal's showering you with gifts."

"He did at first."

"When did he stop buying for you? When he learned about you and me?"

"Not really. Both of us wanted to buy for Hope. Everything else went back into the ranch: buying our starter herds, learning new ways to plant and irrigate, learning about new crops, and buying more land. Toward the last, he hated me too much to want to buy me anything, and by that time it didn't matter to me anyway."

"Gifts always matter," he contradicted. "It means something to know that someone — anyone — thinks enough of you to buy you a present. And speaking of presents and since we're buying for Hope and Jason—" He held up a blue ribbon. "I thought maybe you'd find some use for this. It doesn't exactly match your hair or your eyes, but you said they should match the colors in your clothes."

"Thank you," she murmured. "It's beautiful. I have a dress that will go with this perfectly. I'll wear it at the fiesta when we arrive home."

"Is this a belated celebration for the Fourth of July or something special?" he asked.

"I'm sure they celebrated the Fourth with a fiesta, but they will have another one when we arrive. And it will be most special. Every time I'm away, my return is celebrated with one. Any excuse for playing." Her smile softened her words. "This trip will be no exception. Well, yes, this will be the exception. They'll be thinking about you also. Isn't that a nice feeling? To know they're planning a celebration in honor of our return?"

Before Cord answered, the store owner patted their stack of purchases and called out, "Here you are. Everything's packed and ready to go."

Cord and Floryn returned to the counter where they paid for their goods. Their arms full, they left the dry goods store to walk leisurely toward their hotel.

"We're on the last leg of our trip," Floryn murmured. "Before daybreak we leave for Donaldsonville where we'll be met by Antonio, and from there to the ranch."

Floryn sighed as they disembarked from a stage for the final time. She flexed her shoulders and gazed around at the small town of Donaldsonville, dawn slowly dissipating the grayness of night. "We'll soon be home, Cord."

"*Patrona!*" A small, wiry Mexican, his mustached face wreathed in a smile and almost hidden beneath the shadow of the massive *sombrero* he wore, walked toward her. His spurs jingled with each step he took.

"Antonio!" Floryn exclaimed, her gaze eagerly searching for her daughter. "I'm so glad to see you."

"And perhaps the buggy with the padded leather seats?" Ebony eyes twinkled as he glanced from the dust-covered stagecoach to her.

Floryn laughed. "And the buggy."

"I am glad to see you, *Patrona.*" Antonio swept his *sombrero* from his head and bowed with a graceful flourish. "Without you there is no Fancy Lady. You have been gone far too long."

"Thank you, Antonio. I am glad to be home,"

Floryn said and glanced about. "Is Hope with you? I thought perhaps she would ride in with you."

"*La niña* is fine," he said. "She felt she was needed at the ranch today to help Leanor prepare for your arrival."

"Yes," Floryn murmured, her disappointment dampening the joy of her arrival. "I suppose so."

She turned, bumping into Cord, and realized she had been remiss in making introductions.

"Antonio, may I present my husband? Cord, this is Antonio Perez, the *gran vaquero* of the Fancy Lady."

"*Señor.*" The Mexican spoke politely, but his smile was gone. "Welcome to the Fancy Lady."

"Thank you, Antonio."

As they shook hands, Antonio gave Cord a long, measured look, the black eyes alert, shrewd.

"I have heard much about you," Cord said.

Antonio smiled slightly and nodded his head. Then he turned to Floryn. "You are ready now?"

"Yes."

The warm smile returned to his face. "Then we shall go. We have much celebration planned for you."

"A fiesta," she said.

Laughing, he nodded and began to load the luggage onto the buggy. "One like you have not seen before, *Patrona*. Leanor, Hope, and I planned it, but the ladies, they outdid me this time. The prizes for the tournament are really *magnifico*." He touched the tips of his fingers to his lips and threw a kiss.

"If Hope helped to select the prizes, I can imagine what they will be," Floryn said.

"Ah," he drawled and rolled his eyes, "that is true."

"Antonio, what has she chosen?"

He shook his head. "I promised I would not tell, *Patrona.*"

"Tell me," Floryn said softly. "I won't let Hope know."

Shaking his head, Antonio laughed softly. *"La niña* can tell you when you get home. That's her secret, *Patrona."* He turned to Cord. *"Señor,* you will enjoy the festivities, yes. We will have a tournament and horse racing, a barbecue dinner followed by a big dance."

"What kind of tournament?" Cord asked.

"Spearing for rings," Floryn explained. "An old game brought to America from Ireland."

"Sí," Antonio said with flourish. "When the Irish migrated to Spain in the late 1600s and early 1700s as a result of English persecution, they brought the game with them. We *mexicanos* quickly adopted it as ours and have labeled it *Los Anillos de los Patrones."*

"Rings of the Masters," Floryn murmured, then said, "It is a game for superior horsemen. Each carries a six to eight-foot sharpened pike and rides full tilt for rings that hang by ropes from eight posts spaced about forty feet apart."

"Sounds interesting," Cord drawled.

"Sí," Antonio answered, "and requires great skill. The prize goes to the horsemen who can spear the most rings in the shortest period of time. It is *muy bien, Señor.* You will compete, yes?"

Cord laughed quietly. "Probably I shall watch."

"If *El Patrón* is able, he should always lead his *vaqueros* in the competition," the Mexican informed him stiffly.

Floryn took exception to Antonio's announcement and said quickly, rather defensively, "I have always led the *vaqueros* in the competition. I see no reason why I should not do so this time. I am *La Patrona*."

An enigmatic gleam in his eyes, Cord said, "I'm sure, my dear, if you think about it, you will see the reason behind Antonio's statement."

Floryn did, only too well. And now she knew Cord understood the *gran vaquero's* message also.

"In the past," Cord continued, "because of his physical handicap, *El Patrón* was unable to lead his *vaqueros*. That is no longer true. At this fiesta *El Patrón* can lead his *vaqueros* and should."

Again Floryn had the sinking feeling she was losing the ranch, if not the ranch itself, her position. Even Antonio seemed to be in conspiracy against her.

"Don't look so glum," Cord said. "It's only a game."

"Is it?" she countered.

When Cord's hands closed about Floryn's waist so that he could lift her into the buggy, she tried to twist away from him. His clasp tightened, and he laughed softly.

"Everything is going according to the plan you set in action," he murmured, a smugness in his voice that Floryn resented. "Relax and flow with it, sweetheart."

Moving away from him as soon as she could, Floryn settled into the soft, padded seat. Why must she feel so confused when she was with Cord? She wanted his touch because it made her feel good. She did not want his touch because it made her feel good. She wanted him to be kind and gentle and teasing because it drew her to him, made her remember why she loved him. She wanted him to be brusque and harsh because then she kept

211

her distance, she kept her guard up.

Breathing deeply, grateful for the clean, dry air, grateful he was not touching her presently and she could think clearly, she sat back and closed her eyes. On the one hand, she was glad to be home. She had missed her daughter and wanted to see her. On the other hand, Floryn regretted that she must face the problems she had left behind.

Many people thought West Texas was stark and ugly, but she loved it. True, the land could be hard, but it was always fair. If you loved and took care of it, she thought, it loved and took care of you.

Antonio gave the command, and the buggy lurched forward. At the same time, Floryn pushed her worries behind. She opened her eyes, ready to face whatever the future held, ready to fight for what she wanted, confident of winning.

She had to win. Hope's entire future depended on Floryn, and she promised herself that her daughter, unlike herself, would never be an abandoned child at the mercy of the world.

Fifteen

Prison had never erased Cord's confidence in himself, but it had blurred his concept of self. In restricting trust only to himself, he had narrowed his world. When Floryn had first made her proposition to him, he had been thinking like a convict, like a victim of fate. His thoughts had been only of his freedom, only of clearing his name.

But since the morning in San Antonio when Floryn had willingly asked him to make love to her, he had been thinking about their lives together. Although he did not think about it frequently, he realized that by making love that morning, their relationship had subtly changed. He had manipulated their first consummation after marriage, and it had been no great feat. Both of them were passionate people who gave in to mutual desire. The morning after her accident, she had asked him to make love to her. She had been the assertive partner, not him.

He was unclear of the exact meaning or the true nature of their relationship, but during the journey they had proved they were compatible. They had enjoyed one another's company, and they had some common goals when it came to running the ranch.

The longer he was away from Huntsville, away from the memories of the past nine years, the more he thought about a future, a future with him and

Floryn and Hope. San Antonio had been a turning point for him. As he had nursed Floryn, he realized how much she had come to mean to him. He had begun thinking like a husband, a father, and a provider for his family. He was beginning to broaden his horizons; he was beginning to trust others.

A little surprised by the direction of his thoughts, certainly embarrassed, he smiled to himself. Freedom was heady; it caused a man to think oddly. But he loved freedom; he loved the headiness. He gazed around, drinking in the beauty of the wide open spaces and freedom. Freedom. A wonderful concept, an even more wonderful reality.

The sun on his face, the brush of the wind against his body, Cord rested the back of his head on the soft, padded buggy seat and gazed up at strings of wispy clouds against a backdrop of pure blue sky. In the distance, however, were low, slow-moving, gray clouds, a sign of an impending summer shower. But even that was wonderful and free, an integral part of nature.

The team labored up a foothill, the buggy toppling first this way, then that as the wheels rolled over and around large rocks. When they reached a copse of scrub oaks and mesquites at the top of the incline, Antonio stopped the team.

As never before in his life, Cord appreciated the West Texas summer. He listened to the sighing of the wind, the rustle of the leaves, the chirrups of the insects, the swish of the horses' tails. Sounds he had never really thought about, never really heard or regarded. Sounds he would never take for granted again. Here he was at peace with the world.

"Es bonita, sí?" Antonio said.

"Yes." Floryn gazed into the valley below. "It is beautiful. No matter how prepared I think I am for

214

it, I'm always unprepared for its beauty. I'm surprised all over again."

Cord said nothing, for he, too, was awed with the beauty surrounding him. In the valley below sat the Fancy Lady. It was exactly as he had remembered it, as he had dreamed about and fantasized it. A Mexican *hacienda* — a white native stone building with a red tiled roof — it spread regally amid several groves of trees. Here and there were patches of brightly colored native flowers in neat, well-tended gardens.

"Is it as you remembered, Cord?" Floryn asked.

"Yes."

He uttered the one word only. To say more would have revealed his feelings . . . something he was not prepared to do yet, perhaps never would be.

The buggy moved again, and they slowly descended the foothill. For the first time since he had been released from prison, Cord truly felt like a free man. When Floryn had promised him he could put his past far behind him once he was away from Huntsville, he had thought she was mistaken. Not now. At this moment, he knew it was possible.

As the buggy moved toward the *hacienda*, he looked over his shoulder to see a sunbeam breaking through the thickly leaved trees. Like a golden curtain, it magically dropped on his past. He slowly turned his head and looked forward. In front of him lay the future, bright and beckoning. For the first time he felt optimistic about his future, one that included Floryn and Hope.

Soon they were in the shaded driveway, the fragrance of native flowers lazily drifting to them. The buggy came to a stop in front of the *hacienda*, in front of an arbor that was covered with thick, green vines. Suspended from the top of the wooden frame was a yard swing.

Mesmerized, Cord stared at it. The sounds and odors and sights of spring surrounded him as they had done the first day he had arrived at the ranch. Memories rushed in on him.

Floryn, wearing a white dress, had been sitting in the swing, her honey-gold hair hanging loose about her face and shoulders. On hearing his horse approach, she had looked up, and he found himself staring into the face of an angel. She was the most beautiful woman he had ever seen, and he had fallen in love with her at first sight.

Cord felt Floryn's hand on his arm, and he turned to gaze into her face, into honey-gold eyes that were still the most beautiful he had ever seen. One look at her countenance, at the softness of her eyes, told him that she, too, was reliving the moment they had first met.

"Mira, Patrona!" Antonio exclaimed, rudely intruding on an almost sacred recollection. "Look all about you. We are ready for the celebration, yes?"

Cord and Floryn remembered a celebration of love long ago.

"Something is wrong, *Patrona?*" Antonio guided the team up the tree-lined lane to the house. *"Señor,* something is wrong?"

Cord continued to gaze into Floryn's eyes. Yes, he thought sadly, something was wrong. His optimism faded. Time had passed, and Hal was deceased. Yet the Fancy Lady was Hal's ranch, not his. Cord had never belonged here, even less now. Floryn was Hal's wife, not his. True, she had given her body to him, but not really, certainly not fully, her heart or love.

"You are not pleased?" Antonio persisted.

Cord tore his gaze from Floryn; both looked at the driver.

"No," she said.

Antonio was crestfallen.

"I mean, yes." Looking confused, she shook her head. "Forgive me, Antonio. I am tired."

"And you, *Señor*," the *gran vaquero* said, "do you like?"

"Yes," Cord said quietly.

He sniffed the odor of burning mesquite and barbecue meat. He heard the shouts and laughter of the workers. Everyone was festive and in the mood for a fiesta. Even the lawn. Hanging from the branches of the oak trees, Chinese lanterns, gilded in polished brass and inset with colored glass jewels, swayed in the early morning breeze. One in particular caught Cord's attention. The bright red glass, cut like the ruby, gleamed in the sunlight to remind him of the pendant, of the way it swayed when he held it by the chain.

The pendant. A heaviness settled on his heart. For several hours he had forgotten about it altogether. That was strange because it had been his one constant thought throughout his imprisonment, his one hold to sanity. He was disappointed that the only clue he had to clear his name was gone. Its theft served only to strengthen his resolve to discover the pendant's secret, although its being gone might prove to make his task more difficult.

"Always before, *Patrona*, we planned the celebration for you alone." Antonio cut his gaze at Cord. "But this fiesta, she is special. We planned it for *Señor. Mira!* Look over there!" The Mexican pointed. "That is the tournament field."

Cord looked in the distance to see the posts that sat about forty feet apart. Ropes were attached to the top of each post, in the fashion of a maypole, and attached to the end of each was a ring. Leaning against a frame were about twenty to thirty

217

sharpened pikes, all of them brightly painted.

"This is *Señor* Cord's fiesta," Antonio announced proudly. "Perhaps it shall also be *la fiesta del patrón.*"

"Of course," Floryn said, "for *El Patrón.* He's the new owner of the Fancy Lady." She cut her eyes, refusing to meet Cord's gaze.

"Our daughter owns half," Cord said dryly.

"You control it," she said.

Cord was irritated because Floryn's thoughts were always on the ranch. They shared moments of togetherness but always she reverted to her true self. He ought to know by now that her angelic appearance was a disguise. She was totally self-centered, her one and only thought the Fancy Lady. It was to the ranch Floryn had pledged her forever love, not to him. But, he wondered, how could he fault Floryn when he, too, was encumbered by a past?

Antonio stopped the buckboard, and Cord leaped down. As he had done so many times during their journey from Huntsville, his hands circled Floryn's waist and, disregarding her scowl, he swung her down. Her feet had no sooner touched the ground than the front door opened, and an older woman— her hair plaited and coiled around her head in coronet style—rushed toward them.

"Floryn!" she called. *"Mi hija,* it is good that you are home. We have missed you, yes."

"I've missed you." Floryn hugged the woman, pressing her cheek against her shoulder. When she lifted her head, she looked around. "Where is Hope?"

"Riding," Leanor said, looking apologetic.

"Out riding?" Floryn's voice was dull with disappointment. "Why?" she demanded. "She knew we were arriving today."

Leanor said gently, "Don't be angry. She's a little girl, and she's nervous about seeing . . . you."

218

"I'm not angry," Floryn protested, "I'm—"

"You are worried, yes, and a little disappointed. I understand." Black eyes softened with sympathy.

"Hope wasn't ready to meet me, was she?" Cord said and walked to the arbor. With one hand he gently pushed the swing. His back to the housekeeper, he heard her answer.

"No, *Señor*, she was not."

"Cord," Floryn said, "this is Leanor Santico. The housekeeper, Hope's nanny, and my dearest friend."

"I'm glad to make your acquaintance, Leanor," Cord said. "Floryn thinks highly of you."

Leanor beamed. "I think highly of her, *Señor*. I apologize that Hope is not here to greet you. It is my fault that she is not. I knew she was nervous and when she asked if she could go riding, I gave her permission. I felt that you and Floryn would need some time to yourselves, and I knew the child did. Please, be gentle with her. She is skittish like a young colt, yes?"

"I will," Cord promised.

"Gracias." Leanor clasped her hands together. "I love the child as if she were my own, *Señor*. I was the midwife who delivered her, my hands were the first to hold her, and I have cared for her ever since."

Cord nodded, and the two of them gazed at each other. Cord allowed the ebony eyes to search his countenance for answers to unasked questions. Finally when she seemed to be satisfied with what she saw, she smiled. He did, too.

She said, "Now, I must go. I have much to do if we're to be ready for the fiesta this afternoon."

"I will bring up the luggage," Antonio said, then asked Cord, "Are you staying in *Patrón* Hal's rooms?"

Master Hal's rooms! Although he had been married to Floryn for over a month, Cord did not feel a part of a family. When it suited Floryn, he was her husband or Hope's father. Mostly he was helping Floryn fulfill her ambitions.

Floryn was *La Patrona,* Hal *El Patrón.* Cord doubted he would ever fit into life at the Fancy Lady, but he sure as hell was going to give it a whirl.

Earlier as they had ridden up the side of the foothill, he felt for the first time that he was no longer a convict, no longer the scourge of society, no longer a victim of circumstances beyond his control. He felt for the first time in ten years that he was master of his destiny. He liked the feeling and would not easily let it go.

"*Señor?*" Antonio said. "Where shall I put the luggage?"

"I will share my wife's suite."

With a brief nod, Antonio called several *vaqueros* and gave them instructions. Floryn led the way into the house, stopping in the large foyer.

"I have your rooms prepared." Leanor opened the door at the end of the corridor. "I thought you would wish to rest before the festivities."

"Yes, thank you." Floryn picked up the small stack of mail that had accumulated during her absence and opened them one by one.

As she read, Cord walked through the parlor — a large room with a fireplace and several groupings of chairs and sofas — then peered into the study. With the exception of new rugs and curtains and reupholstered furniture, it had changed little during the passing years.

He walked to the built-in bookcase and stared at the volumes of books. Hal had loved to read and had an extensive library. Cord searched for some of the books he had read when he was here before.

From the corridor he heard Antonio say, "*Patrona,*

Señor Phillips wants to know whether you're going to have a meeting of the ranchers sometime during the fiesta?"

Cord moved out of the study into the hallway.

"No," Floryn said, "I think not. I'm rather tired and want some time to gather my thoughts before we get together. Send Pedro over there now to tell him we'll meet tomorrow afternoon about three o'clock. Afterward we'll have dinner here."

"*Sí, Patrona,*" Antonio said.

Although Floryn's plans did not bother him, Cord was a little irritated that she had not consulted him before making the decision. But he said nothing. In the past she had had to make the decisions on her own, and it would take her some time to get accustomed to sharing authority with him. However, he determined to talk to her about it later in private. Now that they were married, now that he was here, he was going to be instrumental in the managing of the ranch.

She tore open another envelope and gasped when she began to read. Holding the letter in one hand, she raised the other to her mouth.

"Bad news?" Cord asked.

She glanced at him in question. "I—I beg your pardon."

"You're frowning," he said. "Is something wrong?"

"No," she murmured, then added more emphatically, "No." She looked down, crumpled the letter in her fist and shoved it forcibly into her pocket.

"Bad news?" he persisted.

Looking visibly shaken, she shook her head. From the tray she picked up the other mail. "Leanor sent out invitations for the fiesta. These three have declined in writing. Alonzo Jennings, owner of the mercantile company. Henry Beeson, feed store.

221

Tidwell Jones, doctor. Hal made sure that my reputation was ruined. Donaldsonville high society will have nothing to do with me, and they take great pleasure in letting me know it."

"Are we going to have any guests at our fiesta?" Cord asked.

Floryn laughed softly. "Oh, yes. All the surrounding ranchers, the *vaqueros* and ranch hands, and many of the townspeople. We'll have a crowd." But not Lyle and Claudine Hackett!

At the kitchen door Leanor halted and turned. "Do you wish to have lunch served in the dining room or in the master suite, Floryn?"

"In our rooms," Cord answered, not caring that Floryn cast him a glance of reproof. "We want an early lunch served at eleven. If we haven't seen Hope by that time and you have, tell her that we want her to join us."

Leanor nodded.

"Your guests will be arriving at two o'clock," she said. "We have planned games and competitions for the afternoon, a barbecue dinner, and dancing for the evening. When will you want your baths?"

"At one," he answered.

After the door closed behind Leanor, Floryn, holding the letters in her hand, walked to the stairs. Cord remained in the opened doorway where he pulled his watch from its pocket.

"We have several hours before lunch. I'm going to walk around for a while." His gaze strayed to the barn. "Maybe I'll take a ride."

Cord savored the feel of the powerful horse beneath him, the smooth unwinding of muscle. He leaned forward and patted the horse's neck. It had been nine years since he had enjoyed riding such a choice mount. Antonio told him that Floryn had chosen this one especially for him. She had remembered his preference for roans. Again the summer wind whipped against him to brush away signs of his incarceration, reinforcing freedom, somehow returning him to his youth.

His gaze scanned the blue sky to the approaching rain clouds; it rested on indomitable mountains that circled the Fancy Lady. This was his domain now; his to administer and to take care of. He rode not really caring where he went, as long as he traveled, as long as he was free. He followed the meandering creek, brought to life each year by the spring rains, dried out by the summer sun.

He crossed onto the other bank. He rode through harsh country, cactus and mesquite bushes brushing against his trouser legs, the sun beating down relentlessly. He stopped every now and then beneath the stooping boughs of scrub oaks and mesquites. Then he rode into a meadow. A beautiful green meadow, its centerpiece being an old oak tree with branches spread out in majestic splendor.

Their meadow. His and Floryn's.

He slowed the roan. This is where he was headed all the time. The spot he had dreamed about during the past years, that had almost become a shrine of all that freedom stood for.

He hitched the horse and walked to the tree, guided more by memory than by sight. The words that he had carved so long ago were clearly visible and were as overpowering as the memories. He walked closer and as Floryn had done so many years ago, he traced the words, then pressed his palm against the pledge.

"Forever love. June, 1855," he could hear Floryn say.

Cord withdrew his hand.

"Forever love." Floryn's voice was louder, a little more bitter this time. "How ironic!"

That was no voice from the past. Floryn was here . . . in the meadow with him. He turned and thought he had stepped back into the past. He was seeing the woman with whom he had fallen in love. She wore a dark brown, split riding skirt with a blouse almost the same color as her eyes. Her hair, clasped with a brown ribbon at the nape of her neck, hung loose down her back. She pulled off her broad-brimmed hat and brushed her hand through the curls that framed her face.

But this time their roles were reversed. Cord was the nostalgic romantic. Floryn the embittered cynic.

"You're staring at me rather oddly," she said.

"I was surprised to see you."

She walked closer to the tree. "I didn't follow you."

"I didn't think you did, but I wouldn't have minded. I'm glad you're here."

Rubbing her toe against an exposed root, she said, "I wanted to get away for a few minutes, and this is my favorite place. I had—no idea you would come here."

"It just happened."

Cord noticed she kept her distance from him, as if she were afraid of him. Certainly her gaze never quite collided with his.

"It seems like only yesterday that we made our pledge, yet it seems like a lifetime." As she had done that summer long ago, she touched the carvings on the tree. She outlined the words. When she spoke, her voice had a faraway wistfulness to it. "I never dreamed our lives would turn out the way they have.

224

I thought love conquered all. I guess that's the romantic imaginings of first love. Maybe the arrogance of youth."

Feeling vulnerable, Cord turned his back to her, his gaze swinging from the meadow covered in red Indian paintbrushes—the blanket on which they had lain when they first made love—to the sprawling mountain range. Puffy, gray clouds swirled by the sun, momentarily casting the earth in shadow.

"We lost something precious, Cord. Something we'll never regain . . . even if we wanted to."

"No, we'll never regain it. We can only have lost it, Floryn, if we had it. Did we ever have it?"

She shrugged.

"What we shared that summer was wonderful," he confessed, "but it was made even more wonderful because each of us was forbidden fruit for the other."

"In other words, stolen sugar is sweetest."

"Something like that."

A gust of wind blew around them, tearing strands of hair from the confines of Floryn's ribbon and whipping it against her cheek. Gazing into those beautiful honey-gold eyes, drawn by the promise of past memories, driven by the fear that they would never have more than a few stolen moments, Cord moved closer to her. He brushed the hair from her face. Her lips trembled; her eyes shimmered.

Again the summer wind kissed them. He leaned down. From her cheek he kissed away a tear. From her forehead, he brushed a lock of hair. The wind picked up momentum, rustling through the grass and trees. Droplets of rain splattered on them.

"We're going to get wet," he said, his words a close repetition of those Floryn had spoken ten years ago.

"Do you mind?" she asked.

"No. I thought you might."

They melded into an embrace, a shared embrace. Her head lifted; his lowered, and their lips touched — softly, warmly — in the most glorious kiss Cord had ever experienced. Although totally lacking in passion, their kiss was filled with foreverness. It transcended time, returned him to youth and wistfulness. Infused him with the courage to dream and to conquer.

Maybe . . . just maybe they could recapture what they had once shared. He lifted his mouth from hers to gaze at the tears, blending with the rain, to stream down her cheeks.

"Floryn, maybe we can—"

"I—I thought we could, too." He saw no tears, but knew she was crying. The kind of crying that defied tears, that came from the soul. "But—there's so much—"

Shaking her head, she pushed away from him, her eyes sad. She stared at him for only a second before she turned and raced to the bush where she had tethered her horse.

"Floryn!" Cord ran after her. By the time he reached her, she was galloping away.

His boot caught on a root that was slippery from the rain. He stumbled and fell to the ground, then lay there, watching the woman he loved riding away, leaving him alone. He thought he had experienced every facet of loneliness imaginable during the past nine years, but nothing compared to the anguish he felt now. He was more alone than he had ever been during his lifetime.

As he had done to her ten years ago, she did to him.

The rain splattering against her hat, Hope stood on the hillside and watched her mother ride off. Re-

226

luctantly her gaze returned to the man who now stood beneath the magical, forever tree. She hated him. He had no right to kiss her mama. No right whatsoever.

Sixteen

Long after Floryn had galloped away, long after the summer rain ceased to fall, Cord remained in the meadow, thinking. No matter how selfish he might believe Floryn, the Fancy Lady did rightfully belong to her, not to him. She had spoken the truth when she said she was *La Patrona*. She was the one who had sculpted and molded it into what it was, not him, not Hal.

As he had no right to the ranch, Cord had no right to Floryn either. She belonged to the Fancy Lady. That was her first love and always would be. So much did she identify with the ranch that Cord, at times, found himself believing they were one and the same, certainly they were inseparable.

He heard a noise and looked up to see a rider approaching. Thinking it was Floryn returning, his heart skipped a beat. But closer scrutiny revealed that the figure was too small to be hers. Small enough to be a child. Dare he believe it was Hope? The brim of the hat the rider wore was pulled low so he could not see a face, so he could not tell if it were a boy or girl.

Horse and rider drew nearer, and he saw a black braid hanging over each of the rider's shoulders. A girl. Hope? His daughter? She lifted her head, and he saw her. Yes, this was his daughter. The morning sun shone on a beautiful, somber face that was dominated by large brown eyes. They stared at him, at the tree, then at him again.

Stopping the gray, she smoothly slid out of the saddle and tied the reins to a nearby bush. With a carriage and gait like that of her mother, she walked toward Cord, stopping when she stood a few feet from him. She wore a checkered shirt and denim trousers tucked into knee-high boots. In her right hand she held a riding crop which she lightly tapped against her leg.

"You're Hope," he said.

She stared, openly and curiously, and the silence grew between them. Finally she said, "You're wet."

"So are you."

She nodded. "I like being out in a summer rain."

"Me, too."

"Leanor always worries about the rain interfering with her plans. Today she's worried about the fiesta."

"As brightly as the sun is shining now, I don't think she has anything to worry about. Everything should be fairly dry in a couple of hours."

"It wouldn't matter," Hope said. "We'd have the fiesta if we had to tromp around in mud."

He asked, "Do you know who I am?"

She nodded. "I wondered what you looked like."

"What do you think?"

She cocked her head to the side, squinted her eyes, and studied him. Finally with childish simplicity, she said, "I like the patch. What happened to your eye?"

Keeping the conversation on an objective footing which the child seemed to want and which Cord appreciated, he related the events to her, leaving out the goriest of details, yet answering any questions she asked with direct honesty. He imagined she had heard rumors from various and sundry people, and he wanted her to hear the truth from him.

"The fiesta is for you," she announced. "You're supposed to lead the *vaqueros* in the tournament of the rings."

He nodded.

"Have you ever played the game before?"

"Not this one, but I've played similar ones."

"With only one eye can you see the rings well enough to spear them?"

"It's going to be tricky, but I think I can manage."

"If you don't, the *vaqueros* will laugh at you."

"And if I do, I'll have a prize to give you. That is, if you'll give me your favor."

"What's that?" she asked.

"A scarf or something of yours that will bring me luck."

"Are you going to wear a favor from Mama?"

Cord grinned. "I can't imagine your mama letting me be her champion, can you?"

Hope grinned back at him and shook her head. "Mama is good. She's a champion herself. She always wins."

"Maybe this time she won't."

"Probably she will." Hope studied him before she asked, "May I touch the patch?"

Cord's first inclination was to say no, but he bit back the words. Slowly he knelt in front of his daughter and let her stare into his face. She stepped closer, and he could see the sunbeams dancing in loose strands of black hair. Eventually a small hand lifted and an index finger tentatively touched the black leather.

"It's soft," she said.

"It had to be to keep from rubbing my face raw."

"I wouldn't like to be in prison." She drew back her hand and clasped them behind her back. "I never want to be away from the Fancy Lady. I love it here."

"You may have to leave one of these days." He rose.

"I won't. This is my home. It belongs to Mama and me."

"What about your education?"

"I go to school here." Her voice was hard.

"Probably when you're older you'll want to go

230

to a finishing school in New Orleans or back East."

"I can be finished here." Her brown eyes flashed angrily. "What you're really saying is that you're *El Patrón* now, and you have the right to send me away."

"No, Hope, I'm not saying that," Cord corrected. "If I had a mind to send you away, I would do so by the authority of being your father, not *El Patrón*."

Her eyes misted; her chin trembled. "You may be my father, but you aren't the boss or my papa. Papa was *El Patrón,* and everybody around here knows it. You're not going to make me go anywhere."

"I am your papa," he said, "but I don't intend to send you away. If you go, it'll be your choice."

"I don't choose. Half this ranch belongs to me, and I'm going to keep it. It's mine. Do you hear me? Mine."

Although Hope's features were dark like his, she was her mother's child. Her stance, her almost vehement love of the ranch, the possessive and authoritative tone of her voice. All of this was Floryn. Like her mother, Hope identified herself with the ranch.

"I'm here to make sure you get to keep the Fancy Lady."

Hope raked him over with a skeptical gaze. "You're here because of my mama, not me. I saw you kiss her."

He returned her gaze. This time it was he who was silent.

"You've kissed her lots of times, haven't you?"

"Yes, and I hope to kiss her many more times."

Hope strolled to the tree and gazed at the words. "Did you love Mama?"

"Yes."

"But you left her."

"Has she told you about it?"

"She said you had to leave, so y'all wouldn't hurt Papa."

Papa! This was the second time she had addressed Hal as Papa, and it hurt Cord. He had argued with

Floryn, telling her that Hope was a stranger to him, her daughter, not his. At the time he had thought he was telling the truth, but the moment he had seen Hope he knew it was not true. Hope was not a stranger to him. She was part of him, his flesh and blood. He knew her. He loved her. She was his daughter. He was her papa.

The Fancy Lady may have belonged to Hal and may now belong to Floryn, but Hope belonged to him. She was his daughter, and by God he would move heaven and earth to keep her.

"I read Mama's letters to you," Hope said. "She told you about me."

"I've read them, too." Cord wanted to reach for the child. She looked so small and frail, so alone. She reminded him of a little bantam, lost among the larger fowls in the chicken yard, yet puffing out her chest and strutting, fighting for her right to be. He wanted to hold her in his arms, to assure her that everything was going to be all right. But more than years separated them.

"When did you read the letters?" she asked.

"When she came to the prison to see me."

"Then was too late. You should have read them when she wrote them."

"I didn't receive them."

"Little girls need their papas."

"I want to be your papa now."

"I'm not a little girl anymore." She gazed at him for a long time before she turned and walked away.

"Hope," he called, "I apologize for not being here for you all these years. If I could undo the past, I would. If you'll give me a chance, I'll make the future better."

"My life is fine without you." Her back to him, she kept walking, lightly slapping the quirt against her leg. "I don't need anyone to make my future better. I'll do it for myself."

He said nothing because he believed her. His daughter was indeed a product of her parents. Proud. Stubborn. Independent. She would make her future better, with or without him. A fear newly born in him was that she would make it without him.

"Mr. Wallis—he's a friend of my Papa's—he said you were returning with Mama." She spoke over her shoulder. "He said you married her so that you could inherit the ranch."

"No."

She turned slowly so they faced each other again. "Why did you marry her?"

"I told you, but you didn't believe me."

"Tell me again." The order, her tone of voice was an exact duplication of Floryn's.

He wanted to smile, but knew she would not understand his amusement. "I want to help you and your mama."

Skepticism was blatant in her expression.

"Also, Hope, I wanted out of prison so I could find the people who wrongfully put me there."

Skepticism was replaced by an I-could-have-told-you look.

"Mr. Wallis said you killed a whole bunch of people and stole their money." The voice was firm in its accusation, but her eyes questioned him.

"Mr. Wallis has told you what people are saying," Cord answered quietly, "but it's not the truth."

Hope grinned. "Leanor says lawyers always mishandle the truth."

Cord returned her grin. "I'd say Leanor is a wise woman."

"Why are people lying about you and saying you kill people and steal money?"

"Because they believe it," he said, "but it's not true. What is true is that I'm an accused killer, Hope, and unless I clear my name I always will be."

233

Briefly, simply Cord told her the story of Sanchia Guilbert and the supposed San Domingo treasure. He answered the questions she posed. For the first time since he had gained his freedom, he wanted desperately for someone—for Hope—for his daughter—to believe in his innocence. He had wanted Floryn to believe in him. Had she not, it would have mattered but not nearly as much as Hope's not believing him.

Hope's believing him, believing in him did matter. He had to clear his name for his daughter's sake as well as for his.

Hope broke a twig from the bush she stood by, and stripped off the leaves one by one. "Does clearing your name and helping Mama and me mean you're going to leave us?"

No, he wanted to say, I'll never leave you. But he knew he must leave until he had settled his past. Unless he left, unless he cleared his name, he could have no future. His being here was the only way to save the Fancy Lady for Hope and Floryn, but his being here also placed both of them in the shadow of his past, placed them in great danger.

"I don't know if you'll understand what I'm about to say—"

She broke the twig in half and threw it to the ground. "When adults say that to children, it means they're about to do or say something wrong but want it to seem like the right thing to say or do. I know you're not going to stay. You never tried to find out if you had a little girl or not, so why should you stay now? I told Leanor you wouldn't."

She walked to where her horse was hitched. Untying the reins, she swung into the saddle. "I knew you didn't care."

"Hope, let me finish what I was going to say."

"No."

234

Long strides carried Cord to the gray. He caught the reins. "You're going to listen to me."

She lifted her right hand, the one that held the quirt, high in the air as if she were going to strike him, and stared into his face. Her pose, her arrogance and superiority, her anger — all were reminiscent of Floryn. He returned the child's stare. She lowered her hand, then yanked the reins from him.

"You can't make me."

She spurred the gray with her knees and galloped away. After riding a distance, she reined in and turned the prancing horse around. "I didn't want Mama to go get you, I don't want you to stay, and I'm not going to give you my favor. I don't want you winning any prizes for me. I don't want any of the prizes."

Her anguished cry echoing in his heart, Cord watched Hope gallop across the meadow. She reminded him of Floryn, reminded him of the wild Texas wind.

First, the woman he loved, now the child he wanted to love rode away and abandoned him.

Disappointed, angry at himself for having handled the situation so poorly, Cord untied his roan and began to walk. What had begun as a business deal, a simple marriage of convenience was turning into a complicated affair, as complicated if not more so than the search for his past. The search for his past meant finding people who had wronged him. This involved his emotions. He had sworn never to care again, yet here he was letting both mother and child enter his heart. Not only was he allowing them to enter his heart, he was allowing them to possess it fully. His involvement was getting deeper and deeper, making it harder for him to extricate himself . . . if the need should ever arise.

Floryn's words returned to haunt him. Hope was the innocent casualty of this entire set of events, the ones

235

he and Floryn had set into motion ten years ago. Even now she stood to be injured by what they chose to do with their lives.

She stood to be the one most injured by his past.

Cord also recognized that in returning to the Fancy Lady, his life had changed. From now on he wanted his life to be dictated by his heart, by the ties that bound him to his daughter. He wanted to be a father, her father. But how could he be when she evidently hated him and did not want him here?

He wanted her love and respect. He wanted to hear her call him Papa.

"He's not my papa!" Sitting in the bay window of her room, her arms wrapped around knees that were drawn up to her chin, Hope sulked.

"Yes, he is." Floryn carried the parcels she and Cord had purchased for Hope in El Paso to the bed.

"I don't like him."

"You won't know until you meet him."

"I did."

Surprised, Floryn moved closer to the window bench.

"Where?"

"The meadow." She rubbed her cheek against her knees. "I saw you kiss him, too."

"Yes, I did," Floryn said. She had learned long ago to be truthful with Hope. She never told the child more than she asked, but she always answered her questions. "Your papa and I are married, Hope. We're going to live together, so I'm sure you'll probably see us kiss again."

"He said he intended to kiss you many more times," Hope said. "And I suppose you'll be sleeping together? I saw his valise in your bedroom."

"Yes."

236

"Well"—Hope flounced on the bench—"I still don't like him."

"You haven't given him a chance."

"My papa is dead." Hope turned her head to look at her mother, tears glistening in her eyes. "I want Papa back, Mama. I don't want this stranger."

Floryn sat on the bench and gathered Hope into her arms. "Your Papa Hal can't come back, darling, and this man, whether you want to accept him or not, is your papa."

Hope sobbed in her mother's arms. "He's not staying."

"Do you want him to?"

There was a slight hesitation before Hope said, "No."

Floryn knew differently. "I think he would like to."

"We don't need him, Mama."

"I think we do."

"I don't. I want him to leave."

"He can't," Floryn said. "Unless he stays I lose custody of you. He's the only one who can help me keep you, and I'm not going to lose you, darling. You're the most important person in my life."

"What about Mr. Wallis? Maybe he'll help us. He told me he'd like to talk with you."

"Mr. Wallis can't help."

Floryn shivered as she thought about the letter she had inadvertently opened and read before she realized it was addressed to Cord, not to her. A letter Kern Wallis had written to Cord. A letter containing the promise to expose Floryn, to produce proof of her infidelity. She wished Hope were old enough to understand that Kern Wallis was responsible for all the changes, the undesirable ones, in their lives.

"Only your papa can help us."

"What if he doesn't?"

"He will. I believe in him."

237

"Did you believe in him when he rode away and left you alone?"

"Yes, I believed in him then. I still do."

"You loved him," Hope murmured. "That's why I'm his child, not Papa's."

"Yes," Floryn said. She brushed strands of hair from Hope's forehead. "You are a child conceived in love, my darling."

Large brown eyes, framed in thick, dark and curling lashes, focused on Floryn. Equally dark and thick brows, naturally arched, pulled together in a frown. "But he doesn't love us, Mama. He never wrote or came to see us. He didn't even want to know if he had a little girl or not."

"That was wrong of him," Floryn said, "but we must forgive him. Remember, I told you when he left he was hurting. When people hurt, they hide themselves so they can heal. And all of us make mistakes. I did, too, darling. I wasn't a brave woman or I would have told Papa Hal that I loved your father, that I wanted to be with him."

Floryn cupped Hope's face in both hands. "He loves you. I know he does. Right now, he's like you. He's scared."

Hope looked skeptically at her mother.

"He's unsure if you're going to accept him."

"You want him to stay, don't you, Mama?"

"Yes, and I want you to get to know him."

"I won't love him, Mama."

"Will you be kind to him?"

Hope shrugged. "I guess so, but don't make me call him Papa."

Floryn asked, "Would you call him Father."

Hope paused a long time before she said, "If I call him anything, I'll call him Father."

"That's settled," Floryn said. "Let's get dressed for the fiesta. Let's have fun and celebrate."

"I'm not going to change clothes to please him." She eyed the packages on the bed.

"Don't. But you might want to take a look at your gift." Floryn walked to the bed.

"I'll wear something that Papa"—she looked at Floryn who frowned—"that Papa Hal bought me."

"Please, Hope, give Cord a chance."

"I don't want any clothes he bought me."

Floryn carried one of the parcels to Hope, handing it and a pair of scissors to her. "Open it. If you don't like your gift, you don't have to wear it and you can return it to him."

Mumbling under her breath, Hope clipped the binding and tore through the paper. She held up the green and white gingham dress, turning it around and scrutinizing it.

"Ruffles," she scoffed. "I hate ruffles. This looks like the dress Mr. Wallis gave me."

"Kern gave you a dress?" Floryn asked.

"Yes, a brown and white striped one. He told Leanor that it was a birthday gift even though it was late. It's ugly. It looks like the kind that Agnes Jennings wears. I'll bet it was a dress Agnes outgrew and gave away. I hate Agnes Jennings."

"Oh, darling, don't say that."

"I do, Mama. She says bad things. Real bad things."

"It's not things Agnes really believes," Floryn said. "She's repeating what she hears her mama and papa talk about."

"They talk about you, Mama, and say bad things." Hope wadded the dress up and tossed it on the bed. "I won't wear this dress. Not now. Not ever. I'm not going to look like Agnes."

Floryn's heart ached for her daughter. In accusing Floryn of infidelity, Hal had ensured that Hope, an innocent, would suffer also. Floryn moved to the bed, picked up the dress, and carried it to the wardrobe.

"We'll hang it up until you decide what to do with it. Are you going to open the other packages?"

Hope slipped off the bench and walked to the bed. Halfheartedly she pulled at the paper on another package. "Why did you let him buy me a dress? You know I don't like them."

"Your papa didn't ask my permission."

In spite of herself, Hope grinned. "Do you like his patch?" she asked. "I do. It makes him look tough."

Floryn smiled, thinking about Jason.

Hope parted the paper and gazed at the gift. Lifting her head, she stared at her mother with wide eyes. "A shirt," she exclaimed. "A yellow and white checkered shirt. Did you buy this for me, or did he?"

"Your papa bought it. I bought the other two shirts."

"How did he know I liked shirts and trousers?"

"I told him about you." Floryn moved to the bench where she helped Hope take off her boots.

"And he still bought me a dress?"

"He bought the dress for you because he liked it. He bought the shirt because he knew you would like it."

"I do, Mama. I really like it."

Hope peeled out of her shirt and slipped into the new one, racing over to the cheval mirror as she buttoned it.

"It fits me," she cried gleefully, turning this way and that. "I'll wear my new hat, Mama. The one you bought for me last Christmas. And the brown trousers that Leanor just finished sewing for me. And I'll polish my boots, and—" She stopped blabbering to look at her mother. "Are you going to wear something new, Mama?"

"I hadn't thought about it."

Hope brushed a strand of hair from her eyes. "Did he buy you something?"

"Yes, a blue ribbon for my hair."

"Are you going to wear it tonight?"

"Yes."

The childish gaze concentrated on Floryn. "You still love him."

Floryn turned so she did not have to face her daughter's contemplative gaze.

"Don't you, Mama?"

"Yes."

Hope ran across the room and threw her arms around her mother. She pressed her cheek against Floryn's breast.

"Mama, you have me. We have each other. We don't need Cord."

I do.

"We do if we're going to be a family," Floryn said.

"I don't want to be a family with him. I'll give the gifts back to him, and we'll send him away as soon as we can." Hope pushed away from her mother, stripped out of the new shirt she modeled, and tossed it to the floor. "We don't need him. People say he kills people, Mama, and steals their money."

"People say bad things about me," Floryn chided, "but that doesn't make them true. It doesn't make what they say about your papa true either."

Hope hung her head.

"Your papa isn't guilty of those things, Hope. No matter what you think of him, no matter that it seems as if he deserted you and me, he did not murder that woman or those people on the wagon train. He did not steal their money."

"I know." Hope hung her head. "He told me."

"Still you want him to leave?"

"Yes." She raised her head, her eyes shining with resolve. "He doesn't belong to us, Mama. The Fancy Lady does."

"Not without him," Floryn softly said.

Seventeen

Cord did not belong to her and probably never would, Floryn thought sadly as she stood in front of the dresser staring down at the comb and brush set. Yes, they were good together sexually. But was a sexual commitment enough to bind them together through the years?

She closed her hand over the folded piece of paper in her dressing gown pocket. The letter Kern Wallis had sent. The contents of which had kept her heart from soaring when Cord had suggested they make a future for themselves. The contents of which she must confess to Cord.

But not before the fiesta. She wanted tonight with him.

The door opened and closed behind her. She did not turn.

"You've taken your bath?" Cord asked.

"Yes."

She heard his footsteps first, then felt his hands clasp her shoulders. She felt the warmth of his body along the length of hers and leaned back against his strength. It felt so right, so good. If only he loved her. . . .

"Why did you run away from me?" His breath

242

blew tendrils of hair about her neck.

Her hand was still closed about the letter. "I was frightened."

He turned her around. "Of what? The burglars? My past?"

She stared into the rugged face she loved so much. Memorizing each line, each expression, she raised her hand and outlined his brows, his nose, the black patch.

"Our pasts," she said. "I have the premonition that you and I don't have a future together, Cord. Each of us has a past that stands in our way, one we can't get beyond."

"We can if we try." He smiled tenderly. "That's what you told me."

"I thought we could at the time."

"Floryn, I want us to try to make this marriage work. Both of us deserve it and want it."

"The Fancy Lady?" she murmured.

"The Fancy Lady and Hope," he answered. "And for us. You have to admit we're good together."

Although he had not said the words she wanted so desperately to hear, he was admitting that he wanted to stay at the Fancy Lady. He wanted to be with her and Hope and to make their marriage work.

"Yes, we are good together," she said.

"I've been concerned that my past might cast a dark shadow over Hope," he said, "but since I've been here, Floryn, I've felt differently about it. We can and we will put our pasts behind us. We will build a life for ourselves and our daughter."

Cord ran his fingers down the edge of the white dressing gown, grazing her breasts.

"I saw her," he said. "She came to the meadow after you left."

"She told me." Her gaze carefully moved over his

243

face. "What did you think of her?"

"She's beautiful. She reminds me a lot of you. I kept thinking how wonderful it was that you and I conceived her."

A product of our love, Floryn thought.

"We could give birth to more children," she said.

"I've been thinking about that, and I like the idea. How about you?"

"I guess I should have thought about it considering I became pregnant the first time we made love, but I didn't until just now. I've had other things on my mind."

"Do you find the idea so repulsive?"

"No, I enjoy children. I would like to have more." *With the man I love.*

"You're a good mother. You've done a good job with Hope."

"Thank you," she murmured.

"She doesn't like me, and doesn't want me here."

"She doesn't mean it. Having recently lost Hal, she's afraid to love you for fear of losing you."

"It was a strange feeling, Floryn," he confessed. "I had wondered how I was going to react when I saw her. When you told me about her, I felt something inside. But—" He was quiet for a second, then said, "But the moment I saw her, I knew she was my daughter. I love her."

Floryn caught her breath.

"I want to be her papa. I want to make up for all those years that I wasn't here for her." He drew Floryn closer to him and buried his face in the hollow of her neck and shoulder. "Oh, God, Floryn, can I make up for all those years?"

"Yes, but it's going to take patience. She asked me not to make her call you Papa."

"What did you say?"

"I told her she could call you Father."

"That's rather stilted," he said.

Floryn knew he was disappointed. She rubbed her hands up and down his back. Biting back the tears, she held him close. She comforted him.

"It's a beginning."

"I guess I didn't do too well with her today," he confessed.

"You did better than you think. She's going to wear the shirt you bought her to the fiesta."

He lifted his head. "She liked it, huh?"

Floryn nodded. "But she hated the dress and said she would never wear it. It reminds her of the kind of dresses that one of her schoolmates wears."

"Is it so bad for her to look like a little girl? To look like one of her schoolmates?"

"She doesn't want to look like this one," Floryn said, "because Agnes Jennings has been spreading rumors that I'm a whore."

"Jennings," Cord said. "That name sounds familiar. Anyone I should know?"

"Alonzo Jennings," Floryn answered. "The name may sound familiar because he owns the mercantile store in Donaldsonville, but you wouldn't know him. He and his family moved here about three years ago. He and his wife became fast friends with Hal but took an immediate dislike to me."

"Well, I don't want Floryn to look like Agnes either," Cord said, "but I have the feeling she wouldn't even if she wore the same exact dress as the child."

Cord laughed quietly and stepped away from Floryn. Reaching up, he unfastened his necktie and moved across the room to toss it on top of the dresser.

"One of these days in the very near future, our

daughter is going to be a beautiful young lady with more suitors than she's going to know what to do with."

"Yes," Floryn murmured, "she is."

"We're going to be fighting them off." He laughed. "I can guarantee you right now, there's not a man out there who is worthy of my daughter."

"No." Floryn's eyes grew misty. Cord had been tender with her, but he had not shown her the love he was showing for his daughter. While she ached for the same for herself, she was happy he was giving it to Hope.

"She's just like you," Cord said. "She's your daughter."

Yes, she's my daughter!

Standing in front of the dresser, he picked up the piece of blue ribbon and pulled it through his fingers several times.

"The way she talks." He smiled. "Her actions."

"Please be careful with that," Floryn said softly. "A special person bought it for me." She walked to him and pulled it from his fingers to lay it on the dresser. "I'm going to wear it to the fiesta tonight."

He put his arms around her and drew her into a loose embrace, the warmth and strength of his hands and arms easily penetrating the silk barrier of the dressing gown.

"You know," he said, "I don't remember your thanking me properly for the ribbon."

She smiled. "What do you consider a proper thank you?"

"This for starters." His arm tightened and he drew her closer so that she felt the hardness of his body against hers. She had no words to describe the bliss that filled her when he simply held her. It made her feel as if he cherished her. For the moment it chased

246

her fears away.

His lips lightly touched hers, and he whispered, "This next." He lowered his face to cover the tip of her breast and to blow through the soft material. His warm breath sent wave after wave of sheer pleasure through her body.

"Then this."

He parted the dressing gown, the material sliding down her shoulders to reveal her breasts. He stroked her shoulders, collarbone, and neck. She trembled beneath his touch.

"When I think of all the years we've wasted."

The material of her dressing gown draped over her arms and down her back, leaving the front of her body exposed to his hungry gaze. She placed her hands on his cheeks and guided his mouth to hers. At the same time that they kissed, his hands slid under the material of her dressing gown to cup her naked buttocks and to edge her closer to himself.

"Now for the next step." He was urging her down to the floor.

She was moving with him, was on her knees when she heard the rustle of paper in her pocket and remembered the letter. She pulled out of his embrace and rose. "We—we shouldn't."

"Of course, we should, and we are." On his feet now, he circled his arms around her; his lips sought hers.

She turned her face away from him, resting her cheek on his shoulder. Concerns she had pushed into abeyance now rushed in to inundate her. She had accused Cord of being a victim of his past, but he was no more one than she. And hers was about to catch up with and tumble in on her. Ultimately it would damage her more than Cord's had damaged him. She stood to lose him, the ranch, and her daughter. The loss of the ranch she could bear. The loss of him and her daughter would be unbearable.

She had wanted the fiesta and tonight for herself and Cord, and she would have it. Honesty, however, compelled her not to take advantage of Cord again. She would not make love to him until she told him about the letter from Kern Wallis, told him the full truth about the accusations and the loan. She would make her confession tonight after the fiesta so their next coming together could be a mutual one, a sharing of ultimate fulfillment.

Moving out of his arms, she gave what she hoped was a bright smile. "It's time for you to meet our friends and workers. Besides we wouldn't want to hurt Antonio and Leanor's feelings, would we?"

He drew her closer, his mouth exploring her neck and shoulders. "When I'm with you, I don't give a damn about hurting anyone's feelings." To prove his point—if that were necessary—he spread a trail of butterfly kisses along her collarbone. He nuzzled the bath-damp tendrils of hair at the base of her neck. "I want to stay in this room with you forever."

His lips captured hers in a long, drugging kiss, one that strove to drag her soul from her body, one that was succeeding. Unable to help herself, she slid her arms around him, her hands clinging tightly to his shoulders as she melted against him.

Through the open window beginning sounds of festive activities could be heard. Leanor and Antonio giving instructions, musicians tuning their instruments, workers setting up the table and chairs. Odors of the cooking food drifted into the room.

When Cord swung her into his arms, she opened her eyes.

"We can't, Cord." Her voice was thick and raspy.

248

She braced her hands against his chest and shoved him. "We have to be outside to greet our guests. We have enough problems without adding discourtesy to them."

He refused to be pushed away. "At most, we'll just be a little late."

She smiled and caught his face in her hands, guiding his lips to hers for a quick kiss. "Absolutely not. Mr. and Mrs. Cord Donaldson, owners of the Fancy Lady, will greet their guests as they arrive."

Persistent, Cord tumbled onto the bed with her, but she squirmed out of the tangle of arms and legs. A resigned smile on his face, he sat up and thrust his hand through his hair. Floryn moved only enough to pull her dressing gown over her shoulders and to fasten it. Cord finger-brushed hair from her face. He traced her eyebrows, the bridge of her nose, her lips. She was leaning toward him, silently begging for a kiss when the door opened and Hope burst into the room.

"Mama, I want you to help me dress for the fiesta." Her shirt and trousers draped over her arm, Hope's gaze moved about the room as she searched for Floryn. "Why is your door closed, Mama? It's never been . . . closed. . . ." She found her parents. "Before." Hope's words trailed into stunned silence. Her mouth open, her eyes large in a white face, she stared at her mother and father.

Although both she and Cord were fully clothed and were not even touching when Hope entered the room, Floryn felt guilty. She started to scoot off the bed. Cord clasped her hand and tugged. Floryn wanted to run to Hope, to take the child in her arms and reassure her, but Cord held her tight.

"The door's closed because this is your mother's and my private place," he said. "Our rooms. From

249

now on, you'll have to knock on the door before you enter."

"This is my house." Hope's head went up a tad, but her chin quivered as did her tiny voice. "I don't have to knock on doors. Do I, Mama? I never have before."

Working her wrist loose from Cord's grip, Floryn slipped from the bed. "That was because it was only you and me, and both of us are girls. From now on you will have to. Your papa is a man, and—"

"I have to knock on your door, Mama, before I can enter?" Stunned disbelief underscored Hope's question.

"Yes," Floryn answered. At the moment she could not remember a moment when her heart had been heavier.

Hope looked at her mother, her scrutinizing gaze making Floryn aware of her dishevelment, making her feel as if she were undressed and indecent. She fidgeted with the lapels of her robe.

"Now that you have him, you don't want me," the child cried out. "You'll love him and not me."

"No," Floryn and Cord exclaimed at the same time.

"Yes, you will," the child shouted.

Floryn could identify with Hope's cry of anguish. When her mother died, she had felt abandoned. She had been alone and terrified. Although the circumstances were different, Floryn knew Hope felt the same way. She rushed to her daughter, to comfort her, to reassure her, but Hope dodged away.

"Well, you can have him, if that's what you want! I have Leanor. She'll love me and won't shut her door on me. She'll help me get dressed for the fiesta. And I'm not going to wear the new shirt Cord bought for me."

She tossed the shirt to the floor and to emphasize

her anger, her betrayal, she stamped on it. "And I'm never, never gonna wear that ugly dress you bought for me. I'm not going to look like Agnes Jennings."

Hope rushed out of the room, slamming the door behind her. Following immediately, Floryn wrenched open the door and overtook her at the landing. She caught her by the arm.

"Please, Hope, try to understand."

Tears running down her cheeks, Hope twisted out of Floryn's grip. "Can't you see, Mama? He's messing things up. You never let Papa Hal come into your room and touch you like that. You never closed me out of your room."

"No," Floryn said wearily, "I didn't, but your Papa Hal and I didn't have the kind of marriage your papa and I do." She rubbed her hand down the back of Hope's head. "As your papa explained, it's different now. You wouldn't want to walk in when he's undressing or bathing. That would be embarrassing for both of you. And for the same reason he'll knock on your door before entering your room. All three of us are going to have to work together for us to have a family."

"It would work if he'd sleep in Papa Hal's rooms. That's where he belongs until he leaves."

"No," Floryn spoke firmly, "he's my husband and he belongs in my rooms with me."

"I don't want it to work." Hope pushed away from Floryn. "I don't like him in your bedroom, touching you."

"But you promised you would give him a chance."

Hope hung her head.

"You're not going back on your promise, are you?"

"I wish we didn't have the Forever Tree. I'm going to have Antonio cut it down."

"The tree can't be blamed," Floryn said.

251

"I don't like Cord."

"He's your papa."

"I'm not ever going to call him Papa, and I don't like him loving on you. I don't like you loving on him," she whispered. Still holding her trousers, she ran down the stairs and called, "Leanor. Leanor, will you help me get ready for the fiesta?"

Disheartened, Floryn slowly returned to the bedroom. When she had gone to get Cord, her primary purpose had been to save Hope. She had given thought to the child's reaction to Cord, but had foolishly assumed Hope would love her father as Floryn loved her lover, now her husband. In her haste, in her desperation she had not thought it possible that Hope would believe she was abandoning her in favor of Cord. In overcoming one problem, she had created another. Perhaps this one was insurmountable.

She entered the bedroom and closed the door. Bending, she picked up the discarded shirt and laid it across the foot of the bed. "I've never seen Hope react like this."

"She's never seen you with a man before," Cord said.

His words brought little comfort as she thought of her daughter's distress.

"Give her some time. She'll get accustomed to it."

"I suppose so," Floryn murmured. After a moment she said, "Maybe, Cord, until she does get accustomed to you, we should—"

"No. I can understand and sympathize with your feelings, but we aren't going to do that, Floryn. We're married and have already established marital relations. If I move to Hal's suite, you go with me."

"Cord, she's a child. She doesn't understand."

"She's a child, but she understands. She's one smart kid, and if we're not careful we'll be marching

252

to her cadence."

He took Floryn into his arms. She rested her cheek against his chest, taking comfort in the firm, steady beat of his heart.

"I think I know how she feels. Abandoned. Terrified. Lonely. That's the way I felt when my mother died. I was even angry at her for having left me and at God for taking her."

Cord held her a long time before he said, "She'll come around. Give her time. Remember, you told me not to underestimate our daughter."

She nodded her head against his chest.

"Now, I'm giving you the same advice."

"I should go help her dress."

"Isn't she old enough to be dressing herself?"

"Normally she does."

"Then let her today, or let Leanor help her . . . if she needs help. You can check on her after you're dressed."

Floryn slowly nodded her head. She moved to the dresser and picked up her brush. Combing her hair, she twisted it into a coil at the nape of her neck. Its only adornment was the blue ribbon Cord had purchased for her in El Paso.

By the time she was through, a knock sounded. She crossed to the door and opened it. "Leanor," she breathed.

The older woman smiled. "I knew you would be worried, *mi hija,* and I wanted to let you know that Hope is fine. She and I had a long talk about mamas and papas." She held her hand up, the thumb and index finger almost touching. "She's still sulking a little bit, but not much."

"Thank you, Leanor." Floryn breathed easier than she had since Hope burst into the room.

"May I have her new shirt? She was telling me

253

about it."

Floryn crossed to the bed and picked up the piece of yellow and white fabric handing it to Leanor.

"And, Floryn"—the ebony eyes twinkled with understanding—"do not let Hope's actions cause you to be angry with *Señor* Cord. What he did and said to the child were correct. She should not be bursting into anyone's room. She has been allowed too many liberties in the past. It is time she had a papa to love and to discipline her."

"Are you telling me that I failed her?" Floryn asked.

Leanor shook her head. "No, you were her mama, and a fine mama you are, but she needs her papa also. It's going to take her a little while to get accustomed to him, but she will."

When Floryn closed the door, Cord said, "Do you feel better?"

She smiled and nodded her head. "For a minute there, I thought you were going to say I told you so."

He grinned. "Well, I was thinking it."

"Hal would have said it again and again. In fact, he would have gone into a rage, shouting at me. Long toward the last he seemed to take great pleasure in berating me."

"I'm a Donaldson," Cord said, "but I'm not Hal."

"No"—Floryn admitted—"you're not."

"While we're getting dressed," Cord said, "why don't you tell me about these people I'm going to be meeting shortly?"

"They're friends," she said, "who have stood beside me through thick and thin, who refused to believe Hal's accusations about me. The ones who defy convention for their friends. We're going to need them when we start moving the cattle to market, and they'll be there for us."

254

She returned to the dresser and straightened the ribbon in her hair. Then she picked up her timepiece and wound the stem.

"They are strong-minded and determined men and women who have agreed that nothing will stop us—not the war or anybody hoping to gain from it. We have agreed to consolidate our cattle, so we can be among the first to get our herds to market."

She turned around, the white material swirling around her ankles.

"You and I, Cord," she said, losing herself in her dreams, in her ambitions, "we're going to be the leaders in a new generation of ranchers. We'll blaze new trails. The Donaldson name as well as that of the Fancy Lady will be so common, school children will know about them several hundred years from now."

"I'm not interested in being remembered two days from now much less two hundred years," Cord said. "I'm interested in you and me and the here and now."

Floryn moved toward him. "Then listen to the here and now. Texas and Texans are money poor, but they're rich in land and cattle. Millions of head of cattle which you and I are going to convert into money—into U.S. currency. The Yankees are hungry for meat, for our cattle, and we're not going to wait for them to come get it. Come next spring, you and I will lead the largest migration of cattle to market that the world has ever seen."

"I've never seen your eyes so dreamy and your face glowing with such animation and love," he said, "not when you make love to me, not when you talk about Hope. Only when you talk about this damn ranch."

"I love the ranch," she admitted, "because it provides for my life." She moved to the wardrobe. "Without it I would be nothing, would have nothing, but I

255

don't love it to the exclusion of everything as you love to accuse me of."

"You faulted me for not consulting with you about the money I offered to pay Tony and Kid for riding out to Norwell's place. But today when you sent a message to the rancher about the meeting, you didn't consult with me."

"No, I didn't," she answered. "If it bothered you, why didn't you say something?"

"I realize that in the past you've had to make these decisions by yourself and that it's going to take time for you to change. From now on, Floryn, I won't be excluded."

A navy blue split riding skirt across her arm, a matching calico blouse in her hand, Floryn closed the wardrobe door. "I apologize," she said quietly. "I didn't mean to exclude you. But until you become acquainted with the men and have readjusted to the ranch, I think it's better that I make the decisions. As you pointed out, I'm the one who's been here running the place. I know what's going on, what needs to be done and when. And the men recognize me as their *La Patrona*."

"And what do they think I am, Floryn?" he asked dryly. "Your stud?"

Openmouthed, Floryn stared at him. "I have never thought of you like that and still don't. You're the one who kept pushing for . . . intimacy. Remember, that was part of your bargain." She was dry-eyed. But she knew for a fact hearts cried, for hers did. "Perhaps you're voicing your own guilt when you keep referring to yourself as a stud."

He glared at her. "I want it understood that I'll be the doting husband, the father, and the courteous host who meets your friends tonight. But I will also be *El Patrón,* and no decision about

256

this ranch will be made without my approval."

Floryn ran her hand down the side of her skirt, smoothing it over her hips. Vulnerable because of the recent run-in with Hope, now this one with Cord, she took refuge in aloofness.

"You may call yourself *El Patrón* as much as you wish, but that does not make you the master of this ranch. I have been *La Patrona* for the past twelve years. None of the ranch hands will easily switch their loyalty to you."

"They will," Cord said. "That I guarantee. According to Antonio, all I have to do to get their loyalty is win the tournament."

"He was speaking symbolically."

"But the truth, nonetheless."

"I generally win the tournament," she said.

"Not this time."

"We'll see."

She returned to the wardrobe and pulled out a pair of boots. Once she was completely dressed, she twirled in front of the full-length cheval mirror.

"That becomes you." Cord leaned against the door frame. "And it looks like the Floryn I remember."

"I rather like being unhampered by petticoats."

"In that outfit you look like *La Patrona*."

She leveled a hard, direct gaze at him. "I am *La Patrona*, and always will be."

Eighteen

"*Señor* Cord! *La Patrona!*"

Cord and Floryn stood together on the veranda, while the *vaqueros* and ranch hands shouted their names repeatedly. In a swell of enthusiasm, they also waved and threw their hats into the air. As if to support the verity of Floryn's statement, they addressed him as Mister, Floryn as the mistress.

Cord chose to see this as a challenge rather than an obstacle. He would win the trust and confidence of the ranch hands and of the surrounding ranchers. He would win for himself the title *El Patrón*. Along with that he would win their respect.

He looked through the crowd of smiling faces. Among the ranch hands were a few business people from Donaldsonville and many of the owners of smaller ranches. He saw Leanor and several of the *vaqueros* whom he had already met. He searched for Hope but did not see her.

Wearing new black Spanish cut trousers, vest, and a black and silver *sombrero*, Antonio moved onto the veranda to stand beside them. He held up his hand to quiet the crowd.

"Today is a great day for the Fancy Lady. Our *Patrona* has returned and brought home her husband, *Señor* Cord."

Cord noticed that Antonio did not address him as *El Patrón*.

"According to the ancient tradition," Antonio finished, *"Señor* Cord has agreed to ride in the tournament."

After more hurrahs and whistling, one of the *vaqueros* yelled, "This year, *Patrona*, you may not win all the prizes."

"What makes you think I won't, Pedro?" Floryn shouted, joining in the jesting.

"We have *Señor* Cord."

A subtle way of saying they hoped he would become *El Patrón*, Cord thought.

Pedro stepped closer to them and held out a yellow and red pike to Cord. "I made this especially for you, *Señor*. With it you shall win the tournament."

As the man handed him the pole, Cord realized that although the tournament was a game, a layover of medieval jousting and a part of the archaic feudal system under which Mexicans still lived, it was a significant event in these peoples' lives. It symbolized a new beginning, as much for them, as for him. From this moment forward he was embarking on a new life. No longer was he an ex-convict, a victim of injustice at the mercy of a fickle fate. He was master of the ranch, master of his destiny.

He was *El Patrón*.

"Thank you," he said. "I will do my best."

"Viva, Señor Cord!" the *vaqueros* shouted vigorously three times. Again *sombreros* flew through the air.

When the shouts silenced, Antonio said, "You will speak to them, *Señor?"*

Cord looked at Floryn. "Why don't you?"

"It's your fiesta, not mine," she said flatly.

259

In an undertone he asked, "Do I detect a hint of jealousy?"

She glared at him. Cord chuckled and stepped forward. The crowd grew quiet.

"Ladies and Gentlemen, while I'm saddened by the death of my uncle, your *Patrón*, I'm glad to be here at the Fancy Lady. I can never take my uncle's place, but I promise to make you a good *Patrón*. My wife, my daughter, and I want to welcome you to our fiesta. The people of the Fancy Lady have worked long and hard to prepare this fiesta for you. We have entertainment in the form of games and dancing and food to your heart and body's content. Now, let the tournament begin . . . and may the best man—"

He deliberately turned to Floryn and grinned.

"—or the best woman win."

"What are the prizes?" an older man, dressed entirely in buckskin clothing, shouted. "Always makes the game more exciting to know what you're fighting for."

"That, Zeke, has been kept a secret. The only ones who know are Hope and her mother." Cord had no difficulty in remembering the man's name. Zeke Phillips's manner of dressing made him stand out from the rest of the ranchers. "You'll have to ask them."

Zeke turned to Floryn who said, "Since Hope planned the fiesta, I'll let her tell you what the prizes are."

When the child did not immediately step forward, Floryn called her name . . . several times. Then Cord called her, his voice sharp. Hope stepped from beneath the arbor and sullenly walked to the veranda. Cord noticed that she was wearing the new shirt he had bought her in El Paso. Possibly she had had a change of heart; more probably her vanity overruled her sentiments.

Looking directly at her mother, Hope said, "The horseman who gets the most rings in the shortest period of time will receive the deed to the lower meadow."

Floryn gasped, and Cord turned to look at her.

"The lower meadow," he said. "Our meadow?"

Floryn nodded.

"What's the meaning of this, Hope?" he asked.

Her mouth agape, Floryn stared at him as did the child.

"Hope?" His stern voice demanded an answer.

Hope drew up to her full height and cast him a defiant gaze. "It's mine. Papa gave it to me for my fifth birthday. I can do with it what I want. I don't want it anymore."

Floryn tried to push by Cord to reach Hope, but he caught her wrist and held her forcibly by his side. Looking at the crowd, he smiled.

"Folks, please move on to the playing field. We'll disclose the prizes there. I think my daughter and I need to have a little talk."

The crowd laughed, many of them nodding their heads in understanding, and began to move away. Floryn—obviously angry—and Cord remained on the veranda with Hope. When the three were alone, Cord spoke.

"Please explain this, Hope."

"It's mine," she repeated. "I can do with it what I want."

"Why do you want to give it away?"

"I don't like it anymore."

"What if your papa or I don't win the tournament?" Floryn said, her tone worried. "We'll lose the Forever Tree."

"I hope so," the child answered. "It's not my meadow. It belongs to you and —" She looked at Cord. "And to . . . him."

Cord realized that as the pendant was symbolic of the key to unlock his past, thus his future, as the tournament game was symbolic of a new beginning for the Fancy Lady, the tree in the meadow was also symbolic. For Hope it represented him and Floryn and their love for each other, a love that she was a great part of, but one she felt left out of presently. With his returning to the ranch, Hope felt as if she were being pushed out of the nest . . . and she was not ready to try her wings.

"I'm not going to let you do this," Floryn said. "We're going to give the calf as we had planned to do."

"No," Hope exclaimed, her dark eyes flashing.

Now Cord knelt down. "Do you understand, Hope, that you may lose your property altogether?"

"Yes," came the sullen reply. Then: "Why do you care? You have my mama and half the Fancy Lady."

Cord looked at her for a long while before he said, "You're right. The property is yours to do with as you wish."

"What?" Floryn scowled her disapproval. "You have no right, no say in this. I will not let her do this."

Her eyes glinting as if she enjoyed their arguing, Hope looked from Floryn to Cord.

Having observed Hope's reaction, Cord said, "The property belongs to Hope?" When Floryn nodded, he turned to the child. "You can do what you wish, but in doing this you stand to lose the meadow forever."

Hope looked confused.

"I'm sorry I wasn't here for you when you were a baby and a little girl," he continued. "I regret it, Hope, but I'm not going to let you try to make me feel guilty about past mistakes that cannot be changed. I don't want you to put the meadow up as a prize. If you do and if you lose it, you won't be hurting me. You'll be hurting yourself."

"I don't want that old tree," she muttered.

"Do you wish to leave it as the grand prize?"

Hope looked down. Cord caught her chin and turned her face to his. "It's your call," he said.

"Leave it as the grand prize." Her voice was barely audible.

"Cord," Floryn cried, "can't you see—"

"It's settled." Cord rose. "Now, the three of us— Hope, you in the middle—are going to walk to the tournament field."

He held his hand out for Hope, but she did not take it.

"Hope."

"I'll walk on the other side of Mama," she said and moved to her mother's side.

"No, you'll walk between us," Cord said.

Hope glanced at her mother. Although stiff-faced, Floryn nodded. When the three of them reached the field, Cord ordered Hope to call out the prizes. This done, he permitted her to run to Leanor. Once Hope was gone, Floryn gave vent to her fury.

"How could you have allowed her to do that? She's a child and doesn't know better. You do."

"She fully understands what she's doing," Cord

answered. "She's going to learn she's not going to manipulate or make me feel guilty."

"She's a little girl," Floryn iterated.

"That's no excuse. Children grow up, and I don't want her to grow up thinking she can manipulate and control other people. It's up to us to show her how to correct her attitude now. And, my dear wife, she's old enough to know that you and I feel guilty about the past, about her conception. She's going to play it to the hilt and push us as far as she can. Well, she's pushed me as far as she can, and she needs to know that."

Floryn glared at him but made no retort.

"*Señor* Cord," Antonio called, leading Cord's mount to the starting line. Red and yellow streamers had been braided into the roan's mane and tail.

"I hope *La Dama de Suerte* rides with you."

"Thank you, Antonio," Cord said. "Perhaps she will. Lady Luck and I seem to be on a much better footing here of late."

Before he mounted, Cord saw Hope and Leanor in deep conversation. Hope ran to him.

"I didn't mean what I said yesterday about the favor."

Cord said nothing.

"Can I give one to you and to Mama?" she asked.

He nodded.

She pulled a scarf from her pocket and handed it to him. "This is my second best one. It's red and yellow and matches your pike," she said. "I'm giving Mama the best one."

Cord acknowledged with a nod. Taking off his hat, he tied the scarf—pirate style—around his head, long silk ties hanging down his back.

"That is good, *Señor*," Antonio said. "You look like one of the early Spanish buffalo hunters."

After Cord donned his hat again, he swung himself into the saddle and looked down at Hope. A breeze stirred, the silk scarf gently brushing against his cheek and neck.

"Thanks for the favor, Hope."

Her brow furrowed in thought, she said, "Yesterday you promised that if I gave you a favor, you would give me the prize you won."

"I said that," he admitted, "but your behavior today has changed the rules. I'm going to keep whatever I win."

She chewed her bottom lip. "Mama's unhappy with me, and I want to give the property to her."

"You should have thought of that before you declared it a prize. Would you like to have your favor back?"

She hesitated a long time before she finally said, "I hope you lose and Mama wins."

"She's not going to win, Hope, and you've lost the meadow."

"Mama won't let you keep it," she said, not far from tears. "She's *La Patrona.*"

"I'm *El Patrón.*"

The sun was setting by the time the tournament ended, and although Floryn had been tough competition, Cord emerged—just barely—as the winner. Grinning from ear to ear, Antonio swaggered to the front of the crowd to make the announcement that was immediately lost in a flurry of flying hats and huzzahs. Cries of *"El Patrón"* filled the air.

Cord's pleasure over winning the competition did

not compare to his pleasure at being called *El Patrón*. Winning the game, being called *El Patrón* was symbolic. He knew the *vaqueros* called him this to signify their respect of his skill and concentration in winning the tournament.

But it signified more for him. Managing the Fancy Lady was real. It was his responsibility. Success or failure rested squarely on his shoulders. It would take more than skill to make the ranch a success, to win the loyalty of the *vaqueros* and the neighboring ranchers. It would take a love and devotion like Floryn's. But he would do it.

He and Floryn would do it . . . if she would let him. If not, he would do it by himself.

Cord happened to look up at that time to see a piece of blood-red glass on one of the lanterns reflecting the sunlight, and it reminded him of the pendant. But the thought of not having it no longer made him feel sick at his stomach. Surprisingly, he was thinking less and less about it, about its secret.

His thoughts seemed to be centered more on the Fancy Lady, on Rule's joining him and the two of them working together. He missed the old man and would be glad when he arrived.

When Hope handed Cord the deed to the lower meadow, Floryn's heart cried for her daughter.

"Thank you," Cord said.

The crowd clapped. Hope sulked, and Floryn smiled through stiff lips.

"The second prize goes to Floryn Donaldson, *La Patrona* of the Fancy Lady," Antonio shouted. "Truly *el día maravilloso* for the Fancy Lady."

266

There were more whoops and hollers of congratulations.

After Floryn accepted the black colt, Antonio announced that dinner was ready. Rehashing the events of the day, the crowd quickly dispersed and moved to the serving tables. Hope, still sulking, darted off. Floryn moved to follow her, but Cord caught her wrist and pulled her back.

"I'd like for you to stay with me," he said. "A wife should be by her husband's side. *La Patrona* with *El Patrón.*"

The caustic tone of his voice caught her attention, and she gazed into his face. The streamers of the silk scarf blew behind him, the brim of the black hat casting a shadow over his face, making his features seem hard and unyielding.

"Hope needs some time and space to herself," he said.

Floryn twisted her arm, but his grip tightened. "You really know how to make friends."

He laughed. "I'm not doing bad for a new papa, am I?"

She looked at him sarcastically.

He ignored her. "I've enjoyed the day. Your neighbors are nice, and I'd forgotten how much fun it is to play."

"And to win," Floryn said.

Again she tried to wiggle her hand free from his, but he retained his hold on her. He walked close to her so that their shoulders rubbed together. She moved away from him. He simply moved closer to her.

"My, my. Do I have two sulking little girls on my hands?"

A breeze stirred, again blowing the scarf against

267

her skin, tantalizing her with the promise of his touch, flaunting his victory.

She caught her breath, exhaled, then said, "You had an opportunity to win Hope's confidence today."

"I took advantage of it," he answered. "I'm teaching her that she's not going to manipulate me, nor is she going to make me feel guilty over past mistakes. I didn't play her game which should win her respect. In time I'll win her love."

"Are you going to keep the lower meadow?"

"Yes."

He guided her away from the serving tables to a quiet and secluded part of the lawn where they were surrounded by tall, flowering bushes. Although they were away from the crowd, lantern light spilled onto them.

"Someday when she's old enough to appreciate it, I'll give it back to her," he said. "Sometimes things must be taken from us before we realize their importance."

"You're thinking about your freedom?" she said.

He nodded. "I've been thinking how I've enjoyed today, the games and the socializing. I know Rule is going to enjoy it, too. He would have been out there helping Leanor cook."

"I really miss him. I'll be glad when he gets here." After a pause, she ventured, "How are you feeling about the loss of the pendant?"

"I don't think about it as much as I used to," he said. "I'm sorry it's gone because it was my only clue, but it's gone. That's that." He smiled. "You cut quite a figure out there today, Mrs. Donaldson."

He moved and a limb from one of the bushes knocked his hat off. Floryn reached up and caught it. Holding it, she stared into his face.

268

"You were quite dashing out there, too," she murmured.

"I thought you were going to win," he confessed.

"I should have," she answered, "but I didn't. I thought about what you said, and the Fancy Lady does need its *El Patrón.*"

"Are you saying you deliberately lost?" He lifted a brow in question.

She outlined the black patch and brushed in the fullness with the tip of her finger. "Yes."

His soft laughter mocked her. "If you could have won, you would. You wanted the deed to that property that much, Floryn Donaldson. You'd love for me to believe you were responsible for my being *El Patrón.* That would put me further in your debt."

Taking the hat, he tossed it aside so that it landed on top of a bush. He moved closer, his chest pressing against her breasts.

"Being further in my debt wouldn't be bad," she whispered, momentarily pushing aside thoughts of Kern Wallis's letter.

"No?" he murmured. He began to take the pins and combs out of her hair, the coil unwinding so that her hair hung freely.

"If you were," she said, "I would allow you to redeem yourself by doing penance."

He felt her breath warm on his chin; her fingers provocatively kneaded his arm. Her lips were a hair's breadth away.

"What kind of penance?" he asked.

"This."

She clung to his arms, tipped her head to the side, and brought their lips into perfect alignment. Just before their mouths touched, he saw her dark lashes lying against her creamy cheeks. Her mouth

269

was soft and warm and responsive. It moved over his, coaxing, demanding a response from him.

"You're a wanton woman." His lips barely lifted from hers. "Do you know what you're doing to me? Can you imagine the effect you're having on a man who has not made love to a woman in two weeks?"

Her hand eased between their bodies sliding down to rest on him. She pressed her palm over his arousal.

"I can feel what I'm doing to you," she whispered. Her fingers teased him.

He enjoyed the pleasure. "I want to ravish you," he muttered.

Her other hand touched the black patch. "I want to be ravished."

Both of them were playing with fire, and Cord cared not. He was aroused and felt lustfully primitive. Proud to be a male, he wanted to take her here and now.

Cradling her head in his hands, he breathed her name, cherishing it, savoring it. Floryn had always been the only woman for him. She was his equal, and in her he found fulfillment. Her hands continued their assault on his body, as his mouth captured hers in a long, hungry kiss.

He was heady—from having won the competition, from having freed himself of the bondage of the past, from having this woman in his arms—and heard himself groan.

Or was it Floryn?

Everything they did seemed to be synchronized. She wound her hands about his neck, twining her fingers together below the knot of the silk scarf, that he yet wore. His fingers combed long honey-brown tresses, rediscovering their thick and silky texture.

270

Breaking the kiss, but not the spell they had cast for themselves, he drew back to look at her. In the muted light of the oriental lantern he saw her face clearly. She was staring up at him with wonder written on her face. He felt her heart beating against his, keeping the same erratic time. She had set him on fire.

"If all believers knew that penance was this wonderful, I think they would be inclined to sin more often."

She smiled at him, a soft smile that did wonderful things to his insides. Again she touched the patch; she traced her fingernail along the line of silk that banded his forehead.

"You look like pictures I've seen of pirates," she said. "Or of the gallant Spanish buffalo hunters—buccaneers of the plains."

"And you are the lovely young maiden whom I've stolen off a richly laden Spanish ship and whom I must ravish," he said, joining in her game. "To maintain my image of a rogue and rake, lady, I would that I could take you here and now."

Again they kissed . . . and they kissed. Finally they drew apart. Floryn, remaining in the circle of his arms, placed both of her hands on his chest and gazed up into his face. In the distance they heard the musicians tuning their instruments.

"Although this distresses me sorely," Cord said regretfully, "I cannot claim you, but shall have to wait till later. I have a feeling that if we don't show up pretty soon, we'll have the entire assemblage hunting us. But, I promise before this night is over you shall be properly ravished by a buccaneer."

Another long and satisfying kiss later, he untied the scarf and stuffed it into his pocket. Floryn

271

reached for his hat and resettled it on his head. Hand in hand they ran from the bushes to join the reveling crowd.

Briefly Floryn thought about Kern Wallis's letter and remembered her resolve to confess to Cord before they made love again. Once before she had been given a moment in time, and she had turned it loose. That moment was gone, lost forever. She would grab what pleasure she could.

Confession could . . . would . . . come later.

Nineteen

"This young man may be your prize, Floryn, but I'm not going to allow you to monopolize him all evening."

Cord felt the tap on his shoulder and turned to see an older woman — a widow and the owner of an adjacent ranch — whom he had met briefly earlier in the day. Mildred Hudgins wore her thick white hair pulled back into a chignon at the nape of her neck. The austerity emphasized gaunt, angular facial features. Like Floryn, she was dressed in a blouse and split riding skirt, a black and gray one.

"I want to learn more about this man you've just married," Mildred said.

Floryn said, "I may not want to give him up."

"Don't figure you do," Mildred retorted, "but I don't figure you have any say-so." She nodded her head toward the buckskin-clad man headed their way. "Zeke's wanting his dance with you. Looks like I got the best end of this deal."

"I'll say you did," Floryn murmured.

"I always look forward to my dance with you, Floryn," Zeke said when he was closer, his eyes twinkling. "And when I saw Mildred cutting in on you and taking your man, I figured this was my chance."

All of them laughed. Moving into Zeke's arms, Floryn mouthed to Cord, "Ravish me." Cord winked

273

at her as the two couples whirled away from the other.

After Cord and Mildred had danced for a while, Mildred said, "How does it feel to be the center of attention?"

Cord gazed into shrewd eyes that were locked to his face.

He shrugged. "Everybody' s curious about the man Floryn got out of prison to be her husband."

"Yeah," Mildred drawled. She dropped her lids so he could no longer look into her eyes, "You're right. They are curious. Kern Wallis has done a lot of talking about you, and none of it good."

"I haven't heard a good thing said about Wallis today," Cord commented.

"Maybe we could find something good if we wanted to waste a lot of time thinking," Mildred said, "but we figure we don't have the time to waste to find so little good about him."

Being led by Mildred, more than leading her, Cord soon found they were dancing away from the crowd.

"Getting back to you," Mildred said. "I believe most of us are more than curious. We're interested in you."

"A fine line of difference between the two," Cord said.

"But a difference."

"Interested in knowing whether I'm innocent or not?"

"Not really." She laughed as she said, "I don't know that this says much for our character, but anytime Wallis is against something, we're for it. In regards to you, we've counted on Floryn's judgment. She's a good judge of character. If she says you're okay, we accept it. I think most of us want to know what kind

274

of man you are inside and if you're strong enough to help us." She cocked her head to the side. "Are you?"

"Probably not."

"Good. If you think not, then I'm sure you must be."

"Mrs. Hudgins—"

"Mildred. We don't stand on ceremony around here."

"Mildred, I'm married to Floryn, father to Hope—"

"Well, Mr. Cord Donaldson"—again she interrupted him—"Floryn has needed a husband for a long time, and Hope has needed a father. At times a man can be a good, neutralizing force in a woman's life. I'm glad you finally came home where you belonged."

"I'm here for them," Cord said, "not for the valley."

"Way I see it, they're sort of one and the same."

"I'm certainly not a gladiator for anybody."

Mildred said, "I don't rightly recollect my history, but I don't think we're looking for a gladiator. We need someone a little more impressive, someone with a little more clout. You know, someone like David who slew Goliath."

Cord grinned. "I repeat, you have the wrong man, Mildred. I'm not a giant slayer either."

"We'll see."

"I believe Floryn said you have a spread close by?" Cord attempted to change the subject.

She nodded. "The Bar-H, but if we can't get the cattle to market pretty soon, I won't. Kern Wallis has the mortgage on my place, and he's ready to foreclose. He's already forced one of us out. Lyle Hackett. Reckon you've already heard about him?"

Cord shook his head.

"Owned the livery in town. He was killed last

evening when his horse threw him. Broke his neck. Claudine—his widow—had taken as much as she could. Before the sun rose on a new day, she sold out lock, stock, and barrel to Kern Wallis." Mildred sighed. "God only knows what's going to happen to us."

Kern Wallis again. The man's name had cropped up repeatedly and frequently during the afternoon and evening. Cord looked at the group of men and women who danced around them. Most of them hated the attorney.

Mildred's gaze followed his. "We're all in the same fix."

"Is that why you feel loyalty to Floryn?" Cord asked. "She's your salvation?"

Mildred gave him a long and measured look. The already angular features became even sharper as did her tone when she spoke. "Young man, I resent your asking that question, but I'm going to overlook it this time because you're new here and have a lot to learn. We're with Floryn because she's our friend. We're sticking together—all of us, Floryn included—because none of us has a chance alone."

Mildred pulled away from him. "I'm tired of dancing. Let's walk awhile."

"If it's all the same with you—"

"It ain't," she barked. "I want to talk some more with you."

"Don't you mean *to* me?"

Mildred chuckled. "Reckon I do."

Never looking back to see if he followed, she started walking and did not stop until they stood outside the lantern light, a good distance from the revelry.

"I like and respect Floryn," she said. "She's my friend. Her first husband was also my friend, one of

276

my best friends. I never approved of his marrying Floryn because he was an old man, and she was a baby, only sixteen. But he did. She took care of him, and he took care of her."

"Even when he falsely accused her of infidelity."

Walking farther into the dark, Mildred did not answer straightway. "I don't rightly know if he accused Floryn falsely or not. I never caught Hal in a lie, and he said he had proof. But it made no matter to me if he did or not. He shouldn't have treated her like he did. He should have known that Floryn would want a man."

She spread her hands in exasperation. "My God, that's the way it is with the animal kingdom. It don't matter that we're humans. That's life. Hal was blind to some aspects of life, and that blindness ultimately caused him great grief."

Stopping beneath an oak tree and crossing her booted feet at the ankles, Mildred leaned against the trunk. She took a pouch of tobacco from her shirt pocket and rolled herself a smoke. Then she extracted from the same pocket a match which she struck against the tree. She held the flame to the tip of the cigarette, her face illuminated in the light. She inhaled deeply, then exhaled.

"You think Floryn was guilty of infidelity?" Cord asked.

Mildred inhaled a second time, the tip of the cigarette lighting up again to reveal the coarse features of her face. She shrugged and exhaled. Darkness now concealed her.

"Makes no difference what I think, but you're not asking that question of me. You're asking it of yourself."

What the woman said made sense, Cord thought.

"Have you lived a celibate life for the past nine

years?" Mildred asked, then said, "You don't have to answer that because it ain't a bit of my business. I just wanted you to give the question some thought before you let yourself get all caught up in the local gossip about Floryn and start getting judgmental."

"She told me about Hal's accusations," Cord said.

Mildred grunted. "All I have to say is this. It shouldn't matter to you. You weren't part of her life then. She wasn't part of yours. What matters is how the two of you make it from here on."

Mildred took several drags on the cigarette before she spoke again.

"You got your work cut out for you, son, and your task is far from easy. There's a mighty big difference in being called *El Patrón* and in being *El Patrón*. The one you have to watch out for is Kern Wallis. He's not an evil man, just a greedy one, out for all he can get. And he wants this valley."

She walked around, moving to stand in the pale moonlight. "And if we don't do something about it, he's gonna get it. He's one of the few who's profited from the war. If we can get our cattle to market we'll get about thirty-five dollars a head. He's offered us seven dollars and fifty cents. That's what I call stealing. Kern calls it good business."

She dropped her cigarette to the ground and crushed it with the toe of her boot. "When Floryn spurned Wallis's attention, he promised he would get even. He thought he had broken her when Hal accused her of being unfaithful. But he underestimated her. She's been stronger and smarter than him on every count. And he's underestimated the rest of us. With or without your help, we're gonna keep our property. With your help, we'll do it quicker and easier. And you've got a big stake in this."

She clapped him on the shoulder. "Well, I had my

say. Now, let's me and you get back to that fiesta. We got a lot more celebrating to do."

Hope in his arms, Cord easily ascended the stairs to the bedroom. Holding a lamp, Floryn walked ahead of him. Light flickered down on him and the child.

"Is the fiesta over?" Hope snuggled sleepily against Cord's chest.

"Sure is," her mother answered. "And about time. It's going to be morning soon."

"But it's still night now?" Sleep slurred her words.

Floryn laughed. "Yes, you have plenty of time to rest."

Hope's lids drooped and by the time they put her in bed, she was slumbering soundly, not even awakening when Floryn put her nightgown on her. After she and Cord kissed Hope good night, Floryn blew out the lamp and they slipped out of the room.

"Are you sleepy?" Cord asked.

"Not really," she answered. "I don't know when I've felt this charged up and full of energy."

"I feel the same way." He put his arm around her, and she leaned her head against his shoulder. "Let's go riding."

"Riding," she repeated with breathless anticipation. No doubts assailed her tonight. She had promised herself she would seize the moment, and she was going to. She stopped walking and turned to stare at him. "Now?"

"Now. To the meadow."

"I'm . . . not sure."

"When did you start calling our tree the Forever Tree?"

"Hope started it. After you left, I rode to the

279

meadow nearly every day. I guess I always hoped that you would return to me. I dreamed that one sunrise I would see you riding up. After Hope was born, I brought her with me. As soon as she was old enough to notice the carving, she wanted to know what the words were. Every morning she would come bounding into my bedroom, wanting me to take her to the Forever Tree."

"This morning we'll watch the sunrise from there."

"Cord, I need to talk to you—"

"You can later. Tonight is fiesta, a time of celebration."

Yes, she thought, *it is.*

He pulled the scarf from his pocket, letting it flutter through the air, before it looped around her neck. He gently tugged, bringing her closer to him. "I'm going to ravish you."

She trembled with expectation. "I don't think—"

"Like buccaneers of old, I shall abduct you." He swept her into his arms, and Floryn locked her arms around his neck. "This night you shall be properly ravished. I promised."

As he carried her down the stairs, Floryn felt his strength, the pull of his muscles. When they reached the veranda, she slipped out of his arms and they ran to the stables where they quickly saddled their horses. They raced each other to the meadow, enjoying the early morning wind against them.

Floryn's horse was in the lead, the roan behind, but as they splashed across the creek, Cord caught up with her. Looping an arm around her waist, he pulled her in front of him and held her close. She embraced him, and they rode until they were beneath the oak tree.

She laughed as his mouth hovered over hers. "We're here at the Forever Tree. I suppose you

280

have me where you want me."

"No," he murmured, "not quite."

He reined his horse in and both slid to the ground, still damp from the brief shower on the previous day. If he did not mind, then neither did she.

Her prayers had been answered She had had this night with Cord. She had this sunrise in which her dreams could come true. Cord would be with her in the meadow.

"I've waited so long for this." His lips teased her ear. "It seems as if it's been forever since we made love."

"Forever," she whispered, the word a repetition of what he said, a reinforcement of her love for him.

He guided her to the tree, placing her palm over the pledge, placing his hand over hers.

"Forever," he whispered.

She sighed and turned, her back to the tree. He faced her, clasping her hands in his, palm to palm twining their fingers together. He raised her hands above her head and gently pressed against her, trapping her between him and the tree.

He stared at her for long, still seconds, the moonlight and shade of the leaves casting his face in darkness. An excitement as she had never before felt skittered through her body.

"You're mine," he murmured.

"Yes," she agreed, as he stirred a primitive response in her.

"I'm going to set your body afire tonight, my captive."

"And what are you? Pirate of the high seas? Or buccaneer of the plains?"

"That doesn't matter." His lips played with hers as he pressed the hard, lean length of his body against hers.

"What matters is that I'm a man determined to have his way with you."

Floryn trembled and opened her mouth, but he did not take her lips in a full kiss; he played with her; he tormented her.

"And I am a woman determined to have my way with you."

"A battle of the sexes." He chuckled, the sound low and sensuous.

She was surrounded by sensuality, by heat, by hardness. As she stretched against the tree, she felt primitive and lustful and wanton. Again she promised herself tonight and its pleasure with no regrets.

His mouth possessed hers. His kiss was hungry, savage, but not rough. His tongue was rowdy and undisciplined, but not vicious. He gave pleasure as he ravished.

"I am a man determined to set you afire with the flames of passion that flow through him."

"I receive it," she whispered, "and freely give you mine."

Floryn closed her eyes, giving herself to the fantasy world they created, giving herself to the desire that thickly flowed through her body.

"Tonight, I am going to make you my woman."

"Yes," Floryn heard herself say, wondering if this guttural voice could really be hers. "Yours. I want to be all yours. I want you to be all mine."

He lowered his head, and with his mouth he undid the first button on her blouse. Floryn gasped when the moist warmth of his breath touched her skin. She twisted beneath him. His teeth gently nipped her heated flesh.

From the cleft between her thighs, heat began to swirl in widening circles. She struggled for her arms to be freed, so she could participate in this stormy exchange of kisses. When he did release them, she plunged her hands into his hair, twining her fingers through it to hold his mouth against hers. Groaning, he dipped his head and kissed her neck.

"I think," she breathed, "that I am already afire."

"Nay, lass, you don't know what fire is yet. At the moment you're nothing but kindling."

"I would be more," she cried.

"You will be," he promised.

He lowered his hands to unbutton her blouse and to push the material from her shoulders. Her undergarment followed. Again he paused to gaze at her. She reached out to undress him.

"No," he said. "Stand still, captive. I'm ravishing you."

Exhilarated, Floryn did not move as he continued to gaze at her moon-touched body. She looked at him, wishing she could see his expression, wishing she could know what he was thinking.

"Have you ever done this to a woman before?" she whispered, feeling deliciously decadent.

Cord laughed, again touching threads of awareness in Floryn that she was not aware she possessed. "Would it matter?"

"Not as long as I'm last."

"You're the last." After an infinitesimal pause, he added, "You're also the first."

Her heart sang. "I'm glad."

"Me, too."

Piece by piece he slowly took off the rest of her clothes, deliberately brushing her skin with his fingers and his mouth as he did so, deliberately murmuring words that built up the fires of desire. When she stood naked in front of him, he caught her hand and led her out from beneath the tree into the full glow of heavenly light, that of both moon and stars.

283

"I am burning up with yearning and desire," she confessed. "I feel that fire and I are one."

"Not yet," he said, "but you will be."

Again capturing both her hands, he gazed at her. Then he took her into his arms and held her. She felt the graze of his leather vest against her breasts and her nipples hardened. Want—painfully, acutely—speared through her body, taking residence in her nether parts. Her stomach quivered; her legs buckled. Had he not been holding her, she would have fallen to the ground.

He kissed her, winding his hands through her hair. She parted her lips, savoring the sweet taste of his tongue, savoring the feel of smooth, worked leather against her heated flesh. While she clung to him, his lips stroked the corner of her mouth, the hollow of her neck, her closed eyes.

She had wanted, had dreamed of this, and while it was happening, it did not seem possible. But reality was the strength of his arms as he embraced her, the feel of his lips as he kissed her, the hardness of his body against hers. Reality was his never making a declaration of love, but she accepted what he offered. Reality, in this case, was substantial, a better bedfellow than fantasy and dreams and memories.

As she slipped her hands into his pockets, her fingers moved past the silk scarf in one pocket, his knife in the other, to close around his arousal. Although fabric was between their flesh, Floryn felt the searing touch of him. Evidently he felt the same. He caught his breath; he shuddered.

"Now it is my turn, my lord."

"Nay"—his voice was thick and sultry—"you are my captive."

She withdrew her hands from his pocket, pulling out the contents. She draped the scarf around his

284

neck and stepped back from him. In buccaneer fashion she tipped the closed knife, glinting silver in the moonlight, to his chin.

"I have the dagger. I'm in control now."

"So you are."

"You are my captive."

"So I am."

"Undress for me."

As slowly as he had undressed her, he undressed himself, beginning with boots and socks, then moving to the black leather vest. Pleasure thickly, hotly flowed through Floryn as she gazed at his hands. They seductively rubbed, fingered, worked the leather as if it were her body. She had never felt so wanton, so debauched in her entire life, had never in her wildest imaginations dreamed she would behave like this. But she enjoyed the sexual forays. She reveled in her sexual freedom, in her ability to lust without feeling guilt, to accept it as a beautiful part of their coming together, to accept lust as a part of her love for Cord . . . as an integral part of love itself.

She enjoyed Cord. She had always thought him handsome, but he was beautiful as he stood naked in the moonlight. Clearly defined under the satin sheen of his skin were his muscles. Rock-hard, their craggy edges were smoothed by night shadows. Her gaze slid down his torso, seeing him strong and ready for her. He moved toward her.

"Not so fast, captive," she said, amazed at the raspy sound of her voice. "Turn around and put your hands behind you."

"Ah, maiden," he murmured, his voice the same texture as hers, "I fear this ravishment is more than I bargained for."

"Perhaps better than you would have bargained for," she whispered.

"Better," he agreed. "Better—far better—than I had anticipated."

Dropping the knife, she reached for the scarf, loosely tying his hands. She twirled him around and stepped closer to him. Not once touching him with her hands, she lightly pressed herself to him, hot, naked flesh against hot, naked flesh. As he had tormented her, she tormented him. Her lips played with his mouth, his chest, his stomach. She caught the smooth contours of his desire in her hands and caressed it.

Her hands moved to cap his shoulders and she guided him to the ground so they knelt facing each other. His hands still behind him, Floryn now combined hands and mouth to continue the slow assault to his senses.

He moaned softly; his body trembled.

Then she felt his arms around her as he set her from him.

"I should have tied you more securely," she teased.

He draped the scarf about her neck, the silk lightly touching her sensitive breasts. She pulled it off, bent, and picked up the vest. She slipped into it and leaned back, thrusting her breasts forward. The black leather, barely covering her, gleamed provocative in the moonlight.

"If I were a pirate, my love," he said in that sultry voice she loved to hear, "and you were my captive, this is all I would allow you to wear."

"It's more than I would allow you to wear," she answered.

Both laughed, their voices husky with love. They were captives to the passion that flowed through them. He rose, swept her into his arms, and began walking with her.

"Do you know where I'm taking you?" he asked.

286

"Yes," she whispered, her lips meeting his in a sweet, tender kiss. "To our bed of Indian paintbrushes."

"Where we first made love," he said.

Floryn smiled. They had ravaged and ravished each other. Now they would make love.

"We can only smell and feel the flowers now, but in the morning we'll share the glory of dawn with them," she murmured.

Tonight, she thought, *we'll share the glory of our love with them.*

He knelt down with her still in his arms and gently laid her on the mat of flowers, their softness holding her, their fragrance surrounding her as did his arms.

"You're worth waiting for," he confessed.

"You are, too."

She ran her fingers along his back, glorying in every remembered detail of his body. Her hands cupped the muscled hardness of his buttocks while he kissed her breasts and in turn sucked her nipples. Feeling her need for him deep in her abdomen, she moaned. His mouth was honeyed nectar, his fingertips fire and ice as he explored her eager body. She strained against him. To delay any longer was madness, yet she still wanted to see him, to touch him everywhere. She had a need for this as much as for the taking, for the fulfillment.

Pushing him down gently, she said, "Let me."

And then, leaning over him, she kissed his chest, tracing the curve of his pectorals, laving his nipples. She feathered his body with her fingers and her hair. Moving down, she found his navel and drew designs around it with her fingers. She pressed her tongue into it while her hands stroked his thighs, drawing closer and closer to the heat of his swollen sex.

"Oh, God, Floryn."

She caressed his shaft, gently touching the glistening tip. It was beautiful, straight, broad, eager to thrust into her body. She was eager to receive it.

Cord groaned. Catching the vest in both hands, he pulled her on top of him and kissed her hard. Then he turned so that she was lying beneath him on the blanket of flowers.

"Now, it's my turn," he said. "I'm going to kiss every inch of you."

He began with her fingertips, kissing the tips of each, then slowly sucking each one in turn, bringing back vivid memories of the day he had wiped the ointment from her fingers, that he had caressed her hands with his. Only this tenderness with his mouth was so much more delicious. So much more so. Moving on, he nibbled and laved the sensitive skin of her inner arm. She trembled as he reached her breasts, as he moved the leather aside with his face.

She whispered his name as he continued the slow movement down the curve of her breasts, then up again, in teasing circles. His mouth, his tongue, and the leather patch all rubbing her, all exciting her. As her body turned hot and cold with pleasure, she instinctively turned her head, seeking his mouth, his jaw, his temple. Her blood began to pound.

His lips moved lower, his tongue skimming over her stomach and dipping to the curve of her thigh, until she was shuddering convulsively, a victim now of her own desire and of the taste of heaven he had already given her.

Passion sprang out from him, from her, mixing together in a sudden, breath-stopping fury. Her bones seemed to liquefy, degree by degree, until she wondered why she did not simply melt out of his hands. Her mind, that had been swirling with needs, clouded with a pleasure that was softer, truer, than any she had ever imagined.

He was on top of her, pressed against her from breast to ankle, his mouth on hers, hot yet soft and lazy. Against her belly he was hot and hard and not at all lazy. Eagerly she opened her mouth, and when he thrust his tongue within, she met him fiercely. She rotated her lower body, alerting him to her readiness to receive him fully. His hands stroked from her waist to her hips. With his knee he separated her thighs and settled his stiff penis there, where it belonged. She gasped, arched, and welcomed him into her.

She had never been so driven to touch a man before. With her fingertips and her palms, with her lips and her tongue, she discovered him. A forceful urge came to hold him, to wrap tight around him and hold on. To never let him go.

He thrust fully, hard within her. Her moan merged with his. Damp flesh pressed against damp flesh as they moved together. She had never felt so strong, so utterly weak as she did now, joined as closely as was conceivable with Cord. With his face pressed against her throat, she could smell his after-shave cologne, mixed with the pungent, earthy scent of passion. Her mind and body drained of everything but sensation, she arched and gasped in indescribable delight. They moved in rhythm to each other, for each other.

Time passed. Time stood still. Time ceased.

"Cord." His name burst out of her as she was carried away by a climax so strong, so intense, that she was left limp and dazed in the aftermath.

"Floryn!" He tensed on top of her, then his body shuddered in an answering climax. He collapsed, panting. He kissed the side of her neck. "Oh, God, Floryn, we're good together."

We're good together. Her joy, her pleasure died within

289

her. The same words he had spoken to her that day so long ago at the penitentiary. The day he had suggested she become a prison whore. How quickly Cord could turn a moment from tender to bitter. She squeezed back the tears.

She would have moved away from him, but he held her close. Her heart crying, her eyes dry, she gazed at the morning gray sky that was soon filled with gentle pink streamers. At the very bottom of the eastern horizon, a tiny golden dot promised another glowing sunrise. Quietly she lay, not speaking, hardly daring to breathe as dawn dauntlessly rent the last vestiges of darkness, cloaking the world in a brilliant and golden light.

Yet her heart was heavy, shadowed with grief.

After they bathed, they redressed.

"You've been quiet." He caught her shoulders and turned her to face him. "Did I disappoint you?"

She had promised herself she would not beg. When . . . if . . . he spoke of love, he would do so freely. And he would be the first to admit his love. She had admitted it first ten years ago, not so this time. "Making love with you is always pleasing," she answered.

He pulled her into his arms. Heart against beating heart, they looked into each other's face.

"I will always make it so," he murmured and lowered his head.

Floryn knew that pride demanded she turn her head, that she refuse his caresses, his lovemaking, but she wanted and needed him. When it came to Cord Donaldson, she had no pride.

He kissed her, the kiss slow and leisurely, yet it brought a new sensual onslaught. His hand slid down her back in a soft, tender caress. Floryn touched his ribs, explored them through the material of his shirt,

290

while their tongues mated. Cord broke the kiss, pulling slightly away from her so he could look fully into her face. Floryn gazed back steadily.

The awesome beauty and tenderness of his expression took her breath away. A feeling of *déjà vu* swept over her. She was eighteen again, and they were standing in the meadow after having made love for the first time. He cherished her; he loved her.

Finally Cord spoke, low and husky. "I've never wanted a woman like I want you, Floryn. You're in my blood."

I want to be in your heart, she cried.

After another long, drugging kiss, she twisted her head away from him to say, "We must return to the *hacienda*. We have a meeting with the local ranchers this afternoon."

"Yes," he murmured, "we do."

He stroked his fingers through her hair, and she looked into his face, into his darkened expression. There was something profound and sincere there, something deep and desperate, yet Floryn could not decipher what she saw and sensed.

Each said they had to return to the house. Each knew they must. Yet both delayed.

He kissed her hungrily, then rained kisses upon her face and throat and chest, as if he could not get enough of her or as if he were afraid this moment was just that, only a moment and there would be no more. A day at a time was all that he had promised. Floryn felt and shared his fear, his need. It fueled her response to his caresses.

Her heart was bursting with joy and breaking with sorrow. She loved this man, and the pain of loving him was nearly unbearable. Yet bear it she would.

She thought about Kern Wallis's letter and knew that today she must make a full confession. She

291

would do so as soon as they reached the *hacienda*. She would give Cord the letter, let him read Wallis's accusations, then tell him the full story.

Her night of fantasy was over. Today she faced the real world.

Twenty

"*Buenos días*," Leanor said as Floryn walked into the kitchen. "You are up early, *mi hija*."

"I never went to bed," Floryn confessed, memories of her and Cord's lovemaking bringing the warmth of pleasure to her cheeks. "Cord and I spent the night in the meadow. We watched the sunrise."

"I'm glad," Leanor said. "I like your man."

Her lover, Floryn thought, but not her man.

Stopping at the stove, Floryn poured a cup of coffee and walked to the door where she stood gazing out.

"He is a good *Patrón* and will get better in time," Leanor went on. "He is also good for Hope and for you, *mi hija*. Your cheeks are glowing this morning, and you look like a woman who has been loved."

"Do I?" Floryn murmured, saddened because she had been made love to but was not loved.

She could not have asked for a more wonderful sexual experience with a man, with Cord, but she wanted more. She wanted the love that would make their coming together complete, love that would give her hope that they had a future together.

"Why are you not happy?" Leanor asked as she removed a large mixing bowl from the cabinet.

"I'm not sure I understand happiness anymore," Floryn answered. "When I get something I think will

293

bring me happiness and peace of mind, I find it brings problems of a different kind."

Leanor chuckled. *"Sí,* that is life. Think how boring life would be if we always worried about the same problems. New ones bring variety. It helps if you think of them as challenges."

Floryn grinned. Leanor had a simple philosophy about life, and it served her well. "Presently, I have one gigantic challenge. I have to tell Cord about the accusations and the loan, and I'm afraid he won't believe me."

"He is a passionate and possessive man," Leanor said, "so at first it will seem that he does not believe you. But he does. He's a man who wants to be loved." Lightly sprinkling the big ball of dough with flour, she patted and continued to round it. "Cord Donaldson is a passionate man in everything he does, and he does nothing he does not believe in."

Floryn cast Leanor an amused gaze. "Where did you get so much insight on Cord Donaldson?"

Leanor flashed her a big smile. As quickly it was replaced by an unreadable expression. *"La Curandera.* She talked with the cards about him."

Floryn laughed. "You and Angelita are priceless, Leanor."

"Sí, we are." From the dough, Leanor pinched off small pieces, deftly twisting and fluffing them in her hand, before she dipped them into grease and wedged them into the baking pan. "But I believe in Angelita. She has the sight."

"Yes," Floryn mused, "she does. And she's probably right about Cord. He is a passionate man. But I believe he wants lust more than love."

"Lust is passion, and only a fine line separates lust and love," Leanor said. "Perhaps that is why my people are happier than you *anglos.* Because we believe lust to be an honest emotion, a facet of love, we accept and

294

enjoy it. *Anglos* have a morality that calls for labels and categorizing. You seem to divide something until it has no character anymore."

"Like splitting hairs on lust and love?" Floryn teased. *"Sí."*

Floryn poured a second cup of coffee. "Perhaps you're right, but the way I see it there is a big difference between lust and love. The commitments for lust are purely physical, and Cord can give that. Love calls for a commitment of the heart, and I'm not sure Cord has one. If he does, he doesn't want to involve it in his affairs."

He had changed a great deal since they had married. He smiled more frequently and his remarks were less cynical, but he would never be a soft, trusting man. Age as well as injustice and prison had seen to that. They had tempered his gentleness, his tenderness. They had obliterated his ability to trust anyone but himself.

She feared her belated confession would only reinforce his distrust and the barrier that separated them. Whether it did or not, she could delay telling him about the accusations and the loan no longer. As the thought flitted through her mind, she clasped the timepiece that hung about her neck and stood a moment longer, hoping for, wishing for courage to be true to her convictions.

"I'll be in the study." She set the cup on the counter and walked out of the kitchen.

Floryn had not been gone from the kitchen long before Leanor experienced a tightness in her chest, a shortness of breath, and dull pains in her heart. Holding her chest, she dragged a chair close to the door and sat down.

Closing her eyes, she breathed in deeply many

times, and she prayed to the Blessed Mother. She had work yet to do. She could not go, not yet.

Once the pain had subsided, she rose and walked to the cabinet. She quickly mixed with water the herbs Angelita had given her and heated them.

The door opened and Antonio entered the kitchen. "You are pale, Leanor. What is wrong?" he asked in Spanish.

"It is nothing," she replied, also speaking her native language. She poured the drink into a cup which she promptly drained. "I am an old woman, and I tire easily. I must rest more frequently."

"Yes," Antonio agreed. "I understand. The fiesta, she has left all of us happy but tired, no?"

Leanor smiled and nodded. "Sit," she ordered, "your breakfast is ready."

As she put the food on the table, Leanor remembered the last time Angelita had looked at the cards for her. She had studied them, frowned, then hastily reshuffled. She spread them a second time, the frown deepening on her aged face, her gnarled, arthritic hands as quickly covering them. But not before Leanor had seen the card of death, not before Leanor had seen her friend's trembling hands. Angelita had given her a reading, but failed to mention that particular card.

Since that day Angelita had refused to read them for Leanor, and she had been plying Leanor with medicinal herbs and giving her charms and potions to ward off evil spirits. This they would do. But Leanor knew they would have no effect on the Angel of Death, for he was sent by God.

Leanor walked out of the kitchen to stand on the back porch. Holding on to the post, she held her head back and closed her eyes, absorbing the brilliance, the warmth of the sun.

Sunshine streamed into the study. Floryn stood there, her eyes closed, savoring the warmth against her body. Last night, moonlight and romance had softened and gentled truth. Today sunlight, brilliant and golden, revealed its sharper edges. Moving to the fireplace, she gazed first at the Oriental silk screen that hid its darkened face, then higher at the mirror. Idly she ran her fingers around the ornate frame as she gazed at her image.

Nervous, she adjusted the collar of her pale green and brown striped blouse. She straightened the brown grosgrain ribbon on which her timepiece was suspended. Finally she stared into a frightened face that stared right back at her, into darkened eyes full of questions and doubts rather than assurance. She ran her hand over the smooth coil of hair at the nape of her neck and sighed deeply.

She knew Cord deserved to know the truth—the whole truth. She found that she had little courage and even less resolve. If she knew for sure Cord would never learn the lurid details about the accusations, if they would not come back to haunt her and him, she would not make her confession. But fear, not bravery, prompted her action. She would have Cord learn about them from no one but her. She owed that to herself . . . and to him.

Footsteps in the hallway alerted her to someone's arrival. Not Cord. They were too soft. She saw the reflection of the housekeeper in the mirror as she entered the room with a tray in her hands.

"Your coffee." Leanor set the refreshments on the table between the two reading chairs in front of the fireplace.

"You're pale," Floryn said, scrutinizing the housekeeper's face.

Leanor laughed and waved her hand dismissively. "You are imagining it, *mi hija*. I am fine."

"Perhaps you should see the doctor."

"I have *La Curandera*," Leanor said stubbornly. "Her medicine is strong."

"All right," Floryn said doubtfully. "If Hope should awaken while I'm talking with Cord, please don't let her interrupt us. Our discussion is quite important."

Leanor nodded. "She's not likely to. I think she is like me. The events of the last few days have caught up with her. The anticipation of her mama and papa coming home. The fiesta. She will sleep a little longer, yes."

Leanor moved to where Floryn stood. Lifting her hand, she brushed her fingers through the soft curls that framed Floryn's face. "You are worried for nothing, *mi hija*, about your *esposo*."

Floryn gazed into eyes that were large black pools of understanding. "I'm worried about you also," she admitted.

"Don't be," Leanor said softly. "God takes care of us."

"Sometimes I wonder," Floryn said.

"He does. I promise. He will take care of you and *Señor* Cord."

"I don't know what I'll do if Cord should decide not to stay."

What am I going to do if he never loves me? was the question that frightened her, that ate at her insides.

"It will be all right," Leanor assured her. "Cord is not going to abandon you. He will stay."

Will his staying be enough for me?

Always before Leanor had been able to reassure her, not so today. "I hope so."

Inside Floryn trembled, and although she had not run from a confrontation before, she wanted to do so now. She herself was about to pull the foundation out from beneath her world.

Kern Wallis was a smart man, an opportunist. He would not easily give up in his quest to control Fancy Lady, to control the entire valley. And he had already made great inroads. He now owned all of Lyle Hackett's property, including her note.

The Fancy Lady was his, Cord thought as he surveyed the ranch from the bedroom window. The knowledge filled him with pride. It endowed him with a sense of individuality and importance, of belonging. Long ago Rule had told him it was time he headed home. Maybe . . . just maybe he was home.

He heard the soft knock and Leanor's gentle call. "*Señor* Cord, Floryn is waiting in the study for you."

The thought of Floryn waiting for him stirred Cord's senses and caused his imagination to take wing. Striding across the room, he opened the door.

She smiled. "The coffee has been served. Hurry down, before it gets cold."

"Coffee. No one makes coffee like you, Leanor. I can smell it all the way up here." He sniffed appreciatively. Then asked, "Do I smell biscuits?"

She nodded, her smile growing, the black eyes twinkling. "I am glad you came home, *Señor*. You are good for the soul of an old woman." As if he were a small boy, she reached out and patted his arm. "Now, hurry downstairs."

Cord hesitated for a second. He liked Leanor, found himself liking her more as time passed. She reminded him of his mother. Not the way she looked or her manner of speaking, but the way she acted, the wisdom she spoke, the gentle, firm way she governed the house and them. The love and care that exuded from her. Since he had been at the ranch, he had learned she had no children of her own, no family except them, yet she was a mother.

"Leanor, you're a special woman." Yielding to his feelings, he caught her in a bear hug. As quickly he released her and stepped back.

299

The small hand, the top slightly wrinkled and lined with dark blue, strutted veins, lifted. A callused palm cupped his cheek. Black eyes, that seemed misty, gazed at him. "You are a special man. I am glad you returned to your home. This is where you belong. Floryn and Hope need you."

Again as if he were the child, she the mother, Leanor patted his cheek. His mother had done that also. When he had begun to think of himself as a man, it had irritated him. Today the gesture touched him deeply, touched a part of his heart he had thought lost forever. Smiling, he covered her hand with his.

"Go now, *mi hijo.*"

My son. Cord liked the soft "me-ho" sound. Like bright sunshine the words filled his heart with warmth and light.

"Go to your *esposa.*"

Go to your wife. He liked the sound of that, too. Thinking of his wife filled him with pleasure.

Leanor and Cord walked to the landing together. With a smile, they parted there. She headed toward Hope's bedroom. He stood a moment longer looking at her as she stood in the door and gazed at the sleeping child. Even at this distance he could see the love on her face for Hope. He saw the tear roll down her cheek. Feeling as if he were intruding on her privacy, he moved down the stairs toward the study. He stopped in the doorway to gaze at his *esposa.*

Floryn, presenting her profile, stood in front of the fireplace but gazed out the window. She was one of the most beautiful women he had ever seen. Tall and slender, she stood erect. She was a strong woman, a determined one, and he was proud of her. Today she was radiant, and it was more than being bathed in sunshine. He wanted to believe it was the radiance of a woman who had just made love.

Her honey-gold hair shimmered with a life and vital-

300

ity of its own. Not even the austere coil at the nape of her neck could subdue the rebellious curls at her temples. The dark brown riding skirt emphasized her height, her slenderness. Both blouse and skirt emphasized her gentle curves.

"Good morning again," he said.

She turned. Raising her hand to tuck a curl into the coil, she pulled the material of her blouse taut against her breasts, breasts that only hours ago had been naked and swollen pressing against his chest.

"Good morning," she said softly. "Please close and lock the door."

He grinned wickedly. "Are we going to have an assignation in the study? One we don't want Hope to burst in on?"

"I wish we were," she answered.

He strode toward her. "We can."

He took her into his arms; she went willingly. How wonderfully they fit together. Smiling down at her, he gazed at the shape of her nose and chin, at her high cheekbones, the classical lines of her oval face. Lowering his head, he covered her mouth with his, eagerly savoring her female taste and softness, enjoying as if he had never tasted it before. Her breath warmed his cheek. Her hands moving to his chest, she clasped the vest.

Clinging to him, she parted her lips, and he entered the sweet warmth of her mouth. Last night he had plundered, had taken. This morning he was gentle and soft. His love strokes fragile and delicate. She shivered beneath his searching hands and tongue.

Cupping his hands around her buttocks, he pulled her pelvis to his body, sliding his knee between her thighs, glad she was wearing a split skirt to grant him easy access to her most private places. Then, supporting her with his arms, he began to lower her to the floor.

"No, Cord." Her protest was weak. "We — we can't do this."

"Of course we can," he answered. He lifted his head and looked down into her flushed face and molted eyes. "Don't you want to?"

"Yes," she whispered, and stared at him with large, round eyes. Her gaze moved from his face to his shoulders, down his chest, to the lower part of his body. "Yes, I want to with all my heart, but I must talk with you first."

"Why? When both of us enjoy this so much more?"

She reached out to touch his cheek, to run her finger along the bottom edge of the patch. "Before we make love again, I must talk to you."

"Pretty serious?" he said.

She nodded.

"All right." He stepped away from her.

"Do you want some coffee?"

"I'll take a cup."

As she moved to the table, he settled into the chair and stretched out his legs, crossing them at the ankles. He leaned over and lazily cut two biscuits, filling them with butter and jam. He took a bite, chewing and swallowing.

Her gaze thoroughly encompassed him one more time; intently she looked at him. Her actions were so deliberate, he also glanced down at the black trousers, vest, and white shirt he now wore. When she said nothing, he wiggled one of his feet and grinned.

"I cleaned and polished my boots. The toes are shining."

A small smile touched the corners of her lips, but her eyes were sad.

"You're not going to eat?" he asked, taking another bite of the hot biscuit.

"Not right now."

After stirring a liberal amount of cream into her coffee, she slipped her hand into her pocket and withdrew a letter which she handed to him. Laying his biscuit down and wiping his hands on the napkin, he took it.

"This was with my other mail yesterday when we arrived," she said. "I opened it accidently. It wasn't until I had begun reading it that I realized it was addressed to you, not to Hal."

Cord unfolded the paper and began to read.

"I started to give it to you then," she continued, "but decided to wait until after the fiesta to talk to you about it."

After he finished the letter, Cord refolded it and looked at her. "What's this about our owing Wallis money? Is it true?"

Floryn drew in a deep breath. "It's true."

"Why, Floryn? As much as you hate the man, as badly as he's treated you, why did you become indebted to him?"

"I didn't—not to him," she said. "When I learned the provisions of Hal's will, I knew that I would move heaven and earth before I'd let Wallis have Hope and the Fancy Lady. My only hope was to find you, but I didn't have the money. The only thing I still owned was my herd of horses."

She ran her finger around the rim of the cup that sat on the mantel. "I went to an old friend, Lyle Hackett, and asked him to make me a loan."

"The man who was thrown from his horse."

She nodded.

"Didn't you realize you were jeopardizing the Fancy Lady? Didn't you care?"

"I cared, Cord. Dear Lord, but I cared. I was trying to save Hope. I had to decide which was worse, my borrowing the money and finding you or Kern Wallis ending up with the Fancy Lady and with Hope. Had it only been the Fancy Lady . . ." Floryn rubbed the side of her face. "Perhaps I would have reacted differently.

But I was not going to let Wallis have Hope. I was not."

She paused and lifted her hand to the base of her throat where she fiddled with her collar. "Claudine didn't want Lyle to use the herd as collateral, so he gave me a loan on my signature alone. But he and I had an understanding."

"How could you have done this?" Cord asked. "You're the woman who brags that she single-handedly saved the Fancy Lady. You should have a better business head on you, than this?"

"Lyle was my friend. I trusted him," she said. "He agreed that if I couldn't get the money immediately, we would work something out. He wanted my prize foals."

She took several swallows of her coffee. "Lyle wouldn't have done this to me."

"What?" Cord asked, his voice rather curt, "died on you or demanded immediate cash repayment on the day the note is due?"

"Demanded immediate payment," she answered. "I wouldn't have expected Claudine to sell everything—at least not on the day after Lyle died. I can't believe she had the funeral in the morning, sold everything, and took off on the afternoon stage." Shaking her head, Floryn broke off.

Cord felt the walls of the room closing in on him. "My God, Floryn, this man—your friend—just died. Yet you're sounding exactly like the woman who stood in front of me at the prison, so manipulating and calculating."

"No." She turned hurt, soulful eyes on him. "I didn't mean it to sound like that, Cord. I knew Claudine wasn't as committed to our cause as I am, but I never expected her to let me down like this, to sell me out to Kern Wallis."

Whether it was logical or not, Cord felt that betrayed by Floryn, by this surprising turn of events. He had listened to Floryn's rhetoric about trusting, about rehabilitating himself once he was out of prison. At first he had tossed it aside; then he had begun to think about it.

"I can't believe you didn't tell me about this. Not after we agreed that the basis of our relationship would be honesty."

"I wasn't dishonest," she defended. "I just didn't tell you everything. I truly thought everything was going to be all right. Lyle and I had already agreed that he would have the pick of my foals or any horse he wanted from my herds. Cord, my herds are the best in Texas. Now that Wallis owns the livery maybe he'll—"

Cord looked at her. "Yes?" he drawled.

"No," she said quietly, "—I guess not."

"You said we were running short on money, but I had no idea. All that shopping that we did in Huntsville and more in El Paso. If only I had known." He walked to stand in front of her and gazed down into her face. "And you did know and you didn't stop me, Floryn."

"I know it wasn't prudent of me or even businesslike," she said, her voice tremulous, "but it had been so long since I'd been able to spend money on clothes for Hope. I just wanted to buy her something. And I wanted to buy for you. And I wanted you to buy her something. I knew she would like having a gift from you."

Unable to bear the sight of her tears, and oddly understanding her need to buy for those she loved, he turned his back to her. He walked to the window, bracing his palms against the windowsill and looking out.

"How much do we have left?" he asked.

When he heard a little voice tell him how much, he spun around.

"That's all! No more!"

She shook her head and quickly began to tick off the items she had bought, the money she had spent for each. The New York detective. Her clothing. His clothes. His parole guarantee. Their shopping sprees and trip.

He moved until he was standing in front of her. He caught her by the shoulders and pulled her closer to him. He spoke in a controlled voice, but it belied the emotions that broiled within him.

"You spent how much for clothes before you came to see me?" he asked, giving her a shake with each word he spoke.

Her face was white, her eyes round. "I — I wanted to look pretty . . . for . . . you."

"Floryn" — he shook her more firmly this time — "why didn't you use that brain of yours?"

The cup and saucer fell from her hands to the floor. Her coil came unloose and slid down her back, silken strands of hair grazing Cord's fingers that bit into her shoulders.

"Because I'm not like you." She threw her head back and glared at him through those wide-opened eyes. Her voice trembled slightly, but she was defiant. "I have a heart, too, not just a mind. I know it's a fault, but I allow it to influence me."

Only when he heard the quaver in her voice did he realize he had frightened Floryn. He took a deep breath, turned her loose, and stepped back.

As quickly she stepped back from him, hugging herself. Out of the whitened face, she continued to stare at him, accusingly. This, too, added to his growing list of frustrations. He breathed in deeply several times, regretting his outburst.

"I wasn't going to hurt you," he said. He walked to the desk, then around it, trailing his fingers over the polished surface.

"I didn't mean for this to happen, Cord."

"We're going to have to get some cash," he said.

"We have no collateral."

"We'll have to get some."

Cord understood that Floryn had borrowed the money in good faith from a trusted friend who had agreed to her paying him back with foals and that he had no reason to be angry. Yet he was angry, at her, although she had no way of knowing that her note would be sold to Wallis. At himself. At the situation. At the world in general.

When he was in prison he had been told what to do and when to do it. His entire life had been manipulated by others. When he gained his freedom, he had thought life would be different, at least that there would be a little more equity to it. At this minute he felt as if the circumstances set into motion by Floryn were manipulating him. In a strange sort of way he felt as if she were manipulating him . . . even though she knew nothing about the Guilbert jewels.

The Guilbert jewels. Something Cord had not mentioned to a soul during the past ten years. This was his secret.

All these years people had been harping on the San Domingo treasure, one that was nonexistent as far as Cord knew. But there were the Guilbert jewels — the priceless heirlooms Mathieu Guilbert had given to Cord as payment for escorting Sanchia safely to New Orleans.

Now Cord was going to be forced to go get the jewels. And he was leery of doing this. He had the feeling that he was being watched. Perhaps his paranoia came from so many people having warned him to watch his backside. Nellie. Norwell. Jack Willowby, the warden. Shelby Martin. Even Rule.

If he were being watched, he would lead whoever it was — if anyone — to the jewels. That was all he had left in the world.

Yes, he was angry. Angry at the world for putting

him in such a position.

Yes, he was irritated. Irritated because Floryn had waited until now to tell him the truth, waited until her back was against the wall to confess and it made her seem less than honorable.

"Tell me something, Floryn," he said, breaking the long silence that had stretched between them, "would you have told me about the loan had this not happened?"

"I don't know," she answered.

"I figure you wouldn't have."

He walked to the door. Laying his hand on the knob, he said, "If you're finished, Floryn, I promised Antonio that I would meet him —"

"No." She cleared her throat. "I'm not. There's more."

Twenty-one

"More," Cord said dryly.

"Yes," she said, "more."

Breathing in deeply, he raked his splayed hand through his hair. Leaning back against the door, he crossed his arms over his chest and waited. He could tell from the expression on her face, from the tone of voice that he was not going to be pleased with what she said.

"Kern Wallis"—her voice was clear and steady—"has in his possession written and signed statements that Hal considered proof of my infidelity."

"Written and signed statements," Cord repeated, wondering how much more he was going to be hearing today. A loan. Now signed statements. Proof of Floryn's infidelity. "Like signed confessions of . . . of—"

"Yes," she answered.

Written charges of infidelity! Somehow it seemed far worse, far more incriminating that they were written. Yet the news of the accusations was old, something he had known from the beginning. So why was he discomfited to find the accusations were in print? Why were they settling so heavily on his shoulders? Illogically, their being signed lent a certain amount of credibility to them.

"How long have you known about these?" he asked curiously.

"Two years." As if she read his mind and knew he was wondering why she had not told him, she said, "I couldn't take the chance of your not believing me, and in your frame of mind when I first saw you, you would have disbelieved me."

Cord did not deny the accusation; he could not, for it was the truth. Even now he felt as if she were pushing him to the edge of credibility. He was reeling from the double blow—blows he felt that were below the belt. The kind of blows he would have expected from the scum he was around in prison, not from the woman to whom he was married.

And again she was confessing because she knew he would learn about these signed confessions tomorrow when he met with Kern Wallis.

It seemed a matter of her having to rather than a matter of her wanting to because it was the right thing to do.

"When I came to the penitentiary, you were cold and hostile to me," she said. "I didn't trust you, so I didn't tell you about the written testimonies."

"Why not later?" he said.

"By then I was afraid of losing you," she admitted. "And Hope . . . and I . . . we needed and wanted you." She paused, then added, "If I were given the same set of circumstances I would do it over again without a second thought. No one will take my daughter away from me without a fight."

"You weren't afraid of losing me personally," Cord corrected.

Always Floryn's feelings for him came down to want and need. While he did not fault her for that, he felt that they had made no progress at all during their time together. Nothing had really changed. Oh,

310

yes, they were sleeping together and making sex, but he still felt as if he were a pawn in this game Floryn was playing.

"You were afraid of losing what I could do for you," Cord continued. "It was always a man, not a particular man, who could get the Fancy Lady for you, who could save your daughter for you. In this instance this man's name happened to be Cord Donaldson. But it never was Cord Donaldson, *the* man."

"That's not true."

"It damn sure is," he snapped. "You were considering Kern Wallis if I turned you down."

"I was bluffing. I didn't really consider him."

Floryn looked forlorn, but she had a knack for looking like that when she wanted something. Beneath the disguise of dejection he saw her pride, her defiance.

"Well, my dear wife, you'll never have to fight for Hope by yourself again," Cord said. "From now on I'll be fighting for my daughter. No one is going to take her from me. The Fancy Lady belongs to *her*, and by damn I'll keep it for *her*." Cord crossed the room and sat in one of the wing chairs. "Tell me about the accusations."

Floryn shrugged. "I don't know much about them. I know they exist. I've seen them, but I've never been allowed to read them. I guess Hal was afraid I would destroy his evidence if I got my hands on them. And I would have because they are lies, Cord. Outright lies."

If Cord understood anything, he understood injustice. He knew what it was like to be the victim of a vicious lie and to be unable to defend himself.

"The charges were a figment of Hal's imagination with no substance until Kern Wallis came along," she continued. "He's the one who convinced Hal I was unfaithful. It's not all his fault, but he has a lot to answer for. From the minute he walked into this house, he determined to have the Fancy Lady and me. When I spurned his advances, he swore he would get the Fancy Lady and would ruin me in the process. He's spent the last three years doing just that. He weaseled his way into Hal's confidence and did everything he could to discredit me. Kern Wallis paid these men to lie about me."

As Floryn stood here and confessed, as she confronted the demons that plagued her, Cord's admiration for her returned. He had told Mildred only last night that he was no giant slayer; yet, here he was — after all she had told him — wanting to slay all the giants in Floryn's life.

But she really did not need him for herself. She was a strong woman accustomed to fighting her own battles. She had let no one, nothing deter her from seeing him. She had climbed the quarry, she had borrowed the money so she could free him.

From the beginning she had believed him, had believed in him . . . the man branded a mass murderer and a thief.

Even if she had slept around, what was her crime compared to murder?

"How did Hal convince the court to declare you an unfit mother? Did any of these men appear to testify about having had an affair with you?"

"No," she said, "there was no need. Hal owned and controlled everybody in and around Donaldsonville. He produced the letters and they served to prove my unworthiness."

After a long silence, she said, "Do the written confessions make a difference to you?"

"No."

312

She knelt by the chair, and he felt the soft pressure of her hands on his arm. She lifted her head so that he was staring into her face.

"Your confiding to me only when you were pushed against the wall does. Is there anything else you need to tell me?"

"No," she said slowly, quietly, "I've made all my confessions. Do you believe I've told the truth about them?"

"Yes."

"I'm glad."

He shrugged, his expression enigmatic. "It's no more than what you did for me. You believed me, and the crime I was accused of committing was far greater than yours."

"I know you," she said.

He had thought he knew her.

He pushed out of the chair. "If the discussion is over, I need to go. I promised Antonio that I would meet him at the stables in an hour. He's going to show me around the ranch."

She reached out and caught his arm. "Cord—"

He pulled away from her clasp. "Floryn, if we're going to save this ranch, one of us has to work. And saving the ranch . . . for Hope . . . was the reason I was brought here, why my freedom was purchased."

As if she had been struck, Floryn jerked back her hand and stared at him. His voice was hard and cold, the words insulting. Yet she had known the risk factor when she had married him with these dark secrets in her past. She had known he might revert to the stone-quarry man when she confessed about the loan and the signed statements. And he had.

She watched him walk to the door.

While Cord's accusation that she had married him because he could save the ranch and Hope, hurt, it

313

was also the truth . . . in part. In her heart of hearts she knew she married him because he was Cord Donaldson, because she was still in love with him. From the beginning he had refused to accept that she cared for him. He always relegated their lovemaking years ago to lust.

That, too, was partially correct. From the beginning she had been physically attracted to Cord, and it had been a stunning attraction. But Floryn had always felt—and still felt—more, much more. She needed him as she had needed no other man. She wanted him with the same intensity and exclusion.

Her needs and wants had nothing to do with her capabilities and independence. She knew she could live the remainder of her life without him, she could fight her own demons and giants, but she did not want to. She wanted someone to stand beside her, to cheer her when she was sad, to support her when she was weak, to laugh with her when she was happy. She wanted Cord to enhance these same characteristics in her. She wanted him to be an integral part of her life as well as an integral part of her sexual pleasure.

Deep down Floryn knew Leanor's words were true. Cord professed only to wanting her, but he needed her, too. Because she loved him, she could give him support and comfort. Because she was strong, she could help him fight his dragons, she could heal his wounded heart and soul, and she could bring him light and peace of mind. All of these things she wanted to do for him; she wanted him to do for her.

His hand, that big hand, that could be so gentle, closed over the doorknob.

Perhaps she was asking for the impossible. Cord Donaldson had always been a hard man. He was even harder now that he had been in prison. Nellie

314

Stratford had been right when she said Cord loved no woman. She was also correct when she said that Cord married Floryn but was not married to her. Perhaps he would never love Floryn, but she still had faith that one day he would see her as his helpmate.

And Floryn did believe in miracles.

She rose from where she knelt beside the wing chair. "Will I see you at lunch?"

He shrugged.

"And then he galloped right up to the pole and speared the ring," Hope said, having talked incessantly through lunch. She took a bite of her carrots, chewed them thoroughly, and swallowed. "I thought maybe he couldn't see so good with only one eye, but he can. Maybe it won't be so bad having him around here for a little while, Mama."

Floryn smiled, but her gaze continually returned to the window. She watched for Cord.

"Do you like the patch?" Hope asked.

"Umhum."

The door opened and Leanor bustled into the room, clearing the table. "Remember, I'll be gone this afternoon. I have refreshments in the kitchen safe. And I shall be back in time to serve dinner."

Floryn nodded.

"Is Cord going to be at the meeting, Mama?" Hope asked.

"Yes," Floryn answered and returned to the table.

She wished Lyle Hackett were going to be there, too. His death, his wife's selling out and leaving had been a hard blow for Floryn. And her concern was not only the money. Hackett was a strong man respected by the community. He was a strong opponent to Hal Wallis.

Although the neighbors had been her friends and had supported her, she knew they could not stand up against Wallis and his demands much longer. By holding their mortgages, he had them over the barrel and was threatening to foreclose. She had known that Cord would infuse them with a new spurt of defiance and resolve. They reckoned he was a tough man who could and would deal with Wallis, that he was the man who could do the impossible. If anyone could drive cattle to a faraway market, Cord Donaldson could.

Yes, she thought, Cord Donaldson could do it. She had faith in him.

She wished he had as much faith in her.

"He's not going to let me have the meadow back, is he?" Hope asked.

Pulling herself back to the present, back to Hope and her endless barrage of questions, Floryn said, "You'll have to talk to him about that."

Hope played with her fork for a little while before she said, "I wish I hadn't done it, Mama. I really do like the Forever Tree."

"I'm sure you do," Floryn murmured. "Why don't you tell your father how you feel about it?"

Sighing, Hope laid the fork down. She propped her elbow on the table and rested her cheek against her palm. "Because."

"Why because?"

"Just because."

They heard a horse galloping toward the house.

"Maybe that's him." Hope jumped up and ran to the window where she pulled the curtain aside and pressed her face to the pane. "It's him, Mama. He's come back."

While this had not been the best day for Floryn herself where Cord was concerned, she was glad to

316

see that father and daughter were making progress. Hope was captivated by her father.

The front door opened, steps sounded down the corridor.

"Hello, Father," Hope said. "I saw you ride in."

Floryn raised a brow in surprise. She had asked Hope to call him Father, but this was the first time she had heard the child address him directly. Although *Father* was rather stilted and formal, it was a step in the right direction. Certainly it was better than *that man*.

"Hello, Hope," he said.

He whipped off his hat and pegged it on the back of the nearest chair.

"Where've you been?" Hope asked.

"Riding."

"Where 'bouts?"

"Here and there," he answered.

"What'cha got behind your back?"

"A surprise."

He brought his hand to the front of his body. "A bouquet of flowers."

"Indian paintbrushes," Hope yelped and clapped her hands. "I know where you've been. You've been to the Forever Tree."

"Yes," he said, his gaze on Floryn. "Do you like them?"

"Oh, yes," she squealed. "They're my favorite flowers. And Mama's too."

He held them out to her. "Here you are."

Floryn remembered the bouquet he had bought her in San Antonio. That seemed such a long time ago, as if it happened to two other people. Taking the flowers from her father, Hope left the room. Cord sat down at the table.

"You've already eaten?" he said to Floryn.

"Yes, you were late, and we didn't know if you were coming or not."

He nodded and began to fill his plate. Floryn walked to the buffet and busied herself with straightening the candle holders and refolding the linen napkins. Every so often she would glance in the window to her right to look at Cord's reflection. Shortly Hope returned with her bouquet in a vase of water. She set it on an empty pedestal table.

"So, young lady," Cord said to Hope, "you and Leanor are going into town this afternoon."

"We're gonna be gone while you're having your meeting," Hope answered, "but we'll be back for supper."

Hope stretched out her arms, the sleeve of her shirt riding high on her arm, to pick up her glass of milk.

Cord caught her wrist. "When did you get that bruise on your arm?"

"The other day before you came. I fell off the seesaw at school," the child answered. Setting her glass on the table, she twisted her arm so she could view the wound also. "It's not a good seesaw like the one Agnes's father built for her. Hers won't break."

Again Hope lifted her glass of milk and took a swallow. "But I don't seesaw on Agnes's anymore," she said. "Since Papa Hal died, her mama and papa won't let me play with her 'cause they don't like Mama."

"You have your own seesaw, don't you?" Cord asked.

"Umhum. But Agnes's papa built hers for her. Antonio built mine."

"It's not the same, is it?" Cord said softly.

"Well—" Hope leaned back in the chair. "It's nice when papas do things for their children."

"Hope," Leanor called from the kitchen, "if you plan to go with me, you better come help me clean up the dishes."

"Coming."

While she finished drinking her milk, Cord picked up his coffee cup and walked into the kitchen. By the time he returned, Hope was wiping the white mustache from her upper lip. Then she shoved her chair away from the table, the legs grating against the floor. Singing, she skipped out of the room.

"What time is the meeting going to start?" Cord asked.

"Two o'clock," Floryn answered. "I have a list of all the people who will be here and some notes I've made. Since you'll be in charge of this, would you like to look it over?"

They exchanged looks.

"Political move?" he asked.

Would he always be suspect of her motives? Floryn wondered.

"Not altogether. You're *El Patrón*," she said without rancor, "you're the one to officiate."

He nodded, and they walked out of the dining room into the study. As if he had been doing it all his life, Cord sat down behind the desk, Floryn stood behind, and they looked through the stack of material she had amassed.

She opened the map and spread it on the desk. "There are several routes we can take," she said, running her index finger over the black lines. "Here are the ones I've marked, the ones I think will be the best and the safest, not necessarily the quickest."

One time when she was pointing, her arm accidently brushed against him, and he moved away from her. She tried to make sure she did not touch him again.

By the time they had discussed the advantages and disadvantages of all possible routes, Floryn was sitting in one of the wing chairs in front of the desk.

"We're taking a big risk," she said, "by driving our cattle to the railhead in Missouri. It's never been done before. And Kern Wallis is offering us seven dollars and fifty cents a head. Sure money."

"What are you saying?" Cord asked.

"What do you think we should do?" she asked. "Should we risk it all on the chance that we'll get these cattle to market or should we accept Wallis's offer and make our drive next year?"

His elbows propped on the desk, his fingers bridged in front of his mouth, Cord said, "Are you actually interested in my opinion, or is this just a question to generate talk?"

"I want to know," she said heavily. "I honestly don't know what to do."

"Let's go to Sedalia," he said.

"Good morning, Mr. Donaldson." An elderly man stopped to speak to Cord as they passed each other on the boardwalk in front of the general store in Donaldsonville. Smiling, the man extended his hand. "I'm Pastor Whitmore."

"Pastor." The men shook.

"Welcome to Donaldsonville." The light gray eyes were friendly; they seemed sincere. "I hope we see you in church one of these Sundays."

"You never can tell where I may show up."

"I look forward to seeing you at my place," the minister said. "Please give Mrs. Donaldson my regards."

Promising to relay the message, Cord bid the pastor a good day and continued walking until he stood in front of Kern Wallis's office. Cord knew he was the center of attention, and his knowledge did not stem from conceit. The townspeople were blatant in their curiosity. Some wandered onto the boardwalk and stared at him. Others peered through windows and opened doors. Others hid behind curtains and window shades. And the meeting with the minister was not coincidental, was it?

Cord looked at his watch, then slid it back into its pocket. Opening the door, he walked into the small room. His gaze swept around the office before it settled on the dapper man who sat behind the desk.

"Kern Wallis?"

"Yes." The attorney's gaze slowly slid down Cord's body, taking in the white shirt and black vest, lingering on the two Navy '51 Colts. Wallis pulled off his spectacles and rose.

He was a big man, a powerfully big man, and reminded Cord of Orwen Baxter. Both of them were built like locomotives. Whereas Orwen was older and rusted out, Wallis was young and sleek. The suit did not disguise his trim, muscular physique.

"I'm Cord Donaldson." He stripped off his gloves and slid them beneath his belt. "You're expecting me?"

"I am." The attorney looked at the wall clock.

So did Cord. One minute after ten.

"You're right on time."

Cord hung his hat on the clothes rack close to the door.

"Welcome to Donaldsonville." Wallis extended his hand, an extremely large hand that easily gripped Cord's, that gripped firm and hard as they shook. "How do you like your new home?"

Morning sunlight beamed into the office through

321

the window to the back of the attorney.

Cord dodged using the word home. He had never had a place he had called home. The prison had come the closest to being that. Every time he thought he was about to find this illusive place, he learned he was farther away than he had ever been. He had begun to think there was no home for him.

Even now he was wary of thinking of the Fancy Lady as home. He feared that to do so would guarantee its being taken away from him. Maybe that was why he was wary of loving Floryn. He feared he might lose her again. If they moved from the physical plane of lust, to an emotional plane, as he suspected Floryn wanted, he might have a greater opportunity to keep her. Rather than being in his bed only, she would be in his heart. It was easy to leave a bed without regrets, not so the heart.

But Cord did not allow himself to linger on such thoughts.

He glanced up to see Wallis looking at him expectantly, and he searched his mind for the thread of conversation.

"The Fancy Lady," Wallis said. "How do you like her?"

"I've always liked it."

"She's beautiful," Wallis said. "But even if she were not, anything would beat prison."

"Almost anything," Cord answered.

"I'm sure you were happy when your parole came through."

Cord simply looked. No need to answer the obvious.

"Sorry I didn't meet you sooner at the fiesta. I pressed for an invitation, but Floryn refused to send one." Wallis smiled. "Of course, I can understand. She dislikes me because as Hal's attorney I represented his best interests, which she felt went against hers."

"She has a point," Cord said.

"Heard you and some of the ranchers had a meeting yesterday at the Fancy Lady," Wallis said.

"We did, but I didn't ride all the way into Donaldsonville for small talk, Mr. Wallis. You and I have some business to take care of and I want to do it as quickly as we can. I need to get back to the Fancy Lady. I have a great deal of work to do."

"The ranchers would like for you to think my offer is small talk, but it's not, especially not in the light of their . . . and your present financial straits," Wallis said. He reached up to brush his hand over immaculately combed and greased hair.

"I can handle my financial affairs without your help," Cord said.

"I'm prepared to give cash for your herds. Seven dollars and fifty cents a head in U.S. currency."

"We're all aware of your offer," Cord said. "We discussed it last night, but our minds are made up. We'll drive the cattle to market ourselves where we can get thirty-five dollars a head."

"Which railhead?" Wallis asked.

"Sedalia."

"My God, do you know where Sedalia is?"

"Pretty good idea," Cord replied sarcastically. "One of us had a map. Another could read. And we were extremely fortunate to have had with us one man who had actually made the trip there and back."

"A man traveling from here to Sedalia is different from a cow, from a herd of cattle, making the same trip. This is a harebrained idea if I ever heard one. How many cattle do you think will survive that long, hard trek to Missouri?"

"I'll let you know when we return," Cord said.

"They may be offering more than I am," Wallis said, "but you'll be paid only for the cattle that make it."

Cord had thought about that long and hard, and even longer and harder since Floryn had asked for his advice on the cattle drive.

"We figure we have a good chance of making it come spring. Anyway, it's a risk we're willing to take."

"How about my giving you ten dollars a head," Wallis said. "A guaranteed amount."

Cord shook his head.

After a pause, Wallis said, "Well, I wish you luck, and you're going to need it. Mr. Donaldson. I don't suppose I need to remind you when your note is due?"

"No, Floryn told me." No matter how matters were between him and Floryn, Cord would not allow the attorney to make slurs or innuendoes about her. The attorney would never know what the true state of affairs between them was. It was none of his concern.

"Good. Let's you and me get to business. Coffee?"

Cord shook his head, pulled a chair to the front of Wallis's desk, and sat down.

"Maybe something stronger?" Wallis suggested.

Again Cord declined. "I'll just read the papers transferring the property to Floryn, and if everything reads right, I'll sign them. As I said, I'm in a hurry."

"Before we go into that," Wallis said. "I need to discuss a related matter with you. One that will probably change your mind about deeding any of the Fancy Lady to Floryn."

Twenty-two

When Kern Wallis sat down, he squirmed into a comfortable position, the chair creaking and squalling beneath his weight. His elbows resting on the armrests, his hands—again Cord noticed how big his hands were—loosely twined in his lap, he gazed steadily at Cord.

"Mr. Donaldson, because of a promise I made to Hal as his attorney and because I'm the estate's attorney, I have to relate certain facts to you before I can allow you to transfer any of your inheritance, especially if the transfer is to Floryn."

Surveying the man across from him, Cord crossed a leg over the other to rest his ankle on his knee. He had certainly been surprised when he finally met Kern Wallis. He had imagined him to look and to be like *Slick Willie* Webb Pruitt.

"Are you going to tell me there are stipulations which say I can't do as I please with my half of the property? That I cannot give or sell it to Floryn?"

Leaning back in the chair and rolling his pencll in his hands, Wallis smiled slightly. "Hal wanted to make such stipulations, but I advised him against it."

Did you now? Cord wondered.

"They may have kept you from doing anything with the property for a few years, they may have kept Floryn from getting a share of the Fancy Lady, but eventually you could have gotten a reversal of the decision. There are always legal ways around stipulations."

"Especially if one has money," Cord murmured scornfully. "In this case, though, the most important thing was to take guardianship of Hope from her mother. Hal knew Floryn would get over the ranch, that eventually she would get more land. But Floryn would never get over her loss of Hope and would never be able to replace her daughter."

Once more Cord and Wallis sized each other up.

"Again, Mr. Donaldson"—the attorney's voice was hard—"that was Hal's decision, not mine. He had to do what he thought was best for the child."

"And best for the child according to Hal was either you or me as her guardian rather than her natural mother. At the time, two unmarried men, one of whom Hal hadn't seen in ten years and knew nothing about."

Wallis fiddled with objects on his desk. "When Hal drew up his will, he was not sure you could be found. He had tried unsuccessfully many times during the past nine years to locate you. But he wanted you, his only living heir, to inherit along with Hope."

Cord noted that Wallis did not include Hope as one of Hal's living heirs.

"How did you locate me?" Cord asked.

Wallis, looking at Cord, rubbed his hand down the sides of his mouth. "A private detective."

"You should have hired the same one Floryn did. Hers found me quicker."

"I had no doubt we would find you," Wallis said. "It was simply a matter of time."

"That was Floryn's fear. Time was running out."

"For her or for you?" Wallis asked, his eyes narrowed.

"For both of us," Cord answered.

"Hal believed his wife to be a greedy, grasping woman," Wallis said. "And I do, too. He has a few facts he wants me to give you. Facts he felt you had a right to know before you made any decisions concerning the sale of the property. What you do with the facts, Mr. Donaldson, is your concern. None of mine."

The man was different from Webb Pruitt. Both were smooth, but Pruitt had a closed gaze. Wallis appeared to be open. Both were businessmen. Pruitt was calculating. While Cord would not go so far as to say Wallis was guileless, he did think he seemed to be less devious.

Mildred had seemed to think Wallis's one tragic flaw was his greediness. He wanted to own the entire valley.

Wallis spoke. "What I'm about to say is extremely delicate and is not necessarily a reflection of my feelings. Nor is it an attempt to demean your wife."

As Cord stared at the attorney across the desk from him, he thought back to the events in the study the previous morning and was glad Floryn had told him the full story.

"As I stated in the letter I wrote to you when you were in the penitentiary," Wallis said, his words intruding on Cord's thoughts, "Hal wrote Floryn out of the will because he felt she had been unfaithful to him."

"When?" Cord asked.

"When what?" Wallis swiveled back in the chair.

327

"When did he learn she was unfaithful or when did he write her out of the will?"

"Both," Cord said.

"He wrote her out of the will two years ago."

"Why two years ago rather than ten years ago?" Cord asked.

"Hal forgave Floryn for her indiscretion with you, and he accepted the child as his. It was her transgressions in the latter years that brought such unhappiness to Hal, but it was a particular transgression that caused him to write her out of his will and have her declared an unfit mother. A transgression he learned about two years ago."

"So far there have been a lot of fingers pointing at Floryn, a lot of talk about having proof of her infidelity, but I've heard or seen nothing that convinces me of her guilt."

Wallis took a key from his coat pocket and unlocked the top drawer of his desk. He removed a brown portfolio that he opened and from which he extracted a packet of papers.

"I won't go so far as to say this is proof, but these are signed statements, witnessed by impartial observers." He held them up. "People can lie in writing as well as by mouth."

"Why didn't you send these to me when you wrote me?" Cord took the papers from Wallis.

"I didn't want to take a chance on their being lost," Wallis answered, "the mail being what it is."

"You didn't even mention them," Cord said.

"No, I thought it would be to my best advantage to wait until you arrived here to let you see for yourself."

"The decision to take guardianship of Hope away from Floryn was based solely on evidence in these confessions, yet not one of these men testified against her in court?"

"Any of these people would have stepped forward, but the judge didn't feel the necessity. He knew several of these men personally and believed their testimony. The details of the case were kept confidential because Hal didn't want to hurt Hope or damage reputations any more than he had to."

"He was interested only in damaging Floryn's," Cord said.

"He was interested in the truth, Mr. Donaldson," Wallis said. "These documents are yours now to do with as you wish. As I said before, my obligation to Hal and to the estate is to inform you."

"Yet you waited until after I married Floryn to let me see these, before you told me about them," Cord said, remembering Floryn's hatred of the man, her accusations about him and his character. "Was this a deliberate ploy on your part?"

"Meaning what?"

"Let Floryn think she's won and then jerk the rug from beneath her feet."

"I'm not going to dignify that with an answer."

"What role did you play in obtaining these statements?"

"Nothing after I hired the private detective for Hal. In fact—" Wallis rose, slipped his hands into his trousers pockets and walked to the long table against the far wall. "Hal Donaldson was my friend. I tried to get him to stop this because it was driving him insane. The more he heard about Floryn's supposed behavior, the worse he got, the more abusive he became to her, the more determined he was to make sure she was punished for her sins."

Cord looked at the papers he held. "It's strange

that with her having so many supposed lovers, my wife never conceived another child save the one I gave to her."

Wallis searched through the bottles before he picked up and poured himself a glass of whiskey. "Are you sure you won't have something to drink?"

For the third time Cord declined.

His whiskey in hand, Wallis wandered back to his desk but did not sit down. He adjusted the shade on his window and gazed out. Across the street in front of Jennings's Mercantile, Cord saw a little girl jumping rope, and he wondered if it was Agnes Jennings. Her long blond braids bounced each time her feet touched the planks. When he noticed that her dress was covered with ruffles, he thought of Hope and smiled. He also wondered what Agnes Jennings's seesaw looked like.

Wallis said, "There are those in Donaldson who loved Hal and who believe Floryn is guilty of infidelity. They would argue that there are ways a woman can get rid of an unwanted baby."

"What are you getting at?" Cord demanded.

"Floryn has had a Mexican witch doctor in her employ since she married Hal and came to the ranch. A woman who knows potions and herbs. One who used to work at the cribs in El Paso and dispose of unwanted babies."

"This is the *curandera* Floryn told me about?" Cord said.

Wallis nodded his head. "Of course, let me point out again, Mr. Donaldson, it's a matter of one person's word against another. I just want you to be aware of both sides of the story. Since you've married Floryn and have come back here to live, you're going to be hearing it. If I know human nature, you'll feel the prejudice of those who dislike Floryn."

"Thank you for telling me, but I'm still unconvinced," Cord said. "Is there anything else you're obligated to inform me?"

Wallis paused fractionally before he sighed and said, "I had hoped it would not come to this, but yes, there is." He reached into the drawer and pulled out a small bundle wrapped in brown paper and securely sealed. "These are private and personal papers Hal left you."

When Cord took them, Wallis also handed him another letter. "This is the document I had to sign, swearing that before I allowed you to transfer any property to Floryn, I would give you Hal's package."

Cord skimmed Wallis's document first, dropped it on the desk, then looked curiously at the bundle he held. "What is it?"

"I don't know. Hal never confided in me," Wallis answered. "The only person who does know is the judge. Hal went into a private session with him. The decision to take custody of Hope away from Floryn was based on this piece of evidence. Hal gave me instructions on what to do with it and when."

Cord reached for the letter opener.

"If you recognize your uncle's handwriting, you'll see the way he guaranteed that you could tell if the original binding had been tampered with."

Cord nodded. He cut his way through several layers of paper to reveal a letter and a smaller package on which the words *Do not open until you have read my letter* were written. Cord laid the items on Wallis's desk and unfolded the letter. Leaning back, he read.

Hal informed him of Floryn's unfaithfulness and accused her of being a *femme fatale* who had lured every man she met into her bed. For years, he claimed, he had overlooked the men in her life because he understood human nature and loved Hope. He considered the child the apple of his eye. Knowing Hope was Cord's child, that she was a Donaldson, Hal felt that she was his child also.

Two years ago, George Greeve, the former foreman of the Fancy Lady, had returned demanding money. He admitted to having an affair with Floryn and agreed to sign a confession in return for money. In his own writing, he confessed he had been Floryn's lover after Cord left. He also confessed he was Hope's father. Further evidence uncovered that Floryn had periodically sent him money through the years. Blackmail money for his silence.

If Cord wanted proof of that, Hal informed him, he could check the ledgers. With the outbreak of the War Between the States, Floryn had no money to send George. Thus, he came to the Fancy Lady, hoping to blackmail Hal also.

The unopened packet contained Greeve's signed confession and two notes Floryn had written him. Hal wrote that Greeve was no threat. Shortly after he left the Fancy Lady, he died.

Hal's letter continued. After Greeve's confession, Hal had Kern Wallis hire a private detective who began an investigation of Floryn. He was the one who collected the other signed statements. Hal had hoped they would be enough evidence to keep Cord from signing over any of the Fancy Lady to Floryn. Had it been, Kern was instructed to destroy this packet and no one would know there was the possibility Hope was not Cord's daughter. Whether she was a Donaldson or not, Hal wrote, he loved the child as his own and left her one half the Fancy Lady. Forever she was his daughter.

Cord opened the packet, glancing at the two notes Floryn had written to the former foreman, then unfolding Greeve's written confession. Each word the man wrote sliced Cord to his very heart and soul. As much as he had liked George, as much as he had respected him, Cord could not bear the thought of Floryn and the man having slept together, of their having made Hope.

Yet, this man whom Cord knew, whom he trusted had written and signed the testimony. As far as Cord knew, George had no reason to lie about it.

The spirit flagging out of Cord, he refolded the letter and held it for a moment. Everything he read substantiated Hal's belief that she had been unfaithful to him, that she had indeed made love with George Greeve. Based on Greeve's letter and Floryn's two notes, Cord could even understand the judge's decision to take Hope away from her.

Floryn had not mentioned Greeve to him, had not even hinted she had been accused of sleeping with him. That he claimed to be the father of their child. Only yesterday she had sworn that she had told him everything. Yet he was learning about George Greeve today.

Why had she not told him? Then he remembered her telling him that she had never seen the statements, had only heard about them. Had she no idea this one was here? Surely she would suspect that he would learn about George. Was this another instance of her not telling him something until she was pushed against the wall? Cord feared this was so.

Yet he could not forget Floryn's telling him repeatedly that he was the only one who had made love to her. She had all but sworn it to him. Something deep within Cord wanted to believe her, needed to believe her.

Cord curled his hand into a fist. By God, Hope was his daughter, Floryn his wife. He could not undo the past, but he damn sure had something to do with the present and the future.

Cord looked at Wallis. "You haven't read this?"

The attorney shook his head.

Cord bundled everything together and slipped it into his shirt pocket. "Well, Mr. Wallis, if you have those papers ready, I'll read over them."

His elbows propped on the desk, his hands bridged in front of his mouth, Wallis stared a long time before he said, "So you're going to go through with it? None of this convinces you?"

"I'm going through with it," Cord said, choosing to answer the first question rather than the second. "These men could have been paid to lie about her."

Cord could not imagine that Greeve would have sunk so low. If he had, the former foreman was a much different man than Cord had thought. When Cord had known him, he had the impression that George Greeve was an honorable and trustworthy man.

"They could have lied," Wallis said slowly, "but did they? Always, Mr. Donaldson, there will be that question in your mind."

"Mr. Wallis," Cord said, "my wife's past belongs to her, as mine belongs to me. I didn't marry the Floryn of yesterday; I married the Floryn of today. I have no doubts, no questions about this woman."

Wallis lifted his brows in surprise. "Mr. Donaldson, I believe you're making a grave mistake in put-

334

ting so little confidence in Hal, in what he discovered about your wife. If she were unfaithful to him, she'll be unfaithful to you."

The words struck home with Cord. If Floryn had slept with George Greeve, she had not been unfaithful to Hal, she had been unfaithful to him. She had never slept with Hal, never professed to love him; therefore, she could not be unfaithful.

But what did Cord expect? He had ridden away and left Floryn, a young, naive, and pregnant girl, to face the world alone. If she were unfaithful, could he blame her for turning to George? A part of him could. Another part could not.

Wallis said, "Your uncle wanted you to have this property."

"My mind's made up." Cord's words were as direct as his gaze.

Wallis shoved the papers across the desk. "Here they are."

Cord picked them up. When he was through reading, he leaned forward, picked up the pen, and dipped it into the inkwell. Whether Floryn had made love to George Greeve or not, a bargain was a bargain. He had promised her one half of his share of the ranch if she would buy his parole, and that bargain was not predicated on her virtue. He would keep his word. After he signed his name on the document, he shoved it across the desk.

The attorney's fingers touched the edge of the paper and he slid it closer to himself. "Please be aware, Mr. Donaldson, that many of the good folks of this town regard your wife as a promiscuous woman, and they doubt the paternity of her daughter."

"Please be aware of this, Mr. Wallis. I don't give

a damn what the good folks of this town think. Even if I did, I couldn't stop their thinking. I will not, however, tolerate anyone's calling Floryn promiscuous from this day forward, and believe me when I tell you that Hope Donaldson is *my* child."

Cord rose, sunlight falling fully on him. It beamed on the Navy '51 Colts with the ivory grips. As he removed his gloves, he casually placed a hand on his gun belt.

"If ever I hear anyone make such charges against my wife or my daughter, they shall answer to me. Also tell these hypocritical bastards that I play by my own rules."

He slid his hands into the gloves and flexed his fingers.

"There's nothing soft or easy about me. My enemies have accused me of having no conscience. I wouldn't go so far as to say that about myself, but I do confess my sense of justice is different from the average man's."

"I understand," Wallis said.

"How do I go about getting guardianship of Hope returned to her mother?"

Wallis raised his brows. "You'll have to petition the court. That will take a little while."

"I have plenty of time."

"Do you want me to file the petition for you?"

"No, I think perhaps it would be a conflict of interest for you. You were Hal's attorney, not Floryn's. I would always feel like you were representing Hal's best interests rather than mine, Floryn's, or Hope's."

"Do I take this to mean that I'm no longer to represent you in any capacity?"

Cord nodded.

"Possibly you're not aware, Mr. Donaldson, that I have been handling all of Hal's business for the past two years. Hal found Floryn to be careless in her managing of the ranch. While the accounts are accurate, Floryn did not have a business head. As a result, Hal shifted that responsibility to me. I have all his ledgers and financial papers."

"I'm sure my uncle appreciated all that you did for him, Mr. Wallis," Cord said. "I would appreciate your sending me all the estate property as soon as possible."

"I will," Wallis said, his expression hardening. "But I want you to know, I'll be more than happy to work with you, as I did with your uncle. The two of us can come to some agreement and between us can administer the Fancy Lady."

"As I said before, Mr. Wallis, I'll do it on my own," Cord said.

Wallis's eyes and mouth became thin slits in his face. "Under the circumstances I doubt you can do it on your own but hope you can, Mr. Donaldson. Within the next few days, I'll send you all your property."

Cord walked across the room and was passing through the doorway when Wallis spoke again.

"I sincerely believe you're going to regret this decision, Mr. Donaldson."

Twenty-three

He would probably regret this tomorrow, Cord thought, laying down the hammer and rolling his aching shoulders. A few weeks away from the chain gang, and he was growing soft.

When he had returned from his meeting with Kern Wallis this morning, he had planned to give the signed statements to Floryn and after she had read them, confront her about George. But she had been gone. Antonio was working the cattle; Leanor was busy with the house. Even Hope had deserted him. She was visiting with Mildred. Restless, he had wanted something to occupy both his hands and mind. He had begun to work on Hope's seesaw.

His gaze swept over the backyard. Strewn about were lumber, bags of nails, and building tools. He brushed his arm across his sweaty brow, lifted the patch and blotted the skin beneath. This was one of the many disadvantages of wearing a leather shield. In the summer it was hot, miserably hot, and tended to chafe the skin around it.

He kicked remnants of wood from his feet as he walked to the water pail hanging on the back porch. He was reaching for the dipper when Leanor stepped out of the kitchen.

"How about a glass of cool lemonade?" she asked.

Cord smiled, murmured "thanks," and took the

338

glass she handed him. In a few deep gulps he slaked his thirst. Planting a palm against one of the porch columns, he stood in the shade and enjoyed the cool. He also surveyed his work with pride.

"Did Floryn say when she would be back?" he asked.

Leanor shook her head. "She is sometimes gone all day when she rides. That is the way she handles her worry."

"She was worried about my reaction to Wallis's accusations," Cord said more than asked.

"*Sí,*" Leanor answered. "*Señor* Wallis is the one who turned *El Patrón* against her. You and Hope are the most important people in her life, and she's afraid of losing you. She's afraid *Señor* Wallis will succeed in turning you against her."

"Why doesn't she have more faith in me?" he asked.

"Faith comes from loving. She has never been loved, and those whom she loved have let her down."

If the words were meant to be an accusation, Cord did not know, but he accepted them as such. Long after Leanor returned to the house, he stood on the porch, pondering what the housekeeper had said. Floryn had often faulted him because he believed in himself only. But she was no different. Their secret fears had made them wary, made them draw up within themselves. Each restricted his trust to himself.

Cord looked at the swing that Antonio had hung for Hope, at the smaller seesaw the *gran vaquero* had built. He looked at the larger one he was building. As he had worked today, he thought about creating a small playground. A slide, he thought. That would be fairly easy to construct. A merry-go-round. He remembered one he had seen years ago. With the right equipment and tools, he could build Hope one.

He could see her standing on the merry-go-round, the wind on her face and in her hair as she spun around. Straight and proud, her head held high, she would be queen of her domain.

"What are you building?" Floryn asked.

He looked to the side of the house to see her walking from the barn area.

"You've been gone a long time."

Floryn pulled off her hat and slapped it against her leg, a fine haze of dust swirling through the air. "I rode across the border to meet with *Señor* Luna. He's the one I've been talking to about sheep herding."

She was still nursing her plan to become a sheep rancher.

Shucking off her gloves as she stepped onto the gallery, she laid them and her hat on the shelf above the washstand. After she filled the tin basin with water, she bent over to splash it over her face and on the back of her neck, the movement pulling her trousers tautly across her buttocks and thighs. Nicely rounded buttocks!

She straightened and flexed her shoulders, material now pulling over her breasts, also nicely rounded and alluring. Like tiny, many-faceted diamonds, water droplets glistened on her face when she returned to the edge of the porch. The afternoon sunshine colored her hair gold, and the breeze gently riffled the moistened curls around her face.

"I didn't know you were a carpenter," she said.

"There's a lot about me that you don't know."

"Yes, there is."

She stepped off the porch and meandered through

the maze of lumber and tools. She leaned against one of the sawhorses.

"The transfer of the property is complete," he said. "I gave you the acres you asked for."

"Thank you." She kicked a small block of wood, following it around the yard. "I wondered if you would change your mind after talking with Wallis."

"No, our deal wasn't based on your fidelity. We made a bargain. Maybe if I had known you were going to consult with a sheep herder, I might have reconsidered giving it to you."

Her expression was guarded. "As you pointed out to me before we left Huntsville, your word is final since you own one fourth of the ranch and control Hope's half interest."

"I gave you one hundred and fifty thousand acres. It's yours to do with what you want."

Smiling, she picked up the hammer and swung it several times, the material of her shirt pulling tight against her back as her arm moved forward, against her breasts as the arm went backward.

"You don't mind the sheep?" she asked.

"Yes, I do," he said. "They're a stinking lot, but the property belongs to you. I'd like to request that before you actually begin your sheep herding you talk in more detail to me about it."

She gazed at him a long while before she nodded her head.

"I have something else for you," he said. "The statements. They're in the top drawer in the study. Do with them what you will."

He waited to see if she would tell him about George.

"Thank you, Cord."

Evidently not.

He moved back to the seesaw foundation platform—about the size of a large food crate—he had been working on. Picking up a plank, he laid it across two sawhorses and measured.

"I put some other papers in there, also," he said, keeping his voice casual. "Personal papers that Hal gave to me in case the confessions didn't convince me of your infidelity."

"Personal papers?" she questioned.

"More about your infidelity," Cord answered. "You'll probably want to look through them."

Still she said nothing about Greeve.

"Is it really over?" She stood beside him.

"As far as I'm concerned."

She nodded and blinked back tears. After a while she asked, "Is what you're building a secret?"

"A seesaw for Hope." Strong sure strokes of the saw cut the plank, wood powder flying through the air, little particles clinging to his eye patch. The end of the board dropped.

Leaving the plank, he moved a few feet to pick up a split log. He placed the flat side on the center of the platform, the curved side upward, and nailed it. He raised his arm, again wiping perspiration from his brow, from beneath the patch.

Floryn was staring at the platform.

"Four steps. Two on either side of the board." He patted them. "This way the kids can climb up and down safely from the center as well as getting on at the end."

"Father, I'm home. Is it finished?" Hope ran out of the house.

He smiled. "Give me a couple more hours."

"Hi, Mama." Her big brown eyes sparkling, her face beaming, Hope bounced off the porch. "Did you see what Father is building me? A real big seesaw. Bigger than the one Agnes has. I didn't know it, but he gave Leanor a list of things to buy him yesterday when we were in town, and he surprised me."

She danced around the yard. "We're even gonna paint it, and it'll be better than Agnes's because hers isn't painted."

Both Floryn and Cord were caught up in Hope's enthusiasm, in her happiness. Looking at each other, they laughed with her. Then as they remembered recent hurts and misunderstandings the smiles faded.

Still Cord did something that surprised him. He moved to Floryn, caught her lightly by the shoulders and pulled her forward. He kissed the tip of her nose. Floryn looked startled.

"Our daughter looks very much like her mother."

Hope beamed. She skipped over to them, catching a hand of each parent. She looked shyly at Cord and grinned.

"Are we a family?"

Cord and Floryn looked at each other.

"Yes, we are, and since we are, I'd like to give you a small kiss like I gave to your mother."

Hope stared at him for a long time before she said, "All right."

Cord planted a butterfly caress on the tip of his daughter's nose. She jumped back, clamping both hands over her face, and giggled.

"Now, you're my angel," he said. "I've branded you."

"You have not," Hope teased.

"Yes, I have. Go look at your nose and see if it doesn't have angel dust on it. That means you'll never be alone. You'll always have an angel with you and no matter what happens we'll always be a family."

Hope giggled again and skipped away. "You're silly, Father."

"Yeah," he drawled, lapping up her enjoyment like someone starved for water.

"But I like it," Hope quickly added. "You've branded me and Mama as your angels."

Cord looked at Floryn.

"Yes," Floryn answered quietly, "he's branded both of us." She walked over to the swing.

"Father," Hope called.

"Hmmm?"

"Will the angel dust wash off when I bathe?"

"No, it's on there forever."

She thought a minute then asked, "Have you put angel dust on Leanor?"

"Not yet," he answered.

"We better. I don't want her to be alone either," she said, then raced off, her mind on another subject. "And she is part of our family, isn't she?"

"She sure is," Cord answered.

Bending over the plank, he tried to forget Floryn was in the yard with him. He tried to concentrate on his building, but he could no longer give it his full attention. Always he was conscious of Floryn.

He scraped the plank with the adz. He would work awhile, then run his hand over the area, almost caressing the plank. Over and over he did this until he was satisfied that it was smooth. He would stop and without moving his head, without giving any indication, he would glance out of the corner of his eye at Floryn.

Rays of sunlight painstakingly picked their way through the branches to shine down on her. A pensive expression on her face, she sat in the swing,

344

her hands wrapped around the ropes, her eyes closed. Using her feet, she pushed herself back and forth.

Hope, singing a little ditty she made up, skipped around the yard, picking up the remnant lumber and throwing it into a wheelbarrow. "See, Mama, I'm helping him," she called out.

Floryn opened her eyes.

"And he's gonna let me help him paint." Hope grinned. " 'Course I had to make him a promise before he would let me paint."

"What's that?" Floryn asked.

"I gotta wear the new dress he bought me. He wants me to wear it to church one Sunday. He's gonna take me."

"Church?"

Cord laid the adz aside and turned outright. Leaning back against the sawhorse, he crossed his hands over his chest. "Since I'm part of this community," he said, "I need to take an active role in the running of it. I've already met Pastor Whitmore. He sent you his regards and invited me to visit the church."

Hope said, "Father saw Agnes in town today, and she was wearing one of her ruffled dresses. He told me I was prettier than Agnes and so was my dress. And he said she would be jealous when she saw me in my new dress. She'll be even more jealous, Mama, when she sees me walking into church with my papa."

This had been a good day for Cord. He and Floryn had laid to rest one of her demons, one that would not plague their relationship in the future. And he had made great strides in getting to know Hope better. She was calling him father and today for the first time she had referred to him as her papa.

His shirt thrown over his shoulder, his body still damp with perspiration and gritty with sawdust, Cord stopped by the study on his way to the bedroom. He stood in the door and gazed at his wife. Her eyes and nose were red and swollen. Even now she sniffed and pressed a handkerchief to her mouth. Scattered over the desk were the papers Wallis had given to him. She held Hal's letter in her hands.

A forlorn expression on her face, she looked up. "I'm sorry you had to see these, Cord. I didn't know — I didn't know Hal had these. I wish you could have been spared this."

So did Cord.

"George was such a good man. So sweet and understanding. I loved him. I really did."

Her revelation shocked Cord; they bolted his feet to the floor. Words she had not said to him since that summer long ago. Yet his heart went out to her. He could understand her loving George Greeve. He was a man worthy of her love.

Yet a part of him was angry that again she had withheld vital information from him, that she had allowed him to believe Hope was his daughter. That she would not have confessed had he not learned about it.

Was this going to be the pattern of their life together?

Floryn looked so lonely and dejected that Cord pushed all thoughts but her out of his mind. He dropped his shirt to the floor and walked to where she sat. Kneeling, he caught her into his arms. Even as his heart hurt within him, even as wounded pride angrily raged, he soothed and comforted her.

She felt good against him. Soft and warm. All woman. Yet all he wanted to do was reassure her that she was not alone. He was here with her; he was here for her.

"I didn't know he was dead. I thought he was—he was—"

She began to sob in earnest.

"I had no idea that the two of you—that you loved—" He could not finish the sentence.

She never seemed to notice. "He was one of the most gentle men I've ever known, Cord. He saved my life and our unborn baby's life, and he almost died doing it."

Again Cord listened and she talked.

"It was in early March," she said, her voice far-away as she remembered, "and one of the children wandered away from the house. One of the Mexican children. My men were looking for her, and we sent for help. But we had to find her fast. It was raining, and we were going to have a freeze. She would have died from exposure."

This was the Floryn whom Cord knew, whom he admired. The woman who would go hunting for a lost child, who would spend the last cent she had on someone else. The woman who cried because her lover, the father of her child was dead. His shoulder was wet from her tears, but Cord held her, would hold her until her grief was spent. She sniffed.

"I had George drive me over to the Mexican village. They have a tracker, Primero, who I knew would find her. He's the best out here. On the way home, the buggy threw a wheel and I fell out. George was unhitching the horse to bring me home when a sudden clap of thunder frightened him. He bolted and ran."

She moved away from Cord and looked into his face. "My pains began. Realizing I was in labor, I ordered George to go back to the village for help, but he refused to leave me. He carried me all the way back. He really loved me and was determined our baby would live."

"Yes," Cord said slowly, studying her expressions, listening to the tone of her voice, the cadence of her words, "it sounds as if he loved you."

He pulled her back into his arms and held her. One thing Cord could . . . would . . . give her was comfort, and that is what she needed now, not questions, not recriminations.

Later when she had gotten over her grief, when she had regained her composure, they would talk.

"It was there that I met Leanor," Floryn finished. "She had taken me and George into her home, nursing him and delivering Hope. Because my delivery was hard, it was a long while before they could move me to the *hacienda*. By this time Leanor was in love with Hope, and I asked her to come with us."

She was quiet a long while before she said, "Can you understand why I love him? Why I'm so hurt by all of this?"

"Why didn't you tell me about him?" He held her tighter and lay his cheek on the crown of her head. "I would have understood your loving him."

Something in his voice evidently caught her attention. A look of surprise on her face, she eased back to gaze at him. "Oh, no," she whispered. "It's not that kind of loving. I loved George like a brother or uncle." She waved her hand over the desk. "None of this is true. I didn't—I didn't—Cord."

"What *is* true?" he said.

He rose and walked to the fireplace.

"Did you write the notes to George?"

"Yes."

"Did you send him money?"

"Yes, but it wasn't blackmail money. It was his. Wages for four months," she said. "During the time he worked for us, he asked me, as did many other of the ranch hands, to keep his money for him. Each time he wrote, he requested one hundred dollars. I still have his letters. He asked me to keep the rest because he was going to return and needed it for his nest egg. Am I going to have to spend the rest of my life defending my virtue?"

Cord was once more beside her, holding her, comforting her. "No," he said quietly, believing her, believing in her.

Yes, he believed her. He believed in her. No matter how recriminating the evidence might be.

Hal had emotionally abused her with these damned confessions, had bruised her heart and soul, would have broken her spirit if she had allowed it. Cord felt as if he had done the same thing. He would no longer.

"I didn't sleep with George, Hope isn't his daughter, and this isn't his confession." Fresh tears ran down her cheeks.

"I believe you," he said, tilting her chin so that she was looking directly into his face. "I believe I'm the only man you've made love to. I believe I'm Hope's father. It doesn't matter to me whether you did or did not sleep with him, Floryn, we're never going to speak of this again. Never."

"Never?" she whispered.

"Never."

"I can't prove those other accusations are lies."

"You don't have to prove them."

349

She picked up George's letter. "I can prove George's is untrue. I'm the one who taught George to read and write, and this isn't his handwriting. This is written in cursive. George had learned only to print."

"Hal lied," Cord said.

She shrugged. "All I know is that someone forged George's letter."

She dropped the letter and it fluttered to the floor.

"George returned," she whispered. "He came back, and I never knew it. Kern did this, Cord. When he looked through the records, he learned that I sent George the money, and he figured out a way to use this against me. When George returned, Kern tried to bribe him like he did the others, but George wouldn't be bribed. Kern killed him and forged his letter."

"Hal said Greeve came to him," Cord pointed out.

"George would have come to him, but by this time Hal already distrusted me and had let Kern take over the bookkeeping. It's natural Hal would have sent George to him for payment, and whatever Kern told Hal, Hal believed and recorded it as if it had happened to him."

"If this were true, Kern would have falsified the ledger," Cord said. "We'll check to see when we get them back."

"I don't have to prove it to know it's the truth. This letter is enough for me. Kern Wallis is responsible for this, as surely as day follows night."

Cord held Floryn in his arms as she worked her way through her grief and regained her composure. Later he eased away and walked to the sideboard, pouring her a small glass of wine.

Gratefully she took it. Several sips later she asked, "What did Kern say about me?"

Sitting in the wing chair, he said, "Nothing I care to repeat."

"I want to know." She paused. "I have a right to know."

Cord repeated in detail the conversation between him and Wallis. By the time he was through, she had refolded all the papers and stacked them in a neat pile in the center of the desk.

"Do you believe I used the *curandera* to get rid of unwanted pregnancies?"

"No."

"I have never had an occasion to use Angelita or any other *curandera* for that purpose," Floryn said. "Had I had lovers, had I gotten pregnant, I would have carried my baby."

With that quiet dignity Cord so admired, she rose and walked to the wall lamp to pick a match out of the container. She moved to the library table and struck the match, dropping it and all the letters, except George's, into a shallow china bowl. Both watched the flames dance in the air, then die down. The paper turned from bright orange to brown, curling up, then shattering into thousands of pieces of gray-black ash.

Gone forever were the confessions!

"I fired Wallis today," Cord said, "and told him to return all the property of the Fancy Lady he had in his possession."

Floryn looked startled. "That wasn't wise."

Cord lifted a brow in surprise.

"He's the only attorney in Donaldsonville," she said, a desperate tone to her voice. "Who are you going to get to petition the court to reverse its decision about my being a fit guardian for Hope?"

351

"We'll get one in El Paso."

"When?"

"As long as I'm here, there's no rush," he said.

"When, Cord?" she pressed.

He scrutinized her. "We'll drive over in a few days."

"I don't want to wait that long. I don't trust Kern. If George is dead—and I believe he is—Kern killed him. He'll do the same to anyone who stands in his way. You're probably next."

"You're worried about Kern's becoming Hope's guardian and getting control of the ranch?" Cord said.

"That, too, but I'm also worried about you," she said. "If I were Hope's guardian again, you would be out of danger. There would be no point in Kern's going after you."

Twenty-four

Ever since Floryn had read Hal's letter to Cord this morning, she had worried that something would happen to him. When they first married, her concern had been that someone in his past would hurt him. Now that concern was that someone from her past was a threat to him as well. She wondered if they would ever be safe.

"Riders coming!" The shout sounded around the *hacienda* about sundown, an hour or so after dinner.

Floryn walked out of the house to the edge of the veranda. Shading her eyes against the sun, she strained to make out the three visitors, but they were too far away for her to do so.

Cord, joining her, focused binoculars. "One of them is Shelby."

"Shelby Martin?" Floryn said. "The deputy I met in Huntsville?" When Cord nodded, she murmured, "I wonder what he's doing out here."

Cord shrugged. "The other one is Rule. I can't make out the third one, but he's too small to be Tony or Kid. Besides neither of them would be riding with Shelby." A little later, he exclaimed, "Jason! Floryn, the second one is Jason."

"Who's Jason?" Hope climbed up on the bannister.

As they awaited the arrival of their visitors, Floryn

and Cord told Hope about Jason. When the three reined in, Rule waved.

"I'll tell you this place is a sight for sore eyes." He slid out of the saddle and pointed to Shelby Martin. "If'en it hadn't been for your friend here, I don't know that we would have found the place today. Right, Jason?"

"Right, Mr. Compton," he said.

"Hello, Jason," Cord said.

A small smile tugging the corners of his lips, Jason swung off the back of the mule. "Howdy, Mr. Donaldson." The boy looked at Floryn and pulled off his hat, a shock of red hair falling across his forehead. "Howdy, ma'am."

"This is a pleasant surprise, Jason," she said.

Hope jumped from the railing to the ground in front of Jason. "Hi. I'm Hope."

Boy and girl sized each other up.

"My daughter," Cord said.

Rule smiled and nodded his head. "You're a'mighty pretty little lady. Look a lot like your ma."

"Thank you." Hope grinned and looked up at Floryn.

"And I reckon I see some of your pa in you, too."

Shelby rolled his eyes in mock horror.

"You do?" Hope exclaimed. "What?"

"The dark hair and coloring," Rule said. "Your height. Yes, sir, you're a mighty fine looking lady."

"My papa built me a new seesaw," Hope bragged. "And after we finished cleaning up, he said he might build me a merry-go-round and a slide."

Looking at Cord, Shelby hiked a brow. "Hasn't taken you long to become domesticated, has it?"

Cord grinned. "Survival tactic. I'm outnumbered by three strong women."

"Mama and Leanor," Hope said, "but who's the third one?"

"You," Cord answered.

Hope giggled. "I'm just your little girl."

"Yes, you are," Cord said softly. "Maybe I can have the merry-go-round finished before we start rounding up the cattle."

"Oh, Father, I would like that," Hope said. "You're a real good carpenter. My seesaw is better than Agnes Jennings's. And nobody has a merry-go-round."

"You bet your pa is a good carpenter, and anything your pa does will be better than what anybody else does," Rule said.

"Shelby," Cord said, "what are you doing out this way?"

"Had to accompany a payroll to El Paso. Thought since I was this close, I'd drop by to see how you were doing. Along the way I found these two."

"Right glad he did," Rule said.

"And so are we," Floryn said. After she greeted Shelby, she turned to Rule, "How's your arm?"

Rule flexed his shoulder. "All fine and dandy."

Cord lightly clapped him on the back. "It's good to see you." Cord motioned for one of the *vaqueros* to stable the horses. "Shall we move to the veranda?"

Floryn, Jason, and Hope led the way; the three men followed.

"Thank you and Mr. Donaldson for the vest," Jason said. He lifted his hands and tugged the lapels. "I'm mighty grateful."

Floryn figured he had been with Rule for several days. He was beginning to drawl his words like the older man, even to walk like him.

"Floryn and I were talking about you today," Cord said. "We wondered if you had received it."

"Sure did, and I would have wrote you, but I had to get moving. When I decided to travel this way, I figured I'd tell you myself."

355

"What are you doing this far west?" Floryn asked.

"If it's all right with you," Rule said, "we'll go inside and sit a spell while we talk. I'd like to have a cup of coffee and some vittles right about now."

"I'll say so," Shelby said. "I'm tired of beef jerky and campfire coffee. Could do with some home cooking."

Rule lightly cuffed Jason on the back. "Reckon you could use some food, too, young fella?"

"Yes, sir," Jason answered. "I'm powerful hungry."

Soon they were seated around the kitchen table, Rule, Shelby, and Jason eating, the others drinking a glass of cool lemonade. Like a mother hen, Leanor bustled around the kitchen, refilling plates and glasses, serving more hot bread and butter. Every so often she would pat Jason on the head.

"Jason caught up with me in San Antone," Rule said in between mouthfuls. "I stayed over a few days longer than I intended, so's when he told me his story, I offered to let him travel with me. Always safer with two than one."

"I'm looking for a job," Jason announced. "I figured I'd work as a ranch hand."

"Does your ma know you're out here?" Floryn asked.

Jason dropped his head, then lifted it. His eyes were sad. "My ma's dead. She caught a fever." Jason struggled to hold back the tears. "Nothing Doctor Pritchard did could save her. She died real quick like. Doc said that was because she had no resistance. I stayed in Huntsville for a while but figured I'd best head on west. Figured I wanted to be a ranch hand instead of an errand boy. While I was working in San Antone to get money to shove on, I met Rule. I was right glad when he offered to let me travel with him."

Floryn pressed her hand over Jason's. "I'm sorry about your ma."

Jason lowered his head and nodded. "She was—she was a good woman."

Floryn's heart ached for the boy who was trying hard to be a man. "I didn't know her very well, but I know she was a good woman, Jason. The owner of the general store in Huntsville spoke highly of your mother."

Jason brushed his sleeve across his eyes.

Cord laid his hand on Jason's shoulder. "Jason, you're welcome to stay here with us. We'd like to have you."

Jason gazed steadily at Cord. "Thank you for inviting me, Mr. Donaldson, but I'm a man now. I need to earn my own way. Don't want to be a burden on nobody."

"You wouldn't be," Floryn said. "We'd enjoy having you."

"Thank you, ma'am," he said. "I appreciate the offer, but I want to make it on my own. I'd be grateful if you could hire me as one of your ranch hands."

Cord and Floryn exchanged a glance.

"Well, Jason," Cord said, "I figure we can always use another good hand. I'll take you and Rule to meet Antonio. He'll help you settle in." He looked at Shelby. "Want to come with us?"

Shelby nodded. "Reckon I will."

As soon as Cord turned Rule and Jason over to Antonio, he and Shelby walked off by themselves.

"I've been worried about you," Shelby said. "Heard about the theft of your pendant."

They walked to the corral and leaned against the fence.

"Found out anything?"

Cord shook his head.

"To be honest, Shelby, I really haven't been thinking about it too much lately."

"Damn," the lawman softly swore. "I wish something would jar that memory of yours."

"Maybe there's nothing wrong with my memory," Cord said. "Maybe it's the dragoon's story. Maybe there just isn't any San Domingo treasure."

Shelby grinned and shrugged. "Could be."

They watched the horses for a while, before Cord spoke.

"Is it usual for you to accompany a payroll?"

"Nope, sure isn't," Shelby answered. "There's been a rash of robberies lately, what with the returning soldiers."

He took the makings for a cigarette out of his pocket.

"Wasn't going to tell you this, but we figure Kid Ferguson threw in with a gang of outlaws."

"I didn't figure Kid to be stupid," Cord said. "I thought he had learned his lesson."

The cigarette rolled, Shelby stuck it into his mouth and lit it. "Although we don't have any proof, we think Norwell and Pruitt are running the gang. It's a pretty slick operation. We haven't been able to get anything on them, but I'm hoping Kid will be the weak link. I've been on his tail ever since he left Norwell's place a week or so ago."

"He's out here?" Cord asked.

Shelby nodded. "Keep an eye out for me, will you?"

By the time Cord returned, Floryn had sent Leanor to her room to rest, had finished cleaning the kitchen, and was on the back porch hanging the soiled dishcloths.

"Tony sent a message through Rule," Cord said.

"He'll be here in six to eight weeks, and Kid isn't . . . coming."

"The guest bedroom is ready for Shelby," she said.

"He's sleeping in the bunkhouse. He'll be leaving early in the morning and doesn't want to disturb us when he leaves."

"Howdy!" Mildred Hudgins rounded the house. "I came to get that foal. Antonio said he'd be ready today."

"He is," Cord answered.

"Would have been here sooner," the woman said, "but I've been in town."

Mildred sat down in one of the rockers and pulled her hat off, dropping it beside the chair. Her features, always angular, were sharper today as if she were preoccupied with something.

"Is anything wrong?" Floryn asked.

"Nothing new," the rancher answered. "Somebody put a burr under Kern's saddle. He said he's not going to extend my note a day later than it's due. It's either sell my cattle to him at his price or take a real big chance on losing the spread."

"Does this mean you're thinking about selling your cattle to him?" Floryn asked. She knew if Mildred backed down, so would others. Although the woman was unsophisticated, a product of the frontier, she was respected by the surrounding ranchers. They would bow to her wisdom.

"I've been talking mighty big and proud, but I've been thinking about that for a long time," Mildred confessed. "All of us have. Nobody's driven their cattle to market like we're thinking about doing. It's a big risk, Floryn. More so for some of us than others. To be honest I'm scared."

"When does the note come due?" Cord asked.

"Next June." She reached into her pocket and pulled out the tobacco pouch. The cigarette rolled, she licked the white paper and stuffed it into her mouth. Lighting it, she took several puffs. "If only we could be sure this is gonna work."

"But we can't," Floryn said.

"Nope." Mildred grinned. "But I reckon it's a chance I have to take. I want to see the look on Kern Wallis's face when we leave with cattle and return with money."

"Father," Hope shouted.

She and Jason raced across the yard onto the porch.

"Can I take Jason for a ride?"

Floryn noticed that Hope asked Cord's permission, not hers.

"Sure can," Cord replied, "but don't go too far."

"And can I saddle him one of the horses?"

"I don't want one of your horses." Jason tilted his head stubbornly. "I have my mule. I bought him with my own money, and he's good enough for me."

"I'm sure you would prefer your mule," Cord said smoothly, "but he's tired from his trip. Why don't you let him rest?"

Jason thought a second. "Reckon that makes sense."

"Who's this?" Mildred gave the boy the once-over.

Jason pulled off his hat and told her his name.

"I appreciate you taking your hat off," Mildred said, "but you can put it back on. We don't rest on ceremony around here. What'cha doing out here?"

"His ma and pa died recently, and he's headed west. He's going to work for me for a while." Cord gave Mildred a special look that spoke volumes.

She pursed her lips and nodded her head. "Well, if you find you have too many ranch hands, I reckon I could use an extra. Need somebody to take care of my horses especially. Could use somebody to help me

360

get this foal home. Don't reckon you have anybody in mind, do you?"

"Sure don't," Cord answered.

Mildred nodded. "For a while I'd have to pay him with room and board and he'd have to take one of the bedrooms in the house. Later I could give him wages and see about us getting a regular bunkhouse."

"I'm good with horses," Jason said.

"You want to work for me?"

Jason looked up at Cord. "I've already told Mr. Donaldson I'd work for him."

"If you'd like to work for Mrs. Hudgins —" Cord began.

"Mildred," she said, interrupting him as was her custom. "If the boy's gonna work for me, I want him to call me by my name."

"For Mildred," Cord said, "I think it would be good. She needs a man around the place."

"Why, yes." She looked rather surprised. "I reckon I do."

"You don't have a husband or any sons, ma'am?" Jason asked.

"No," Mildred said, her voice softer than Floryn had ever heard it before. "My husband and sons died a long time ago, Jason. They were massacred by Indians. We were on our way to California."

"My pa was killed when we moved out here," Jason said. "I've been taking care of my ma since then. I reckon you need somebody to take care of you."

Mildred cleared her throat and looked into the distance, blinking her eyes rapidly. "Reckon I could at that, Jason."

Jason bobbed his head energetically. "I'd like to work for you, ma'am. When do I start?"

Looking at the child, all emotion wiped from her face, Mildred took a drag off her cigarette. "I figure you have time to ride with Hope. When you get back, we'll take off. How's that?"

"That's fine, ma'am. Just fine."

As he and Hope darted off the porch, they bumped into Rule. Excitely Jason told him what had happened.

"I'm gonna get to sleep in the main house," Jason said, ending with, "She needs a man around the house."

Then he and Hope scampered off. Rule glanced over at Mildred. He whipped off his hat, a strand of sandy gray hair lopping over his forehead, and smiled at her.

"Howdy, ma'am," he said.

"Howdy," Mildred answered, not tacking on her familiar phrase of *put your hat back on. We don't rest on ceremony around here.* She stared at him.

Floryn could have sworn she saw Mildred's hard, angular features softening again, twice in one day. The first had not surprised her. Jason was a child who easily touched people's hearts. This second softening did. Floryn had never known Mildred to be mildly interested in a man.

His eyes twinkling, Rule said, "So you need a man around the house."

"Just hired Jason." Shrewd eyes pinned him.

"Why not hire a man?"

"Ain't had any use for them since my husband died," Mildred answered, her voice a tad softer than usual.

"That's because you haven't found the right one."

"That could be true. Are you interested?"

"In what?" he asked, a decided glint in his eyes.

As if they were alone, they gazed at each other. She took a drag off the cigarette. "A job."

"Do I get a bedroom in the house?" Rule asked.

"Only have two, and both of them are occupied."

"Don't mind sharing," Rule said.

Silence stretched between them.

He added, "But I don't share with boys or men."

During the following days and weeks, Cord and Floryn established a pleasant pattern to their marriage. Their days were filled with work, their nights with pleasure, but Cord never mentioned love. Neither did Floryn. Long after Cord was asleep at night, she would lie awake and wonder about their future. He seemed to think they could continue their marriage on this basis. Floryn was having her doubts.

A marriage of convenience with Hal was one matter. She and he had not consummated their union. They had not been emotionally involved even on a physical level as she and Cord were. Floryn was learning that she could not be content with a marriage based on lust alone. There was a fine line of difference between lust and love, but there was a difference. Floryn wanted to move across it. She wanted love; she wanted all of Cord's heart as well as all of his body.

Each morning Cord was up early. He was gone all day, working long, hard hours and returning only for dinner that evening. He would spend time with Hope before he and Floryn tucked her into bed. Then he and Floryn would go to the study where he worked on the accounts and she did her sewing and mending. Later they went to bed together.

Before daybreak, their routine began again.

Cord enjoyed life on the Fancy Lady. Sometimes he felt hemmed in, but the feeling was a fleeting one. He enjoyed the physical work he did each day out in the sun, in the wide open spaces.

At times he would think of the pendant and wish

he could have learned its secret. There was that small part of him that yearned to have his name cleared, to be exonerated of a crime he did not commit. Floryn's friends had been eager to accept him, but he sometimes wondered if they had not done this because he was a means to an end.

Still that did not bother him all that much either. Prison had taught him not to worry about what he could not change. And he had learned that people thought whatever they wanted to think.

His days were spent with Antonio and the *vaqueros*, with Rule and Tony, as they rounded up the cattle and branded them, as they prepared to move their herds to the railhead in Sedalia.

Sometimes Floryn would break the routine of the day by packing a basket with food and meeting him for lunch. Cord enjoyed these excursions when the three of them spent many a fun-filled hour together, laughing and talking and learning to be a family.

The weeks passed quickly.

The bedroom where Cord and Floryn slept was shrouded in the gray-black of early morning. Floryn lay in the crook of Cord's body, her back nestled to his chest, her soft, round bottom tucked immediately against his most intimate parts. His hand rested on the top of her hip, the thin material of her nightgown unable to conceal her soft curves, unable to stop his mind from imagining, his hand from wandering . . . until heaving pounding on the front door rudely, painfully reverberated through the house.

"Can you believe someone would come visiting this early on Saturday morning?" Cord grumbled.

"It's not that early," Floryn said. "I heard the clock chime eight not long ago."

They heard more knocking.

"Don't you think you ought to get up and answer the door?" she asked.

"Why me?" he grumbled. "I thought we agreed that in this marriage we were going to share and share alike."

The pounding sounded again.

"Only when it pleases me." Floryn pushed at him with her buttocks. "When someone comes calling this early in the morning, it's your duty to answer the door. Could be a bugger-bear you need to take care of."

He trailed his hand over her leg, beginning at the knee, climbing higher, bringing up the gown with him. He loved to feel her tremble beneath his touch; he delighted in listening to her soft purrs and giggles of pleasure.

"Who's going to take care of me?" he teased.

Her hand did some exploring on its own. "I will," she softly replied. "Later, after you've answered the door."

A rueful smile tugged his lips. "I have a feeling *later after I've answered the door* is going to prove to be never."

She smiled sleepily, stretched, and settled back into her little ball.

He bent down and kissed her cheek. Although he enjoyed each caress they shared, a quick kiss on such soft, inviting skin was poor consolation in view of what he planned for them to do.

The knocks were harder this time, their firmness, their timed repetition alerting him to the caller's growing impatience.

Sighing, Cord threw off the sheet and slid out of bed. He hastily slid into undergarments and jeans, closing the bedroom door as he quietly moved down the stairs before the noise awakened everyone. He opened the front door to see a young man standing on the veranda, his face drawn in a scowl. Holding a large wooden box, he shifted his weight from one foot to the other.

Handing the container to Cord, he said, "Mr. Wallis sent this to you. On top you'll find a letter of explanation."

Gently kicking the door closed, Cord moved down the hallway to the study and was soon engrossed in the contents of the box that he had spread across the desk. The general ledgers of the Fancy Lady. Checkbooks. All sorts of personal records, financial and otherwise, that belonged to Hal.

His initial curiosity appeased, Cord pushed back in the swivel chair and opened the letter. The attorney, reminding Cord of the outstanding debt, informed him that it must be paid in full. He ended the letter with a reminder of his willingness to work with Cord and of his offer to buy the Fancy Lady cattle or Cord's portion of the Fancy Lady itself. None of the alternatives suited Cord.

Later—he was not sure how much time had passed—he looked up to see Floryn in the doorway. She was wearing her dressing gown, her hair hanging in waves about her shoulders.

"Good morning." She smiled brightly, her gaze rounding the room, then coming back to rest on him. "Or is it good morning?"

"The morning will probably be good enough," he answered. "I'm not so sure how we're faring."

He could imagine how he looked without a shave and half clad in yesterday's clothing. He raised his hand and rubbed it against his cheek, the beard stubble abrasive to his palm.

She walked farther into the room and glanced curiously at the desk. "What's this?"

"Wallis returned the ledgers."

Her eyes lighting up, she bent over the desk, her

366

hair falling forward to hide her face from Cord. Delicate morning light streamed through the window, seeming to take residence in the honey-gold tresses. He reached out and ran his hands through them, loving the silky feel.

She shuffled through the book, then flipped through the pages. "As I thought." She looked at him.

Cord gazed into triumphant honey-gold eyes.

"Someone has changed the entry." She thumped her finger on the sheet. "According to this, George withdrew all his money when he left."

Cord said nothing.

"Look," she exclaimed. "You can see for yourself."

"I can see." He removed her hands from the opened pages and closed the book. "It's over and done with. Forgotten."

She smiled, and although he was accustomed to seeing the gesture, its brilliance yet astounded him. He gazed in fascination at the fluid mobility of her full lips. Lips that promised pleasure. . . . His eyes dropped lower. A body that promised pleasure. . . .

"Do you think later has arrived?" she asked softly.

Their arms wrapped around each other, they walked out of the study, up the stairs, to their bedroom.

Twenty-five

Later that same day as they dressed for dinner, Floryn said, "How are we going to get the money to pay Wallis?"

She watched Cord button up his shirt and tuck it into his trousers.

"What can we use for collateral?"

Cord fiddled with his collar, then with his necktie. Finally he said, "I have some jewels. It's a matter of my getting to them."

Slowly Floryn moved to stand in front of him. She reached up and stilled his hand as he refastened his necktie. "The San Domingo treasure?"

"No."

Cord lightly capped her shoulders with his hands, but his gaze, his grip was anything but casual. "I don't know anything about the San Domingo treasure. Nothing. These jewels I'm talking about are some that were given to me by Mathieu Guilbert. I refused to accept Mexican money when he hired me to escort his wife to New Orleans."

He spoke slowly. "It was American money or gold and silver. He paid me in priceless family heirlooms, begging me not to convert them into cash. His agent who was to meet him in New Orleans would have given him American dollars. For safekeeping, I buried the jewels in a shallow cave and never had a chance to get them."

"Why didn't you tell me about them?" Floryn asked.

"Until now, nothing in our marriage has hinged on them."

"Where exactly did you bury them?"

"Somewhere between Donaldsonville and the Church of the Angels. I have the landmarks memorized. I'll remember when I see them again."

"When are you leaving to get them?"

"After Tony gets here," he answered. "If your suspicions about Wallis are true, I want Tony and Rule to be here to protect you, Hope, and the ranch."

And, he thought, to protect you from Kid if he were really in cahoots with an outlaw gang and on the prowl out there.

"Do you think you'll be gone for long?"

"I'm not sure."

"I want to come with you."

"You're needed here, for the ranch and Hope."

"Cord, I'm worried." She hugged herself. "Before you leave would you go to El Paso and—"

He nodded. "I've already been thinking about that. I'll file the petition before I do anything else."

"Cord, take Primero with you."

"Primero?"

"The tracker I told you about. He knows this country better than anybody else. Just tell him what landmarks you're looking for, and he'll help you find your cave."

"I know where I'm headed," he said, "and the fewer who know about my leaving, the better."

"Cord—"

"No!"

* * *

369

Two weeks had passed. During this time Cord had gone to El Paso, met with the attorney, and filled out the necessary papers to have guardianship of Hope returned to Floryn. He had located the Guilbert jewels and returned with them to the *hacienda*.

Now Floryn and he were on their way to Piedras Negras to see if they could negotiate a loan. They had been traveling for two days and a night.

Stopped in a cluster of trees near a small brook, Floryn gratefully accepted the canteen from Cord. Although the water was warm, she welcomed its wetness. After she returned the container to Cord, she flexed her shoulders and wiped her sleeved arm across her forehead.

Glad she had worn trousers, she squirmed in the saddle, leather creaking as she moved her body. With gloved hands, she pulled her hat lower on her face, and she looked around, her gaze scaling the rugged mountain range to the right of them.

"How much farther?" Cord asked.

"Not far," she answered. "However, Primero is guiding us a different route than I usually travel. It seems farther. Probably because he's hiding our trail."

Cord gazed into the distance also. He wore his hat low, the upper portion of his face shadowed. The lower portion was covered in the beginning of a thick black beard that only enhanced his virility, that accented his dark handsomeness — oddly enough that went with the black patch. He rubbed his cheek beneath the leather, making Floryn want to reach out to touch him, to caress his skin, to feel his beard against her palm, against her cheek.

"I hope you're sure about this silversmith," he said.

"I am," Floryn answered. "Emmanuel Tellez is an honorable man, a friend whom I trust. If anyone will give us a loan using the Guilbert jewels as a collateral, he will. And if he'll give it to anyone, it will be me. I've helped him and the Juaristas in their fight against the French government."

An Indian rode up on a pinto. His straight black hair, cut shoulder length, was parted in the middle. "We are being followed," he announced.

"How many?" Cord asked.

"Two. Possibly more."

"We'll ride through the night."

The Indian nodded, turned his horse, and led the way. Cord and Floryn followed.

Another night passed, and they continued to move in serpentine formation through the foothills. Morning came. Afternoon. They glared into the midsummer sun, their eyes burning, their throats glazed with dust. Darkness fell, and they continued to move. They had ridden so long Floryn was aching all over, but she did not want to stop, would not stop. She forced her eyes to stay open; she commanded her body to remain in the saddle.

The next morning Primero slowed so that Cord and Floryn caught up with him. He pointed.

"Follow that trail," he said, "and in an hour's time you will be in Piedras Negras. I am going to turn back and pick up those who are behind us. They will follow me rather than you. That way you will reach your destination with no one knowing. Do you want me to come back for you?"

"About midafternoon," Cord said. "We should have our business concluded by that time."

With a curt nod, the Indian rode in one direction, Cord and Floryn in the opposite.

"Men have killed for less than these." Emmanuel Tellez, silversmith, pushed back in his chair and gazed at the jewelry spread on the table in front of him. The gold and silver glistened, the jewels glittered in the sunlight that spilled through an opened window of his shop in the Mexican town of Piedras Negras. "These are priceless pieces. Heirlooms?"

"Yes," Cord answered.

"They are not stolen?"

"No," Cord answered, "they were given to me as payment for leading a wagon train from Mexico City to San Antonio."

"If only they could tell us their history," the silversmith murmured.

"I'll tell you the part I know," Cord said and began talking about Mathieu Guilbert and his wife Sanchia. When he finished talking, Emmanuel Tellez was sitting back, a thoughtful gaze on his face.

"The name Guilbert is familiar," he said. "I remember many years ago a young Frenchman married into an influential Mexican family. The San Domingos, I believe. I do not know them personally, but we share acquaintances."

"Perhaps these are the same people," Cord said.

"With the similarity of names," the silversmith said, "I should think so. I'll see what I can find out about them for you."

"Would you consider holding them as collateral and giving us a cash advance in U.S. currency, *Señor* Tellez?" Floryn asked. "I hate to ask this of you, but we have no one in the States who can help us on such short notice."

Señor Tellez raised his head, wrinkles furrowing his aged face. He brushed a hand through thick, white hair. "I have a feeling that these bring trouble with them."

"If certain people were to find out you had them, you could be in danger," Cord said. "We've tried to be discreet in our coming to you and have used one of the best trackers in the country to hide our trail, but we can't promise you anything."

372

"I see," Tellez murmured, his gaze again on the jewels. "Getting U.S. currency is not impossible, but in these troubled times it is difficult . . . especially on such short notice."

"We can pay you back after we have driven our cattle to market come next spring," Floryn said.

"Perhaps," the Mexican mused, "there is someone in San Antonio to whom I could speak."

Deep in thought, the old man reached up and scratched his cheek. Finally a smile softened the weathered face.

"*Sí*, I will do it for you, *Señora*, and for none other. You have been a good friend to the Juaristas, helping us fight the tyranny of the French government, giving us medicine and provisions when we could not repay you, hiding some of those who were on the run from Maximilian's troops. Mexico owes you a debt of gratitude that I shall be happy to pay back."

He again turned his attention to the jewelry, picking it up piece by piece, studying it with the use of his eyepiece. "I shall hide these in a secret place that no one knows about. I will keep them safe for you."

"Thank you," Floryn murmured.

"*De nada*," he murmured absently. Dropping the lenses, he looked up and held out one of the silver pieces. He brushed his thumb over it several times. "This work is familiar. The design is unusual, the workmanship distinctive. It reminds me of a piece I have seen before."

Yes, Cord thought, it was quite similar to the ruby pendant, the one he had been calling the San Domingo pendant. Even without closing his eyes, he could see the blood-red stone and the unusual markings.

A strange yearning seized him. He wanted his pendant, wanted to know its secret. More, he wanted to be free of its secret.

Tellez shrugged and shook his head. "I cannot remember. Perhaps it is an old man's foolishness." He gently picked up the pieces and laid them on velvet cushions in mahogany boxes. "Now shall we discuss the loan?"

Knowing the jewels would be safe until they returned from the cattle drive and knowing they had the money to repay Wallis, Cord graciously accepted the silversmith's invitation to have lunch at his home. While Cord and Floryn awaited the return of Primero, they relaxed and visited in the cool and colorful patio gardens with *Señor* and *Señora* Tellez.

The appointed time of Primero's arrival came and went; yet the Apache did not show up. Cord was not overly concerned because they had taken precautions not to let anyone know they were coming to Mexico to visit with the silversmith; Primero had also taken great precautions to hide their trail and to lose anyone who might have followed them. By late afternoon they were sipping a glass of wine when a servant opened the heavy wooden gates, and a vendor pushed into the patio.

Excusing herself, *Señora* Tellez walked to the youth and talked with him for a while. Although *Señor* Tellez continued to regale Cord and Floryn with accounts of the civil unrest in Mexico, he kept a close eye on the activities in the patio.

"There are many of us who have fled from the French persecution in Mexico City to Piedras Negras," the Mexican said sadly. "I have. Ramon—the young vendor over there—his father. Many others. We have no use for Maximilian; he has none for us. If we were closer to the capital city, we would be considered enemies to the state."

Emmanuel's gaze kept returning to the boy called

374

Ramon who he explained was not really a vendor but an informant. Using his trade as a disguise, he moved easily and freely through the provinces taking and bringing information to and from the Juaristas.

"In 1855 we found ourselves in a climate similar to the one we have today. Instead of Mexicans being shot as traitors to the French government, we were dragging in people and accusing them of being French spies. If I remember correctly, such was the case with this Mathieu Guilbert. Hard evidence was not necessary for a conviction. An accusation from the right person was all it took."

Finally the lad, accompanied by the *señora,* pushed his cart to the back of the house. Hardly had the cart disappeared from sight, than their host pushed to the front of his chair and snapped his fingers.

"Ramon!" he exclaimed. "He is the one." He jumped to his feet.

Puzzled, Cord and Floryn looked at him.

"I shall return shortly." When he did, he had the boy in tow. "This is Ramon Guzman. He wears a piece of jewelry that is similar to the silver one I questioned. Show them, Ramon."

Ramon pulled aside the neckline of his shirt to reveal a medallion hanging on a long chain. When Floryn saw the pie-shaped piece of silver, she gasped and dropped her glass of wine on the tiled patio. Cord leaned forward.

"May I see it?" he asked, his voice strangely husky.

Emmanuel Tellez had no sooner translated the words, than the boy pulled the chain over his neck and handed it to Cord. Floryn rose and leaned over Cord's shoulder.

As the two of them gazed at the pendant, she said, "I have a feeling of *déjà vu.* It's the same as when I saw it for the first time."

"The ruby is missing," Cord said, "but it's just like

the San Domingo pendant I had."

Emmanuel translated for Ramon. The youth shook his head and spoke rapidly.

"Not a ruby," the Mexican interpreted for Cord and Floryn. "An emerald, reputed to be about twenty carats."

"The same weight as the ruby," Floryn murmured.

Cord nodded and turned the pendant over in his hands to see the strange markings, like those on his pendant.

"You would like to have the pendant?" *Señor* Tellez said.

"Yes."

The silversmith spoke to the boy who nodded eagerly and pulled the chain over his neck and handed it to Cord. Surprised, he looked at Tellez.

"I'll pay Ramon for it," he said, "and we'll deduct it from the loan."

Minutes later, Cord was not only in possession of a second pendant but more information concerning its history. According to the boy, the medallion had belonged to a prisoner, a Frenchman who at his death for treason gave it to a compassionate guard.

Years later, the guard had lost it to Ramon's father in a game of chance. Originally the stone had been a twenty-carat emerald, but that had been gone from the pendant (if it had ever been there, Ramon had interjected) long before the boy's father had come into possession of the jewelry. At his death, Ramon's father had passed it on to his son. This was all the boy knew about the pendant.

With *Señor* Tellez interpreting, Cord asked, "Is the guard still living?"

"Yes," the boy replied. "Like many of us, he is hiding from the French. I do not know his name but I can take you to his village. Do you wish to go?"

As soon as the silversmith translated the boy's

376

words, Cord looked at Floryn, at the anxiety mirrored in her face. Without her speaking a word, he knew what she wanted him to do. He also knew what he must do. He turned back to Ramon.

"Yes," he answered. "When can you take me there?"

"Tomorrow," the boy replied. "We should start early in the morning because it is a three hour journey to the village."

"I shall send some of my men with you," Tellez said.

Cord nodded.

As the afternoon lengthened, Floryn wandered through the garden. Unable to share the men's excitement, she listened halfheartedly to them as they discussed the probability of this being the same man as Mathieu Guilbert, of this pendant being a sister pendant to Cord's, as they laid their plans. Finally she strayed out of hearing distance, but all the foreboding she had experienced in San Antonio returned in full force to haunt her. Once more their pasts—Cord's past—had caught up with them.

She had seen the glow on his face, the purpose, the resolve when he had held the pendant, when he had looked at it. She had thought his obsession was gone, that it had been replaced by her and Hope and the ranch. She understood his preoccupation with the pendant, with his past. She understood his desire to vindicate his name, but she had hoped he had forgotten his lust for revenge. As she had watched him only minutes before she had the premonition that it had only been pushed to the back but never out of his mind.

Floryn was not aware she and Cord were spending the night at the Tellez home until *Señora* Tellez found her sitting by herself on one of the stone benches in the garden and led her to the guest bedroom.

This was the first time Floryn and Cord had enjoyed privacy in days, since they had begun their hunt for the Guilbert jewels. Although Floryn was glad they would have this night, her apprehension about Cord's welfare dimmed the excitement of their sleeping together. She was once more filled with a desperation that came from the fear of losing him, that came from the fear of losing the Fancy Lady.

By the time Cord joined her, Floryn had taken off her riding clothes and had changed into a wrapper *Señora* Tellez had so thoughtfully provided for her. She was brushing her hair. He closed the door and leaned back against it.

"I had to do it." A sense of expectancy and urgency emanated from him.

She stopped brushing. "Had to or wanted to?"

After a pause and a searching glance at her, he said, "Both."

Only now did he move into the room to drop the pendant on the night table. Floryn stared at it, soon learning that it, too, was a spell caster. It compelled her full attention. She slowly moved toward it, laying her brush on the table before she picked up the pendant.

"I still believe these medallions are cursed," she murmured. "Look at the deaths that are associated with them. Sanchia Guilbert and her entire entourage. Mathieu Guilbert."

Don't add yours, Cord, she silently screamed. He said nothing.

She laid down the pendant. "I understand your driving need to clear your name and to solve the mystery of the San Domingo treasure, and I know you're going. But can't it wait, Cord. You've waited nine years. Will a few more months hurt you?"

"I have the boy and the pendant now," he said, his expression closed, guarded, his voice cold. He reminded her of the rock-quarry Cord. "If I don't take this opportunity, I may never have it again."

"This is the only opportunity we have for the Fancy Lady," Floryn said, her anxiety causing her to speak sharper than she would have ordinarily. "The valley is depending on you, Cord. We need you."

"You knew when I was released from prison that my purpose was to find who framed me, who massacred all those innocent people on that wagon train."

Floryn felt him erect the barrier between them again. He was shoving her away from him.

"Yes, but not at Hope's and my expense."

They simply looked at each other; words would have been wasted.

"I'm going," he said. "*Señor* Tellez is going to have the money delivered to you at the ranch. As soon as you get it, pay Wallis off. There will be enough for you to make Mildred a loan, so she can pay off her note. Do that."

"Why Mildred?"

"I've singled her out because she carries a lot of weight with the other ranchers. If we have her solidly backing us and the cattle drive, the others will, too. After you pay Wallis off, you'll have plenty of money left. Clyde Bristoll, our attorney in El Paso, has all the necessary papers to get custody of Hope returned to you."

Accepting the inevitable, she asked, "When are you and Ramon leaving? In the morning?"

He nodded.

Twenty-six

Cord slipped the pendant into his pocket and moved to where she stood. He gazed into her upturned face.

"I know you're angry about my going."

"No, I'm not angry," she said, "I'm furious. And I'm disappointed. And betrayed. I knew we didn't have a marriage based on love. You had made that clear, but I did think you were interested in the Fancy Lady and in Hope. I thought you were going to help me save the ranch."

Floryn gave vent to all her combustible emotions. "Instead you're running off to Mexico to chase tales and rumors associated with that damn pendant. You have plenty of time to do that, Cord. There is no time limit to your parole. There is a time limit on driving our cattle to market. We don't have time to spare."

Cord said nothing, offered no argument, no excuses. She gazed into the somber face. She had believed their relationship was changing and it had, but for the worse. Now they were regressing. Not once had Cord told her he loved her. Not even during their most impassioned lovemaking had he ever said those three simple words. But he used to tell her how good they were together. He was not even saying that now.

She had always feared the pendant was her worst enemy, and now her fears were confirmed. Only hours ago he had seen it, and already he was following it into the dark shadows of the past. She thought of all the needless hours she had wasted worrying about losing him. She should not have. She never had Cord. From the minute he had walked out of that prison, he had been married to his past. He belonged to it, to its secrets, its intrigues, its dangers.

Still she loved him, loved him with all her heart. And a part of her understood his driving need to find that missing part of himself. More, she worried about him. She worried that he would someday move into those shadows and never return.

Floryn's emotions were rising to the surface, and conflicting emotions they were. Paradoxical. She loved him; she hated him. She wanted him to discover the secret of his past; she did not. She wanted to make love to him; she wanted him never to touch her again.

But no matter how contradictory her thoughts, how vacillating her emotions, one remained true and steadfast. She loved Cord.

Ten years ago she had been the one to declare her love first, to make her vow of forever love. She had promised herself that this time, Cord would be the first to say the words. Perhaps that was immature of her. Whether it was or not, she did not want him leaving in search of the pendant — perhaps never to return — not knowing that she truly loved him. Maybe . . . just maybe . . . if she were to let him know how she felt, he would confess his love also, and he would stay with her.

But, a small inner voice warned, *look how quickly he left you in the hotel room in San Antonio when he wanted to check on his gunfighters, how quickly he decided to chase down this present rumor, how quickly he decided his quest was more important than the Fancy Lady. He may not confess to loving you, because he may not love you!*

That was the chance she must take.

"Cord, I — I really care for you." The coward in her could not say the words *I love you.* "I'm worried about your making this trip."

Cord took the brush from her and gently pulled it through her hair, his movements strong and sure.

"I love your hair," he said. "It's beautiful."

What about loving me?

"It smells like fresh flowers, like the Indian paintbrushes in the meadow."

Playing with a strand of hair, Cord rubbed it against her neck down toward her breasts. The whispering touch sent passion flaming through her body. When she trembled, Cord turned loose of her hair and gathered her close to him.

"Just hold me," she begged.

Yes, she knew her heart was fickle where this man was concerned, but she loved him. She wanted him. She leaned against him, feeling again that sense of belonging, that sense of comfort and security, of peace that she felt only with him, that she would soon be without. It seemed at odds with all the pulsating sensations he was able to arouse in her; yet, with him, the calm and the storm went together. As well it should, their love had been conceived in a storm; it was as elemental as the weather itself. As Cord had once told her, he and she were lightning and thunder.

Floryn felt the thump of his heart, the warmth of his body, and she looked up and knew the pleasure of simply gazing at him. Suddenly nothing mattered except him. Her hands went up and around his neck; her lips lifted to meet his.

"Take me, my darling," she murmured. *Take me in love.*

"I've taken before," he whispered, his mouth close

to her ear, "now I'm going to give as I've never given before."

"And I shall give to you."

His lips met hers, and hungrily they joined, as if they had never joined before. Many times they had mutually taken from the other, Floryn thought; other times one had given, the other had taken; this time Cord had said he was giving, and so was she. With both of them giving, their union promised to be one of the most glorious either had shared.

She was now pressed against him, her mouth on his. She ran her hands through his hair, her fingers playing seductive games with the sensitive skin of his head and neck. As he could so easily set her afire with wanting, she could do the same with him. She wanted his blood to be like currents of liquid fire, searing and sensitizing every nerve, every muscle.

"Now, Cord," she whispered. She needed no foreplay.

"Yes," he murmured.

Pleasure coursed through him as she responded so completely to his every touch, her hands doing their own exploration, playing an equal part in this exquisite journey toward their union.

Determined to be the tender lover, he moved slowly, his hands gentle and cajoling rather than demanding. His physical need was overwhelming; it had been days since they had made love, but Floryn was the important factor here, her pleasure, her well-being. He would leave her with sweet and precious memories.

Floryn felt him tremble as his hands carefully explored her with restrained tenderness. She knew from the tension in his body how much that restraint was causing him. She knew because she also felt a terrible urgency, a need unlike any she had ever felt. She loved him all the more.

Raw desire coursed through her, along with an overwhelming urge to give, to present Cord with a gift of her own, to give of herself in a new, selfless way.

They parted. Looking at each other, they undressed. They moved back into an embrace. They kissed. They stroked. They gave, they received pleasure. Their lips kept returning for long, drugging kisses.

When Cord finally lifted his lips from hers, his expression was passion-dark. The intensity of it caused Floryn to swallow. He looked at her as if she were incredibly precious, touched her as if she were. One time before when they were making love he had gazed at her like this, but then he had not seen her as a precious treasure. Now he did. He did not have to tell her. She knew it because her soul, her heart told her it was so. She felt as if she were drowning, drowning in sensation, in passion, in the wonder of revelation.

She also knew at this moment that if she were going to love this man unconditionally, she had to accept him. She could not change him. He had to change for her because he loved her and wanted to change.

Again his mouth took hers, casting away all thoughts save those of him and her and their passion, or did her mouth take his? It mattered not. For the first time, without the utterance of any words, without promises of any kind, Floryn felt deep within her heart that they were loving—not making love.

He scooped her into his arms and carried her across the room. Both of them tumbled into the bed.

"I need you," she whispered. "I want you. Now, Cord."

I love you, Cord, with all my heart.

As if she had spoken her declaration of love, Cord

raised up, as did she. She returned his steady gaze. He was the most compelling, most ruggedly handsome man she had ever seen. His face was both craggy and gentle, his body rock-hard. She let her gaze wander from his face to his chest to his abdomen. With trembling fingers she ran her hands down the line of black hair that led to his erection. Her hand stroked the satin smoothness of him, and she felt him tense.

Tenderly his hands caught her shoulders and he guided her down onto her back. He shifted his body so that he was over her, looking down at her with a face, softened and filled with an emotion she hoped . . . she prayed . . . was love.

She raised her lower body up, reaching for, meeting him. He entered and she was swept with billows of exquisite yearning. She felt herself tighten around him as his body started moving in a gentle rhythm that passion soon quickened, and he carried her along with him. That same expectancy — yet always a mysterious expectancy — built within her until she thought surely she would burst into flames of sheer happiness.

She cried out. Then she clasped his back, holding on as the flames died down, as the bright orange glow subsided into a wondrous peace and contentment that spread throughout every inch of her body. She wanted never to turn him loose. She kissed his shoulders, tasting the salty glaze of perspiration on his skin.

"Floryn," he whispered.

She waited in anticipation for his avowal of love.

"Thank you."

Always she was disappointed.

"Thank you."

She would not dwell on her disappointment. She had much to be thankful for. In the deepest recess of her heart she felt that Cord cared . . . still cared for her. Perhaps it would never be love, but that was a risk she had taken when she married him.

Stretched and cradling her head in the nook of his arm, she decided to take another risk. "Cord," she said, "I love you."

She waited a long, heartrending time for his answer.

"I'm not sure what love is, baby. When I was twenty, I did. I had all the answers then. Now I don't, but I have special feelings for you, Floryn. Very special feelings."

While this was not the declaration of love Floryn had wanted to hear, they were honest words that described Cord's changing attitude and emotions toward her. They were an affirmation to what she had felt when they made love. Still his confession was heavy. He still had a great deal of emotional baggage to sort through before he recognized that he loved her . . . or that he did not love her!

The latter thought she quickly, totally pushed out of mind. She could not . . . would not . . . accept such an alternative.

"When I was younger," he said, still speaking slowly as if searching for the right words, "I vowed forever love to you, but it didn't last. That wasn't enough. I don't know if what I feel for you is enough now. Enough for you."

"Things are different now."

She twined her fingers through Cord's and held their hands up. She remembered the times he had caressed her hands, had brought such exquisite pleasure to her. She brought his hand to her lips and kissed it, feeling the crispy hairs against her tender skin.

"We can make our marriage work, Cord. We can."

"I'm not talking about making a marriage work,"

he said. "People who don't love each other can do that. I'm talking about loving, Floryn, about all that goes with it."

"Love makes way for itself," she softly said, repeating wisdom she had learned from Leanor.

"Perhaps it does," he said.

"It does," she promised, wanting to take the uncertainty from his voice, the loneliness from his gaze. These did not fit this man of hers, the one hewn from the rock quarry. They did not fit the strength that emanated from him. Or maybe they did. Maybe this was the underlying foundation of his strength. He was a man who felt things strongly, who did everything passionately, who loved deeply.

Accepting that they were making progress in their relationship even though he was resuming his quest for the secret of the pendant, sated sexually, Floryn was able to push away momentarily her fears for her husband's life. She took confidence in the fact that love would make way for itself. Drowsy, they snuggled together and were soon asleep.

A soft knock on the door awakened them.

"*Señor* Donaldson," Emmanuel Tellez called, "your friend, the Apache, is here. It is urgent that he speak with you."

Cord threw back the covers. "I'll be right down."

"Something's wrong," Floryn murmured.

"Why don't you wait here?" Cord suggested.

"I'll do my waiting while you're searching out the secret of the pendant," she said, her earlier sense of well-being shattered. "Right now. I want to know."

He did not argue with her. Out of the bed as quick as he was, she was soon dressed in the wrapper and both of them were moving toward the parlor.

When Cord opened the door to the small room, he

saw no one. Then Primero stepped out of the shadows into the fall of lamplight. The massive Indian dwarfed the room, but it was not his size that caught Cord's attention. It was his wounds. His shoulder and leg were bandaged.

"What happened?" Floryn demanded, rushing past Cord.

Primero looked up at Cord. "I was ambushed. The one who chases you has hired an Indian tracker also. That is why I did not come for you sooner. To keep your whereabouts secret, I had to be even more careful and cunning. Finally I doubled back and returned to my village."

"Do you think you were followed here?" Cord asked.

"I was followed to the village, I made sure of that. But not here." Primero shook his head, a rare smile touching his narrow lips. "To *anglos* one Apache looks like another. I sent another warrior, bandaged up, out of the village within a short time. According to reports I received, he is being followed. He will lose those who follow him in the mountains." Primero's expression grew somber. "But we cannot be too careful."

Floryn came awake slowly, aware that, while sleep still lulled her mind, life tingled through her body. She shifted, stretched and slowly opened her eyes to a room filled with first gray light of predawn. She reached for Cord, but he was gone. Her gaze went around the room and found him gazing out the window, his long, fit body clearly illuminated in the moonlight.

"Cord."

He returned to the bed and drew her to him. He held her close. "I want to know the secret of the pen-

388

dant. At the same time, I'm afraid of what I'll learn."

"What are you afraid of?" she asked softly.

"For ten years I've lived for the day when I would learn who had set up the ambush. Would learn why everyone on the train had to be massacred. Would learn the secret of that damn pendant. Would know the truth about the San Domingo treasure. That was my reason — my entire — reason for living. That was the sum total of Cord Donaldson."

Some of Floryn's happiness dissolved. "You're afraid that in learning you'll no longer have a reason for being. You're afraid you'll have no identity."

He shrugged as if embarrassed that he had spoken about his fears, that he had shared something so intimate with her and revealed his vulnerability.

Floryn was engulfed by sadness. She doubted that she and Hope and the Fancy Lady would ever be enough for Cord. "Until you find the answers to these doubts and questions," she said, "there isn't room in your heart for love, or me, or Hope. You must find the answers. You have to in order for you and me to have a future, to find out if you can and do love me."

"I don't want to ruin what we have, Floryn."

Her heart hurting, she said, "Then you must learn the secret of the San Domingo pendant. We can't live the rest of our lives under its shadow. I told you I didn't want you to go, and a part of me doesn't. But you have to, Cord. In order to love me, in order to find me, you must first find yourself."

"Floryn, more than anything in the world I want to tell you that I love you."

"You want to tell me because you know I want to hear it," she said sadly. She blinked back the tears. At the same time that she loved him for wanting to make the declaration, she was also irritated with him for thinking she wanted less than his love itself.

"Please don't say it until you really mean it, Cord, until you really feel it. I don't want empty promises and hollow words. I want your love, your unconditional love."

"If I were to love a woman," he said slowly, his hands touching her face sweetly, "you are the one, the only one."

"You're the only man I shall ever love," she vowed. She had always known he was her only love.

He turned her so she lay on her back; he leaned over her.

"I love you," she whispered. "Take that with you wherever you go, and know it will bring you back to me safe and alive.

"Thank you," he murmured huskily, and she wondered if she imagined the tears in his voice.

He bent and covered her mouth with his. Soon his lips and hands were guiding her down pathways they had traveled before, but he made them new again, made them more delightful than they had been on the previous journey. His hands knew where and when to touch her. They caressed her like the wild Texas wind.

When the time came, she opened to him eagerly, her hunger as great as his. Their coming together this time was a tender fierceness that left her with a peacefulness she could remember never having felt before. Maybe it was the wonderful feeling of physical fulfillment he had given to her. Maybe it was because she hoped she had conceived their second child.

Whatever it was, she knew deep inside that she had finally turned a corner. Her healing had begun, and she owed it to the man she held in her arms.

Now she would help him heal. She would teach him to love again.

Twenty-seven

For a second time Floryn heard the soft pelting sound on the pane of her bedroom window. It sounded like hail or pebbles hitting against the glass. But it was not raining, so hail was out. Pebbles? Curiously she walked across the room and peered into the yard. In the moon-dappled shadows she saw the tall man who stood below, his arms outstretched. Her husband whom she had not seen in three weeks.

"I'm home," he said in an exaggerated whisper.

"Cord," she cried.

Whirling around, she dropped her hairbrush to the floor and raced toward the door, pausing only long enough to grab the nearest lamp. Catching the skirt of her wrapper and hiking it to keep from tripping over it, she bounded out of the room and down the stairs as fast as slippered feet would allow. When she reached the bottom landing, she fairly flew to the door, her only stop now to place the lamp on the hall table. She muttered when her hands fumbled on the bar and lock. Finally she heard the slide and grind of metal, the whoosh of the heavy oak swinging open, and she stared into the grizzled—but infinitely handsome and welcome—face of her beloved.

Murmuring his name over and over, she melted into outstretched arms to lay her cheek against a chest hard as pure rock. She listened to the steady, heavy pounding of his heart that convinced her he was all human. She absorbed his heat, his strength, his presence. Then she pushed away, her arms everywhere on him at once, his face, his shoulders, his arms, his face again.

"Oh, Cord, I've been so worried."

She now cupped his cheeks in her hands, strewing kisses all over his bearded face. She laughed. She cried. She did both at the same time. In the glow of pale lamplight that spilled from the hallway onto the veranda she looked at him.

"I thought I heard the horse, but I couldn't be sure. I was getting ready to go to bed, and I—I thought it might be Rule. He was over visiting with Mildred, and—"

With a grin Cord hauled her back into his arms, and his lips captured hers as he kissed her long and deep and thoroughly as he kissed her into silence. Then he kissed her again, and again.

As her hands had swept his body, his now swept hers. She felt them everywhere at once, and they felt so wonderful, so right. She was pressed against the wall of the house; he was pressed into her. She felt the entire hard length of him from shoulders to thighs. And she wanted to feel more.

"Three weeks," she murmured, in between kisses. "Three weeks without a word. I was worried sick. I'm so frightened of those damned pendants. I could see—"

"I could see your beautiful smile," he said, his voice thickly flowing over her. "I could smell the flowers in your hair. I felt you lying in my arms at night."

He pulled back and gazed at her with wonder and softness.

"I wanted you, my darling," he murmured, his voice expressing that same wonder, "wanted to make love to you, but most of all I missed holding you and talking to you. I missed your laughter." He touched her lips, his rough finger lingering at the corner. "Oh, God, Floryn, it's so good to be home."

"It's so good to have you home," she whispered, brushing her hands through the thick growth of hair on his face. She touched the dusty leather patch. "I'm so glad you're here."

"Me, too." He gave her a quick kiss. "Wait here for me, baby. I have a surprise for you."

He slipped into the house. Minutes later he reappeared, his arms laden with clothing. He grinned, that slow grin that tilted his mouth smugly.

"You hold these," he said.

"What are they?"

"Towels, washcloths, and clean, dry clothing and other things. You'll see."

As soon as he had transferred them to her, he swept her into his arms and walked toward the barn to the water trough. "I'm too dirty to go to bed and too randy to stay away from you, so I'm going to let you take a bath with me."

"Oh, really," Floryn whispered, locking the clothes between their bodies as she wound her arms about his neck. "What makes you think I want to bathe with you?"

He chuckled. "Just a feeling I have. I'd like to say it's a heartfelt feeling, but I think it's more physical."

They laughed together, and in the dark they stripped off their clothes and slid into the trough. Floryn sat between his thighs, her back resting on his chest, as he reclined against the back of the trough. Lazily he ladled water over her breasts. Floryn squeezed his thighs, testing the strength of hard muscles beneath the hair-dusted skin.

"Dear Lord," Cord muttered softly, "I didn't know how exhausted or how blessed I was until right now. This is the most wonderful feeling in the world."

"What?" Floryn teased. "Sitting in the barnyard water trough taking a bath in the dead of night?"

Even his chuckle was sleepy. "No, holding you in my arms. Just holding you."

"The first order of the night," she whispered when he became too still, "is to bathe."

"That's so, Mrs. Donaldson." His mouth was at her ear, nibbling on the outer edge. "And that's what we're going to do, so we can get out of here. I don't relish being caught naked in the barnyard water trough in the light of morning."

Quietly, playfully, but with no lack of gusto or enjoyment, Floryn bathed him. They dried off, but did not redress. Once more Cord piled clothing in her arms and swept her into his arms.

"Now to the second order of this night."

Before Floryn realized his intentions they were in the barn. The clothing distributed evenly between them, they climbed into the loft and closed the door and sealed themselves off from the world. As they had the knack of doing, they created their own time and place.

Naked, they lay down on the blanket he had so thoughtfully provided. They faced each other, touching only with their lips. Then Cord touched her breasts, her sensitive, swollen breasts as he received her into a mouth that was gentle and erotic.

Sighing with pleasure, she separated her legs to make way for him. He pressed his open hand over her mound, then slid it between her thighs.

394

She reached for him. Beneath her questing fingers he was hard and smooth and warm and already brimming with passion.

They caressed each other into a glorious frenzy. Much later, they lay facing each other, replete and languid.

"I love you," she whispered.

"Floryn—"

She laid a finger over his mouth. "It's all right," she whispered. "I just wanted to say it."

He held her tightly, and they lay together for a long time without speaking.

"Are we going to sleep out here?" she asked.

He sighed deeply. "As much as I would like to, I don't want to be awakened before dawn with people coming in and out of the barn." He rolled over, kissed her a dry, fleeting kiss, and got up. He caught her hands and tugged her up also. "We better dress and get inside."

They were moving quietly down the hallway, when the door to Leanor's bedroom opened and she stepped into the hallway. Light from the bedroom lamp was to her back and did not illuminate into the hall.

"Floryn, is that you?" she asked, peering into the darkness.

"Yes."

"What are you doing up at this hour?"

"Cord's home." Floryn laughed. "We're trying to get to bed. He—he took a bath in the water trough."

By this time Leanor had reached into the room for the lamp and was holding it high, light spilling on Cord and Floryn.

"Ah, yes," Leanor drawled, her eyes moving from Cord to Floryn, "if only I had had lamplight to see by before I spoke. It looks as if you took a bath in the trough also."

"She did," Cord said, "and she's thoroughly compromised me." His husky chuckle joined Leanor's as he took the lamp from her and handed it to Floryn. Capturing the housekeeper in a bear hug, he swung her around.

She laughed and squealed, playfully pounding his chest with her hands. When he set her on her feet, her face was alight with joy. "I'm glad you're home, *mi hijo.*" The obsidian eyes twinkled.

"It's good to be home. I am bushed."

"And hungry?"

"Yes, ma'am. Hungry for some of your biscuits and a cup of your coffee."

Soon they were seated around the kitchen table. Between bites of food which Leanor piled on the table as if she were feeding all the ranch hands, he told them about his trip to the interior. He and Ramon had located the guard, but the old man had added nothing new to the story. He did confirm, however, that the prisoner was Mathieu Guilbert, that he had been shot to death by the Mexican government as a traitor and the pendant had belonged to him.

His meal finished, Cord pushed back in the chair and dug the pendant out of his pocket. He was gazing at the silver medallion when Leanor refilled his cup with coffee for the last time. He tossed the jewelry on the table where it wobbled on its curved side before it finally fell flat. Lamplight flickered on the pie-shaped silver pendant. Three sets of eyes were riveted to it.

Aged hands reached out, tentatively touched the medallion, then hurriedly retracted as if burned.

"Madre de Dios," Leanor gasped.

Floryn glanced up to see the housekeeper's stricken face. "What is it?" she asked.

Shaking her head, Leanor struggled for breath; she clutched her chest and slowly bent double, collapsing to the floor.

"Leanor!" Floryn was on her knees beside her friend.

Her face ashen, Leanor gasped, *"La Curandera."* Her hands frantically clawed at her throat and chest.

Cord slid to the floor beside them, he and Floryn working to unfasten Leanor's clothing.

"Go get the *curandera* and send for the doctor," he said. "I'll get Leanor to bed."

Cord swept the woman into his arms.

"Not the doctor," Leanor weakly said as she fished her crucifix from the neckline of her gown. As if it were a lifeline, she clutched the gold cross in her hand. "Angelita and Fath—" Her voice grew faint.

"The priest?" Floryn asked.

"Sí," Leanor whispered, her lids resting against pasty white skin cheeks. "I would confess and have the last rites."

The only light in the bedroom was the pale glow of the hall lamp that filtered through the opened door. Incense burned in bowls on every available table, and Angelita sat in the corner chanting, running her rosary through her arthritic hands. The mixture of heat and odors was nauseating, but Floryn did not budge from Leanor's bedside, nor did she attempt to stop the ritual the *curandera* performed. Leanor believed in her. That was enough for Floryn who had been keeping vigil ever since Cord left to get the doctor and the priest.

Floryn had cried until she thought she had no tears left. Dry-eyed and hurting, she held Leanor's hand as if she could will her friend to live, as if she could send her life force into the weakened body. Alternately Floryn begged God to heal Leanor. She begged him to stop the pain and suffering. She begged him to do what was best.

Moving to where Floryn sat, Angelita laid her gnarled hands on her shoulders and gently squeezed. "I have done all for her that I can. She is in the hands of God. I will return to my cabin and pray."

Floryn nodded.

Angelita stepped closer to the bed and touched the tips of her fingers to Leanor's forehead and to her heart. She leaned over and kissed the rosary Leanor held in her hands.

"*Vaya con Dios, mi amiga,*" she whispered.

"*Sí,*" Leanor whispered. "I go with God." Her eyes flickered open, then closed as if the effort were too much for her. Her lips moved slightly, her voice frail, she said, "*Padre?*"

"He'll be here," Floryn assured her. "Cord went for him."

Leanor nodded, and after awhile said, "Open the window, *mi hija,* I would look out and see the stars."

Floryn flung open the shutters, glad for the rush of air. Although hot summer air, it was clean and fresh. It breathed of life, not death. When she returned to her chair, Leanor was gazing outside. She was breathing better and seemed to be stronger. She plumped her pillows, then reaching out caught Floryn's hand in hers and gently squeezed.

"I love you, *mi hija,* as if you were my own child," she said. The obsidian eyes, made darker and fathomless by the muted light that filtered into the room, fastened to Floryn's face. "I have been with you all these years because I loved you and you needed me. Now my work is finished and I must go."

"No," Floryn cried, "I don't want you to."

Leanor breathed deeply. "I don't suppose any of us want to go, but it's time. The Lord has sent his angel for me."

Floryn rested her head on the side of the bed and cried, big sobbing gulps that echoed through the room. She did not mean to, but could not stop herself. She knew she should be strong for Leanor, as Leanor had been strong for her during the past nine years. But Floryn loved the woman like a mother and did not want to give her up. She did not know what life would be like without her gentle laughter, her wisdom, her guidance, did not want to know.

For the third time in her life Floryn felt the acute pain of abandonment, first her mother, then Cord, now Leanor. It mattered not, the reason for their leaving. What mattered was their leaving her.

"I love you." Floryn sobbed. "Don't leave me."

"I love you, but I must go. I'm not leaving you alone. You have Cord now. He loves and will take care of you." Leanor ran her hands through Floryn's hair. She brushed her temples, her cheeks. "I love *la niña* as if she were my own child, also."

Floryn wiped her tears and sat up to look down at the peaceful woman. The old hand lifted and cupped her cheek.

"I must make my confession," Leanor said.

"The priest will be here soon," Floryn whispered.

Leanor shook her head on the pillow. "I want to tell you."

"Please wait for Father. It's taking so much effort

399

for you to speak," Floryn said, brushing strands of black hair from Leanor's face.

"I must talk. For so many years I have kept my silence. The words have been locked in my heart. Perhaps that is why it is hurting." She closed her eyes, waited a moment, then said, "Nine years ago a young pregnant woman stumbled into our village. She was exhausted and delirious and soon went into labor. She told us a wild tale about all her people having been attacked, all killed but her. I delivered her baby, but could not save her. Her only thoughts were for her child."

Leanor's face twisted in pain, and she raised a hand to her heart. She breathed deeply a time or two, then relaxed.

"Why are you telling me this?" Floryn asked. "You have been a midwife all your life. Why must you talk about this particular birth, Leanor?"

Leanor pointed. "Open my chest." Falteringly, she gave instructions for opening the secret compartment. "You will find the items which the mother left for her child. Get them for me."

In a matter of seconds, Floryn was kneeling at the foot of the bed over the opened trunk. She reached into the secret compartment to pull out a small gold wedding band and a medallion. Even in the dull light, she recognized the shape of it and felt as if her heart had stopped beating.

Old fears gripped her anew.

She rose and moved into the hallway where the lamp burned brightly and held the pendant close to the light. A third San Domingo pendant. This one was inset with a diamond about the same size as the ruby.

A diamond. An emerald. A ruby.

"The mother had nothing on her." Leanor's weak

voice barely reached Floryn. "She was so weak, she could not even tell me her name. She was dressed as a servant, but she had the pendant. She talked as if she were educated and were of the nobility. She said she had disguised herself so no one would know who she was because her life was in danger. She and her husband were considered traitors, and she was traveling to New Orleans where she would meet his people. But she never spoke their names."

Tears rolled down the side of Leanor's face. "The pendant . . . it belonged to her baby. She had a pendant herself, she said, but it was lost. She mumbled something about three, one for each of them. I did not know what it meant then. Now, I do. She, her husband, and the baby each had a pendant."

Apprehensive, the grasping, vicious tentacles of fear twisting about her heart, Floryn now held the ring up and peered inside to see if she could find an inscription or any initials. She did. Dear God. SG. Sanchia Guilbert. This pendant belonged to Sanchia and Mathieu's child.

Floryn rushed back into the room and sat down beside the bed. "You recognized this when you saw the one Cord had. That's what frightened you."

Leanor nodded.

"What happened to the baby? Did it die also?"

"No, the babe lived. I promised the mother that I would care for her child," Leanor said. She opened her eyes and gazed into Floryn's. "The babe was born on March 1, 1856."

Floryn's chest hurt; she could hardly breathe. The heat, the obnoxious odors . . . fear . . . were suffocating her. "Just a few weeks before Hope."

"Sí."

"You must tell me where the baby is," Floryn said.

401

"She is here, *mi hija,* with you."

At that moment Floryn's world fell out from beneath her. She swirled down, down into a black, bottomless cavern. "Hope," she whispered. "Sanchia Guilbert's daughter is Hope?"

"*Sí.*"

"No," Floryn cried and shook her head until her hair fell down. Fear caused her voice to escalate. "No, that can't be true. I won't believe it. Hope is my daughter. Do you understand? Hope is my daughter."

"*Sí,* Hope is your daughter," Leanor said, her voice strong, firm. "You are her mother."

Floryn's anger, born of despair, drained out of her as quickly as it arose. She stood and walked to the opened window. Now she was numb, numb all over. She gazed outside but saw nothing; she felt nothing. Yet her mind was awhirl. Hope—her Hope—her daughter—was not her daughter. She swallowed the hurt that knotted in her chest and throat.

"My—my baby—" she said, pushing the words through equally numbed lips. "What happened to my baby?"

"Your daughter was stillborn," Leanor said.

"No. That cannot be."

How quietly she spoke. How composed she was. Did she have any grief left for her and Cord's baby? Did she and Cord really have a baby? How wrong this seemed. No funeral. No mourning. No baby. No . . . Dear Lord, she silently cried, help me. Her fingers bit into the windowsill, only the pain of the wood against her skin making her know she was alive and not dead.

"You were injured in the accident," Leanor explained, "and after the baby was born, you were unconscious for many hours. I sent George to get

402

La Curandera, and she gave you medicine. She told me to talk to you. Thinking the baby was yours, she told me to put it in your arms. That the child would heal you."

"So you gave me Hope."

"Yes," Leanor said, "I gave you Hope. For me, it was the right thing to do. You wanted your child so much. You needed your child. You had so much love to give, and Hope needed love, your love. She needed you, *mi hija.*"

Unable to stand, fearing she would also collapse, Floryn pressed her forehead against the wooden frame. Hot tears scalded her cheeks. Grief for all things merged into one, and she mourned.

Minutes later, Leanor asked, "Will you forgive an old woman?"

Her eyes and lips swollen, her nose stopped up, Floryn wiped her tears away and returned to the bed to place her arms loosely around Leanor. "Why didn't you tell me?"

"I didn't think anyone would ever know," she answered. "And deep in my heart, I felt that you were Hope's mother."

"Hope is so much like Cord," Floryn said, making her last desperate bid to reinstate her old world, her old set of beliefs, to bring back into her life the security she had established for herself. "She must be his daughter. She must be."

"She's very much like you," Leanor said. "The color of her eyes." She breathed heavily and smiled wearily. "Perhaps the old woman bungled up the job, but God knew her heart was right, so he worked out the details."

"Yes," Floryn said, "your heart has always been right."

"I don't apologize for giving you the baby,"

403

Leanor said, "but I'm sorry I deceived you, that I didn't trust you. Please forgive me."

"I forgive you." Floryn sobbed. "And I thank you. I don't know how I would have faced life without Hope. She is my life."

Leanor brushed strands of hair from Floryn's face. "You and Cord are her life, too, *mi hija*."

Floryn smiled.

"Didn't I tell you that God takes care of us?"

"Yes," she murmured.

Leanor breathed quietly, easily. She held her rosary in her hands, her fingers moving reverently over the crucifix. "All is well. I'm going to sleep now."

Tears burning her eyes, Floryn nodded. Returning the pendant and ring to the chest, she tiptoed out of the room. She went upstairs and wakened Hope, quickly explaining to her that Leanor was ill and the two of them were going to sit with her until Papa returned with the doctor.

Floryn sat in the chair beside the bed, Hope sat on the bed. She laid her little hand over Leanor's and patted. A few minutes later, Leanor opened her eyes and smiled up at Hope.

"*Mi hija*," she murmured. She lifted her hand and touched her cheek. "What are you doing up?"

"Visiting you. Mama said your heart was hurting."

"*Sí*, it is tired."

"Leanor," she said in a teary voice, "has the Lord called you to come clean his mansions?"

Leanor tried to smile. "*Sí*."

"Are you scared?" the child asked.

"I was," Leanor said, a beautiful peacefulness radiating her face and her voice. "I told the Lord I was, and he said not to worry. He would send a friend to help me find the way and to keep me company."

"Who?" Hope asked.

"An angel."

Tears running down her cheeks, Floryn watched Hope lean over to plant a quick kiss on the tip of Leanor's nose.

"Now you're ready to go, and you'll never be alone," she said. "I gave you some of my angel dust. That way I'll always be with you."

"Angel dust?" Leanor questioned.

Solemnly Hope nodded her head. "Papa gave Mama and me angel dust, and I'm giving some to you. That way we'll always be together. We'll always be a family." Her little voice wobbled. "Won't we?"

The old hand reached up to touch the little cheek, to cup it. "*Sí, mi hija*, we'll always be a family."

Not long after daybreak, Cord rode up to the house with the doctor. He was hardly out of the saddle when Hope burst out of the door.

"Papa!" she cried and threw herself into his arms. "Papa! The angels took her to heaven."

Tears burning his eyes, Cord held the sobbing child close to his heart. He felt a new vulnerability that came from loving a child, from loving his child unconditionally, from giving her the whole of his heart. Hope cried into his chest and clung to him. She had called him Papa but he was not sure if it was from grief or love. At the moment, it mattered not because the two emotions had merged to become one.

He carried her inside, held her in his lap, and rocked her as Floryn and Angelita prepared for the

405

burial. By mid-morning, he placed the spent, sleeping child in her bed, and he and Floryn sat in the parlor.

"The priest will be here as soon as he can," Cord informed her. "He was giving last rites in a neighboring village."

Glad Cord was here, that she did not have to face her grief alone, Floryn rested her head on his shoulder. She had accepted Cord's comfort when she grieved for George Greeve. Again she accepted his comfort, but this time she also gave comfort. Cord needed it also. Unstintingly, unselfishly they gave to each other.

Twenty-eight

Floryn stood in the parlor in front of a pedestal table arranging the bouquet of flowers Cord had picked for her. She found it hard to believe that a month had passed since Leanor's funeral. The house had returned to normalcy with a new and much younger housekeeper, but everyone still mourned the loss of Leanor, especially Floryn.

Leanor had been more than a housekeeper and nanny. She had been Floryn's dearest friend. Her confidant. This morning Floryn stood in the parlor thinking about Leanor, more specifically thinking about Leanor's confession. The farther removed she was from the funeral, the more Floryn found herself thinking about it, pondering what she should do. As of yet Floryn had not told Cord, could not bring herself to.

She had told him they could not live the remainder of their lives in the shadow of the pendant. Now she was not so sure. Perhaps the shadow would be better than its reality, less harsh. Perhaps the shadow offered life, whereas reality did not.

Looking at the desk, she saw the pendant Cord bought from Ramon. Although Floryn stood in the warm sunshine, she shivered. She was cold and frightened. She had always had a fascination for the pendants, but at the same time, she had an aversion to them. And that aversion had grown through the past months. She truly believed they were cursed. So many deaths could be attributed to them. Yet they held the secret of Cord's past, his future . . . their future.

She moved to the table and picked up the pendant.

Like her, Cord had no claim to freedom until he proved his innocence, until he revealed the secret of the San Domingo treasure. If she gave him the last pendant, Hope's pendant, Floryn felt an obligation to tell him who Hope really was.

Floryn had promised to help him heal, to bring peace into his troubled soul, laughter into his heart, light into his soul. In telling him she reneged on her promise. Yet duty, integrity, honesty compelled her to do something that would pull the newly laid foundation from his world. And she feared the consequences.

Floryn thought she and Cord had climbed the highest and roughest obstacle in their marriage, but it did not compare to telling him that Hope was not their daughter—not their flesh and blood. She was not born out of their love.

"Here you are," Cord said, standing at the door. "I've been looking all over for you."

She smiled sadly. Before she lost courage, before she let another day pass, she reached into her pocket and extracted the medallion. "I have something to show you." She walked to the desk and laid it down.

Cord stood beside her. Both were silent a long time as they stared at the two pieces of jewelry. He ran his finger around the diamond while Floryn related Leanor's story to him. When she finished, he said nothing—absolutely nothing. He played with the pendants, positioning them so that they formed two-thirds of a circle.

But he was not interested in the medallion.

He had never doubted the paternity of his daughter. Never. Not from the beginning. The minute Floryn made the announcement, he believed. Easily he had believed. Immediately. He wanted, had needed to believe it.

Locking his grief within his heart as he had done for so many years, unable to share it, he walked to the window and stared out, seeing nothing.

Floryn followed. She pressed herself to him, laying her cheek against his back. He was rock hard, tense.

"Don't shut me out," she begged softly. "I need you as much as you need me. I love you, Cord. I'm here for you."

He turned, and she saw his tears.

They did not hug each other; they clung, clung as their world spun out of control around them. They clung because they had each other.

"Damn it!" He hugged her so tightly his arms bit into her flesh. Floryn held back her cry of pain, knowing that the pain he suffered was much greater. She felt his tears on her neck, and she cried with him. "She is our child, Floryn. She belongs to you and me."

"I know it," Floryn agreed, her eyes red and swollen from days of crying, from days of grief.

"Maybe Sanchia Guilbert gave birth to her, but you've raised her. We love her."

The two of them talked about Hope, about the playground, her dress with ruffles, her calling Cord Papa, about the angel dust.

His eyes blazing, his hands cupping her shoulders, he said, "We're a family, Floryn, bound together by love. Nothing, nobody is going to take Hope away from us."

Floryn tiptoed, and through her tears she planted

409

a kiss on the tip of Cord's nose. "We all have angel dust on us, don't we?"

Again they held each other, so tightly there was no space between them. Then he loved her, and it had nothing to do with sex. He comforted her. His lips lay against her forehead, and he frequently kissed her lightly in between whispers of comfort, in between promises that everything would work out. They would have their daughter. They would be a family.

"One day we'll tell her," Cord said. "We'll let her know how much we love her, how much she means to us."

Hurriedly they talked. They laid plans; they relaid plans.

"Cord," Floryn finally said, "what about Hope's relatives?"

A new fear seized them. Hope had relatives, her own flesh and blood. The San Domingos in Mexico. The Guilberts in France.

"They might want to—they would have a right to take her."

Cord looked at the table, at the hundred-faceted diamond that mocked him. "Revenge is truly double-edged," he whispered bitterly. "The very evidence that may prove my innocence is that which may take our daughter from us."

"Are we willing to take the risk?" Floryn murmured.

Both stared at each other; then at the same time said, "Yes."

Cord slowly expelled the air in his lungs. "We have to. We owe it to ourselves and to Hope."

Several days later when Antonio announced the arrival of Emmanuel Tellez, Cord looked up from his desk in surprise. He had known Tellez was going to make them a loan, but had not expected the man to deliver the money himself, nor had he expected him to visit this soon—only eight weeks after they had entrusted the jewels to his care.

"Show him in," Cord said.

Shortly Emmanuel Tellez entered the study. With him was a tall young man whom Cord did not know.

"*Señor* Donaldson," Tellez said, "please pardon an unannounced visit, but I felt the fewer who knew about this the better. You expressed an immediate need for your money. Since it was such a large sum, my personal secretary, Alfredo Comacho, and I traveled to San Antonio for it and decided to deliver it ourselves on our return trip to Piedras Negras."

"We certainly appreciate this," Cord said, marveling that it had taken them such a short time.

"No more than we appreciate all your wife has done for our cause."

"*Señor* Tellez," Floryn said, walking into the room, "we're delighted to see you. I know you're tired from your journey. May I offer you some refreshments?"

"At the moment, *Señora*, I am seeking the comfort of a quiet room and a soft bed."

"I can furnish that," she answered. "Would you accept our hospitality and stay over tonight?"

"Most graciously," he said, "and I would go further to ask if we might stay longer. On the way here, we were attacked by marauding Indians and several of my men are wounded. They need nursing and time to recuperate."

"Of course, I'll see to their needs. You and Mr. Comacho will sleep in the house. I'll show you to your rooms later."

Emmanuel smiled and nodded his head enthusiastically. "If it is not too much trouble, as soon as we

411

have made the transfer of money, I would like to go to my room. I am very tired. I have been traveling continuously for the past four weeks. My old bones need more rest than they did a few years ago."

"Surely," Floryn said. "If you gentlemen will excuse me, I'll see about the sleeping arrangements and the evening meal."

"Indians attacked?" Cord said more than asked.

The Mexican nodded his head. "There was no contest between us. We far outnumbered them, but they took their toll. Three of my men were wounded. As a result we have traveled much faster than we would have."

As Floryn left the room, Tellez turned to the young man and motioned for him to hand Cord a small leather valise. "Let's count this and sign the papers. I will feel much relieved to have this in your custody rather than mine."

Cord walked to the desk where he unfastened the traveling bag and took out the money. The three of them counted it; then Cord and *Señor* Tellez signed a receipt.

Floryn returned to the study as Cord locked the money in the safe. Afterward they drank a glass of wine, relaxed, and talked. Eventually Emmanuel Tellez rose.

"And now, *Señora,* I am ready to go to my room and rest."

He returned to the desk to pick up his valise. As he removed it, the bottom dragged over the two medallions. Hearing the clink of metal, he looked down, then leaned even closer.

Surprised, he said, "Another one?"

"Yes," Cord answered. "I learned of it about a week ago."

"So interesting," Emmanuel Tellez murmured.

412

He dropped the valise to the floor and picked up the diamond inset pendant. By this time Alfredo had joined his employer and was inspecting the pendant Cord had purchased from Ramon. The secretary turned it over several times, squinted at it. Then he moved to the window and held it up to the light.

"*Señor* Tellez"—he returned to the table, laying the pendant down—"may I see that one, please?"

Excited, but also cautious, Cord observed both men. Floryn came to stand beside him, curling her hand around his arm. She, too, watched.

The secretary examined both sides of the pendant, picked up the other, and subjected it to as careful a scrutiny before he laid them down again, pushing them together.

"There is a map on one side, writing on the other."

Floryn's hand trembled against him. His heartbeat quickened.

"The marks," Cord said slowly.

"Latin," Alfredo answered.

"How simple," Floryn marveled.

So simple that Cord wondered at all the mystery and secrecy in which it was shrouded.

"I studied Latin at the university," Alfredo said. "But one piece is missing, the pivotal piece."

"What words can you make out?" Floryn asked.

"Mathieu Guilbert," he read. "Something about a valley. It reads as if the spot marked on the map is where something valuable is hidden. But I can't be sure. As I said, the most important piece is missing."

"The San Domingo treasure," Floryn breathed.

Ever since Alfredo Comacho had announced the day before that the writing on the pendants was Latin, Floryn had been filled with a sense of expect-

413

ancy. Somehow the shadows around the pendants seemed to be dissipating. Even though she and Cord were willing to explore their secrets to prove his innocence and to find the illusive San Domingo treasure, they could not. The pivotal piece was missing—the ruby pendant.

Later that afternoon when Tellez and Comacho were taking their siesta, Cord worked on the ledgers in the study. Floryn, having finished instructing the new housekeeper, had seen Hope and Rule off. The two of them were riding over to Mildred's to help with the branding. Smiling, wondering what kind of job Jason and Hope would do, Floryn carried a tray with two glasses of lemonade to the study.

As she passed the front door which stood open, she saw a rider dismounting and hitching his horse to the post. She set the tray on the hall table and moved further into the entry hall.

"Shelby," she said.

"Ma'am." The lawman doffed his hat, then swatted it over his dusty body before he walked any closer to the house. "Is Cord home?"

"Yes, he's in the study."

"I hate to bother you, but I need to see him."

"This way." She turned, Shelby following.

As they passed the tray, he said, "Let me, ma'am."

When the two of them walked into the study, Cord looked up. Laying his pencil down, he rose.

"This is getting to be a habit."

Shelby nodded curtly and tossed his hat on the floor close to one of the wing chairs.

"Please sit down," Floryn said to their guest. "Would you care to join us for a glass of lemonade?"

The lawman's gaze quickly riveted to the sideboard.

"Or whiskey?" Floryn tentatively offered.

414

"Believe this dry throat of mine could use the whiskey, if you don't mind, ma'am?"

Quick strides carried Cord to the table where he poured his friend a drink, then handed it to him. Floryn, a glass of lemonade in hand, sat across from Shelby.

"Is this a pleasure visit?" Cord took his drink from the tray and moved to sit in the chair behind his desk.

Shelby shook his head. In one swallow he emptied the glass. "I caught up with Kid, but he got away."

"Kid Ferguson?" Floryn asked. "What do you mean caught up with him?"

Shelby nodded and gazed through narrowed eyes at Cord.

"I didn't tell her," Cord said.

"Kid Ferguson is a wanted and dangerous man, ma'am."

Shelby rose and tipped his empty glass toward the sideboard. When Cord nodded, he crossed the room for a refill.

"Yes," Floryn said, "I remember your warning us about him when we were leaving Huntsville." She also remembered Kid's cocky attitude the day Cord had talked with him and Tony in the hotel room in San Antonio. "What has he done?"

Shelby drank his second glass of whiskey slower. "For one thing, he's the one who stole Cord's pendant."

"So," Floryn drawled, "he's the one." She glanced at Cord who sat back and listened, weighing all that was said.

"Yes," Shelby answered. "I had him holed up in an upstairs room in a cantina in Mexico. Before he got away, he told me he had been hired by Pruitt before Cord was ever released from prison. He was to follow

415

Cord and to report his every move to Pruitt. In San Antone Norwell tried to hire Kid also. But he made the mistake of describing the pendant to Kid and of telling him how much it was worth. Kid forgot the big picture for looking at the pendant. He decided to steal it for himself."

"He's the one who followed us in Mexico," Floryn said.

"Could be," Cord said.

Shelby's head turned from Floryn to Cord. "Following you?"

Cord told Shelby the story of the Guilbert jewels, from his having received them to using them as collateral for a loan.

"You don't have them here with you?" Shelby demanded.

"No," Cord replied, "I've already exchanged them for cash."

"Reckon Kid thinks you might have them?" Shelby pressed.

"I don't know." Cord leaned back in the desk chair, rubbing his cheek beneath the eye patch. "If he were the one following us, he might have seen them. Why?"

"I've trailed him back this way, and I don't put anything past Kid."

"You think he's on his way to the ranch?" Cord said.

Shelby nodded. "I suspect that he and Esteman are working together."

"Tony's working for me," Cord said.

Shelby's face hardened, his eyes narrowed into a thin line as did his mouth. "Damn it, Cord! I told you before you left Huntsville that you couldn't trust those two. Remember, I'm the one who caught them the first time. I know their kind."

"I know their kind, too," Cord said.

"You know them as convicts," Shelby grated. "God, Cord, you sound like one of them."

"I was."

Shelby drew in a deep breath and released it. "I'm sorry, Cord," he apologized. "I don't know what made me do that. It's just that I'm worried about you and your wife."

The room was quiet for a long time before Cord spoke.

"Why didn't you get the pendant from Kid when you had him cornered?"

"I did," Shelby answered. "He had a little *señorita* who pulled a fast one. She got him a gun, and before I knew what had happened, he shot me. Left me for dead. When I came to, he had taken anything I had of value, including the pendant."

"It's a shame you don't have it."

Surprised, Floryn gazed at her husband.

Cord motioned for his friend to join him at the desk. He opened the drawer. "Let me show you something."

Shortly Shelby was gazing at the two pendants. "My God," Shelby exclaimed. "There's three of them, and they fit together. Look at that diamond!"

"Fit together is only the half of it," Cord said. "It's what you get *when* you push them together. On the one side, you have a map. On the other you have Latin writing."

"I'll be damned!" Shelby breathed the expletive. "All the time these scratches were Latin writing."

Cord briefly told him the interpretation of some of the words on the pendants.

Shelby clenched one of the pendants in his fist. "Damn it, Cord! If only we had the third one. We would know where the San Domingo treasure was buried."

"At least, we would know the secret of the pendants."

"I don't believe this," Kern Wallis murmured.

Sitting at his desk in a pool of sunlight, his broad shoulders hunched over, he looked from Cord, to Floryn, back to the money on his desk.

Floryn, sitting in front of the desk beside Cord, was delighted to witness the attorney's apparent discomfort, his speechlessness. This was one visit she had been anticipating for a long time.

"Our receipt," Cord said. "For a debt paid in full."

"We have guests awaiting us at the *hacienda*," Floryn said.

"Of—of course." Wallis picked up his pen. "So, you're going through with this cattle driving business?"

"We are," Cord replied.

Floryn felt quite victorious as Wallis wrote the magical words on the paper that released them from his grip. One by one she and Cord were cutting the ties that bound them to their past. She looked out the window, at the morning sunlight that brightened the street of Donaldson.

Hope was jumping rope on the boardwalk immediately outside the attorney's office. Of her own accord she had put on her new green and white gingham dress and black patent shoes, and her long brown hair, pulled from her face with a large green bow, was hanging in soft waves down her back. Today she looked to be far removed from their precious little tomboy. She was their little girl. No matter which, tomboy or little girl, Hope was always their daughter. When this was all over, they had promised they

418

would tell Hope about her birth parents.

Floryn's heart felt bright and warm. Ever since Shelby's visit yesterday, she had begun to feel better, even about the pendants. Knowing that Kid was the one following them, the one who had stolen the pendant, lifted some of the shadows and helped her start to put matters into their right perspective.

Not that she reckoned Kid to be any less dangerous. It was that their enemy now had a name, a face, a voice. He was not part of the shadows anymore. And Shelby had promised to stay close in case they needed him. Floryn felt much better knowing that he was around.

"Here you are," Wallis said.

Cord reached for the receipt, read and handed it to Floryn. She read it, tucked it into her reticule, then pulled out two letters. Holding them in her hands that rested in her lap, she landed her last blow. One she had wanted to land for many years.

"Cord brought the written accusations home to me, Kern, and I read all of them."

The attorney squirmed in his chair. His eyes on the letters, he reached up and ran a finger around his collar as if it were biting into his neck.

"Including the one George supposedly wrote," she added.

"I don't know anything about the testimonies," Wallis said testily. "That was Hal's doing, Floryn."

"We understand that," Cord said, "but Floryn and I wanted you to know that someone forged George's confession."

"Forged," Wallis stuttered, his gaze again bouncing back and forth between them. "Why—why the man could write. I know he could. When he—when he came to get the money from Hal, he talked to me about writing home to his sister."

"Yes, he could read and write," Floryn said softly. "I taught him how. I even have two letters he wrote me. Look at them, Kern."

She leaned forward and laid the two documents on the table. If they had been a rattlesnake coiled ready to strike, they could not have appeared more daunting, more dangerous. Three sets of eyes were riveted to them.

A suspicious gleam in his eye, Wallis slowly reached for them and opened one. After a quick glance, he dropped it to the desk, picked up the second one and opened it. He tossed it with such force it slid across the wooden surface, stopping before it fell to the floor.

"What does this have to do with me?"

"George could only print, Kern," Floryn said, keeping her voice soft. "He never learned to do cursive. That confession was in cursive, and the writing looks very much like yours."

Bright red spots on his cheeks, Wallis rose and walked to the window where he fidgeted with the shade.

Cord said, "In Hal's letter he said George had died shortly after leaving here. Since Floryn is certain the confession was not penned by George himself, we believe there may have been foul play concerning his death also. Perhaps murder."

"Murder!" All color drained out of Wallis's face. Like liquid, he slid into his chair.

"I'm prepared to hire a detective in New York who is going to investigate this entire affair." Cord held the unposted letter in his hand. "The one Floryn hired to locate me."

Clearly stunned, just opening and closing his mouth and shaking his head, Wallis looked at them.

"Floryn also believes these other men were paid to

420

sign these confessions. We'll get to the bottom of this matter."

With trembling hands, Wallis shuffled through the money, straightened several sheets of paper and dropped two pencils into a container.

"I don't know about the other confessions," he said. "Possibly the men who wrote them were paid to do so. That was handled by Hal, but I know George Greeve was not murdered."

Floryn tensed and leaned forward.

"How do you know?" Cord asked.

Wallis nervously rubbed the corners of his mouth and chin. "Greeve did return to Donaldsonville, but he didn't go to the Fancy Lady. He was a sick man, real sick. Said he was dying. He'd been under the treatment of some doctor in New Mexico."

Wallis stood. "That's why he didn't go to the ranch. He was afraid of infecting Floryn and the child. Greeve sent word for Hal to meet him in town. When Greeve asked for his money, Hal naturally sent the man to me. He had a box of personal effects he wanted to send his sister with the rest of his money."

Wallis walked over to the sideboard and poured himself a glass of whiskey. By way of invitation, he tilted the bottle toward Floryn and Cord. Both declined. His drink in hand, he walked back to his desk.

After several bracing swallows, he said, "He was coughing and spitting up blood so bad that I let him stay in the room off of my house."

"The shed?" Floryn said sharply. "You put him in that filthy shed back of your house?"

He ignored her and resumed speaking. "I sent for Tidwell, the doctor, but he was out of town. By the time he showed up, Greeve had been dead for hours. I had already figured a way to use him, so I never

told Tidwell why I sent for him. I buried Greeve
then wrote a letter to his sister in Pennsylvania in
forming her of his death. I included in it his persona
belongings and the rest of his money. I didn't wan
her to come snooping and mess up my plans."

The attorney's gaze swiveled between Cord and
Floryn. "If you don't believe me, write her. I told he
about his death. I sent her the things he wanted he
to have, including the name of the doctor he went to
see in New Mexico. You can talk to him, too. I —
changed the ledgers, and . . . well — you know the
rest."

His hands still shaking, he set his empty glass or
the desktop and sat down. "I did not kill anyone. I
won't be accused of murder. You're not going to pir
this on me."

"Maybe you didn't kill Greeve" — Cord rose, hi;
voice hard, his expression thunderous; still he felt a;
if Wallis dwarfed him — "but you sure as hell tried to
kill Floryn, by destroying her reputation and her influence in the community."

His hands rested on the ivory grips of his pistols.

"I didn't do that, *Mr. Donaldson*," Wallis slurred sarcastically. "You did when you slept with her ten year;
ago and left her pregnant. You're the one who sullied
her, not me. You're the one who blazed the trail for
others to follow."

Before Floryn was aware of what was happening,
two long strides carried Cord around the desk. His
face was black with fury, his expression set. He
grabbed a fist full of material and hauled Wallis to
his feet and socked him in the mouth.

The blow sounded through the room, and Floryn
was sure Wallis's jaw was broken. He flew back
against the wall and slid to the floor. Blinking his
eyes disbelievingly, he laid his hand on his mouth.

He withdrew it and looked at the blood on his fingers.

Angry steps moved Cord closer to the attorney who cowered before him.

Cord said, "I told you my sense of injustice was different from most men's. Be glad that my wife and child are here with me. I'm going to be more lenient with you than I would have been otherwise."

Wallis fished in his pocket and pulled out a handkerchief which he pressed to his bleeding lips. "You may have broken my jaw," he grumbled.

"I could have killed you." Cord took a step toward him, and Wallis cringed. "Just like you're trying to kill the life in this valley, just like you tried to kill Floryn. Get that little book of yours out and start writing receipts to these people who mortgaged their ranches through you."

"The hell I will," Wallis spat.

Again Cord rested both hands on the ivory grips of the Navy '51 Colts. "The hell you will is right." To Floryn he said, "Make a list of their names, so he won't miss anyone."

Floryn leaned closer to the desk, and picking up pen and paper, she began to write.

"I think you can help to clear your conscience by giving them clear title to their land, especially when we consider how much you cheated Floryn out of financially and how much grief and humiliation you caused her." Cord's gaze settled on the money lying on Wallis's desk. "I also believe that once you've done that, it would be in your best interest to relocate, Mr. Wallis."

"And if I don't?"

"You will, or you'll be six feet under. That's a promise."

Twenty-nine

Having changed into her riding skirt and blouse as soon as she and Cord returned from their meeting with Kern Wallis, Floryn stood in the front yard, leaning against the arbor. She watched Cord and Hope as they rode toward the Bar-H, moving beneath the arbor to sit in the swing only when they were out of sight.

She was eager for Cord to return. She had some good news she wanted to relay to him. Today she knew with certainty that she and he were going to have a baby. She smiled as she thought about it, about their baby, their second child. Always she reckoned Hope as the first one.

The smile was still lingering when she reached out to pick up her receipt box and tablet. Until Mattie Johnson was trained in her housekeeping chores, Floryn had to do the master planning.

Sometime later, the housekeeper joined Floryn under the arbor. Floryn liked Mattie. She was a young widow who had lost her husband in the recent war. When Floryn had put out word that she was looking for a new housekeeper, Mattie had applied and Floryn was happy to hire her.

After they had completed their conversation, Mattie returned to her chores and Floryn headed for the study. When she walked into the room, she realized that something was wrong. She had an eerie feeling, similar to the one she had experienced when the pendant was stolen from her in San Antonio. She grew clammy and apprehensive. Behind her she heard a noise and knew she was not alone. In that split second she also knew her companion was an intruder. She could not turn around.

"Hello, again, Mrs. Donaldson."

The voice, that haunting voice from the past, only now it was not muffled. Fear, paralyzing fear, gripped her. For her life she could not have moved. Again her space, her sense of privacy had been violated. And this time she was protecting not only her life but that of her unborn baby.

She heard firm steps move over the floor until a man, pointing a pistol, walked in front of her to shut the door.

"Kid Ferguson," she breathed. "So it is true?"

Kid shrugged and returned to stand in front of the desk. "Before I answer that, I'd have to know what was said."

"Shelby said you'd gone bad."

"So the lawman has been talking, has he? Well, what he's saying isn't necessarily the truth. I just figured out where the money is. Pruitt's always known, and in his way so has Shelby."

"The San Domingo treasure," Floryn breathed. "That's why Pruitt was so willing to work with me to get Cord a parole."

"You got it."

"Are you working for Pruitt?" she asked.

"Let's say I'm working for myself."

"You stole the pendant from me for yourself?"

"I did. At the time I didn't quite understand its full value." He unbuttoned his shirt pocket and fished out the silver medallion. He looped the chain on his fingers and let it dangle.

Floryn watched as it turned and twisted; she gazed at the multifaceted blood-red stone. Blood. Death. She had always associated the pendant with death.

"Now I do," Kid said, "and I want all three of the pendants."

"You and everybody else," Floryn muttered sarcastically.

"But I'm not everybody else, and I intend to get them. One way or the other." He moved the Colt fractionally. "I don't want to hurt you, Mrs. Donaldson, and if you do what I say, I won't. I promise. I never wanted to hurt you, but I want the pendants. Please get them for me, and I'll be on my way."

Floryn did not move.

Kid stepped closer. "Get them."

Floryn reached into her pocket and pulled out the key ring. When the drawer was unlocked and opened, she looked in and gasped. "The pendants are gone."

An acute feeling of loss assailed Floryn. Now all three of the pendants were gone. She stared into the empty drawer as if by staring long enough she could conjure up the jewelry.

Kid ran around the desk and peered into the drawer. Muttering expletives, he jerked it out and dumped the contents on the floor. Tossing it aside, wood crunching against the floor as it fell, he kicked the contents.

"Where are they?"

By now Floryn had leaned forward, settled her elbows on the desk, and laid her head in her hands. Kid caught one of her arms and yanked her out of the chair. Glaring into her face, he shouted, "Where are they?"

"I don't know," Floryn answered. "The last time I saw them Cord was locking them in here."

Cursing, Kid pushed around Floryn and restlessly prowled the room. Finally he said, "Get a sheet of paper. I want you to write your husband a note to let him know where you are and who you're with and what it's

426

going to cost him to get you back. I'll get those damn pendants."

Floryn opened the drawer to extract a sheet of stationery and dipped the pen in the inkwell. She had been frightened ever since Kid had spoken to her, but when she saw her hand shaking, she was angry with herself. How dare she let this man reduce her to a mass of emotion.

But bravado would not disguise or erase her fear. She had lost one baby, and she did not want to lose a second. Nor did she want Kid to know that she was with child. She was not sure how he would use the information. She could take no chances on his hurting either her or the baby.

Lowering her hand, touching the paper, and hoping that he had not seen the shaking, she spoke with a nonchalance she certainly did not feel. "We have house guests. They'll think it odd if you force me to leave with you."

"Not really," he answered, his face hard. "The new housekeeper isn't going to know but what I'm one of your ranch hands. And if she notices us leaving that's exactly what you'll tell her. No one will notice that anything is amiss until Cord comes home and finds your note."

"What shall I write?" Floryn asked.

The ransom noted crumbled in his fist, Cord paced back and forth in the study. Floryn kidnapped. Her life endangered again because of those damn pendants. If only he had not moved them. Such an innocent action on his part. At Emmanuel's suggestion, he had given them to the silversmith, so he could make a mold of them. All the time the pendants had been upstairs in the guest bedroom.

"Hope's in bed, Mr. Donaldson," Mattie said from

the doorway.

Cord nodded.

"Is there anything else you'd like for me to get you before I retire?"

"No."

Cord's frustration was no longer over the questions of his past. The present — his fear that he could not save Floryn — had completely obliterated both past and future. He was furious with himself because he may have lost her . . . forever.

He must not lose her. He loved her.

And he had never told her so. He had been too preoccupied with his hatred, with his revenge. As strange as it seemed, he had been in love with his hatred and revenge.

Spurs jingled softly announcing Antonio's arrival. Sweeping his sombrero off, he entered the study. "I left word with the sheriff. He'll give Martin the message if he stops by the office. In the meantime, *Patrón*, what shall we do?"

"I want to take Hope where she'll be safe," Cord said. "I don't want her life endangered. I don't want anyone to kidnap her."

"My village," Antonio said. "I will send for Primero."

Cord nodded, then said, "At sunrise I'll take the pendants to Kid as he instructed."

"I will go with you," Antonio said.

Cord laid his hand on the *gran vaquero's* shoulder. "Thank you, but I want you to stay here. If something happens to me, you'll be needed to watch after Hope and to manage the ranch."

"It is not good for you to go alone," Antonio said.

"I'll take Rule," Cord replied. "If Shelby gets my message in time, he'll join me. I'll get Hope ready."

"I'll send someone for Primero immediately, *Patrón*, and I'll get Rule myself." Determined steps carried the *gran vaquero* to the door where he halted. "I will protect

428

la niña with my life."

Several hours later, by the time Cord had set his affairs in order, Rule, Mildred, and Jason arrived. While Cord talked with Rule, Mildred carried Jason to one of the bedrooms and tucked him into bed. Then she brewed a fresh pot of coffee and joined the men in the study.

The three of them sat together, talking every once in a while, but mostly sitting quietly, thinking. The slow passage of time was marked by the hour and half-hour chimes of the mantel clock.

Cord could not shove the heaviness that engulfed him aside. He had promised Floryn he would not allow his past to put a dark shadow over Hope's life, but it had. Her life could be in danger as was his wife's. He had endangered the lives of the two people whom he loved most, his wife and his daughter.

He and Rule cleaned their pistols; they loaded them. They made sure they had extra ammunition.

Cord paced the floor. He cursed himself for being a fool. He drank more coffee. He paced, he cursed again.

Soft knocks carried him to the door. He was greeted by the solemn face of the Apache tracker. "You sent for me," he said.

Again Cord recounted the story of Floryn's kidnapping and the ransom demands. "I want you to take Hope to Antonio's village for safekeeping. Her life must be protected at all costs."

The Indian nodded, the black eyes glinting even blacker in the lamplight as they steadily held Cord's gaze, as they sealed him a promise to protect the child.

"I'm going with them," Mildred said. "With Leanor having just passed away and Floryn gone, the child's gonna be upset enough. This trip in the middle of the night isn't gonna help. If she has me and Jason with her, she'll get along better."

"Thanks, Mildred," Cord said.

"Do you want me to get her ready?"

"No, I'll do that," he replied. "I want to talk to her myself to let her know what's happening."

The sun was easing into view when Cord and Rule were almost clear of the narrow, rocky passageway. In the distant clearing, they saw the shack Kid had described in his note, an old line shack on the far borders of the Fancy Lady.

"Probably got her inside," Rule said.

"You're right." Kid moved his horse out from behind the outcropping of rocks to ride behind them. "I figured you'd bring this old fool with you, Cord, so I didn't wait in the house."

Cord's hand hovered over his gun.

Kid said, "Don't do anything foolish. I have my Colt pointed at you, and I'll shoot if I have to. Don't give me any notions."

"Where's Floryn?" Cord asked, not even turning his head.

"She's fine. I tied her to the tree in front of the shack. Right now, though, I want you and Rule to dismount."

An Indian, an Apache Cord figured from the way he was dressed, slipped quietly out of the rocks.

"Tie them up back to back," Kid ordered. He moved his horse closer to Cord. "If you'll hand me the pendants Victorio and I will be on our way. We'll put a knife a safe distance away from you. By the time you get to it and cut your ropes, we'll be long gone."

"You don't get the pendants until I see Floryn and know she's all right."

Kid reached up to tug the brim of his hat lower. His eyes narrowed. "You think you're smart, don't you? Well, you're not. I'm not about to let you get close to your wife."

430

"No pendants," Cord said softly.

Kid moved closer to Cord and touched the vest and shirt pockets.

"I don't have them on me," Cord said. "You're not going to get them until I know Floryn is all right."

Kid mulled the words a long time before he said, "I'll let Rule go see her." Then he ordered, "Victorio, tie Cord up."

The Indian hauled Cord off the horse and in a matter of minutes had him trussed up, the ropes binding his arms and upper body more than his legs.

Kid said to Rule, "Walk in front of me and don't get too close to Mrs. Donaldson. Don't try anything. I've given Victorio orders to shoot her if anything goes amiss."

Although he was tied up, Cord managed to twist and roll his body until he was close enough to see Floryn sitting on the ground and tied to the trunk of the scrub oak. His gaze moved thoroughly over her body. Her hair was unkempt, strands having come unloose from the coil to hang about her face; her clothes were wrinkled and soiled; exhaustion darkened her eyes.

"Has he hurt you, ma'am?" Rule asked.

"No."

"How's Cord?" she asked.

"He's fine, ma'am."

"Don't give him the pendants," she said.

"Reckon that's up to Cord," Rule said.

Kid rode back to Cord who had pushed up on his feet and was leaning against a large boulder.

"You've seen her. She's unhurt. Now give me the pendants."

"Let her leave with Rule," Cord said.

"Damn it, Cord! Quit playing games with me. Give me the pendants or we're going to hurt her."

Kid waved his hand at Victorio, and the Indian knelt

431

beside the tree, cut the cords that bound her, and jerked her up. His hand was like a manacle around her arm.

"Give me the pendants," Kid said.

"Let her go first." Cord hobbled closer to her.

"No. You'll just have to trust me."

When Cord continued to stare at Floryn, continued to wonder what to do, Kid motioned a second time to the Indian. Victorio yanked on Floryn's arm. When she did not move with him, he jerked more forcibly and she fell down. He never slaked his pace but continued to pull her behind him.

"Stop," she shouted. "Don't hurt my baby."

Cord froze. Their baby! He knew his wife's greatest fear: losing a second child.

"Stop it!" Cord yelled at the top of his voice. Again he worked his feet, twisting them, jumping, trying to move in her direction.

"My God!" Kid murmured, turning to look at Floryn. He ordered, "Victorio, don't be so rough with her."

Cord's heart beating in his throat, he strained against the ropes, cutting and burning his hands as he worked them. He wiggled one hand to the front so that he could slide it into his pocket. Closing his eyes, he grunted and he worked. Little by little he slid his hands between the pocket placket. With the tips of his fingers he felt his knife.

When he had it open and was sawing at the ropes, he called out, "I'll give you the damn pendants, Kid. Floryn means more to me than they do."

The Indian's grip slackened, and she pulled away from him. Her face white, her eyes large, she started running.

"No," Cord shouted, "don't run, Floryn. Stay put."

But she was running. Because she was looking over

432

her shoulder at the Indian, she was unaware that she was headed straight for a ravine. The Indian gave chase.

"Floryn," Cord shouted again, "stop running."

She paused and looked at him.

Kid took out after her. "Mrs. Donaldson," he shouted, "please stop. You're going to run off—"

Floryn's scream drowned out his words.

"Floryn," Cord yelled, "stop running. You're going to fall into a ravine. Stop running, sweetheart."

Rule drew his pistol and shot the Indian who had knocked his arrow and was aiming at Floryn; then as Kid rose past him, Rule grabbed a leg and yanked him off the horse. The two of them became a tangle of arms and legs as they wrestled and fought.

Floryn continued to run. Cord had cut through the ropes enough that he could move his arms and legs. He took off after Floryn praying that he could reach her before she fell over. As she reached the edge of the ravine, she realized her danger. She looked at him, her face a mask of fear, silently begging him to help her, to save her . . . her baby . . . their baby.

The ropes finally falling from his body, Cord tripped over them, then lunged for her, his arms banding around her body. They fell to the ground, but he rolled over so that she was on top and he took the brunt of the blow. Her arms wrapped around him, and he thought surely she would suffocate him, but at the moment he was too happy she was alive to be worried about his dying. As quickly as he laid her on the ground, he began a thorough examination.

"Dear God, but I love you, Floryn," he exclaimed, his hands moving over her body, finally resting tenderly on her stomach. "I love you. I love you. I love you." He said the words over and over again. "I couldn't bear it if you were hurt, if you lost our baby."

"I'm fine," she cried. "I'm not hurt."

"I love you, darling. I love you."

Again she was in his arms. Forgetting the world around them, breathing heavily, Cord simply held her. She clung to him, crying against his shoulder.

Cord heard a shot. He turned to see Rule pushing to his feet, his revolver in his hand. Kid remained on the ground:

"Is he dead?" Cord asked.

Rule nodded. "I didn't realize the gun had gone off. I didn't intend to."

Shelby Martin rode up. "Good thing you left me the ransom note with your message."

Holding on to Floryn, Cord walked to where Kid lay. Bending over him, he searched until he found the pendant. He gave it a cursory glance, dropped it into his shirt pocket. Then he scooped Floryn into his arms.

Looking down at his wife, he said, "It's time for us to go home, don't you think?"

She smiled tremulously. "I think."

Depositing her on the roan, Cord mounted behind her. Cradling her against himself, he said, "Did you mean it about the baby?"

"Yes."

"You hadn't told me."

"I had only found out. I was going to tell you tonight." He felt the light pressure of her palm against his chest. "Are you glad?"

"More than glad," he murmured, pressing kisses on the top of her head. "More than glad."

As soon as they arrived home, Cord swept Floryn into his arms and carried her upstairs. He helped her bathe and change clothes, then tucked her into bed. While Cord was doing this, Antonio rode to the village to get Mildred and the children, and Rule left on an errand.

434

Later Cord, Alfredo Comacho, and Shelby Martin closed themselves up in the study. Alfredo Comacho sat behind the desk, Cord stood to one side, and Shelby, his hands crossed over his chest, leaned against the closed door.

When Cord moved the pendants together, quiet expectancy fell over the room. Silence was so defined that the scratch of the pen point on the paper resounded throughout the study. After a while, Alfredo laid the pen down, picked up the magnifying glass, and scrutinized the pieces. Finally he pushed back and glanced triumphantly around the room.

"I have done it," he said. "According to *Señor* Tellez, this is a family medallion cast as a whole, then cut into pieces to be given to each family member. In this case to the Guilberts and their child — should they have one."

"Nothing about the San Domingos?" Shelby asked.

Alfredo shook his head. "No, this is just a recording of the Guilbert history."

Cord reached down to pick up the written translation, looked at it, then returned it to the desk. "Thank you, Alfredo. You may leave now."

The door had no sooner closed behind him, than Shelby said, "Go toss your pistols out the window, Cord, and I'll take that." Shelby's Colt was drawn.

"I figured you would."

Shelby hiked a brow.

Cord walked to the window and threw out his guns. "You gave yourself away yesterday when you killed Kid."

"Rule killed him."

"No," Cord said. "When I got the pendant off him, I noticed there were no powder burns on his shirt. There would have been had Rule shot him."

"He was going to kill your wife."

"No, Kid was an opportunist, but not a murderer.

435

He wasn't going to hurt her. He was riding to save her when Rule pulled him off the horse. For a split second it made me question Rule. But he looked too surprised by Kid's death. You killed him because you were afraid he'd tell us that you were a part of this."

"You can't prove that."

"Maybe I can."

In front of the desk, Shelby picked up the paper on which Alfredo had written the translation and briefly glanced at it before he stuck it into his shirt pocket.

"When did you get involved in this?" Cord asked.

"Ten years ago when you told me about your job of escorting this rich Mexican dame into Texas and told me how much they were willing to pay you. I figured it had to be more than saving a woman's life. So I began to investigate the family—the San Domingos. They learned what I was doing and told me about the fortune in jewels she was smuggling out of the country. I tried to get you to cut me in, but you wouldn't. So I took things into my own hands."

"Ten years ago." Cord whistled. "You're the one who was responsible for having my wagon train ambushed and all those innocent people massacred?"

"Had to," Shelby said. "Couldn't leave any witnesses. Of course, you just wouldn't leave things alone. You had to take that Guilbert woman and her maid off."

"And you're the one who chased us," Cord said. "The one who killed her."

"Sanchia Guilbert fought me with a knife. During the tussle the maid escaped."

It was Sanchia disguised as the maid—that was the way she had traveled the entire journey so that no one knew her true identity—who escaped, but Cord did not correct Shelby's misconception.

"She got on your horse and galloped away. I followed for a while, but figured she couldn't be much of a threat. I returned to find you still alive."

"Why didn't you leave me to die?"

"Would have if I had known about that pendant stuffed in your boot. That was all I needed. By the time I found out about it, you were conscious. The only thing for me to do was remain your friend."

"So much for friendship," Cord said lightly, but deep within him he felt like a hot cauldron about to boil over. He had hated during his life and had spent long hours planning his revenge should he ever find the person who had framed him, the person responsible for so many innocent deaths. His hatred and revenge had kept him alive.

Shelby's friendship had been the only light in his life. The only thing in which he truly believed. Now to suffer its loss, to discover that it had been a lie was overwhelming.

"The irony of it all," Cord said, "is that I had lost confidence in every other individual but you. You were my friend. I trusted you."

"I really liked you," Shelby said.

How flippant the words sounded. Cord felt the heat of all his old emotions as they bubbled close to the surface, ready to break lose. He felt as if he were once more incarcerated, as if he were the convict. His world once more became kill or be killed. He clenched his hands at his side. He looked at Shelby Martin's neck and imagined his hands around it, squeezing the life out of him.

"Yes," Shelby said, "I like you, Cord. I just like money better. So did Kid."

Cord took a step. Shelby snapped to attention.

"Don't you push me," the lawman said. "I'll shoot you without a thought."

"I don't give a damn about myself," Cord said. And he truly did not. But he did not take another step. He remembered the woman whom he loved, the woman who was carrying his child. He remembered Hope, his

precious daughter. They needed him. And he care
more than a damn about them. He would do nothin
foolish.

Sensing that Cord had leashed his anger, Shelby sa
on the edge of the desk, his thigh brushing against on
of the medallions. But he was looking at Cord rathe
than at them.

"That ruby pendant was Kid's downfall. He wa
about to mess things up real good. You don't know
what a selfish little bastard Kid was. When he hear
about the pendant and saw the size of the ruby, he de
cided he'd get it all for himself."

"So you and Kid were working together?"

"We were sort of," Shelby said. "Certainly not be
cause I wanted to but because Webb Pruitt was a loud
mouthed son-of-a-bitch and couldn't stay put. When
he learned that Norwell had given you the pendant, h
had to make a trip to San Antonio to see me. He wa
scared we were going to lose the treasure. He was an
impatient man who just couldn't let me handle things.

"Norwell isn't a part of it?"

Shelby shook his head. "Never has been."

"So it was you, Pruitt, and Kid. The three of you
working together," Cord said.

"It just happened that way. I didn't plan it. I had
waited, waited patiently for nine years for the San
Domingo treasure. Old man San Domingo — the last o
his line — promised it to me. And the perfect opportu
nity came when Floryn decided to get you out o
prison. Pruitt approached me, and we decided half a
treasure was better than none at all. Since you and
were friends, we knew you'd never suspect me of keep
ing tabs on you."

Hearing a noise outside, Shelby rose and walked to
the window. Hiding behind the windowsill, he pulled
the curtain back and looked out. Finally he dropped i
and returned to the desk.

"Pruitt turned out to be a big disappointment. Upset because his woman had married old Jack Willowby and run off to New Mexico to try her hands at ranching, he slept with every available skirt. Not only did he sleep with them, but he got drunk and told them his life's story, including stuff about the San Domingo treasure. He paid them to sleep with him; Kid paid them even more to find out what Pruitt was up to. He learned and cut himself in. That's the way the three of us became partners."

Shelby picked up the medallions. When he saw them, he let out a string of curse words.

"I had Tellez remove the stones," Cord said. "So the temptation to steal would be less."

"Too bad you didn't do that sooner. Maybe Kid wouldn't have acted like an idiot and stole them."

Dropping them into his pocket, Shelby moved to the door.

"What are you going to do with me?" Cord asked.

"I'm going to have to kill you," Shelby said. "Sorry, but that's the way it is. Of course, I'll hide the murder by setting the house on fire. That way, everyone will think the secret of the San Domingo treasure went up in flames."

"There is no San Domingo treasure," Cord said.

Shelby laughed.

"When Emmanuel saw the pendants, he vaguely recalled Mathieu Guilbert and began to investigate," Cord said and related in detail the story to Shelby. "According to Tellez, it was common knowledge that San Domingo hired a Texan to massacre the wagon train on which his great-niece traveled. He needed her dead so he could inherit her estate. He bragged that he dangled a fortune in front of this Texan's eyes so he would do the dastardly deed free."

"You're lying," Shelby said.

"Ask Emmanuel," Cord said. "Better yet. Read the

translation Alfredo made from the pendants."

Shelby stared at him disbelievingly, but finally pulled the paper from his pocket. He smoothed it with one hand and began to read. Mathieu Guilbert was the youngest son of Noe Guilbert, owner of the Guilbert Vineyards in the Luviere Valley. The vineyard is mapped.

"The vineyard is mapped! The map is of nothing but a bunch of damn grapevines? The diamond, emerald, and ruby represent the three surrounding mountains." Shelby was so angry he shook. "These are lies."

Cord shook his head. "You were duped, Shelby. Used by the San Domingos. Hired to be their assassin and paid nothing."

Cord sat down in the wing chair and crossed his legs. "I've already sent letters to Pruitt and Norwell, telling them about the pendants and the interpretation. I've invited them to bring a Latin scholar with them and read the inscription on the pendants themselves. This way I can nip this San Domingo treasure myth in the bud."

Shelby raised his Colt.

"I can still kill you."

"If you do, Shelby Martin, you're a dead man," Floryn said from behind. Her voice was dangerously quiet.

Cord turned to see her standing there, clad in her wrapper, her pistol in hand, her gaze pinned to Shelby.

Shelby started to move.

"Don't," Floryn ordered softly. "I mean it. I'll kill you for what you've put Cord through. You made his life a living hell for ten years." She cocked the hammer.

"Don't, sweetheart," Cord said. "He's not worth it."

"You are. Move out of the way, Cord."

Cord took several steps. Shelby remained where he was, but Cord knew the man. He knew he had not given up, that he was planning, calculating his moves.

Then Shelby started to spin around. Before he had pivoted, Floryn shot, the bullet catching him in the back shoulder. He groaned and dropped his pistol. Cord raced to Floryn and took the Colt from her hand and put an arm around her, holding her close to him.

"Get up, Shelby," Cord ordered. Now he aimed the pistol at the lawman.

"What are you going to do with me?"

"Turn you over to the authorities. I sent Rule after the sheriff." Cord smiled grimly. "Be grateful that I'm a changed man, Shelby, or I'd kill you. Knowing the truth is really all I needed. Being exonerated is what I want most. You, Shelby, and what you did to me don't mean anything to me anymore. For nine years I wanted to find you and to make you suffer for all you put me through, but you're not worth the energy or the emotion. I have a life ahead of me with a wife whom I love and a precious daughter. Soon we'll have our second child. I don't have time for hatred and revenge. I barely have enough time for living."

Later after Shelby had been turned over to the authorities, Cord had taken Floryn upstairs to their bedroom, into the master suite where he had had their belongings moved a few hours prior. Floryn had been quiet and withdrawn.

"I hope you don't mind that I switched our bedroom," he said.

"No," Floryn replied.

"I thought it was time that we moved into our rightful place."

"Yes." Moving to the dresser, she picked up her brush and began to stroke her hair.

"You know Mildred and Rule are going to be married?"

"I figured they were."

He took off his vest and hung it on the back of a chair. He was worried about Floryn, concerned that she might be in shock. He had tried several times to hold her, but she had kept her distance.

"Mildred is keeping Hope overnight."

"I know."

"They'll bring her home tomorrow, and we can tell her about the baby," Cord said.

Floryn made no reply.

He looked at her, but her face was expressionless, her eyes lackluster. "That is," he added, "if you want to."

"Yes," she murmured, "I do."

As he talked, he continued to undress. "One of these days we'll travel to France. We'll find these three mountains, the vineyard, and the Guilberts. I have a feeling they'll be glad to see Hope."

Floryn nodded.

"As soon as we get the Guilbert jewels back, we'll put them up for Hope. They will be part of her inheritance."

Floryn smiled.

Clad only in his trousers, Cord reached for Floryn but she moved away from him. "What's wrong, honey? You're not afraid of me, are you?"

She said sadly, "No, I'm afraid of empty promises and hollow words."

"I don't follow you," he said.

"I don't want you to tell me you love me because I'm carrying your child."

He caught her in his arms and hugged her. "My timing was all off," he said softly, "but you ought to know by now that I don't give empty promises or speak hollow words. I'm happy we're going to have our second child, but whether we had children or not, I love you, Floryn Donaldson, and only you. You are the love, the only love, of my life. And you're just going to have to accept my word on that."

"Yes"—she studied his face—"I want to believe you."

"You must believe me," he said. "It's true. I'll prove it, but it'll take me a lifetime."

"That might be long enough," she said, echoing words he had spoken to her long ago.

"Then I better start convincing you right now."

His lips captured hers as he easily lifted her into his arms and carried her to the bed. With tenderness he convinced her. Slowly and infinitely gentle Cord Donaldson loved his wife, and she loved him.

Epilogue

Holding her papa's hand, Hope entered the white frame church and marched down the center aisle between him and Mama.

"In the whole wide world, Mama's the prettiest woman and you're the prettiest girl," Papa had said earlier as they dressed, and Hope believed him. Papa never lied.

Hope liked her new yellow dress — and this time Papa did not buy one with ruffles since she hated ruffles — and black shoes. Her hair, hanging loose today, brushed against her shoulders. Mama had washed and curled it. Hope reached up to touch the big white bow Mama had insisted on her wearing. Hope even liked that.

Peeping around Mama on one side, Papa on the other, she smiled and greeted the people sitting on the pews. She gave Agnes Jennings a real big smile 'cause now Agnes begged to come play on her slide and her merry-go-round and her seesaw.

Papa built all of them for her.

Hope heard the soft mewing sound of a little baby and looked up at Mama. She held their baby brother, Jared. Mama was beautiful, Hope thought. She was always smiling, sometimes laughing with Papa at things that really were not funny. But mamas and papas were like

445

that, Mildred said. Hope guessed they were because Ja
son said Mildred and Rule looked at each other just lik
that! Mama spoke softly to Jared and kissed him, the
she looked down at Hope and smiled.

Little babies needed lots of attention and care, Pap
said. Especially little brothers.

As they scooted into the pew, Hope glanced up t
catch that special look that passed between Mama an
Papa. She liked it. It was warm and full of love. The
looked at her like that, too. Hope smiled.

Mama and Papa had told her that they did not mak
her when she was a baby. They had made another bab
who died just as the mama and papa who had made he
died. That mama and papa and baby were in heave
with Leanor. When God saw Hope without a mama an
Mama without a baby, he put Hope with Mama. Hop
was glad. Papa told her she was very special. She was
chosen daughter.

When Hope sat down, she looked down the pew an
waved at Jason. Then she straightened.

Mama leaned down. *"Mi hija"*— she called Hope tha
now, and Hope loved it; it was special and made her spe
cial — "would you like to hold your brother?"

Hope eagerly nodded her head. He was so tiny an
smelled so good . . . well, sometimes. Mama place
Jared in her lap. Hope brushed the thin cotton blanke
from his face.

"Hello, *mi hijo,*" she whispered, lowering her head an
pressing a light kiss to the tip of his nose. *Mi hijo* — that'
what they called Jared.

Hope wanted to make sure he had plenty of ange
dust. Mama said he was going to need lots of it if he wa
anything like his Papa. And everybody who looked a
him said he looked just like Papa, except Jared had tw
big blue eyes. But Papa had a black patch, and Hop
liked that.

Papa said she and Mama were like the wild Texa
wind. He said quite probably Jared was going to be